AGING
BEAUTY

5/3/19

For

Ali

With warm regards

As ever,

Ted

AGING
BEAUTY

TED GROSS

Library of Congress Control Number:		2019902729
ISBN:	Hardcover	978-1-7960-2011-3
	Softcover	978-1-7960-2012-0
	eBook	978-1-7960-2013-7

Print information available on the last page.

Rev. date: 04/17/2019

To order additional copies of this book, contact:
Xlibris
1-888-795-4274
www.Xlibris.com
Orders@Xlibris.com
787445

In memory of my mother and father

What is hell? I maintain that it is the suffering of being unable to love.

—Dostoevsky

1

From a distance, Alyce Parker appeared as an ageless beauty. As a short, animated woman with the joy of life in her eyes, she was the grande dame of this lavish Crystal Ball and beamed with pride as she delivered a simulated, oversized check of $3 million to the president of Michael Reese Hospital: the proceeds of the evening, the celebration of a great Chicago philanthropic achievement. No one else had ever reached a goal of $3 million. No one had even come close.

On this frigid Christmas night, one thousand guests in black tie and glittering gowns hustled through the hallways of the Field Museum of Natural History, which was surrounded by skeletons of dinosaurs and stuffed elephants and ancient artifacts of bygone civilizations. This large space had been converted into a grand ballroom and now welcomed guests who sparkled like so many diamonds in the sky—Chicagoans who were happy to share the good news of the funds raised, as though they were all Alyce Parker's intimate friends. From where David Rosen sat, in the rear of this cavernous, crowded room, she seemed beautiful without the arrogance of being beautiful. In spite of the recent death of his wife after thirty-five years of a good marriage, he found her riveting.

Rosen was the president of the local, multiethnic Roosevelt University, a haven for Chicagoans eager to enter the middle-class. On a good day, he stood five feet, eight inches tall, but he would have preferred to be six two—a desire that bespoke the meaning of his life. With thick brown hair that he never quite combed to perfection and eyes that were always alert and ambitious, he sat beside his partner for the evening—Janet Barnes, a veteran director of public relations at Roosevelt, where David had been for little more than two years. She was a loyal lieutenant who had insisted that they buy a table at this fabulous annual event. He had been reluctant to travel the social circuit since Debra's death, but in Janet's words, nine months had passed. She said it was time for him to emerge from grief and become an accessible university president once again so that he could do what presidents are supposed to do in modern American universities—raise money and then raise more money.

When the dancing began and he caught glimpses of Alyce Parker close-up, he could see that she was indeed a stunning woman, with large violet eyes and carefully coiffed chestnut hair. She was a self-assured woman with the kind of infectious smile that could light up every room she would enter and invite everybody's friendship and trust.

"Could she become interested in us?"

"I doubt it," Janet told him. "We don't have enough class or panache for the likes of her. We're still considered the little red schoolhouse on Michigan Avenue. But we can always try."

Rosen asked her to arrange a meeting. He had been considering a capital campaign to reinvent a university that labored under a paltry $3 million endowment and an underpaid faculty that taught in the tired, well-worn Auditorium Building created by Louis Sullivan, Dankmar Adler, and Frank Lloyd Wright at the end of the nineteenth century. This iconic edifice—originally a hotel, theater, and office building—was scarcely the natural home for an aspiring university and was in serious need of repairs. A transplanted New Yorker, Rosen, was still an outsider to the royalty of Chicago and needed all the help he could get. Why not Alyce Parker? Why not the best?

She was breathtaking as she danced through the throng of affluent admirers, secure in the distant arms of an escort who was clearly neither her husband nor her permanent partner. Her perfected hair, divorced of any gray, was framing high cheekbones and a bright, approving twinkle that surveyed the hall. Then, as she passed by David and Janet, she concentrated on him for a moment, with the suggestion that he might very well be the only one on that dance floor she did not know. *How old is she?* he wondered. *Precisely how old?* It was impossible to tell. How tall? She was short, with heels hidden beneath her crimson floor-length dress, but not a woman who appeared short. Her eyes connected with his, and it was as if she knew all about him, including the paths that had taken him to a presidency. When he looked for Alyce Parker, she had vanished, lost among the throng of admirers.

After taking Janet Barnes home, he strolled along the festive Michigan Avenue, north of the river and bordered by some of the fancier emporia in America—Tiffany's and Gucci and Brooks Brothers, blazing with Christmas cheer. He did so until he came to his condo at One Magnificent Mile. It was at the edge of the Gold Coast, across from the Drake Hotel and Georg Jensen, and was rising to the heavens until it touched a golden winter moon that warmed Lake Michigan. The condo pool was still open, and he intended to swim his nightly laps until he was exhausted. Then and only then might he be able to sleep without living in the irrecoverable past.

Tonight the ritual didn't quite work. The scent of Debra lingered in this condo they had hesitated buying when they first fell in love with it. "It's a fabulous apartment, Dave, but too expensive. I don't feel comfortable in all this new-found luxury. It's just not you, and it's certainly not me, he remembered Debra said. Her fragrance remained in the bathroom, in the cabinets and drawers, and in their bed. Her dresses still hung in the closet, her coffee cup waited in the kitchen, her diary lay open on her desk (poised for a new entry), and the photographs of them on the Côte d'Azur and the Amalfi Coast kept her alive in him. All that was left were memories—relentless memories. They'd had a good life, and he didn't want to lose her to time despite her premature death.

As he stood at the living-room window overlooking Lake Michigan, he remembered Debra basking on the beach in Amagansett when the cancer first struck. Then came the rush to an Easthampton motel, the vomiting, the doctors, the mastectomy, her chemo, and the assurances that if she were free of the cancer for five years, she'd have a normal life expectancy. When the invitation for an interview from Roosevelt arrived, she urged him to seize it, and they drove to Chicago with the anxious enthusiasm of adolescents, excited by a presidency that was the culmination of his academic career. "You deserve," Debra told him again and again, "to be a university president."

She'd given up her career as director of college placement in the New York City school system. She was persuading David not to worry, as she would find something for herself in Chicagoland. But the cancer returned after five years and metastasized aggressively into her liver. For one year, she struggled to hold on to life, but day by day, he watched her body waste away. In his mind, he could still hear the screeching sound of the emergency van from Northwestern racing through the streets to take her by stretcher to its hospital. She was fifty-seven when she died.

Tomorrow morning, he would take an early flight to New York to visit old friends and colleagues at CCNY. But each time he revisited the city, he felt more and more like a tourist, a stranger to his past. Chicago was home now, and he intended to return to this adopted city for a solitary, sober New Year's Eve alone. He had refused several party invitations. He needed to punish himself and to endure the evening with work. He would strengthen and polish the master plan that he and his colleagues had written for Roosevelt—*Finding the Center*—and focus on his presidential future. Work would be therapy. It always had been. Sometimes it would get him through the night, and sometimes it wouldn't.

2

Alyce Parker lived on Astor Street in a vintage condominium, across from the Cardinal's mansion. Her escort, the CEO of Amoco who had recently been taking her to public events, kissed her discreetly on the cheek good night as the doorman opened the door of his Cadillac. Once, he had suggested staying the night and offered her the possibility of a rich life together, but Alyce resisted the temptation. He and others never quite satisfied her, and she had grown to like her independence and freedom. She thought she was almost too old and too set in her ways to remarry, and she had been badly burned the first time round. It was seven years since Matt's death, and the last few years of their marriage had been spent apart as he struggled alone with alcoholism in their summer home in Wisconsin. At seventy-one, she was reconciled to the realization that the idealized love she'd always sought in her life would probably never happen.

Tonight, she wanted to enjoy the lingering glow of success and the knowledge that the Crystal Ball would never have been so spectacular without her leadership. Then, as she smiled with self-satisfaction, all the other faces faded, and she and this man named David Rosen were alone. They were dancing all alone. His wife had died at fifty-seven, so she was told, and here she lived on to become an ageless beauty. Of all the bejeweled patrons at the Crystal Ball, why was he the one who lingered in her mind? It was as if he was the one in that vast dance hall who seemed to be saying, "I want to see you again. Will you let me see you again?"

Her joy and self-satisfaction were tempered by the grim fear that her brief career as a workingwoman was coming to an end. Shortly after Matt's death, and as a consequence of having socialized with the CEO of Michael Reese Hospital, she'd secured a position as director of the unit that catered to wealthy Chicagoans and visiting celebrities who wanted to keep their illness a secret from the public. It was the perfect job for her. She had never been on salary before, but in all her volunteer work, she was known for her natural executive abilities, her great creativity, sound judgment, and extraordinary charm. She had held the job for seven years, and it had been pure pleasure. She earned a decent salary, but now that income would be gone, and she was no longer as wealthy as she appeared to be. At her age, she should have been preparing to retire comfortably, but Matt had left her only a small home in Cedar Lake, Wisconsin, and beneath her public self-confidence was this nagging financial insecurity that she would not be able to sustain the façade of affluence into her senior years.

Still, she was an optimist by nature and felt that somehow everything would work out in the end. She was beautiful, she was talented, and she was still desirable. Those who didn't know her thought she was at least ten years younger than her actual age. Tonight she was so effervescent she felt eternally youthful and needed to share her triumph. The obvious person to call was her older daughter, Julie, in whom she confided every morning and every night. Their relationship had grown more difficult after Alyce's decision to separate from Matt.

She remembered that evening when she and Matt were sitting opposite each other before the fireplace in their handsome home in Winnetka, which his father had bought for them. Matt had left the prosperous family business, a clothing store in Highland Park, and had failed at one venture after another in search of his fortune. He had philandered; he had become an alcoholic. Finally, unable to afford the mortgage, he was proposing that they move permanently to their summer home at Cedar Lake, Wisconsin, where he promised to attend meetings of Alcoholics Anonymous.

"No, Matt," she told him quietly. "I'm not moving from Chicago to Cedar Lake. I'm too young to wither away."

They never did divorce, and he went to Wisconsin alone and became friends with others from AA until his death, a few years later.

Julie had argued that her mother should have stuck by Matt for better or for worse despite his business failures, his drinking, and his philandering. In her midforties, she still had a romantic childlike concept of marriage and insisted that it was Alyce's obligation to find a way to hold hers together. Despite her father's steady deterioration,

Julie worshipped him and forgave what she considered his foibles and weaknesses. After seven years, the torch burned as bright as ever. The tension between mother and daughter had diminished by now, and they were close—too close from Alyce's point of view.

At midnight, there was no one else she could call. She knew that Julie was sitting by the phone, waiting anxiously, and expecting her to report every detail of the evening. She also knew that if she didn't call, there would be retribution in the morning.

"It was as glorious as I could ever have wanted it to be. Everyone was there. Everything worked out perfectly: the flowers, the dinner, Stanley Paul's orchestra, Tony Bennett's performance. Everything."

"Alyce Parker, the architect and leader of the ball, the planner, the organizer."

"And I loved it, Julie." She went on to describe the details of the evening, and Julie listened avidly, dutifully, and vicariously. "I wish you had come."

"Oh no, no, Mother. Not in a million years would I go. Your extravaganzas are not for me. I don't need to be at the center of every party I go to."

"Don't be mean, Julie, at twelve thirty in the evening, when I need someone to share my joy. The galas are superficial, I know, but they're also sheer joy for me. And they're always supporting good causes."

"Any excuse for a gala," Julie laughed. "I'm sure this one was the best of the best, the climax to a colorful career. But I also hope it's really your last hurrah. You've always given your talents away too easily for nothing."

"Michael Reese has done a lot for me, Julie. It gave me a job when I needed one, and it's helped to pay the rent."

9

"And now it's ended. I'm glad. At seventy-one, you should retire."

Alyce smiled to herself. So smug—Julie thought she knew everything about her life, but she understood so little. She'd be amazed at how close her mother was to the margins. She had always assumed that her father had left enough money and that the Wisconsin home could easily be sold for a profit. Alyce had told her little. Her fragile finances were her private business—a secret even to her daughters and certainly to the world.

"Actually, I'm starting to agree with you. I know you're right. I am tired of being the grande dame of charity balls. It's time to kick up my heels."

She wanted to hang up. Julie had broken her mood of exhilaration, and she knew that if they continued talking, there would be an argument. These days, their conversations always seemed to end with an argument. Julie had drifted from one job to another, like her father, except that she was competent wherever she worked. She was just restless and with no companion except a cat she insisted on naming Matthew.

"Are you coming by for brunch tomorrow?" she asked, hoping the answer might be no.

"Of course, I'm coming. You know me. I'm the dutiful daughter who always brings the croissants."

When Alyce went to the bathroom in preparation for bed, she kept thinking of him—president of Roosevelt University, New Yorker, and widower. Who was that woman with him? She learned that she was a public relations staff member and a convenient partner—no more, no less. *Who is he?* she asked herself. There was so much more to know about him.

3

Everywhere David Rosen went, he encountered Alyce Parker. She was always on the arm of some corporate tycoon or someone who should have been a corporate tycoon. Once, when he was formally introduced to her in the crowded international restaurant of the Drake Hotel, she gazed at him as though they had already met somewhere or should have met. Then he could see the light in her eyes flash on, and at the same moment, they would remember—the Crystal Ball months before, across that crowded dance floor. Once again, their eyes connected; once again, they spoke to each other without uttering a word.

Whenever Janet Barnes tried to arrange a luncheon, Alyce Parker was busy or made herself busy. He learned that she was ending a full-time job at Michael Reese. Although that would soon be ending, she must be ripe for a new adventure. He would see her name and image in *Skyline*, the local rag of high society, and the *Chicago Tribune* or

Sun Times. Despite her demanding job, she seemed to have found time for fund-raising at the opera, the symphony, the zoo, and Michael Reese Hospital itself. Still, he was irritated that she always seemed to find a reason for not meeting. No one was worth all this trouble. Who the hell did this prima donna think she was anyway? What social snobbery lurked in her refusal? But there was more in his desire to meet her than her wealth or access to wealth; he knew that already. There was a vivacity and joy and beauty so infectious, a glow that promised an exciting life beyond his university, and a personal possibility. But at that moment, perhaps the most enticing of all was her priceless access to the movers and shakers of the city. She would make a perfect fund-raiser. As days passed and the university demanded more and more of his attention, he considered her a lost cause, and he buried himself in his work.

In his conference room every Monday morning, the members of David's administrative council—vice presidents, deans, the director of public relations, the head librarian, and other leaders—gathered to present the progress in their individual units and claim their fair share of whatever limited resources there were. Each leader was representing a dimension within David's design of a metropolitan university. He had a vision of a second permanent campus in the northwest suburbs, across the Woodfield Mall in Schaumburg—a two hundred twenty acre spread that would help him create a reinvented, enlarged, and more prominent Roosevelt University. America was becoming a country of city-states and metropolises, and he wanted Roosevelt to become the one that extended outward from

Chicago and over time assert itself as the major private university of the northwest suburbs.

It had taken two years to assemble this group of administrators, his leaders, his team, some old, some new. It was a gang of fourteen that would run the university while he raised the money to help them realize their personal dreams as well as his overarching vision that held those dreams together. He had retained some carryovers from the previous administration, replaceable once the vision took shape, and he had appointed new leaders who shared his purpose and were persuaded, despite overwhelming financial constraints, by his energy and enthusiasm. He was the kind of president others wanted to help succeed. After two years, this was the council of administrative leaders he'd inherited and was recreating. They were eager to help prepare for a capital campaign he needed to realize the dream and to help him implement it no sooner than yesterday. It was easier said than done. There were no resources, no researchers, and no development staff to convert his dream into reality. Every time he felt overwhelmed by this gap and knew he needed a catalyst in private fund-raising, he conjured up the image of Alyce Parker. He was more convinced than ever that she was the kind of person who could help discover the funds to nourish his insatiable ambition.

On his right sat Bob Green, his provost and alter ego, the second in command, and a trusted friend. An older short man with a slight humpback, Green was a former dean of humanities at a Penn State campus in Harrisburg when David had been a provost there. An improbable sex scandal involving a faculty member's wife made him eager to leave the neighborhood of Three Mile Island, the churchgoers, and political conservatives. He and Green had become close, and David knew that he could hand over the day-to-day operations of the university while he developed a fund-raising strategy that would lift Roosevelt from its doldrums.

On David's left was John Anderson, a tall, straight-as-an-arrow former banker from Minneapolis, his CFO. He was without any experience in academic administration but bright as a whip and a fast learner. He was a kind of modest, understated Midwesterner you would trust with your wallet. Beside him slouched Dan Pearson, the vice president for Development, a thirty-year veteran who could boast of only limited raising achievements, although to be fair again and again and as she too sought support to be successful or the leadership to set his imagination afire. David knew this benign veteran had to be replaced, or there would never be a capital campaign worth speaking of. If he could only ensnare the alluring, well-connected Alyce Parker as a volunteer, she could serve as the bridge to a permanent vice president. Alyce Parker was someone who had the snap, crackle, and beauty he needed. She had raised $3 million for the Crystal Ball! Who knew what doors she could open for him—a newcomer to Chicago? She rose before his eyes, dancing across the ballroom floor, as though she were the keeper of the keys to the kingdom.

By Pearson's side sat Mary Henderson, the new vice president for enrollment management who had come from a small Catholic college on the South Side. She brought with her an infectious Irish wit and an optimism that was contagious. "Give me three years," she had assured Bob Green and David at their interview, "and I'll have the enrollments growing by 3 to 5 percent annually."

"You are an optimist."

"Especially about that suburban campus," she winked. "You'll have a gold mine of students once you build that college in the northwest suburbs."

Then there were the five academic deans—a team of rivals for the spare crumbs David could offer each of them. The dean of business was a five-foot-two-inch rotund harridan, with bleached hair and a fiery gaze, panting to have her unaccredited college blessed by the American Assembly of Collegiate Schools of Business as a first step toward her own presidency elsewhere. "Just give me the resources, and we'll have a college you'll be proud of." When, at a meeting of the administrative council, David told her that the university couldn't afford the prestigious AACSB, an accrediting organization that demanded a significant percentage of faculty to be committed to research and, therefore, require higher salaries and lower teaching loads, she cried out before all her peers, "When I was first interviewed, you promised me. You promised me. It was all a goddamn lie! You lied to me!" He wanted to fire her on the spot, but he had no one to replace her with, and he couldn't afford to hire anyone new. Business deans are indeed expensive.

George Roderick, the dean of education, was always eager to please. He had been at Roosevelt for decades and had sent sheaves of scattered proposals, each one more important than the last, to David before his presidency even began. Each proposal was too limited for David's imagined collaboration between his private university and the Chicago public school system. David wanted to bring all the lessons he had learned from the open admissions debacle at the City College in the 1970s and build a genuine collaboration between the schools and the university.

The dean of music, Earl Saunders, was David's closest friend. He was a confidant who was born and bred in Brooklyn and shared similar measures of cynicism, mild paranoia, aggressiveness, and sheer energy reminiscent of so many of his former friends and colleagues in New York City. Saunders had abandoned a dissatisfying career in advertising in Nutley, New Jersey, and studied for an MBA at UCLA when he was in his late forties. David always admired his courage and wondered whether he could ever have done the same in midcareer.

Louise Eggers, a heavyset woman with a sweet, authentic smile, had worked with David at SUNY Purchase just north of New York City and oversaw a college of continuing education that appealed to adult part-time students who had never completed their bachelor's degree and some who wanted online instruction and other innovative teaching methodologies. Roosevelt was their second chance in life. It wasn't just that. She claimed again and again as she, too, sought support from David, that one of the glories of American higher education and a second chance for those who dared to recreate their lives and careers in middle age.

Finally, there was the dean of the college of arts and sciences, Geoffrey Smallwood, who shared David's belief in the centrality of the liberal arts at any university of note. As a Victorian scholar who had drifted into administration, he was an import from the University of Colorado on his way to presidency when he contracted Parkinson's. His associate dean was really doing all his work silently and loyally, and David knew that he would soon be asking her to run this essential college that needed to be the center of his university. It was the college closest to his own background and where his tenured position resided, there in the reliable English department. He had grand plans for the college as the broad home of the humanities, social, and natural sciences by introducing an extensive writing laboratory, an honor's college, a doctorate in psychology, an institute for politics, and other projects. Most of these projects were so ambitious some of the trustees worried they might be unrealistic, given the limited resources available to implement them. "In dreams begin responsibilities," William Butler Yeats, an Irish codger who loved to quote his compatriot, reminded him. David's response, ever idealistic and ever dynamic, was that a capital campaign was needed—the discovery of private support from lost alumni and corporate leaders and foundations to supplement the slow, tedious growth of enrollment. That was why he would be depending on Smallwood's replacement, Associate Dean Lynn Wainwright, who was a loyal champion of David's vision and another lieutenant he knew he could trust with his ideological wallet.

This then was David Rosen's administrative council. These were the leaders he depended on as he scoured Chicagoland and beyond for private funds. There were two others: Janet Barnes, his reliable elderly public relations maven and a closeted lesbian who represented him positively to the world, and Adrian Jackson, the university librarian and a Lincolnesque figure who had been a Jesuit priest. Jackson never uttered a word during meetings but afterward wrote confidential five-page, single-spaced critiques to David of all that had happened with recommendations for improvement.

They're all good people, David thought, *but none of them will provide the funds to fuel my dreams—the pizzazz to electrify my new world that an Alyce Parker can offer.* Of all the units represented, the weakest by far was development, and at this moment, it was probably the most important. He knew few people of consequence in Chicago, but she knew them all. Every time he thought of her, he wanted to find her. She would bring the spark and energy his university needed.

Before each of these leaders was a case statement for a capital campaign that Bob Green and David had jointly crafted, and John Anderson had estimated would cost $50 million. That daunting number would first be shared with the administrative council before he dared present the visionary document of Roosevelt's future to his board of trustees. David knew there would be resistance, as each board member estimated what he himself would be asked to give. But at this early point, he refused to be discouraged. He knew he had no right to drive the university too far or too fast, as he still had no resources to realize the $50 million goal. Slow growth in enrollments would never catch up with the dream. He needed a catalyst—some external force that would galvanize his efforts. As he looked at his council, a group of doubting Thomases and academic leaders, the image of Alyce Parker warmed him as he considered her the wild card, a sudden possibility—fund-raiser, extraordinaire, beautiful, knowledgeable, a traveler among the rich and famous, and (as Buddy Mayer, one of his trustees and the heiress to the Sara Lee fortune and a close friend of Alyce's, had told him) available for a full-time position. She was leaving Michael Reese Hospital and might be looking for a new challenge. A snapshot flashed before his mind: Alyce Parker whirling at the Hilton like a professional dancer, and the kinetic connection that had flared between the two of them, if only for a moment—then flared again whenever they met accidentally and whenever she turned twice to stare at him. Good god, she was bewitching. He would ask Buddy to make the introductions. Just the thought of Alyce Parker warmed him with possibility. *But is it only institutional expedience that drew me to her?* he wondered. *Or is the warmth I feel the stir of emotions I haven't known for years?* Being loveless, was he searching for something deeper than his own avaricious ambition?

I'll need an angel, he thought, *knowing no one is waiting in the wings.* He knew she was someone better than a singular angel. She was a lovely woman who would introduce him to the royalty of Chicago. One by one, he would meet her lifelong friends who trusted her in a way they could never be expected to trust him. Alyce Parker was a Chicagoan born and bred, whereas David was still a stranger from New York and, like most university presidents, a man who lived in a fancy home and carried a tin cup. He was an academic salesman, a charmer, a force of nature, and beautiful. He was drawn to her without her knowing and without having exchanged a word. And part of his attraction, he knew, had nothing to do with the university.

Surveying his colleagues, he tried to fire their imagination.

"Bob and I have called this case for a capital campaign *Finding the Center.* We know it's a stretch, but with hard work and a little bit of luck, we can make it. You guys take care of the enrollments and the classrooms, and Dan I will find funds in the private sector to underwrite these expansive plans, especially the suburban campus."

But, of course, he didn't mean Dan Pearson at all; he was imagining Alyce Parker as his partner.

The council was borne aloft by David's contagious energy and enthusiasm. They wanted to believe their leader would save the institution from mediocrity. They wanted to believe in him; they had to believe in him. As academic administrators, they didn't have to raise or donate the money that would support the overarching vision so that they too could dream, free of charge. The trustees were another matter. They had nothing but praise for the plan, but David could feel their reticence, as each one wondered what a capital campaign of this scope and magnitude would cost him or her personally. Alan Archer, a short, trim man of ebullient confidence, was chairman of the board and CEO of a billion-dollar company that distributed wire and cabling to the world. He knew that he would be expected to make the lead gift. As a man of absolute directness, he believed that what you saw was what you got and what you got was not always what you wanted. He told David privately, "I respect what you want to do, Dave. I'll help you in any way I can, but don't expect a seven-figure gift from me. I have other obligations—personal obligations. I'm committing to one hundred thousand over five years, and that's it." At the public meeting, he put further brakes on David's dreams.

"Before the board signs off on any ambitious campaign, it needs a hardheaded evaluation by a consultant."

The trustees nodded in quick agreement. Any excuse for a delay. When the consultant came, he looked at the meager staff in the development office and Anderson's numbers to see what this ambitious plan would cost. Then he spoke privately to each trustee to determine the amount he might consider contributing. At the end of several weeks, with a long discouraging grimace, he rendered the report that David dreaded.

"You're not ready—not by a long shot. The trustees are behind you theoretically, but they're not ready to step up to the plate in any significant way—starting with your chairman, Alan Archer, who can contribute far more than he's willing to. Most of them are on the board because their CEOs told them to render public service, and all they're doing is guaranteeing modest annual corporate contributions. Most of them aren't even alumni. You'll have to cultivate major donors for the next few years and hope that some angel emerges, or"—the words almost oozed from his lips one by one like sour drops of reality—"you'll have to scale back your goals considerably. Lower your expectations. You'll have to wait a few years until you're ready. You're not ready now."

He knew that the consultant was right. His common sense told him he was being impetuous, impatient, and irrationally ambitious. His will was overriding his reason, but he was not prepared to indulge these indifferent trustees he had inherited. He believed that slowly and tediously he could convince them that the university could become what it should become—a university for Chicago. Patience was not David Rosen's cardinal virtue. And so he sat alone at night and tried to figure out a way through which he could overcome everyone's timidity, fears, and resistance. He'd assumed that when he accepted the presidency of this private university, he would have full authority and power to express an imperial will, with no state legislature and no governor, just a board of trustees resistant to his dream because it would cost them personally too much.

"Lower your expectations," John Anderson repeated in his sobering, sensible Midwestern voice, "and you won't be disappointed."

"No," David tried to convince him. "No, no, I won't acquiesce before I've begun." All his life, he had overreached in search of the heroic in the mundane, and it had worked step by step—from chairman of an English department at the City College of New York to dean of Humanities, to vice president for Development, to provost at Penn State Harrisburg, to dean of Letters and Science at SUNY Purchase, and to Roosevelt University, which he knew would be the last hurrah of his career and his final chance to distinguish himself.

At the center of his master plan for a metropolitan university was the alluring possibility that had arisen: the transfer from a campus in the suburb of Arlington Heights, where Roosevelt had been renting a section of the headquarters belonging to School District 214, to a second campus in nearby Schaumburg that the university could buy. Unocal, the oil company, was leaving the Midwest in six months to return to California and was asking $25 million for its building and property of more than two hundred acres. The Harris Bank was willing to provide a $21 million loan but insisted that David raise $4 million in addition to indicate the university's commitment. "You have to have skin in the game," the vice president smiled at David and John Anderson. They sat opposite him in his office. "We must know that you're financially strong enough not to default on our loan."

Four million dollars? Where would he ever find $4 million for the campus of his dreams? Fund-raisers like Alyce Parker raised that kind of money in one or two galas for Michael Reese Hospital or the Chicago Symphony or Lyric Opera or the University of Chicago or Northwestern. For Roosevelt? Impossible. Whom could he go to? Why would anyone care enough to be a lead donor of a prospective campus out there in Schaumburg beyond O'Hare Airport? Any consultant would tell him he was on a fool's errand. If the chairman, who could easily afford a million-dollar contribution over five years, didn't make a far more significant commitment, what other trustee would ever step forward with a large gift of his own? David wanted that campus so badly he could taste it. He considered it pivotal to the success of his presidency. He knew—oh, he knew—that the campus would be the electrifying force for all his fund-raising and would persuade doubters who had always considered Roosevelt a nice institution to have around in Chicago but not a serious contender. Purchase of that campus would make everything else possible. It would give confidence to hesitant trustees, it would stir alumni to donate, and it would encourage support from local corporations throughout the vast northwestern suburbs of Chicago: Allstate, Baxter, Sears, Motorola, Zurich American, and so on. He needed an Alyce Parker.

"I'll do what I can," Buddy Mayer assured him. "But Alyce Parker is one tough customer. She's a dear friend and an incredible fund-raiser, but she's primarily interested in the arts."

"What about Michael Reese? Cabrini-Green? The Lincoln Park Zoo? I read about her in the newspapers all the time. She seems to be everywhere."

"You've done your homework."

"I've also seen her at the Crystal Ball and other galas."

"I'll try, Dave. I'll try hard to arrange a breakfast meeting."

Buddy was certainly qualified; he had heard from Alan Archer and others. As an inactive Roosevelt trustee, she was the daughter of Nathan Cummings, the founder of Sara Lee. For years, she and her husband, Robert Mayer, an art connoisseur of sorts, had brought up their children in the mansion on a hill in Winnetka, with galleries upon galleries of contemporary art. Next to her estate, in a more modest but still impressive home, lived the Parker family: Alyce, her husband Matt, and their two daughters, Julie and Laura. Buddy and Alyce became the closest of neighbors, and after their husbands passed away, they moved into the city and remained friends. Buddy was rich but homely, smart and kind, a social worker by training who wanted now to save the downtrodden with her fortune, while Alyce was beautiful but pinched financially, although no one in the world would ever know.

"The two of you would make quite a team," she told David. "But as I've told you, she's tired of fund-raising. She wants to call it quits. She is a woman of a certain age, you know."

"Ageless—it seems to me. Just try, Buddy. That's all I'm asking."

"Okay, if you wish. Just give me time to set something up."

David knew that Alan Archer was an admirer of his dream, even though he thought it quixotic; he wanted to help but continued to refuse to make a lead gift. "I'm in for $100,000 over five years. Period." He said it with the determination of a CEO who owns a billion dollar corporation, and David knew he wouldn't budge. "Ask the Auditorium Theatre Council for a $3 million loan."

The theater had always been an integral part of the Auditorium Building. Since Roosevelt opened it again in the 1960s, it had limited success, until a new director recently came on board in the late eighties.

"Three million dollars? Why not? They can afford it. They've made buckets of money since *Les Miserables* and *Phantom of the Opera* appeared, and they're about to score again with *Miss Saigon*. When they were down and out and desperate in the seventies and eighties, Roosevelt bailed them out. They owe us. And they have the money. Someone told me they're negotiating now to bring in *Show Boat* after *Miss Saigon*, which will be another blockbuster. We own that goddamn humongous theater. It's part of our building. It's part of our university. Those profits are our profits—*ours*—to spend as we wish."

Alan Archer's voice rose in moral indignation, but David had learned one lesson about donors. Everyone had suggestions of some philanthropist other than himself; everyone was ready to spend someone else's money.

"If you don't want to speak to them, I will. I'll tell them just how much they owe us."

"No," David insisted. "I'll go."

As the president, David was an ex officio member of the Auditorium Theatre Council, aficionados that were guarding their newfound profits in a theater reborn under the leadership of the recently appointed, young and attractive executive director, Dulcie Grayson. From a group of volunteers serving an ancillary unit of the university that had struggled financially for many years and been beholden to Roosevelt for survival, the council now saw itself suddenly as financially independent and socially superior to the university that owned the theater—*noblesse oblige*. The chairman was Edward Adler, grandson of Dankmar Adler, the brilliant engineer who had worked with Louis Sullivan to design this magnificent theater, which was a 4,200-seat auditorium that soared six storeys high into the heart of the Auditorium Building. The theater was the soul of that edifice, with its dramatic link to the wider world through art and beauty.

He sat in the theater's conference room with fifteen hostile members of the Auditorium Theatre Council. Ed Adler, the chairman, sat beside him. On his other side was the self-assured Dulcie Grayson, a prim, pert, young would-be actress of thirty who was almost wholly responsible for the theater's recent success, and she was its fiercest advocate for independence. She had a dictaphone at the ready in case a transcript might be needed in court. The other members seemed benign enough. Theater lovers were excited by the rebirth of the city's Auditorium Theatre which they now thought of as their own. They enjoyed all the shows and free tickets and black-tie dinners afterward where they could hobnob with celebrities and be tendered public approbation and media coverage that made them seem like a band of angels come to save a city monument when, in fact, the success of the theater cost them very little personally.

"I'm here to request a loan," David began, speaking quickly, much too quickly. "A loan. It's only a loan of $2 million so that the university can purchase a second campus in Schaumburg."

He went on to describe the need for the loan, the possibilities and promises of the second campus, the growing enrollments that would produce more funds and allow the university to repay its loan soon, and the new middle-class audiences from the suburbs that would now be attracted to the theater.

As he spoke with the passion of a desperate president, he was met with stony, silent resistance. When he was finished, the chairman, Edward Adler, turned to him. "We have our own loans that we're trying to pay off for renovations. As you may remember, Cameron MacIntosh insisted that we refurbish all four thousand seats, carpet the floors, and repaint the walls before he'd even consider bringing *Les Miserables* to the theater. Well, we're just now emerging from our own indebtedness."

"I know that you have the funds," David insisted. "I've sat here for two years as an ex officio member of this committee and heard the glowing financial reports quarter after quarter. I know you have the funds, and they all come from ticket sales and not from you or any other single donor—certainly not from this council." His gaze settled on Fred Eiler, a taciturn billionaire who was thin and angular, a Dickensian type who had made his fortune by distributing newspapers throughout Chicagoland. Eiler could easily have been the theater's angel, but he wouldn't commit himself—not yet.

"Those revenues belong to the university, and the university has every right to call upon them. Besides, we're not taking the money permanently. Please don't give me that smile, Fred. Don't mock me. We're not taking the money permanently. I'm simply asking for a loan that will be repaid once the campus is established—soon, sooner than you might think."

No one in that room believed him. No one trusted him. After the rhetoric grew more heated, he burst out vindictively, "This is something out of *King Lear*—a great example of filial ingratitude. There was a time when this council was desperate to meet its budget and the university came through to save it."

Fred Eiler stood and spoke for the first time, "Well, that was then, Mr. President, and this is now."

"The university owns the theater, Fred, and all its assets. There's nothing irregular about a parent company transferring assets from one of its units to another. It's done all the time."

Eiler walked slowly toward David with a smirk on his lips and a document in his hand that could have been a dagger. "Not this time, Mr. President. Not here. Our lawyers have reviewed your request carefully. The revenues from ticket sales belong to us. We earned them, so we keep them. I'm sure your own lawyers will agree."

David left the conference room with a sense of despair. No vice president or dean or director or secretary could console him that day. No trustee. No friend. He needed a wife. But that night, when he dragged himself home, he was met with only a fading ghost that haunted his apartment. He spent the night miserably alone. It was the worst night since Debra's death. He was drinking wine and feeling very sorry for himself. He looked at a shadow eclipsing her, and there in the fog of his imagination emerged Alyce Parker. She was as stunning and assured as she was the moment he first saw her. Then she, too, faded, like all illusions.

More than ever, he was determined to meet her again and to prevail upon her to share his dream.

4

She had come into the Walgreens Pharmacy at Chicago and Michigan on a blustery afternoon in mid-December, carrying packages from shopping along the avenue. She collided with David as he turned to the aisle she was leaving. With apologies profuse, he gave her his cart and helped her transfer her purchases. They broke out laughing.

"Oh god, Alyce Parker. What a way to meet again!"

"Thanks so much," she beamed. She was flustered, embarrassed, and catching her breath. "I've been shopping all afternoon and buying more stuff than I can afford."

"Can I help you?"

"Absolutely. I feel like a damsel in distress."

"You're not a damsel, and you're not in distress. Just a little burdened by the end of winter in Chicago. It'll be April in two weeks."

"I'm sorry it's taken so long to get back to you."

"But you have gotten back to me. Now. Here. It's called destiny." They laughed at each other. "Will you have high tea with me at the Drake? I promise to carry your packages."

"Now?"

"After you're done buying out this Walgreens."

"That is tempting, but I have a hair appointment at five. Then I have to drive all the way out to Lake Bluff to be with relatives for dinner."

"A rain check?"

"Of course. I owe you a phone call. I'll be in touch next week to make an appointment. You still do want to have breakfast with me, don't you?"

"Take a guess."

"I'll call." Then she laughed at herself. "Tell me, Dr. Rosen, why am I always in such a hurry?"

"Because you're in such demand."

On the drive north along the expressway to Lake Bluff, she could not stop smiling to herself. Who is this David Rosen, this handsome man at the peak of his powers? She had done a little research; she had talked to friends about him. He was a widower, a university president, a transplanted New Yorker, an author, and a lonely man. "He must be a lonely man. I should have gone to the Drake with him. I should have followed my instinctual attraction to him. No, that would have been too fast. Drivel. I'm too old to play games. I should have called Sarah, cancelled, and gone with him. He's one of the most interesting men I've met in a very long time. No Matt, no unfocused ambition, no drinking, no insecurity, and no infidelity. He's a cultivated man, someone to admire and learn from and care for. I'll call him tomorrow—no, in two days. Wait. Don't appear too eager."

5

"I'm sorry," Alan Archer commiserated with David the afternoon after David's rejection by the Auditorium Theatre Council. He was calling from Rancho Mirage, California, for an update on David's meeting, but he sounded as though he were in another country halfway across the globe. He was taking a moment after a game of golf, no doubt, before cocktails and dinner with his wife and friends at the Tamarisk Country Club. He felt genuine empathy for David, but he made no gesture to go beyond a few passing words of consolation. They talked for moments. David was listening to him deferentially, and then when Archer suggested that maybe they should postpone this expansion into the northwest suburbs for now, he ceased listening. The man simply didn't really care. The man couldn't understand the dream.

"Look, Dave, I have an idea. I've been thinking about this all week. It's even disturbed my golf game. Can you imagine? Why don't you come to Rancho Mirage for a day or two? I'll host a luncheon, and we'll invite our heavy hitters. You can make the pitch, and I'll be there to support you—all the way."

These trustees had homes in Palm Springs, Rancho Mirage, and Palm Desert: Jerry Stein, the retired CEO of Stein Container, had been on the Roosevelt board since the conception of the university and served now as its éminence grise; Sid Perlman was a retired CEO of a company that distributed industrial components to companies across the country; little Norm Monroe was the CEO of a major financial services firm, and Al Rubin was a rags-to-riches diamond in the rough who had made his fortune in home construction.

"Al gave a million to that temporary space in Arlington Heights, and that was only a third of a school district building—a rented space at that. He got his name high on the ridge where the school stood. He'll certainly want that name perpetuated in a beautiful new college campus in Schaumburg. I'll prime the others before the luncheon. I'll prime the pump for you. Al could become our hero. He ought to become our hero. You never, never know, Dave. Wilder things have happened. I realize you're dispirited now, but you just never know. It might work out."

David let himself believe that the idea might be feasible and clutched it as though it were a lifeline. The five trustees he would meet in Rancho Mirage could provide the $4 million he needed to ignite a capital campaign, without disturbing their lifestyle for a moment. Perhaps they would. Perhaps Al Rubin would make a lead gift and condition it on the others to contribute as well. Or perhaps they would volunteer on their own. Who would know the strange dynamic of fund-raising, the mystery of it all, as one donor challenges another, and dots are connected in the most unexpected ways? David was encouraged when Rubin heard of the luncheon and called to invite him to a party he'd like to throw in his honor at his Rancho Mirage mansion on the Saturday evening of his visit. "You can do some heavy-duty fund-raising, Dave. People give more when they're down here. They're relaxed, retired, sitting on fortunes they'll never need or spend. What the hell are these moguls saving their shekels for anyway? I'll help you, Dave. I'll help you make the case for Roosevelt."

The luncheon was at the Rancho Mirage Country Club, and everyone who was invited came in courtesy of David. The only one missing at the table was Rubin himself. He could be viewed through the large windowed wall, standing patiently near his son on a hillock, with golf club in hand, studying the distance between himself and the little hole in the ground. A caddy was hovering nearby to cater to his every wish.

Although he admired David and welcomed him to Rancho Mirage, Rubin resented the fact that this luncheon had been arranged to target him as a pigeon, and perversely, he took his time on the green to keep his fellow trustees waiting. He was fond of David. Indeed, one morning, he invited him to his suite at the Carlyle Building on Lake Shore Drive—a magnificent condominium edifice that his company had built. He invited for home-cooked scrambled eggs, bacon, and croissants, just a breakfast for the two of them to see how the new president was doing and how he could help, but he was annoyed now at how Archer and his fellow trustees had set him up and were trying to manipulate him. He wasn't about to be anyone's patsy or pigeon.

When Rubin finally arrived at their table, he welcomed David to sunny Southern California. This is a paradise on earth where blue skies are the order of every day, and the temperature rarely rises above ninety degrees or sinks below sixty in the evening, at least from Thanksgiving through May. The other trustees bantered on for a while, sharing their separate experiences on the golf course, discussing politics, telling some pathetic dirty jokes, and basking in a well-deserved life of retirement for which their careers of hard work had prepared them. As dessert appeared, Alan Archer explained to everyone why David had traveled from Chicago, repeating what he had told each one privately. He turned to his president and asked him to describe the special project he had in mind.

The five trustees listened with distant interest, but when David was done describing his concept of a metropolitan university they could all create together and that would be their mutual legacy to Chicagoland, silence fell upon them and all eyes turned away from his. This luncheon was Archer's idea, not theirs, and he felt responsible for its success. He was a five-foot-five, spiffy fighter who had scratched his way toward wealth, and he wanted to help David succeed, for then as chairman, he too would be a success. David turned to Rubin and strengthened the case for a reinvented Roosevelt University.

"Al, you were good enough to give a million for that rented facility in Arlington Heights. The suburban campus bears your name. But now your gift will make the campus into a permanent contribution not only to Roosevelt but

34

also to the community where you've made your fortune. And it'll bear your name forever."

Rubin looked at Archer with a taut smile of condescension. "Forever, Alan? And ever?"

Al Rubin was no fool, and he would not be intimidated or coerced into pledging any significant amount of money—not by his fellow trustees. He fixed his eyes on Alan Archer.

"You're the chairman of this board, Alan. How much are you giving?"

Archer looked at him blankly.

"And you, Jerry, what are you contributing? Sid? Norm?"

So it went, or didn't go.

This was a moment that David would always remember as the one that could have been the turning point in his career and catapult him into spheres unimagined. Instead, all eyes looked everywhere except at Rubin and him.

"What do you guys think I am?" Rubin snarled quietly, grinning at all of them in contempt. "A patsy? A pigeon?"

David would scarcely remember how that luncheon finally dissolved, marked as it was by awkward exits and good wishes that left him standing empty-handed, like a well-dressed, beleaguered beggar whose tin cup is empty.

At Rubin's party on Saturday night, the rich and famous snowbirds from Chicago gathered to drink his wine and liquors. As Rubin introduced David to his friends, he praised him as "my visionary president" who had come to the Midwest from New York with the wonderful concept of a metropolitan university. "It's worth supporting, my friend. It's a contribution you'll be proud of."

Halfway through the evening, the front door opened, and there she was, radiant as ever. She entered quietly and modestly, with Buddy Mayer, as all eyes turned to her. It was as though the partygoers were caught unaware in some old photograph. Time stood still, then Alyce Parker smiled, and the room came alive. She was ravishing; she was as cool as the breeze outside and as fresh as the glow she shed on this ordinary party. Old friends circled her; others wondered who she was. This knockout of an ageless woman, with eyes that lit up the room. It had been three weeks since he'd run into her at Walgreens and one year almost to the day since he'd first observed her at the Crystal Ball. They acknowledged each other instantly.

Others faded from the room, and the two of them smiled at each other like old friends. She waved gently and made her way to him as he sipped a gin and tonic in a corner and tried to look relaxed.

"It's good to see you again. Buddy told me you might be here."

"With a tin cup in my hand, waiting for you to appear."

"You don't look like a man who owns a tin cup."

"What do I look like?"

"A university president. You look exactly like a university president. Impressive."

"Heaven forbid! Does it really show? Can I get you a drink?"

"Unnecessary. Here comes the waiter bearing one on a silver tray, no less."

What next? What could he say now? Buddy had clearly urged Alyce to visit her at Rancho Mirage as her guest once she realized that David was coming to fundraise and would be at Rubin's party. It would seem serendipitous; it would be a happenstance.

"I'm sorry I've been so slow in getting back to you. I've been busy wrapping up my affairs at Michael Reese."

"And now you're a woman without a portfolio."

"A woman who's ready to retire."

"Not necessarily. Will you meet with me?"

"Of course I'll meet with you. Buddy's been urging me to. I've been terribly rude for keeping you waiting. But you'll be wasting your time, Dr. Rosen."

"Dave."

"Dave. I'm not the one you're looking for. I don't belong in a university. I barely escaped the U of C as a student. I just don't see me in your setting—any academic setting. Someone once told me that academics argue so much because the stakes are so little. Is that true?"

The words they spoke no longer mattered.

A curl of her hair came loose. Her eyes remained fixed on his. "I'll call. I promise. This time, I'll call."

"Next week?"

"Next week."

He was in a daze for the rest of that party, but on the plane flying back to Chicago and later, as he settled into his condo and arrived at work on Monday morning, he was still empty-handed. He had achieved nothing. It had been all motion, with no actions and results. What did he need to do to excite the millionaires surrounding him? Was it the message that was wrong? His own impetuosity? The trip had been a failure, except for the brief encounter with Alyce Parker, but that was worth everything. He remembered her every feature with pleasure—her porcelain face, her high cheekbones, her slim figure, her vivacity, and the touch of those slender fingers on his forearm as she promised to call. She made him feel desirable and young again, with his fragile dream still intact.

"What the hell," Dan Pearson consoled David, after he dragged himself into his office.

"This has been my whole history at Roosevelt. These guys have never been asked for real money. They look at Roosevelt like a nice pet to have around the house. They don't take us seriously."

Janet Barnes echoed those words when he took her to lunch. Like Pearson, she had been at Roosevelt for so long that she too was beaten down, expecting very little and looking toward retirement. *I have to replace her,* David thought, *along with Pearson. I have to replace them with younger colleagues who can launch careers at Roosevelt. Fresh blood. Fresh ideas. I need someone with fresh ideas—someone like Alyce Parker—until I can find ambitious young replacements. I can't do this alone.*

Alyce Parker did call him a week after they'd returned from Rancho Mirage, but she said that she could not meet with him now. The folks at Michael Reese Hospital had asked her to stay on a few more weeks until they found her replacement. Before the end of April, she promised, if he was still interested in her, although she urged him to find someone who was more comfortable in the academic world.

The Unocal deadline was eighteen months away. In desperation, he called Al Rubin and prevailed upon him to contribute something if not everything, anything, so that other trustees like those who'd sat round the table at the Rancho Mirage Country Club would follow his lead. But Rubin was adamant. For tax purposes and personal

38

purposes, he could not contribute. "I didn't have to give any reason at all," he said.

On the first day of May, at eleven o'clock in the morning, when David was recovering from a sleepless night and analyzing what new angle he might try, his phone rang. It was Al Rubin. "Okay, Dave. I give up. You've worn me down and filled me with guilt. I'll do a million over five years. But I want you to know, this is only because of you. You. You. You. You are a persistent devil dog. You're a good man, and I consider you my friend. I want you to succeed. I hope this makes the rest of your day a little brighter."

"Thanks, Al. It certainly will."

When David went to work the next morning with a bounce in his step, he shared the good news with Dan Pearson and Janet Barnes, Janet beamed at him, "I have even better news."

"You won the lottery?"

"No."

"Your Aunt Tillie's won the lottery? Or better still, she's left you $5 million in her will and you're donating it to our capital campaign rather than go to the Fiji Islands?"

"No. Better than that."

"What could be better than a bequest of $5 million from Aunt Tillie? Or was it Aunt Lillie?"

"Neither. Alyce Parker has agreed to meet with you at the Pump Room, Friday morning for breakfast at eight."

"I'll take it." He smiled. "Congratulations. It's only taken eight months—"

"Don't hold grudges, Dave. You'll see. Don't let your ego get in the way. This elusive lady will be worth the wait."

6

The Pump Room was the legendary hideaway, where well-known people cut deals or propose marriage or begin professional relationships. It was Alyce's favorite restaurant in Chicago. On each wall bordering the entranceway, photographs celebrated gorgeous movie stars and other celebrities who had interrupted their trips from New York to Los Angeles to cavort for an evening in the windy city, the second city, Chicago, crossroads of the country. Their signatures were scrawled across airbrushed photographs so that patrons wouldn't forget who they were. If important enough, these celebrities sat in booth no. 1 with Irv Kupcinet, the avuncular gossip columnist who would give them inches of favorable ink in the next issue of *The Sun Times*. And this was the legendary spot—yes, the very booth beneath her window where she had enjoyed those early moments of a courtship and a marriage that promised hope and great expectations. It was where Matt had proposed to her fifty years ago and where they celebrated whatever new adventure he claimed would make them rich beyond their wildest dreams.

On the morning that she waited for David, business leaders were isolated soberly in silos of the restaurant, reading *The Chicago Tribune* or *The Wall Street Journal* or *The Sun Times*. She was the only woman in the room, sitting in the booth that she and Matt had reserved as their own, poised and cheerful in the glow of sunshine that flickered through the window. She was facing North State Street and was sipping coffee like an habitué. Everyone in the restaurant and in the Ambassador East Hotel that housed it treated her like family.

"Why have I kept this man waiting as long as I have? Rude, rude, unforgivably rude," she scolded herself. "And so uncharacteristic of me. Why has he been on my mind when I scarcely know him? Why am I meeting with him at all, after all these months? Is it only to pursue a job I know I'll need if I want to maintain my lifestyle? Or is it something else as well? Why do I feel so uncertain, so unsettled, so nervous, and why, oh god, why am I attracted to him at all?" She remembered that his hair, especially on the sides of that handsome head, needed to be brushed more firmly. If she was his partner, she would definitely buy him a brush—a nice one, French, for style.

She remembered standing naked before her mirror that morning, studying her aging face and waiting for the cosmetics to conceal its slight imperfections. She had thought of David as an attractive man, a focused leader, as she was told, with a sense of purpose—unlike Matt. She was vaguely ashamed of her insecurities and social snobbery. Roosevelt would be a fine institution to work for.

She wanted to be admired by everyone, but now, on this morning, she wanted to be admired by David Rosen. Why? Why, David Rosen? She didn't even know him. Seventeen months had gone by since the Crystal Ball and weeks since she'd seen him at Walgreens and then at Al Rubin's party.

Sitting in the corner booth that she had shared with Matt when they were in their twenties and hopelessly in love, she remembered how curious she'd become about David Rosen and how she had even studied his website, which listed all the books he'd written, politically liberal studies of ethnicity and the American dream, and finally the upward thrust of his administrative career. Here it was another year gone by, time was flying, and she had turned seventy. Unlike her dead husband, she considered herself a sensible liberal, just a little left of center, although the newspaper she read each morning was *The Wall Street Journal.* Could she fit in at Roosevelt? Of course, she could. She could fit in anywhere. Hadn't she volunteered for reading programs in Cabrini Green? Hadn't she worked for the Red Cross during the war? Hadn't she tried to help the Auditorium Theatre Council resurrect its great democratic space for people of all classes? Hadn't she always written large checks for charity when she could afford to, even though Matt always objected to her excessive generosity? "Money down the rabbit hole," he would grouse. But now, it was no longer a matter of choice. She could no longer afford to be selflessly charitable, but she could work for a nonprofit organization in a cause she championed. A university? A university as gritty and liberal as Roosevelt? Who ever thought she'd even consider a university? But this adventure was something new. It was something different, wasn't it? She needed a decent salary to continue appearing as she had always appeared—affluent and independent. She kept trying to convince herself that she would be wise to accept his offer, if he made one. Why not? What had she to lose? And she smiled mischievously. It didn't hurt, did it, that she also found him so personally attractive?

She'd taken time to dress for the occasion so that she would look younger than her years. She had chosen her beige St. John suit to wear and the simple silver necklace from Jensen's that Matt had given her many years ago, when he was on the brink of success as a stockbroker and they were still more or less in love with each other. The day before, she had taken time to have her stylist prepare the thick auburn hair that graced those strong high cheekbones and color it to hide the emerging gray. Her thin nose was an improvement over its original; her clear brow and her neck bore no visible wrinkles; the ineffable smile brightened the room like a touch of early morning sunlight, and the scent hovered round large, friendly eyes that sparkled with perennial optimism. She was pleased with how she looked for someone seventy-one. She felt beautiful, agelessly beautiful, and she knew the power of her beauty after a lifetime of admirers told her so.

Sitting in her corner of the Pump Room, she felt her eyes grow moist as she remembered the lost years with a troubled husband. Her head was swirling with anxiety and some self-doubt—until a shadow swept across her vision. David Rosen was standing on the steps above the floor of the room, scanning it, searching for her, then finding her, soon appearing before her, and smiling as though there were no one else in the world he'd rather be with than Alyce Parker. He seemed youthful, more attractive than she remembered, dressed in a dark suit and a blue shirt with a subtly patterned crimson tie, his light-brown hair slightly askew and definitely in need of a brush, eyes darting, grinning at her as though they were old friends who hadn't seen one another for a long time. Why, she wondered, had she ever hesitated meeting with him in the first place?

"I ordered coffee," she apologized. "I hope you don't mind."

"I didn't keep you waiting, did I?" he said nervously, glancing at his watch. "We did say eight o'clock?"

"Oh, you're on time. I'm the one who's early. I have a habit of always arriving beforehand when the appointment is important."

"I'm flattered to be considered important."

"Come, come, Dr. Rosen. You're the president."

"Of a small university."

"Your modesty is charming. I'm sorry I've been so hesitant. I've been—"

"We do keep missing each other, don't we? Or bumping into each other accidentally."

"You must think I'm playing hard to get. It's just—"

"It doesn't matter. My PR person keeps telling me that you're well worth waiting for. And she's never wrong."

"We'll see about that. I've been under stress leaving Michael Reese—"

"And wondering what the next job will be?"

"Something like that."

He leaned forward and almost touched her hand to reassure her.

"Roosevelt could be the next job."

She smiled. "Whoa . . ."

She observed him as his eyes wandered to other early birds at other tables and then settled on her with the kind of look every woman desires—one of admiration and respect and gratitude.

"Why do I feel as though I'm the luckiest man in this room?"

She held him in her gaze, smiling a little at his glibness, but she was pleased nevertheless.

This meeting was an interview of sorts she knew, but as their eyes connected, it was far more than that. It was the smile of two people who know immediately, upon their very first encounter, that they will have a future together.

"By now, you must feel like a Chicagoan."

"I came to this strange city in September 1988. It's seventeen months to the day."

"In a city very different from New York."

"A friendlier city. A city that's more accessible."

"But less exciting?"

"Exciting enough for me. When I need New York, I visit friends and colleagues from my former life."

"It must be hard to go home again."

"Harder and harder. The city grows naturally dimmer—like a fading love affair. And you? You're a lifelong Chicagoan, aren't you?"

"Do I look it? Do I look that Midwestern? Solid and stable and reliable—and just a little dull?"

"I wouldn't exactly call you dull, Alyce Parker."

"Alyce."

"If you're dull, there's no hope for the rest of us."

"In the spirit of full disclosure," she said matter-of-factly. She could already feel her blood racing, and she needed to slow down. "I was born and bred on the South Side before it became the dangerous South Side. After the war, my husband and I moved to Winnetka on the North Shore, next to Buddy Mayer's mansion, on the hill above Green Bay Road. She was the rich one in the neighborhood. Our home was more modest. But it did have a white picket fence and two gorgeous girls. Mine was the usual fairy tale."

"It sounds like paradise. A lot more comfortable than living in an attached brownstone in East Flatbush, Brooklyn, with an aunt and uncle in one bedroom, an Orthodox grandfather in another, and my brother and me in the third."

"Did the grandfather have a beard?"

"A long one. He also had a skullcap and a perpetual grouch. The grouch was important. He thought it made him look like a wise patriarch thinking deep thoughts. He spoke in Yiddish and broken English, depending upon his mood. Your life sounds so American—far more idyllic than mine."

"Not quite. But that's what it was supposed to be when we started out."

"What does your husband do now?"

"My husband?" She hesitated. "Matt? Oh, he's been dead for seven years."

"And before that?"

"He worked at a variety of things. Off and on. On and off." She smiled cryptically and picked up the menu to indicate that this was a subject she'd really rather not pursue—not at this first extended meeting, however appealing David was proving to be. Crossing her mind were images of Matt, fresh out of Brown, an heir to wealth, living in his parents' mansion in Glencoe, the air force down south and his passion to be a pilot, tuberculosis, the

46

end of one dream and the quest for another, and failing at each new enterprise until he was too sick to work anymore. Women, liquor—it was all too distressing and complicated to discuss with this self-confident, ambitious university president.

They took their time ordering. She recommended the eggs benedict, claiming that they were the best in town.

"But you have to like eggs."

"I didn't, until now. Now I'm finding eggs appealing, especially when they're eggs benedict."

She broke out laughing. "Oh, you're too much."

"Your reputation is on the line." He looked up at the waiter. "Eggs benedict, please. I understand they're the best in town."

"That's what everyone tells us," the waiter boasted. "It's Mrs. Parker's favorite dish."

Friends had told her that he'd lost his wife shortly after coming to Chicago, but now, months later, as she watched him, whatever pain he must have suffered seemed to have diminished. When she first learned of his tragedy, her interest in him had risen.

His hair needs a light brushing. She smiled to herself. He was a handsome man, intelligent, ambitious, and with eyes that never left hers. He was the kind of man you instinctively feel you can trust.

"You've accomplished a great deal in two short years."

"I've tried."

"No, it's true. Roosevelt is known everywhere now. I hear about it all the time in a way I never did."

"The university's being reinvented," he said, encouraged by her words. "At least that's what I tell everyone." He put a packet he'd brought with him on the table, and smiling in self-deprecation, he withdrew his plan *Finding the Center*. "Witness my master plan."

"In two short years?" She laughed. "Some of us would just be settling in."

"It was in my mind before I arrived. It was also in the minds of Roosevelt administrators who sent me packages of proposals that they must have known would never be realized. Their dreams were bound up in thick manila folders before I even came. There's probably more in this master plan than anyone could ever accomplish in one presidency. I know that."

She smiled and waited before she spoke again, looking at him evenly. Moving awkwardly in her place, she tried to shake loose her spontaneous attraction to him, searching for a way to appear more like a businesswoman.

"Tell me why I'm here, President Rosen."

"President Rosen. Oh, no. You make me sound like an institution. My real friends call me Dave."

"Tell me. Why am I here?"

"To help me make it happen."

"It? Roosevelt?" She braced herself. "I'm not a rich woman, Dr. Rosen."

"Dave."

"Dave."

"Your personal situation has nothing to do with what I have in mind. Nothing. Believe me."

"Then why am I here?"

"To work with me. You can help make this master plan a reality."

"I can? Whoever told you that?"

"Everyone. You're a legend in this town, but especially Buddy Mayer, your lifelong friend. She's urged me to see you—she and so many others. Your reputation precedes you." He pushed the packet slowly toward her. "Just read these materials and tell me what you think. Even if you don't wind up at Roosevelt, I'd value your opinion."

She could feel his attraction to her and was flattered. It went far beyond her ability as fund-raiser. It was the power of her beauty, her magnetism, her poise, and her optimism. She had seen its effect on other men, and she carried it naturally like a hidden gift, a source of power. He was different from all the others—confident in himself, without the arrogance of being confident. Still, she felt distant from academia, even though she had struggled through the University of Chicago, starting as a seventeen-year-old who was intimidated by intellectuals but became, by her senior year, the most popular if not most brilliant girl in her class—the beauty queen, Betty Co-Ed. Everyone thought of her as stunning, and boys were afraid to approach her for a date. When they did work up the courage to ask her out, they found her lovely and lively and unpretentious and compassionate and intelligent enough. She was a short pixieish girl who became pretty and then matured into a beauty, with a smile that was infectious and invited friendship. She could see that the magic had affected him too. He was hooked.

He warned her that Roosevelt was not the U of C by a long shot; it was just a relatively small local university with a host of fiscal anxieties and a class of people that had returned for a second chance in life—people she had never known in her own youth or adulthood.

"If you do turn me down, I'd like to see you again, in any case. I'll come as a human being then, not as the pompous, pretentious president of a university."

"You're not—"

"I'll brush my hair. I can see it bothers you."

"Oh no, you're lucky to have a head of thick brown hair."

"I may not even wear a tie. How's that?"

"Oh, you are good." She leaned back and laughed. "You are a determined man on every level, aren't you? I am flattered, and I'm sure we will see each other, one way or the other. I'd like that, especially if you take a moment to brush your hair. But you exaggerate my abilities. I know so little about your university—just gossip. The conflict with the Auditorium Theatre Council, for example, and the wish to spread your wings to the suburbs."

"You've done your homework, haven't you? The first needs explanation, and the second you should believe."

"Is that so?"

"The theater belongs to the university, but the council doesn't quite agree with me."

"Be careful." She winked. "I might be a spy. I might report you to the enemy. I was once tight with the Auditorium Theatre Council. Many of my friends are still serving on the council. They paint you as a philistine, interested only in the university, not the theater."

"But you don't believe that."

"I don't know enough. I don't want to believe it. Now that I've met you, I certainly don't want to believe it. The rumor round town is that you're going to have to go to court."

"Exactly—and the lawyers will grow filthy rich. But I'm not a philistine, and I do believe in the long-range goals of the theater."

She smiled and wanted to assure him that she did believe him.

"I do," he insisted. "The second bit of gossip is absolutely true. I want Roosevelt to spread its wings into the northwest suburbs and grow into a metropolitan university."

"Make no small plans." She smiled, noticing a smidgen of butter on the left side of his lips and instinctively wanting to wipe it away with her napkin. She didn't want to believe some of the rumors she'd heard about his desire to appropriate theater funds. That was not the man she was looking at with growing fondness.

"This master document is called *Finding the Center*. Help me find my center, Alyce Parker. Somewhere in the soul of me, there is a center."

"You don't have to convince me."

"Just read this first draft. You'll see what I mean. You're a quick study."

"I am?"

"I can see it in your eyes."

"Whoa," she said, raising her hands in self-defense and fearing that they were moving too fast too soon. "This is getting to be more than an interview."

"What *is* the color of your eyes? Deep gray? Blue?"

"That depends on the beholder."

"They're too deep to be just gray. I vote for blue, maybe even a touch of violet. Read my plan. You are a quick study, I know. At least, that's what everyone tells me. It's a rumor I've heard all over town. Just coming over here, the cabdriver was saying . . . When did you go to the University of Chicago?"

"In the late thirties. They took in the underaged in those days. I was a mere toddler."

"The brightest of the bright."

"Everyone except me."

"I doubt that. As a girl, then you just weren't supposed to be aggressively intelligent."

"How kind you are."

Now I've given away my age, she reproached herself. *Naked. Numbers. Approaching old age. When does old age begin? I hate the idea of it—growing old. This is no country for older women. I know that. I'm beyond the physical interest of men. They no longer desire me, although they used to line up. And now David Rosen has lined up. He still finds me attractive. Why do I need to pass this interview? To impress this man I don't even know and to want him to desire me? Why do I even care? Why am I nervous and insecure? Why does he have to be so appealing, with a slight bit of fuzz just below his chin that his razor missed this morning, all fire and brimstone, with the passion of a thirty-year-old starting out in life full of energy and purpose, determined to conquer?* For no reason, she remembered someone at a recent party—Josh, an older man: "How's your sex life?" "Not so hot" was the rapid response. "But I have great memories." More and more, her life at seventy-one was becoming a series of memories and snapshots of desire, passion, and almost love.

"You're a very lucky woman to have made aging a mockery."

"Really? Don't ask me my age."

"Fifty-nine. My age."

"You're a very kind man, Dr. Rosen."

"You're an ageless beauty. Look, I'd better become presidential again and return to the reason we're sitting here before I get myself into trouble."

"As you were saying?"

"Roosevelt's not Chicago or Northwestern," he admitted. "It's not even DePaul or Loyola. But it does have great expectations."

"The university has? Or David Rosen has?"

"There's no difference between the two. Roosevelt— c'est moi."

By the end of the hour-long breakfast, Alyce's head was also spinning. He had made her feel young again. She agreed to review the materials he'd prepared. She warned him of her other obligations—volunteer work at Michael Reese now that she was retiring and then the Lyric Opera and Lincoln Park Zoo. There were other obligations as well—family obligations. She had no time for Roosevelt; she knew so little about the institution or about fund-raising in higher education. But as a courtesy to Buddy Mayer and to him, she did agree to take his thick packet home. The more she uttered these disclaimers, the more she betrayed her attraction to him.

"My packet of possibilities." He smiled. "Just keep an open mind, Mrs. Parker."

"Alyce."

"Alyce." He smiled, rolling her name between his lips. "Alyce Parker. Alyce Parker. Alyce. It takes practice. I keep reminding myself to see this as strictly a business arrangement."

"No more than that?"

"What would you say?"

"I'd say let's wait to see."

"And I'd say I know already."

"No, you don't. You think you do, but at this moment, you really just want to use me."

"Which is a good excuse for seeing you again, soon."

At the coat check, he helped her with her winter coat—not quite mink but some other fur. It was modest but more expensive than the usual winter coat. Outside the door, in the bitter winter cold, her hair lost its control and danced freely in the frigid, windy air.

"You're quite a salesman."

"We'll see how successful a salesman I am when we speak again."

"If—"

"*When* we speak again."

"Yes. One way or the other, we will see each other again, won't we?"

"If I have anything to say, we will."

Their eyes connected once more in a way that had little to do with Roosevelt University or a master plan for its revival or any of the other pragmatic ways of the world. She hadn't met anyone quite like him for a very long time. No one had even come close. Her beaux were all CEOs or vice presidents cut from the same cloth. David Rosen seemed so alive and comfortable in his own skin that she felt a little weak within herself. She had never experienced a connection quite like this, not even when she was in her early twenties and Matt was pursuing her, trailing as always behind her other would-be lovers. Matt was the sensible choice then—or so it seemed. Matt was homebred and comfortable. Fifty years later, now, this feeling was distinctly different. Once again, she was young. Her hair crossed her face like a silken curtain, and she pulled her headscarf tighter round her reddened cheeks so that she left him with the image of those dazzling eyes. She knew, oh she knew, the effect she was having on him—and he on her.

A cab was waiting to steal her away. She thanked him formally for the breakfast. "I'll call you once I've read your materials."

"And try to remember me as someone other than a university president."

"That, sir, will not be hard to do."

As he helped her into the cab, she knew that beyond her skepticism and doubts about Roosevelt, she would not turn him down, whatever was in the packet she clutched.

She might be misleading herself, she knew. He might be just a charmer—an ambitious president who was beguiling her for her extraordinary fund-raising abilities. But she didn't want to believe that.

"You'd have to be crazy to take a job like this," Julie, her daughter, admonished her.

"Why?"

"Because Roosevelt is a second-rate university not worthy of your talents."

"That's easy for you to say. You are aware that I'm currently in a stage of unemployment."

"Oh, please, Mom. You don't need this kind of downscale employment. Academic employment. Ugh. Plebian employment. Whining, cynical liberals. This David Rosen sounds like a seductive devil out for what he can get. He simply wants to use you—to exploit your talents. Can't you see that? At your age, you deserve better. You deserve retirement. I'm sure you have enough—"

"I do? And how would you know that, Julie?"

"Dad must have left you with plenty—"

"Your sainted father left me with nothing but debts. I've told you that again and again, but you refuse to believe it.

He burned through our savings with all his cockamamie schemes to grow rich fast so long as he didn't have to work hard. He left me with a mess of debt. If you don't know that by now, you haven't been paying attention. Your father is the reason I had to grab the salaried job at Michael Reese in the first place. Didn't you know that?" Her voice bit the words in suppressed anger. "Are you blind? That's why I'll have to find something now."

"I don't believe it. Dad would never have left you completely high and dry."

"Oh, no? Wake up, Julie. Wake up for once in your life. Your glorified view of your father has never quite matched reality."

"Don't start denigrating him to me. We'll never agree. He was your husband, he was my father—there's a difference. He was always good to me. Please don't take this job, Mom. I know it's wrong for you. It's beneath you. Roosevelt has no class. It's a university that'll take in anyone who applies. Open admissions. I know they took me into their paralegal program and look where I'm at now. Unemployed. Between jobs. Just like Dad."

"That's not Roosevelt's fault."

"The place caters to older part-time students who've lost their way in life."

"What's wrong with that as a mission for a college?"

"I'm sorry. The place has no class, and you are the essence of class."

"Class doesn't pay for the lifestyle I've grown accustomed to."

"Oh, please stop crying poor. You've been living pretty well. Astor Street isn't exactly Stony Island Boulevard.

A beautiful furnished apartment. I don't see how your lifestyle has been affected."

"Not yet."

"Let me ask you something. Do you know anything about Roosevelt? I mean, its history? Its struggles?"

"Yes, I do."

"The place started out with a rebellion of the president and faculty against YMCA trustees—your socialite friends, now grown old. They wouldn't let Negroes use their swimming pool."

"I know all that, Julie."

"Who knows? They were probably right. The radical faculty resigned from the YMCA College and took over the Auditorium Building after the war."

"I know that. You don't have to lecture me. I was there. I was on the Auditorium Theatre Council for three years when you were a child. I know its history. Why shouldn't Negroes use the swimming pool?"

"Please, Mother."

"Why shouldn't they?"

"Please you're talking to me."

"Why shouldn't they?" Alyce clasped her forehead with her free hand. She recalled the struggle to reopen the theater, which had been the home for the symphony and opera at the turn of the century before it was forced to close down. Bea Spachner, her good friend, had asked her to serve on the council together with others who struggled to raise money so that the tired, tattered colossus of a theater—4,200 seats—could open again and be restored to its former glory. But it never did find its focus, so Alyce went on to more solid, more prestigious, and less troubled institutions.

"Do you know what this new president of Roosevelt, this immigrant from New York, is trying to do?" Julie snarled. "Now that the theater is finally succeeding, he wants to use its profits from *Les Miserables* and *Phantom of the Opera* to open a second campus in Schaumburg."

"I know. I know. I've read his materials."

"Well, that's just not right after all their work. All these university presidents are egomaniacs who have edifice complexes or football teams or dreams of expansion. Penis promotion, I call it. Megalomania—bigger is better. That's the disease of university presidents these days. They're not educators anymore. They're entrepreneurs, accountants, fund-raisers, salesmen, hucksters. Don't go near him or that university, Mom. It's a losing proposition. I don't want you to demean yourself."

After these testy exchanges, Alyce inevitably would call her younger daughter for the support she needed. Laura had relocated herself in St. Louis as a designer for Plunkett's Furniture and was trying to put her life together again as a forty-five-year-old woman who could support herself. After listening to her mother's doubts and fears, she said simply, "Mom, do what's good for you. Don't listen to Julie. She's trying to make you into an old woman before your time. You'll never be an old woman. Do what will make *you* happy."

What a comfort Laura could be! What a contrast to her sister. She had been through hell and back: sexual molestation by her uncle Ben at the age of seven; a wild, rebellious adolescence; pregnancy at twenty; surrender of her infant boy to adoption and a year-long residence in a psychiatric home to restore her sanity; marriage then to a talented cinematographer who took her to Hollywood; a drug scene that led her from taking to selling coke; and

God knows what else. After the bitter divorce, she returned to Chicago, worked at Plunkett's Furniture, and then the transfer to St. Louis. When Alyce rolled the clock back and remembered the darkest moments of her life with Laura, she wondered what had gone wrong with her girl and why she had lost control, and she blamed it all on Matt. He was off tilting financial windmills after he'd abandoned his own father's clothing business and drifted from one entrepreneurial disaster after the other.

But when she was totally honest with herself, she also wondered whether she, too, might be at fault—at least partially at fault. She was a mother lost to philanthropy. Laura's journey had indeed been rocky, but now she was living a quiet existence in a small nondescript rented apartment, with one or two women at Plunkett's she could call friends. She was still as thin as a twig, a pretty, caring woman who finally gave comfort to her mother after so many years of having plagued her with grief.

As Alyce sat with the document, *Finding the Center,* she wasn't thinking of her daughters' reactions to Roosevelt University or to David Rosen. She wasn't thinking of Roosevelt. At seventy-one, she was remembering David and imagining him as a lonely widower who had no woman to check him out. Could she be falling for this man at this stage of her life? He was searching for the center of his university, but he was also searching for his own soul. As he'd said, it was somewhere at the center of himself. She, too, had been searching for her center—the need for unconditional love that had never been satisfied by Matt or the men who were her escorts after his death.

She closed David's master plan and smiled to herself and wondered, *What would it be like working with David Rosen?*

7

After Al Rubin's reluctant gift of one million dollars, David still needed three more to secure the bank loan of twenty-one million before June of the next year. Unocal, the company that owned the property, would have returned to California by then, and it would have left behind two hundred twenty-five acres of prime land and well-maintained buildings that with the appropriate architectural conversion could become a choice suburban campus northwest of Chicago, where some of the finest school districts thrived. He felt the pressure of a deadline that was now only four months away, but that seemed to be closing in on him. Even if he could raise the $3 million and secure that bank loan, he would then need to find still more funds to turn the plot of land into a university campus. David felt that it marked the test of his presidency and, in a sense, his entire career, maybe even his life.

Everything had been a preparation for this achievement. He knew that the full expression of his vision, captured so eloquently in the shiny packet he'd given to Alyce Parker, would demand a capital campaign of at least $50 million. That worried the trustees who, as never before, would be asked to contribute. It concerned the faculty too. They had never been challenged to think so ambitiously, and now they had to develop enrollments to demonstrate that there was vitality within the core of the university that trustees and donors could support. These anxieties increasingly troubled David, who worried about where the money would come from. Growing enrollments? Private fund-raising? These were his self-created responsibilities now—his and his alone. As he grew more anxious about his ability to raise the necessary funds, he kept returning to the image of Alyce Parker, who rose in importance when he saw no other way to reach his goal but who also had become of equal importance to him personally. He wanted to meet her for dinner after work, to take her to Steppenwolf and the Symphony and the Opera, to know her darkest secrets, and to have her in his bed and share his anxiety and then make love to her as often as age would allow and lie beside her, sharing her warmth.

8

She reread the report several times and was eager to help him and to be with him, but this decision was too important, especially at this late stage in her life, for her to make alone. She consulted those closest to her: Josie Strauss, who listened carefully and ended the conversation by wondering why she needed the job and if should she just retire and find some retired executive to care for her in both of their retirements; Bootsie Nathan, who worried about the quality of Roosevelt and wondered how much Alyce knew about the uncharted territory of academia; Laura, who told her to follow her instincts but to wait until she was dead certain if she had the slightest doubt; and Julie, who repeated her rejection of David Rosen and continued to insist that it was just a bad fit between Alyce and him, between her mother and this man's Roosevelt University.

Doubt and caution, despite all her years in fund-raising, clouded her instinct to say yes. As she wrestled with her decision for the next few days, she found it hard to distinguish between the fear of failing in an academic world she did not know and her attraction to the man who was offering her an exciting opportunity—and possibly himself. In the end, her reason overruled her instinct.

She called his office in the late afternoon and was startled when he answered himself.

"Dr. Rosen? This is Alyce Parker. I'm sorry if I'm calling so late."

"Not at all. For me, it's just the middle of the day."

"A workaholic."

"All my life."

"Look. I must ask your forgiveness for failing to thank you for the stimulating breakfast we had."

"You're granted absolution, especially if you're calling to tell me we'll be working together."

There was an inevitable pause and then, "I've read your document by now, and it is compelling. It's visionary and ambitious, but I'm not the fund-raiser you're looking for."

"Why not?"

"I just don't feel comfortable in academia. All my fund-raising has been in the arts—"

"And everywhere else."

"You've done your homework." She laughed. "Please don't press on. It's hard enough to say no to you as it is."

"Will you see me once again? I won't wear a tie, I promise."

"No, I can't. You're too persuasive."

"Then will you see me if I promise not to say a word about Roosevelt University?"

"No, Dr. Rosen. Both of us know that won't work."

"Why not?"

"Because we'll wind up talking about nothing but Roosevelt University."

"Try me."

"No, it won't work, and you know it. You're an engaging man with an engaging plan, and I wish you the best of luck. If I can help you in any small way, I'll be happy to."

9

When David hung up, he was disoriented and upset. He had thought for certain that she would accept his offer. He saw Bob Green standing at the entranceway to his office. It was late March, and the temperature outside hovered in the callous teens. Snow was falling heavily outside his office window. Bob was dressed in a heavy overcoat and a Cossack hat that made him like look a poor Russian peasant out of a Tolstoy novel. He had a stuffed briefcase in hand. He was going home and leaving David alone in the building. Immersed in the depressing numbers of his budget, half-hidden by a lamplight on his desk, David glanced up at his friend to bid him good night. Bob could see that he was in a sour mood and approached him.

"What's up?"

"Oh, nothing. Just another day of nothing. She turned me down."

"She?"

"Alyce Parker."

'Oh, I thought it was something serious. I've been wanting to talk to you about her. Come to the Hilton with me. Let me buy you a drink. We both need a drink."

"I can't, Bob. I don't need a drink, and I certainly don't need tea and sympathy. I need to put this budget to rest."

"It'll wait for the morning. Those shitty numbers will still be shitty. Let me worry about them. That's what a good provost is supposed to do: relieve the anxiety of his president. You know the cliché: "Provosts say no, presidents say yes and make all the victory speeches.""

They walked two blocks south to the Hilton Hotel through mounting snow that made driving and even walking treacherous. In a corner booth, they ordered two scotches on the rocks and recalled their bucolic days at Penn State Harrisburg. Bob Green looked like a quiet academic soul, but beneath his benevolent smile was a raging bull who wanted to see the world now, live now, before it was too late. At Penn State, his wife, Teddy, had left him for another faculty member, and he went on to have an affair with Paula, the wife of that same faculty member. Only in academe. It was a scandalous mess on a small campus—wife swapping *in extremis.* Bob was glad to escape to Roosevelt when David urged him to assume the key internal role of his administration. In the last two years, he and Paula had gone to the Antarctica and the Galapagos, with plans for Iceland and the Canadian northwest. Given his hunched back, his bald head, his soft voice, and short height, Bob Green was the last man one would suspect of having been embroiled in a sexual scandal or of believing in *carpe diem.* At Roosevelt, he was the leader everyone could depend upon: steady, solid, smart, and compassionate—especially toward David, his compatriot, his coauthor of the master plan, and his friend.

"Dave, you're driving yourself nuts."

David listened.

"Our plan is a bold concept of what Roosevelt ought to be, but it can't be now, nor in the short span of your presidency. Ten years will it be? You must know that's true. Too far, too soon. The consultant's right. Anderson's right. I'm right. You have to get used to incrementalism, frustrating as it might be. Stop torturing yourself. You can't carry this burden alone."

"With a little bit of luck—"

"In the form of Alyce Parker? You're dreaming."

"She does know everyone. I just have to make the case persuasively enough."

"Careful, my friend. There is no silver bullet. She's no silver bullet. Let's build a development staff from within and find a vice president for Development who comes out of academia and can build a department to support a capital campaign and *then* create a second campus. There'll always be the possibility of a second campus. That should be enough of a legacy for any single person, even you. Right now, your vision's way ahead of reality. A university, especially one with no money, is like a tugboat—it turns slowly. No part-time lady, even though she may know every millionaire in town, can deliver on what you demand."

"What's your problem with Alyce Parker?"

"I have nothing against her. She's lovely, beautiful, and classy. But she doesn't belong at Roosevelt. You're lucky she turned you down. Her telling you that she doesn't know enough about academia is sheer bullshit. She just doesn't want an association with plebes like you and me. She belongs in a small college like Mount Holyoke or Vassar. She'll collide with the culture of Roosevelt."

David could see that his friend had finally realized he was too stubborn or vain to hear the truth that he feared himself.

"Don't drive yourself nuts, Dave. She's not your silver bullet. You're playing in the big leagues when you dance with her."

"I don't know. I was thinking of a part-time position, at most, reporting to me."

"Just be careful. She's a beautiful, intoxicating woman. I can understand—"

"It's none of that," he lied. "This is all about a jumpstart, a catalyst."

"Just be careful. That's all I'm saying, my friend. Be careful. Get her out of your head. We'll reserve enough in the budget to attract a first-rate replacement for Dan Pearson, and then we'll build a development staff— appointment by appointment."

David listened to the plodding voice of his friend, but he knew that he was not done with the pursuit of Alyce Parker. What had gone wrong? He could sense she had been on the edge of accepting his offer; he just had to find the right way to allay her fears. She was indeed, he was convinced, his silver bullet.

As the clock in the lobby read midnight, they gathered their heavy coats to leave the hotel.

"Let me drive you home, Dave."

"No, no, thanks." *Thanks for nothing,* he really thought. *Thanks for the caution. Thanks for mediocrity.* "I need to walk home."

"In this blizzard?"

It was a formidable mile and a half to David's condo. He could scarcely see three yards ahead of himself as he walked home alone. He wanted to be cold. He wanted to walk home alone. As he broke through the blinding whiteness and crossed the bridge over the Chicago River to the shops that were closed for the night, all he could think of was Alyce Parker—the encouraging smile that shone through her eyes, the hope and promise and change she embodied, and the excitement that made him want to be with her. When he thought of her, his body warmed, his blood raced, and he knew he had to have her as his partner. But what kind of partner would she be? Professional or personal? Or both?

His days were consumed with anxiety as he wondered whom he could turn to. The evenings were still lonely and long. *Why have a dream at all*, he asked himself, *if you have no one to share it with? Why go home if there's no one to go home to?* In the middle of the night, he had confessed his hopes and fears with Debra, but it was two years already since her death. Her image had now grown fainter and fainter.

He began socializing to overcome the hard loneliness of the widower. His new friends in Chicago, most of them trustees, invited him to dinner parties where they paired him with wealthy widows or divorcees or sprightly spinsters who also craved companionship. At Irene Albright's vintage condo on Lake Shore Drive near Burton, he found himself in a dining room with nine other guests. Irene was a trustee with lovable, almost-comical hauteur that resembled a carryover from the age of Victorian England. With aplomb, she tinkled a little bell for the butler to bring out the next course of her elaborate dinner. She had insisted on introducing him to a well-coiffed blond heiress who kept describing her winters in Palm Beach, her travels to the Orient, and her admiration for Ronald Reagan—a man who looks like a president and acts like a president and has a genuine love affair with Nancy. He smiled at her vacantly and thought to himself, *What in hell am I doing here? Who is this vapid woman so different from anyone I've ever known?*

Joan Reed was another trustee and a vice president at Aon. She was in her midforties, aging gently but inexorably, and had never found someone to marry her. She invited him to lunch and asked him, "What is your most distinctive, promising unit?" When he answered "The Chicago Musical College and the Auditorium Theatre Council," she urged him to lead with that potential strength. "Then the more traditional academic colleges will follow. Success breeds success." A week later, Joan Reed called to say she just happened to have an extra ticket to *Nabucco* and asked if he cared to go. Dinner in the green room and then the opera?

Others, so many others—they blurred in his mind. He placed an ad in the personal section of *The New York Review of Books*, but the responses were from other academics lost in the woods like him, and none of them compared to Alyce Parker. He tended to measure all others against her. Like a stalker, he found himself searching the papers for her name, her photo, and every tidbit about where she was and what she was doing, until he couldn't find her and began to agree, reluctantly, with Bob Green. Alyce Parker was no silver bullet; there was no silver bullet. Whatever personal chemistry he had imagined between them was illusory, a farfetched fantasy. She was a gorgeous woman and probably had that magical effect on everyone she met.

Then just when the evenings could no longer mask his fear of failing, the personal and professional dots connected, like so many separate stars that cluster to form a constellation.

She thought of Buddy Mayer—the daughter of Nathan Cummings, the founder and CEO of Sara Lee, and a close friend of Alyce, as far back as Hyde Park and the U of C. She was the heiress to that huge conglomerate of pastries and lingerie, and God knows what other domestic delicacy one might desire.

Buddy was a long-standing but inactive trustee of Roosevelt. David had tried to engage her philanthropically, but her primary interests were health care and contemporary art, and in the early months of his presidency, he had little to offer. She and Alyce became the closest of neighbors in Winnetka, and after their husbands passed away, they moved into the city and remained good friends. Buddy was rich but homely, smart and kind, and a social worker by training who wanted now to save the downtrodden with her fortune, while Alyce was beautiful but pinched financially, although no one in the world would ever know. Buddy told David that she would continue to try to broker a relationship between Alyce and him—and finally, she was successful in inviting both of them to her suite at the Ritz Carleton.

The walls of her elaborate suite featured Pollack, Lichtenstein, Jasper John, and others. It was as though he was entering the formal gallery of a small family museum of contemporary art—a sacred and munificent place where he didn't belong. Alyce Parker had been there for some time it seemed, sitting comfortably on the sofa and sipping tea. She was slim and youthful as always in a simple light

71

blue dress that ushered in spring and contrasted with the multicolored images of the paintings. As he approached her, he felt like kissing her cheek spontaneously and impetuously, but he didn't dare. For a dizzying moment, he wondered whether he had come to solicit her services as a professional fund-raiser or simply to meet her again, to woo her again, and to renew their obvious attraction to one another.

"I believe you two have met before." Buddy smiled.

"Thanks for agreeing to see me."

"Buddy is very persuasive." Alyce smiled. "So are you. She's been working me over for the past few days."

"And here I come, with tin cup in hand."

"I don't see a tin cup. Do you, Buddy?"

"Oh, the cup's invisible," he said. "We presidents are discreet. I've really come to see you."

Buddy served a *salade nicoise* that had been prepared by her cook. Then, after a few words meant to relax her guests, she sat back and let David and Alyce rediscover each other. He listened to her as she described a reception and concert she had been to the night before. "It was to greet Daniel Barenboim as the new conductor of the CSO. He played Mozart's Twenty-First Piano Concerto as well as conducted the Symphonie Fantastique. Just fabulous. When we thought the evening was over, he reemerged on stage, dressed informally, and began to serenade us with piano favorites from Spain and South America."

"I should have been with you."

"Yes, you should have. You would have loved it."

"Next time."

Who was with you? he wondered. *Who? I would have taken you to the Rhapsody adjacent to Symphony Hall and eaten dinner with you before the concert then held your hand while Barenboim played, and afterward I would have been the one to drive you home.*

For a moment, he forgot that he was here to persuade her to be his fund-raiser. They chatted randomly, as he turned on all the charm he possessed, sensing she might be on the verge of accepting his offer. When they turned to the subject of Roosevelt, he assured her that she would be working with him directly to develop the groundwork for a capital campaign he had in mind, occupying the role of senior advisor and reporting directly to him—to him alone.

As he rattled off the names of trustees and others who could be approached for major gifts, she knew them all on a first-name basis and added anecdotal perceptions of her own, brief personal revelations of each prospective donor that could not be found in any resume, as if she were a social historian of the Chicago elite. At intervals, their glances locked, and the truth shone in both their eyes, as if they both recognized the beginning of a love affair.

Buddy smiled as Alyce turned on her infectious charm. She had read the materials he gave her several times since they'd met, and she clearly was impressed. Now she was listening to him go on about a reinvented Roosevelt. He was speaking too quickly and eagerly, like most university presidents eager to make the case.

He thought he could feel her bending toward him like a lovely tropism prepared to flower; he could sense she might acquiesce and perhaps had even made her decision already. Best of all, he wanted to believe that her acquiescence was triggered by her growing attraction to him.

The phone rang, as if planned. Buddy left them alone to take the call in her study. David and Alyce sat closer to each other on the sofa as the cook cleared the table. He felt inadequate before this stunning woman in Buddy Mayer's affluent apartment surrounded by all these original paintings that made it seem like a salon. She was too beautiful for him. He was the supplicant—out of his league, an impostor. She was too rich for him and too important, even though she didn't act so. Why was he losing control of his emotions? Why did he want to take her hands impulsively and kiss them? Was he falling in love with her?

"And what did the consultant you brought in say about your capital campaign?"

"He says we're not ready."

"They always say that," she assured him. "They're always a downer at first, looking for a client. He'll help you get ready and then want to run the campaign for you."

"He warned me that we have no lead gift—no major donors lined up, not enough staff, not enough researchers, a weak alumni base, and so forth. Too much, too fast. Oh, this devil goes on and on in his infamous, negative report. It's enough to discourage any president."

"But not you."

"Not yet. I didn't come to Roosevelt to be discouraged."

"But he's probably right, isn't he? Fund-raising requires patience, lots of patience, a strong foundation, and a measure of good luck."

"More than a measure. It needs a dynamo like you to create the luck. I don't believe that luck just happens randomly."

She laughed and raised her hands in defense. "I'm no miracle worker, Dr. Rosen."

"Dave."

"Dave."

"I'm no miracle worker, either, but together—"

"We can work miracles? Oh, you are a good salesman, Dr. Rosen."

"Dave."

"Sorry, I keep forgetting. Dave. Dave. Dave. Will you share the infamous document of this consultant with me?"

"It'll only discourage you."

"I'm not easily discouraged if the goal is worthwhile. Like you, I'm an idealist in search of a dream, but mine is different from yours. I'm probably more of a realist. I need to know the truth, as bad as the truth might be. Who was it that said, 'If you don't know where you're going, any path will take you there'?"

He looked at her with a new intensity and assured her. "I know where I want to go. I just need help getting there. I need you."

Beneath the banter, he kept feeling sensations deeper than the professional. This seemed true for her as well. By the end of the two-hour luncheon, with Buddy Mayer having returned from her timely phone call, Alyce Parker agreed to give his offer serious consideration. She held the consultant's report tightly in her hands, but whatever she might read in those grim, discouraging pages, he sensed that he had persuaded her to take a chance with him. He had come along at the right moment in her life and he in hers. Buddy winked, as if reading his mind and agreeing. She was pleased at her role as matchmaker.

"I'll call you tomorrow morning at ten," she told him as they bid each other goodbye. "We'll talk again tomorrow morning. I'll have read this report by then."

10

"I still think you're making a serious mistake," Julie persisted. "You're selling yourself short. You're running scared. You're always letting people take advantage of you. But since your mind is already made up, make sure you demand a decent salary."

"Like what?"

"Like twenty per cent more than he's prepared to offer you. Negotiate. You'll be worth more than his whole goddamn staff put together."

"Oh, please, Julie. You sound like a business agent."

"I wish you'd let me be yours. I'd make this disaster worth your time. Milk him for all he's worth. You're too soft, Mom. You're always too soft and generous."

Alyce listened to more of Julie's hectoring, but after a while, she no longer was listening.

All afternoon and evening, she reread David's case statement and the consultant's bleak response.

The vision expressed in Finding the Center is indeed powerful, she thought, *and personal.* The document linked the future of the expanding metropolis with that of his university: a campus in the city and a campus in the suburbs that formed a metropolitan university; an honors college; a first-rate conservatory; a real estate institute; a hospitality management program; an accreditation for the business college; a consortium of local colleges and universities working with the Chicago public schools; and an acquisition of John Marshall Law School, perhaps, and National Louis University, now riddled with presidential scandal and debt, and Shimer College and George Wilson College. She was awed by his hunger to be heroic. So what if the vision is more than any leader might accomplish. His boldness endeared him to her. This was a man who wanted more and still more—that was certainly more engaging than accepting the dull goals the dullest men set for themselves. A vast auditorium theater that would be a coliseum for the city and a biomedical program with Rush Presbyterian Medical School for minority students—why not? She would help him turn his dreams into reality and, thereby, capture his love completely.

The consultant's report was as discouraging as David confessed it would be. The university needed a campaign chairman of citywide stature; there had to be far more significant donations from the trustees; corporations must be engaged; the number of staff, especially researchers, had to be increased dramatically; and enrollments needed to rise so that potential donors would have confidence in the university. It would take at least three years to prepare for the contemplated $50 million capital campaign, and even then, the goal might be an overreach.

She would be seventy-four by then—old. But at this moment, she felt like a young woman falling in love for the first time in her life. She didn't care about age. As some sage once said, it was only a number. Most importantly, she could sense that David Rosen was surely falling in love with her too.

In bed, she couldn't sleep. The Ambien didn't help, nor the hot chocolate, nor the newspaper with its relentless, oppressive, and embarrassing stories about Clinton's philandering. She lay awake and let her mind wander across a lifetime with a man she once thought she could learn to love unconditionally. For her, love had always been absolute and idealized, even when she was in her late teens and early twenties. As she wrestled sleeplessly, she remembered how she had gone from one beau to another until she met Matt—the handsome young aviator who was waiting for her and would care for her, who came from a wealthy family and would provide for them forever, and who loved her more than she ever would be able to love him.

From adolescence onward, Matt Parker had always waited for her. Being a year ahead of her in high school, he was a quarterback with tawny hair and a perennial smile. He was a handsome, adventurous boy who loved skiing and hunting, and he adored her unwaveringly. But she was always seeing others, she was forever courted by other young blades, and as her prettiness turned to beauty, she was in high demand among them. Matt went off to Brown, and she to the U of C. They separated from each other for months, but they were together whenever he returned to his home in leafy Glencoe, just north of Chicago. After graduation, when she was chosen by Elgin

Watch to represent the company at the New York World's Fair, she spent six weeks in the summer of '39 with her mother along as chaperone. She dated the scion to a famous real estate family, a *New York Times* reporter who would become one of its prominent editors, and the son of a large furniture mogul from Bangor, Maine. A scion who was visiting New York fell madly in love with her for a month and urged her to marry him. However, after a chilly visit with her mother to the family's mansion in Bangor and then the mediocre Dun and Bradstreet report of her father's assets, that romance like all the others fizzled, and she was brokenhearted. "The very rich." She laughed afterward to console herself. There was a trace of envy within her. "The very rich are different from you and me."

All during these roller-coaster escapades, the local and reliable Matt Parker saw her whenever he returned from college and waited until she was ready for him. With the outbreak of the war, he joined the air force and trained at Williams Field in Arizona. A handsome flyboy was on his way to becoming a pilot, the fantasy of his boyhood. After she and her mother accepted his invitation to visit, he piloted them on a local flight to nowhere, which young Alyce thought of as something out of a Hollywood romance. "Flying high in the sky," she sang to Matt in his little plane, "is my idea of nothing to do." In his dapper, tailored uniform, he escorted them to the officer's club for dinner and catered to their every wish. He was crazy about Alyce, and unlike the other fleeting romances she'd had, he seemed steady and constant and unconditionally in love with her.

In his convertible, he drove her to a bar for a drink after her mother had gone to bed. The Arizona evening was still stagnant and humid. She didn't know whether she loved him, even when they danced slowly to a three-piece band's scratchy rendition of "Smoke Gets in Your Eyes" or lingered in his car, and she let him touch her in secret places she had never let any other man dare go. She wanted him too; she pleasured him too. However, some inadequacy at the center of him held her back.

He proposed in the Pump Room, and they celebrated the wedding ceremony a few months later in Arizona for a few close relatives and friends. A candlelit dinner for twenty. Unlike others, Matt wasn't the one who made her heart spin, but she tried to talk herself into reciprocal passion and hoped that in time, it would come. He brought her flowers, he took her to fine restaurants, and he felt lucky to be married to so desirable a woman. However, for her, the passion couldn't come, and she never felt entirely safe with him. After two years in Arizona, Matt had a routine procedure to puncture a blister, and he suffered the collapse of the lung on which it rested. He was diagnosed with tuberculosis at twenty-six.

She stared at him in the hospital bed, confused and scared, with a toddler in tow and a second baby six months away.

"We'll be all right, Matt." She comforted him, brushing his golden hair from his eyes and kissing his fretting brow. There were tears in his eyes. "We're going to be all right."

"Stay with me, Allie. Stay close."

She kissed him again and again. "I'm not going anywhere. We're in this together."

"It's not fair, Allie. I'm only twenty-six."

They returned north and existed in the sumptuous Tudor home of his parents, under the control of his mother, a domineering matriarch, while Matt labored for his father in the clothing store he was expected to inherit. The thriving enterprise was his for the taking, but he hated the routine work. He was an adventurer. He was someone who was restless and would never lose his sense of having failed before he began in life. Through years of growing discontent, he began to have martini luncheons, and the depression that he'd suffered from his recovery only deepened. Matt was no longer the man she'd married. Then inevitably, there was the affair with one of the young salesgirls.

Smiling at her at the foot of the bed was that young woman of years ago. What was her name again? Alyce couldn't remember. She wore a skintight black sweater that hugged her full breasts and thin, flat waist, and she let her thick dark hair flow to her young shoulders. Her eyes constantly followed Matt wherever he went in the store. Soon, he was driving her home after work.

Alyce suspected the worst. She told Matt's father that she wanted the girl fired. She personally would replace the tart until he found someone else. The old man understood immediately, but when he finally did let her go, Matt was furious. There might or might not have been a subsequent affair, but Alyce never trusted him again. His drinking grew worse, and his complaints about a boring, predictable life in Parker Clothing Store in Highland Park were more grating than ever. He wanted to create his own business and his own fortune; he wanted to start at the top and not simply wait until his father bequeathed him the company. "It's like living death in that place," he muttered to her. "I'll be fifty by the time I take over." And then he mixed himself another drink.

What a contrast to David Rosen, she brooded. *He's a man so centered, so strong, so singular in his ambition, racing like a thoroughbred from professor to president.* She noticed that he didn't drink. She wanted to believe that he had no issue of philandering and no apparent weakness. It wasn't the prospective job of fund-raiser that she needed, remembering her rocky marriage. It was more than that. David Rosen was someone she could trust.

She turned to her daughters for solace, but they were of little comfort. Julie had become a willful spinster, with a fierce temper different from her mother's disposition as night from day. When her first boyfriend jilted her, she never recovered, and like her father, whom she continued to idolize despite his inability to discover a career, with his drinking and philandering, she drifted from one job to another—a sales woman at Saks, a dental assistant, a paralegal, and a surgeon's nurse. All Julie had now, at forty-seven, was a small house with its picket fence in Winnetka; a Honda Civic; her unemployed younger sister Laura, who was living with her after returning from a disastrous divorce in California; and her mother who called her every evening at eight o'clock and visited her on Saturdays to garden in the front and back yards and have lunch together at Betsey's and Frank's.

Laura was always Alyce's favorite, but she was troubled from childhood onward, and as much as Alyce loved her, she was a continual concern. When she was eight, she was taken by Matt and his relatives to their Wisconsin retreat while Alyce remained home for a charity event. Upon their return, it was clear that something radical had changed the little girl. She was different, quiet, and withdrawn. Alyce never did discover what had happened that weekend, but

Laura's sudden change and her suspicion of child abuse by Matt's cousin Jack, a taciturn, elderly bachelor, led Alyce to take the girl to a psychiatrist—Bruno Bettelheim, of all people. "Wait until she's thirteen or fourteen," he advised, "and moving through puberty." She waited, but by then, Laura was into drugs, alcohol, and wild behavior. Alyce could see that she had inherited Matt's addictive personality.

Now, as Alyce remembered those years, Laura's adolescence was a blurry nightmare. She refused therapy and lived with secrets never shared. She had a natural talent for interior design but was rejected by Rhode Island School of Design and went instead to Moore College in Philadelphia. Suddenly, after her sophomore year and for no reason Alyce could ever discern, she quit and returned to Chicago to live alone, rarely seeing her parents and working at Marshall Fields to sustain herself. In the evenings, she hung out with other lost souls of the Gold Coast and Streeterville. Alyce never did discover what she was up to in the evenings and on weekends.

One night, Alyce and Matt were in town attending a benefit, and afterwards, they decided to stop by for a surprise visit to Laura's apartment. Matt had become a faded, depressed man as a result of his many business failures, but Alyce held on to the marriage. Divorce was too tragic and final to consider. Months had gone by without contacting Laura, and Alyce sensed that something was awry. Matt waited in the car as she entered and found her daughter with some guy in bed, stoned and drunk. She went ballistic and dragged her into the car.

The next morning, at breakfast, Laura told her and Matt defiantly, "I've had a bastard."

"What?" Alyce screamed. Yes, she had seen Laura six months ago and had suspected pregnancy. "If I didn't know any better," she had laughed at her daughter who was three months along at the time, "I'd think you were pregnant" But she hadn't seen her since she'd been too busy with her charity work, and now she was filled with inchoate anger and confusion and failure and guilt at her own neglect. There had been phone calls, but no personal contact. Laura never seemed to want to come home, and Alyce, brokenhearted, had buried herself in philanthropy. "What in hell did you think you were doing?"

"I just wanted to see what it was like to have a child," she smirked, shocking, taunting, and enraging them.

"And where is the baby now?"

"We've given him up for adoption. Chuck wanted to marry me, but after watching you and Dad, I don't think I want to marry."

If ever she wanted to smash her across the face, that was the moment. But she knew that Laura was deeply troubled by what had happened. Once in the early hours of the morning, she heard a distant sound in the dimly lit basement and approached; then she paused at the head of the stairs as she listened to Laura playing a heartbreaking Joni Mitchell song over and over again:

> Child with a child pretending
> Weary of lies you are sending home
> So you sign all the papers in the family name
> You're sad and you're sorry but you're not
> ashamed
> Little green, have a happy ending.

Alyce went to where she was on the floor beside her tape recorder and knelt beside her. "Tell me everything, Laura, tell me everything. Please, please, please let me help."

When Alyce begged her for the name of the adoption agency, with the promise that she'd take care of the infant in the short term, Laura refused. She simply turned to her mother, awash in tears, and confessed, "Mom, I'm one sick babe."

She agreed to enter Chestnut Hill, a psychiatric retreat in Maryland. She was there for more than a year, improving slowly, but after visiting her every few weeks, Alyce and Matt could no longer afford the care. They told her they'd have to find a state-supported sanitarium, and when Laura heard that news, she instantly recovered and was ready to return to the land of the living. She stayed in Julie's home on Pine Street and remained a withdrawn woman, without any incentive to work.

Now it was seven-thirty in the morning, and Alyce was exhausted from having had so little sleep. The phone rang; it was Julie. She didn't answer. She wouldn't answer. She didn't want conflict at this moment; she had to prepare for David Rosen. She let the phone ring itself out, and instead of an argument, she showered for twice as long as usual, as if to dig into her pores and wash away past difficulties and disappointments and guilt.

There she stood, naked and physically imperfect in ways that no one else would ever see or know. She had fallen breasts; a slight paunch, however much she exercised; and a touch of gray hair where no gray hair should ever be. She'd have to get to her hair dresser pronto. She then wrapped her aging body in a white terry cloth bathrobe. The skin above her inner arm, between her elbow and armpit, was beginning to sag. Should she return to her plastic surgeon? Perhaps her trainer could help tighten the muscles, or had they, too, surrendered to aging? As she reached for her hair dryer and then the makeup that would try to mask all human imperfections, the phone rang, and once again, she let it ring itself out.

In the mirror, she studied herself. Five years had gone by since she first noticed a hint of wrinkles along the lines of her neck, a settling in of her jaw, a sliver of loose skin under her chin, thinning eyebrows, and dark circles that were creeping in below her eyes—circles that had never been there before. She'd panicked five years ago at the prospect of aging and sought out a Dr. Gilmore in New York—the best in the country for a face lift. She couldn't afford him, but she afforded him. Afterward, she rested up alone on a vacation in St. Martins, listening to the Marshallin in *Rosenkavalier* who had stopped all the clocks in her house one day as if that act alone would prevent her from growing older. (And the Marshallin was only in her thirties!) When she returned to Chicago, even her closest friends didn't notice the slight change in the structure of her face. It was just enough for them to say, "Lordy, that vacation certainly did wonders for you. You look years younger, Alyce. How in God's name do you do it?"

How much longer will this beauty last, she wondered, *before it all begins to crumble? What magic will I find to replace it? Where will I find another job like the one this president is offering me? Who else will hire a seventy-one-year-old woman? Will I ever be desirable enough for David Rosen? Does he want me only for my Rolodex, or is he attracted to me as a woman, as a beauty whose beauty hasn't yet faded entirely? When it does fade, when the ageless beauty becomes an aged beauty, will he still want me? He does want me for myself. I know that. I can feel that. This is more than a transaction. He is attracted to me. I may be older, but I'm not old, not yet. If I don't seize this now—*

The phone rang again. This time, she answered.

"Are you okay, Mother?" Julie fairly shouted in reprobation. "Where have you been? Didn't you hear all my phone calls this morning? Did you hear them, and you just choose not to answer? I was worried to death. I thought something might have happened to you. I was ready to drive in to see if you were okay—a heart attack, a stroke, you never know at your age. Why won't you wear that pendant I gave you? Then you can call me whenever you fall or have an attack, and I won't be worried to death. Are you there? Are you there? Mother?"

"I'm here."

"I've had further thoughts on why you can't take this job."

"I don't want to hear them."

"What do you mean you don't want to hear them? They're important."

"I don't want to hear them."

"You have to hear them. They're crucial."

"No, I don't have to hear them."

"Mother—"

"I'm going to hang up, Julie. Please don't call back again this morning."

11

At exactly ten o'clock, as promised, she called. She would work with him—with him directly, she insisted, and not through Dan Pearson and the development office. Of course, she would still keep everyone in the loop concerning donors she was introducing him to. Gently but firmly, she reminded him that they would need to discuss the terms of her appointment. She was tired of volunteering for so many organizations free of charge. Her daughters were constantly berating her for donating her talents to the wide world and being exploited. She explained to him slowly that she was not a rich woman. It was with a touch of embarrassment, as if she were stripping away one of her most important veils. "It may seem that way." She laughed. "I may look like a wealthy woman, but I'm not. I'm just your everyday workingwoman."

She confided that she just left her full-time salaried job at Michael Reese, so this opportunity did come at the right time. However, she added she was sure he would understand that she had to be compensated. This could not strictly be volunteer work. She was not, as she repeated several times while stumbling awkwardly over her words, a rich prima donna. She promised with a chuckle not to break his limited bank account. She knew the university was impoverished, but she couldn't give away her services free of charge anymore. She wasn't getting any younger, and she was sure he would understand. Then she drew in her breath, as if she were distressed by the vulgarity of this mundane matter of money, and she waited for his response. She would really rather discuss some of these details in person than on the phone.

"You've given me a lot to digest." He laughed. She could feel him suppressing his obvious excitement, and she hoped it mirrored his desire to know her as a woman as well as a fund-raiser. Her words might have been matter-of-fact, full of confidence, and even business-like, but the softer music beneath those words was clearly a prelude to romance. She could feel it, she wanted it, and she imagined him. It was a dream come true; and she could sense by the lilt in his voice how much he wanted her.

"When can we meet to discuss details?"

"Whenever you say."

"Tonight?"

"If you wish."

"At Café Spiaggia?"

"I'll be there. At seven o'clock?"

"Do you know—"

"Oh, I know where Café Spiaggia is, Dr. Rosen."

"Dr. Rosen? No, no, no—that will not do. I thought we'd gone beyond pompous professionalism. Dr. Rosen sounds as though I'm an institution. We have to end this formality. All my good friends call me Dave."

But she would not call him Dave.

"In time," she suggested, smiling to herself. "In time."

12

All during the time that Debra was dying, David had relied on Café Spiaggia—an informal, cozy hideaway adjacent to the celebrated four-star restaurant on the second floor of his condominium complex. He would leave work as early as possible, take out dinner for the two of them, and sit with his wife of thirty-five years who was shriveling each day before him. She would always be dressed when he came home with dinner and then listen patiently to the details of his day, trying to manifest interest in people she didn't know or hadn't even met. Finally, she would share with him whatever book or magazine article she had been skimming slowly during the hours when she wasn't napping. She read less and less as her breast cancer worsened and finally lodged in her liver, until she stopped reading altogether and spent most of her time staring vacantly at Lake Michigan, the Midwest waterway that went on and on endlessly it seemed into eternity.

Never once did she complain in those dwindling winter days. Instead, she strained to be optimistic about her condition, until she no longer could pretend. She grew quieter and more withdrawn with each passing day. After dinner, he would sit by her side in the bedroom, close to her. They would watch television together as she rested, scarcely observing the images on the screen and breathing softly and faintly until he kissed her closed eyes good night. He would then return to whatever work was awaiting him, and then, exhausted, he would stumble to her in bed, feeling her warmth diminish with each passing breath.

In the café, he knew the receptionist, the waiters, and chef by name. During the harrowing days and nights of Debra's dying, they formed a kind of local family for him in the absence of one. This night, he arrived a few minutes before seven. He ordered a mojito and nursed it while he waited for Alyce Parker.

She came moments later, harried from the winter snow as she withdrew her hooded coat and tossed it onto the seat of the booth opposite him. His heart jumped as he observed her every gesture. She brushed her hair back to give it a semblance of order and quickly composed herself, catching her breath and laughing, smiling at him, blowing into her hands for warmth, and murmuring, "Oh, this March madness. We should be in St. Martins."

"I'm ready."

Impetuously he wanted to engulf her hands and press his lips against them for further warmth.

As always, she looked vibrant, alive, and ageless, although he now knew that she was seventy-one. He didn't care about the differences in their age anymore. Her loveliness obscured practicality, common sense, or reality. She was dressed in tailored gray slacks, a thick black turtleneck sweater, a simple silver necklace with earrings to match, and a ring that was not a wedding ring.

"Well, finally, hello, hello," she greeted him, shaking his hand, settling herself in the booth. "Am I late?"

"No, no. I'm the early one. Whenever I have an important date, I'm always early."

"Seems to me I've heard that line before." She broke out laughing. "We're both early. Now why would that be?"

"We must like each other. You look ravishing."

"Hey, hey." She drew in her breath, "Slowly, Dr. Rosen—Dave—Dr. Rosen. I'm confused. What *is* your name? What should I call you? I thought this was strictly a business dinner."

"It is, but that doesn't stop you from looking ravishing."

When the waiter approached, she pointed to David's drink and said, "I'll have one of those." Within moments, she was apologizing that she had brought up remuneration so abruptly in their phone conversation—how vulgar he must have thought she was. He listened to her words without quite hearing them, as they gazed at each other with mutual attraction. Connection, connection—he loved it. How often does one connect with another human being so quickly? It was magical. He almost touched her fingers, but she gently pulled her hand away.

"Thanks for coming. You don't need to apologize. I always assumed you'd be on salary." It was not entirely true. "It's cleaner that way. I don't believe in exploiting people." He mentioned a reasonable stipend, and she hesitated for a moment, wondering. He imagined whether she would begin to negotiate, but she held back and didn't quibble.

"Let's wait a year to see what I can do for you. If I'm half as successful as you think I'll be, we'll renegotiate my contract, and I'll be as tough as my daughters say I should be." She flexed her muscles like a fighter, and both of them turned their smiles into nervous laughter. Quickly, as she found the subject awkward, she hunkered down to business. "I can be one tough lady, you know."

"I don't believe that for one minute."

"You'll see. I've read all your impressive materials by now. And they are impressive. But your consultant is right to slow you down. We'll need three years before we can think of anything that resembles a capital campaign. I'll need time to understand this strange new world of Roosevelt University, and it'll take months to introduce you to my world—to philanthropists who have become my personal friends and know nothing about Roosevelt. It'll take time for you to earn their trust, however much they may trust me."

"I would trust you for any recommendation, sight unseen, but I know what you mean. I've been there at CCNY, under more difficult circumstances. But Roosevelt is a private university, and that is a distinct help, isn't it? You only have me to worry about."

"That doesn't sound too dangerous now that I'm getting to know you. But remember, you're not entirely independent either. You do have trustees."

"Let me live with my innocence for the moment—or my idealism. I like to delude myself that I'm the captain of my fate."

"I do hope you'll be the captain of your fate. But a bureaucracy is a bureaucracy, public or private, isn't it? Stubborn and recalcitrant. The important point is that fund-raising is personal, not transferable. I can give you a head start with our city's royalty, but that's about it. I grew up with these people. Many of them have been my friends for more than sixty years. They trust me. But finally, you'll have to earn that trust yourself, personally."

"With your help," he said, thinking that sixty years ago, he wasn't quite born, and she was already twelve years old. Looking at her closely now, her wide eyebrows, her hair slightly askew, and her eyes as brilliant as those of a woman far younger, he refused to believe that she was a day older than him.

"With my help."

As the dinner warmed them, they became increasingly comfortable with each other, buoyed by several glasses of Pouilly-Fuissé.

"You must have had second thoughts about staying in Chicago when your wife grew ill."

He bridled at her directness. "You know—"

"Buddy mentioned it. I'm sorry. I don't mean to intrude, but it must have been awful for you to carry on in a strange city, without friends."

He had never confided easily about private matters with anyone, and however drawn he was to her, however empathetic she was toward him, he certainly wasn't about to share Debra. He'd always carried that grief deep within himself, beyond tears, beyond words, like a precious trust. Sharing it would seem a betrayal—a posthumous betrayal. He leaned across the table and gazed at her. "How many men have told you how beautiful you are?"

"I've lost track." She laughed, brushing off his remark as hyperbole. "Dr. Rosen, you're mixing a personal element into this appointment. That's dangerous."

"Is it? I'm sorry. I've been waiting a long time for you to say yes. I'll have to keep reminding myself to separate business from romance."

"That would be a beginning."

"Tell me, how did you arrange to have violet eyes?"

"They're not violet—just working blue. Oh, you're irrepressible. We need to have a compact before we go any further."

"I understand."

"I'm not so sure you do. If this is perceived as anything more than a business relationship, it won't work with your colleagues—or with you and me. I'll be the subject of rumors and resentment."

"You're asking me to be inhuman."

"No, no. The other may come—in time. For now, I'm just asking you to be sensible."

At the end of the evening, they stood in the lobby of One Magnificent Mile, adjacent to David's condo building, which rose sixty stories high into the sky. They were less awkward than when they'd begun the evening but with her openness and he was still pleased with her and attracted to her every gesture. There she stood before him, looking up with affirmation, her dark hood framing that crystalline face, while he was searching for a way to say good night when he didn't really want the evening to be over.

He offered to take her home by cab, but she wanted to return alone to her condo at the end of Astor Street, a stone's throw from North Avenue and Lincoln Park, across from Cardinal Bernadine's estate at the end of the Gold Coast.

"No, no. I can't let you walk home alone."

Over her objections, he hailed a cab, and in moments, they were at her building. Racing round to her door of the cab, he helped her out and kissed her cheek good night, as the doorman smiled at them.

"Thanks," he murmured. "Thanks for everything."

She paused then smiled. "My pleasure."

13

In the hallway of her condo, she stood in front of the closet mirror and wondered what was happening to her. Then she burst into tears and laughter and tears and laughter once again. *To me?* She laughed at herself. *This is happening to me? At my age? Why, this is absolutely indecent, Alyce Parker, you whippersnapper. You should pick on someone your own age.* And she cupped her face, laughing into her trembling hands. *O God Almighty, he's everything I've ever wanted.*

It was midnight. Her emotions were so out of control she had to talk to someone—someone she could trust, someone who would empathize with her and not judge her, and someone who would confirm her decision unequivocally.

"I'm afraid of my emotions, Laura. I'm afraid of letting myself go at my age. I've never felt this way at any time in my entire life—not when I first met Matt, not even when I decided to marry him, and not even when I was walking down the aisle."

Laura listened without uttering a word. When Alyce had finished her confession, full of doubt and fear and intense excitement, she heard her daughter's adamant advice and took it.

"Go for it, Mom. This man sounds marvelous. Go for it. You may never have another chance in your life. I have just one question. Does he feel the same way about you?"

"Absolutely."

"That's all that counts. I just don't want you to get hurt again."

14

David was whirling with delight. She was a gift from the gods of Chicago. She was beautiful, more so than the plastic Hollywood imitations of beauty; in a way that academics never were; and vivacious, as no one her age dared to be. More than a magical fund-raiser, she was a woman he could love for the rest of his life.

How could he be so lucky?

The ghost of Debra visited him in his restless sleep, floating through his dreams like an animated conscience and smiling gently.

"You deserve her, David. Let yourself fall in love with her, as you once loved me. She's a wonderful woman. She'll make you happy. No guilt. Please, no more guilt. I had you for thirty-five wonderful years. The rest belongs to her."

Dan Pearson was not pleased with David's decision to hire Alyce as his personal assistant.

He had every right to be annoyed. David had mentioned the meeting with Alyce Parker but hadn't really consulted with him as to how she would fit into the administrative hierarchy of fund-raising. Pearson was, after all, the long-standing vice president for Development and had been David's point man in philanthropy—his representative to the community of Chicago. He had served Roosevelt for forty years and was an old-time political and social liberal. He was a seventy-year-old veteran who had agreed to remain in a transitional role until David oriented himself and found someone to replace him. Anyone involved in fund-raising, he told David, should be reporting to him, but David wasn't listening. Over time, Pearson had been beaten into a career of low expectations. If ever there was an example of the Peter Principle at work, it was Daniel J. Pearson.

"She's only a consultant," David assured him.

"To you."

"That was one of her conditions, Dan. I'm sorry. She knows she has to keep you in the loop. She will. She's a team player. She's not coming to take over your role."

"That's what they all say at the beginning. Did you ever see Alec Guinness in *The Man in the White Suit*? Remember? He asked those in charge, 'Can I have a corner of your laboratory?' Before you knew it he'd taken over the laboratory. Alyce Parker is just a rich, spoiled lady who probably thinks she can wave her magic wand over this poor pedestrian university and help you reinvent it. But let me tell you, Dave. I've been here for forty years, and reinvention isn't on anyone's mind anymore—not on the mind of the trustees or the faculties or the students or the alumni or Chicago. Don't count on miracles, my boy. There is no silver bullet. Take it from me. Take it from someone who knows. There is no silver bullet for the problems of this university."

"Well, maybe she will help us reinvent it, after all. Maybe she'll find the donors we never knew were there."

In a soft voice, hovering somewhere between bitterness and weariness, Pearson answered him, "Maybe she will, and maybe she won't."

David couldn't believe Pearson's self-protective narrowness. He couldn't believe that the tired vice president didn't appreciate how lucky they all would be to have Alyce Parker join their beleaguered team. Didn't he see the magic of this woman who now was on his mind all the time?

He shared his enthusiasm with Bob Green, who at least understood the dream, although he, too, was troubled by Alyce's appointment. Their friendship had lived through skirmishers at Penn State, and by now, they knew each other's mind before it was even made up.

"Dan Pearson's days are numbered," Bob assured him. "He may want to be at his second home in Sarasota full-time, don't you think? But who will replace him? Will Alyce Parker replace him?"

"No, never. She'll only be a consultant, a partner, to me. Part-time."

"Only?" Bob smiled, skeptically. So the word had already spread. "Be careful, my friend, now that your relationship has become more than professional."

He knows, David thought, tightening his muscles. *How does he know? Who else knows? Is it all that obvious—the joy in my eyes, my buoyancy, and my demeanor?* He let the comment pass as though he hadn't heard it. What else was he to do but find a catalyst to his dream of creating a great university, with some fresh, new external force and some winner.

"I don't know who can replace Dan Pearson. We have so little to offer any decent development director—so little staff, so few resources. Nothing. We have nothing."

"We'll make it, Dave," Bob assured him. "One way or the other, we'll replace him, and," he added slowly, "it shouldn't be with Alyce Parker. Dave—"

"Bob, I don't want to discuss this."

"Okay, I understand. I know you too well, you stubborn son of a bitch. This has already become really personal. But as your friend, I have to tell you it's a mistake to bring her here. I don't blame you for being bewitched. She's an extraordinary lady, a beautiful lady, and I would be knocked off my feet too. I'm sure she'll be helpful, but she doesn't belong here. It's the wrong fit. You'll create more problems than we need."

"Stop," David muttered angrily. "I don't want to hear objections or warnings, as well intentioned as they may be from you or anyone else. I know exactly what I'm doing. If you think I came here as president to wait five or ten years to build a development staff that can handle a $50 million campaign, you've got another thing coming."

"Okay, okay. It's that serious. I have uttered my final word on the matter."

He rose and walked stolidly toward the door, then he turned. "Be careful, Dave. Don't hurt yourself. And always remember, you have my phone number in case you need to talk."

His office had a lonely and fearful air after Bob Green left. *Of course, he's right*, David brooded. Anyone in administration would echo his warning, but I don't care.

I'm not losing Alyce Parker to the whim of bureaucratic correctness. And Alyce is right too. If we see each other as a couple rather than as colleagues, I will be blabbing on about the university anyway, like a man obsessed.

Be honest with yourself, he reprimanded himself. *You want it all. You want her to be your silver bullet, your fund-raiser extraordinaire, and your lover. She brings you status and prestige in the broader community. All in one woman.*

When Dan Pearson told him he was definitely leaving at the end of the academic year, David advertised in *The Chronicle of Higher Education* and had a plethora of applicants, all of whom demanded more staff in the development office, more researchers, more resources, an alumni base, major donor possibilities, and corporate support—a broad financial foundation before any major action could be taken. David only offered himself, a high salary, and the help of his consultant, Alyce Parker.

15

Within weeks of her appointment, Alyce furnished David with a list of personal contacts and their brief biographies—a fifty-page treasure trove worth its weight in Chicago gold. It would prove to be a list of potential donors far more prominent than Ron Grillo's collection of local south side businessmen. Hers included wealthy entrepreneurs, real estate moguls, venture capitalists, and city officials whom she knew personally—blue-ribbon leaders who were the city's equivalent of a royal court. She was pleased with how easily she had adjusted to Roosevelt and how helpful she could be to David. As president, he gave her immediate access to the university and proved to be an amenable partner. He was prepared to give her all the support she needed, but what she liked most was that he was there, in the same building, just an office away. She was careful in how she used her access to him and was keenly sensitive to how easily she could be perceived by Ron Grillo, his development staff, and the faculty at large as a privileged princess. But everywhere she went, every thought she had was really about him, and she wanted to believe that he was sharing her growing love.

She began to go with David to luncheon interviews for a new vice president of Development, but not even her charm and vivacity worked on these savvy young men and women, who were working their way up the career ladder. After one of these luncheons, when David was particularly despondent, she came up with an unexpected suggestion.

"Let's go to a movie."

"A movie? What are you talking about? It's two o'clock in the afternoon."

"When I was a kid, I always felt I was playing hooky if I saw a movie in the afternoon."

"And you feel like playing hooky today?"

"With you. What's playing?"

He bought a paper at the corner newsstand and read off possibilities.

"*Basic Instinct.* That's it. I've heard—"

"It's only another erotic thriller," he said. "Sharon Stone and Michael Douglas."

"But that's it! Perfect escape. Perfect for a sunny spring afternoon. An erotic thriller. It's a lot more thrilling than returning to work, isn't it?"

"Absolutely, but not at two in the afternoon."

"That's when it's most thrilling." She clutched his hand. "When it's unexpected."

They were clearly turned on and emerged into the sunny spring afternoon to walk toward her home. All the way, she clutched his hand and sensed his rising expectations.

"Come upstairs," she murmured to him as they approached her condo. "It's time for you to see my digs."

16

As she opened the door of her condo, David prepared himself to be dazzled. They were greeted by a puppy. Alyce had anointed her Duchess. He watched the dog bark and move restlessly in her arms, licking her cheek and, finally, staring at David with a suspicious glare, as though he were invading her territory.

"Duchess, this is Dr. Rosen."

"Well, good evening, Duchess," he bowed in deference. "I'm pleased to meet you." A softening sniff suggested reluctant acceptance. "It's good of you to let me share your space." He turned to Alyce. "I didn't know—"

"How could you know? I took her from the kennel just three weeks ago. She's my adopted grandchild. No one has ever welcomed me like Duchess, as you can see."

"Now that's what I call unconditional love." His eyes roved the room, taking in its elegance, comparing it to his own increasingly barren quarters. "I can't believe that I've never seen where and how you live."

"There's a time and place for everything." She smiled.

She hugged and held the puppy, a Yorkshire terrier, tight against her breasts as they entered the condo. It was a richly furnished two-bedroom spread, with the foyer leading to a large living room that could have been on window display at Saks or Neiman Marcus and served as a model for how you might want to live if you had all the money in the world. He marveled at her exquisite taste and felt a little like an imposter—someone who was now circulating in the world of the rich and important. This was not just a glimpse of royalty at the International Club or some other fancy restaurant. This was the real thing. His attraction to wealth and power and beauty and glamour was personified in Alyce Parker. He smiled inwardly as he gazed at her. *What a lucky man I am to be able to call her my own.*

Facing him were a cream-colored sofa and puffed up cushions with the same soft cool shade of off-white, a large glass coffee table, and spotless matching arm chairs that looked as though they had never been sat upon. Dominating the living room was a stately Steinway grand piano that stood before a window overlooking Lake Michigan; beside it was an antique music stand, with Chopin, Mozart, and Beethoven at the ready, waiting to be played. On top of the Steinway were photographs of Alyce with Tony Bennett, Alyce with Itzhak Perlman, Alyce with Harry Belafonte— each one celebrating a benefit for one charity or another.

"Such fun," she boasted in a lighthearted way. "Fund-raising has exposed me to the most talented people. I've kept in touch with all these celebrities. They're friends by now. Buddies of mine. This is what you and I have to bring to Roosevelt, Dave. Panache. We have to make fund-raising fun."

Is she for real? he wondered. *Who is this woman whom I've fallen in love with? Part of her is a sophisticated, cunning, beautiful actress. She's a grande dame that sees the world as a stage, a gorgeous lady who wishes she is truly wealthy and sends out the impression of actually being so. Another part is girlish and pretty and optimistic—and plastic. At seventy-one!* He hadn't yet put the parts together, but he knew that her skin, her trim figure, her healthy hair, her bright-violet youthful eyes, her persistence, her intelligence had all fused together in his mind and overwhelmed him and informed his sexual desire for her.

Standing in the middle of the living room, David let his eye travel upward to the portrait of a prosperous, self-satisfied English baron peering down at him as though he was measuring his worth and wondering whether he might be a gold digger taking advantage of his favorite descendant. The baron seemed mummified in the Victorian era, high up there on the wall, overlooking his ancestors and preserved forever above a gas fireplace that she turned on to create light and warmth, sending a glow across the entire room.

"Your grandfather?"

"Oh, no. He's not a relative. I just thought his serious bearing would give the room a certain gravitas. Of course," she added, quickly, without a flicker of cynicism, irony, or self-consciousness, touching David's cheek with affection, "he *could* be my grandfather."

He smiled inwardly at her attempt to recreate herself; but he checked his instinct to be cynical and critical. Gently, he put his arm around her shoulders and drew her closer to him, touching her hair with his lips.

"Maybe in time you'll adopt him."

"Or he'll adopt me. I've always wanted to be adopted."

"By whom?"

"By a rich, cultivated, important man like him and by a warm, loving mother. I had neither in my life."

"And now all you have is someone who isn't rich and only reasonably cultivated."

"Only reasonably cultivated? Ho, ho, ho, Dr. Rosen. Don't underrate yourself." She smiled up at him and touched his cheek. "I'm not complaining."

"Nor am I."

He brought her closer to him, as they gazed up at the painting. Then he turned her slowly to face him, drawing her away from her self-created past and into the powerful present and the joyous future that was beginning to stretch ahead for the both of them. He kissed her lovely, luminous face and felt tears welling up into his eyes, for the first time since Debra's death. Could this be happening to him? After all these years? Was he capable of living in Alyce's world and loving her as he knew she needed to be loved? Whatever hesitancy he might have felt before vanished in a heartbeat, and hungrily he kissed her on the lips.

She pulled away a little, drawing her breath, and muttered, fearfully. "Wow ... Wow ... Slowly, David. Slowly." She drew her breath. "Come see the rest of me."

On the walls of the narrow hallway that connected her bedroom and her office were photographs of Alyce at a variety of charity affairs. She identified each one with quiet pride, as he put his hand on her shoulder. More personal photos followed: Alyce in a Red Cross outfit taken when she was a professional volunteer and helping, in her own small way, to win the Second World War; Alyce at a U of C football game in the thirties when she was selected as Betty Co-Ed, the university's equivalent of Miss America; and Alyce at the New York World's Fair, where she went to celebrate her graduation. He was struck by the degree of self-celebration spread across those walls, for he had never thought of her as a narcissist, but he banished that thought before it was fully formed and held her ever more tightly. He wanted no negative perception to mar her virtues, her beauty, and his lust for her. At every stage of her life, she had clearly been magnetic, and now she was drawing him further and further into her magical kingdom.

In her office were further revelations. Above an antique desk, behind an intricate wire trellis, was a photo of Matt Parker in a starched-white air force uniform. He was a young tawny-haired pilot of twenty-five, handsome and confident and carefree. There were also recent photographs of Julie and Laura. Beside them was another photograph of her family, with the two girls in their late teens standing confidently behind their parents like proper young women. Their middle-aged father looked prosperous and self-satisfied in his dark-blue suit while holding a poodle in his lap, and Alyce, in a prim black-and-white dress, had her hair carefully coiffed while holding a twin poodle. She was stunning then, too, but had not yet possessed the beauty that deepens for some women as they age. She seemed to be happy in that photograph.

All these memories surrounded her. *There must have been happy moments in that long marriage—moments of joy*, David reflected. He was envious of them, envious of a past he did not know, and so he pulled her closer to him. He wanted to

111

wipe her past away, start anew, and own her completely. At seventy-one and fifty-nine, he realized that was impossible, but still he wanted to obliterate her past so that she could start with him. He tightened his hand on her shoulders and turned her around so that he could kiss her brow, then brush the wisps of hair from her face, and finally kiss her on her lips.

In turn, she held him tight.

"You do have a colorful past."

"These are the images I show in public. The memories are buried within me. It's been a long time since I've given myself to someone else."

"That time has come, my dear. Your daughters are almost as pretty as you."

"The girls are now single women in their midforties—still attractive, unmarried, and terribly alone. I just regret—I suppose it's one of the deepest regrets in my life—that I'll never be a grandmother."

At that moment, he didn't want her to be a grandmother. He wanted her to be Sharon Stone in *Basic Instinct*.

Her moist eyes surveyed the room, as she absorbed a life of affluence or at least the appearance of affluence—even by now he couldn't tell which it was—that seemed to have withered with time. Then those mesmerizing large eyes focused on him again, and she snapped to attention like a cadet saluting him.

"Enough of me. Enough of the past. It's time for a drink. I think we're on the verge of something larger than either of us could ever have imagined."

"Business or love?"

"What do you think?"

She touched his lips with her fingers to silence him.

"Dubonnet? Is Dubonnet all right?"

"Dubonnet is what I've been craving all day and night." He smiled. "How did you know? When I woke up this morning, I asked myself what I would like to drink as a nightcap, and believe it or not, it was Dubonnet—with my favorite lady, alone in her condo."

"Dubonnet it is." She laughed. "*Un peu*. Now you have to imagine us—the two of us hand in hand. We're sitting at Deux Magots on Boulevard St. Germains. It's midnight, and we're watching Parisians parade by. We're in our twenties—"

He cupped her face and kissed her forehead.

"In our twenties? That couldn't be—"

"Well, in any case, we're ageless. Isn't that what we vowed to be? There's no disparity between us. We're seeing Paris for the first time."

"Exactly," he murmured, bringing her still closer to him.

"Like the opening scene in *The Sun Also Rises*."

"How did you know that?"

"You forget. I was a U of C English major. The only difference is that I'm no *poule*—or even a Lady Brett Ashley. And you, my dear, have not been wounded in the war."

"How would you know?"

She smiled mischievously. "A woman always knows. Look at yourself." And she trotted off for the drinks.

While she was gone, he sat perched on the edge of the dark-brown leather sofa and closed his eyes. Her every gesture had been perfect, a warm invitation to erotic love. He wanted her badly, relishing sensations he hadn't known for years; imagining her naked body beneath his; fantasizing; feeling himself harden as though he were young once again, priapic again; and starting life all over. How did he ever come to deserve this extraordinary woman? How lucky could he be at this stage of life before it was almost too late to love? How often was anyone granted a second chance? And here she was, prepared to offer herself to him. He could not have enough of her.

She took him in the study where she spent most of her time, whenever she was home. Across from him sat stolidly a large television screen, and by its side, there was a cabinet for music. Above on the wall were more photos of family and friends, including a picture of pretty, dark-haired Julie, with her jaw set between a half-smile and an air of hostile certitude. *She must be a handful*, he thought. Laura had the dull eyes of someone who had lost her way in the wilderness and someone who had known a fair share of self-inflicted wounds that had not entirely healed. To the right of the entrance on the wall loomed a large portrait of Alyce in her younger years, resplendent in a full-pink gown. She certainly had the prettiness of a younger woman, but as she'd aged, she had become even more beautiful, more interesting and complex, and more mysterious, waiting for him all her life. He knew how lucky he was to have found her—the elegant beauty of the Crystal Ball whom he had finally captured as his own.

On the wall opposite the door stood a walnut bookcase that was filled with works methodically alphabetized and selected, as it appeared, by some Book of the Month Club committee. The dust jackets were untouched, the pages were unopened, but the knowledge of the world was there for discovery and seemed stately in its perfect order. Beside these packaged books were the classics of Alyce's college days. In his mind, he saw her racing from class to class—a young pretty colt with hair flying in the wind, a conscientious student in those hallowed classrooms, and a student a little intimidated by the austere intellectuals but smart enough to graduate with honors. He couldn't believe that someone who was so tender and receptive would love him.

Above those shelves glared the huge, threatening head of a lion mounted on a thick wooden frame. His distrustful eyes were glaring directly down at David, watching his every move, getting ready to pounce if he ever got out of line, and proving to be a danger to his mistress.

"Don't anger Malcolm," Alyce warned him. With Duchess as a guardian by her side, she had silently returned, bearing a tray of Dubonnet and cashew nuts. "He has a terrible temper."

"I can see," he said, taking the tray and placing it carefully on the coffee table. He brushed her hand then held it. "Does he growl, too, to tell you what hour it is?"

"Not yet. He's in training. He hasn't learned to tell time yet either. But he is jealous of anyone I bring here, especially if it's a handsome man."

"I'm a man last time I checked, although I'm not sure about the handsome part." He raised his glass to the dead lion. "I'll be careful not to annoy him. It must be comforting to have a patron saint in your own study protecting you. Where did he come from?"

"The wilds of Kenya. On a safari with Matt and the girls. One of our best moments. It was in 1969, after we made a bundle on Archer stock. We were rich for a moment—a passing moment. Matt was a good marksman. He became a latter-day Hemingway but without a talent for writing. It was quite a triumph for him playing Hemingway. He loved it. He even grew a beard for a moment. It was probably the high point of his life. I could barely hold my own rifle steady."

"Good old Malcolm. He growled when I first approached him, but we're good friends by now, aren't we, Malcolm? At least I hope we are."

"Over the years, he's learned to be less possessive. He's come around to the reluctant agreement that any friend of mine is a friend of his."

"Like Duchess." The puppy was now in her favorite spot, the corner of the sofa, awaiting for her mistress to stroke her to sleep. Instead, Alyce invited David to her side and scooted the dog away. He could no longer control himself, and the emotions simmering within him suddenly rose to a boil. He was by her side, holding her and running his hands across her breasts. He was growing more passionate and was kissing her insatiably, his erection hardening more than it had for a long time. His heart was pounding so eagerly he was sure she could hear it. She responded with equal intensity and let him do whatever he desired with her, drawing him into her bedroom and letting him remove her dress, her bra, her panties—a woman who hadn't made wanton love for years and now closed her eyes with passion and gratitude. Her arms were around his neck, her breasts arched into her chest, and her wet tight vagina closed in on him as he entered her and kept repeating. "I love you, oh god, how much I love you."

Afterward, she stayed curled in his arms.

"Stay with me tonight, Dave."

"Funny," he said. "I was thinking the same thing."

Naked, exhausted, ageless—they fell asleep in each other's arms.

In the morning, after he returned home to dress for work, he stared at Debra's photograph—the only one he kept for himself in his bedroom. It was an image of her when she flew as free as the wind on the beach at Amagansett, bursting with such joy just moments before she had that first attack of breast cancer when she was only fifty. The picture still showed her wild light-brown hair before she lost it all. (My beautiful soprano, he'd smile at her.) She had a perfect figure of a woman before the cancer traveled from her breast to her liver and ate away at her innards and made her into a skeleton. Her vivacity and youth and joy surrendered to resignation and depression and ultimate decline at the age of fifty-seven.

His condo had been haunted by an echo of loneliness since her death, as if he believed his suffering might serve as penitence for having survived her. But time had passed, and his wounds had abated somewhat, although the scars would clearly never fade completely. He brought a chair to the windowed wall that overlooked Lake Michigan and Oak Street Beach across the avenue and tried to understand what was happening to him.

Across the lake, a fog threatened rain. Debra's image, once so vivid that he would actually talk with her in the evenings as a way of keeping her alive within him, had faded into an ever-receding past. Once so intense, the memory of her had dulled with time, fading and yielding to the dominant presence of Alyce dancing across the Crystal Ball's floor or sitting alone with him at Le Colonial for dinner after a day's work or strolling home hand in hand or sitting on a bench at Lincoln Park and feeling the spring welcoming or lying naked in bed with her like last night and feeling his heart pound like a teenager.

He remembered one of Debra's final lucid comments and repeated it to himself again and again, as if it might assuage his residual guilt. "Don't live alone, Dave, after I'm gone. Don't punish yourself. Find someone. Find someone who'll make you as happy as we've been."

17

David's private office phone rang later in the morning.

"I want to thank you for last night," she murmured.

He laughed. "The pleasure was all mine."

"I have good news. I think I may have found a solution to your quest for a vice president of Development."

"Really?"

"Seriously. There's an article in today's *Tribune* about the appointment of a new president at Xavier University."

"So?"

She reminded him of a conversation they'd had with Mary Henderson, who had been vice president for enrollment management at Xavier when the former president used university funds for personal purposes—a second home in Michigan.

"What was his name, David?"

"Robert Grillo."

"Yes, yes. Remember how Mary went on about his leaving in disgrace and how lucky Roosevelt would be to snare him?"

"What are you getting at?"

"Speak to Mary about whether it makes sense to talk with him about his career plans."

"You're not serious?"

"I certainly am. He's probably looking for another presidency, but until he finds one he could solve some of our problems."

"God, you are incredible. About last night, can we continue—"

"We will, I promise. Tonight if you wish. But take care of this first, Dave. Trust me. Take care of this first. You won't think straight until it's taken care of."

18

He walked down the long corridor to Mary Henderson's office and closed her door softly. She looked up from her desk, slipped off her glasses, and smiled at him as a friend. They had worked well together and trusted each other, respected each other, and relied on each other. Her position was critically important in an enrollment-driven university. If the numbers and algorithms on her computer screen didn't show growth, no significant fund-raising would be possible. Since coming to Roosevelt, she had led the effort to increase enrollments by 5 percent annually, and she had delivered as promised. She had staffed an adjacent office with young, energetic Irish women who always seemed to be smiling. They'd come as Mary's acolytes from St. Xavier, a quiet little Catholic College on the South Side, where Mary had spent thirty years of her impressive career. She was edging toward retirement now, but as a strong advocate of David's dream and as a friend, she wanted to help him succeed. She promised to extend her career for three more years.

"The numbers look good for next semester." She smiled up at him. "The numbers look better than ever."

"You've kept your word."

"Just give me three years, and I'll turn round those enrollments," she had said when David first interviewed her.

He sat heavily in the chair opposite her. In the two years they had worked together, he would always come to her when he had an issue that troubled him, and he would always leave with less weight on his weighty heart.

"Tell me more about Ronald Grillo."

"Ron? My good friend Ron?"

"That's the man I have my eye on."

"He's a good man, all things considered, a little taken with himself but essentially a good man. He was more or less a successful president, and we worked well together, until he did a very foolish thing."

"Which is why I've come to you."

"To learn about the foolish thing?"

"To learn the worst."

"I don't know all the details, but it involved buying furniture for his country home with the college's money and then claiming afterward that the house would be used for fund-raising and entertainment. Something like that. I don't know all the gory details. There'd been other expenditures put on the college's tab that I never knew about—an expensive condo in the heart of Chicago and other things. After the furniture incident, the trustees acted faster than I'd ever seen them act. Ron was gone by the next board meeting."

"A presumptuous man."

"And a little arrogant. A little taken with himself. You're not thinking—?"

"Yes, I am."

"Oh god. What does Dan Pearson have to say about being replaced?"

"He's been eager to retire ever since I arrived. Nirvana for him is Sarasota. He's told me he wants to be out of here by June."

"Well, I will say one thing. Ron Grillo is a terrific fund-raiser. And you're the president. You'll keep him in check on his desire to live lucratively. He won't get carried away with himself while you're president."

"That's all that I needed to hear. What's he doing now?"

"Looking for another presidency. What else do former presidents do? Once a president, always a president. At this moment, he happens to be free—between jobs, as they say. His wife is a math professor at St. Joseph in the western suburbs. They don't want to leave Chicago."

"Perfect. Will you sound him out?"

"To see if he's interested in becoming our interim vice president for Development? Is that what this is all about?"

"How did you figure that one out?"

"I can read you like a book, Dave. Of course, I'll speak to him. Ron Grillo would make a terrific fund-raiser for your"—she caught herself—"for *our* capital campaign, if only to get it launched."

"That's what I thought too."

So Alyce was right, as always. What an amazing woman I've found—my lover, my problem solver. I owe her everything. And she still wants me, me despite my self-centered exploitation of her talents, despite my obsession with my work. This beautiful, generous woman still cares for me. Beware, David Rosen. Don't take her for granted.

He stood naked before his bathroom mirror. It was the early morning before his breakfast with Ronald Grillo. He studied himself as he rarely ever paused to do. He was fifty-nine and still vibrant—although he had a paunch where there had been none before, little breasts that could have been those of a young girl, hair that had grown significantly grayer, and something that bothered him, a little bald spot at the back of his head, the size of a skin-toned quarter, that had just emerged. He brushed his hair back to conceal it, but he never quite succeeded. There were still wispy strands of hair falling apart, leaving the bald spot in place. When he was an adolescent, the barber had plowed through his wild thick mane with a thinner just to be able to manage it. His legs had been so strong then. He was a runner in his adolescent years; he ran five miles each morning – five minutes per mile. His vision had always been perfect, although in his forties, his eyes did surrender to reading glasses, and now he would have to have them strengthened. It was trivial, stupidly trivial, but significant enough for him—aging, inevitable aging.

Still, despite these signs, he thought with some vanity. He was a fine specimen of a man—reasonably thin, almost handsome, playing vigorous tennis twice a week, with a mind as alert as it was when he was young, except for a lapse now when he could not recall a name, a book, or a movie. But if he were patient, the name would reappear in the circuitry of his brain. Acceptance—that was the hardest part of growing old.

19

"I still worry," Alyce confessed to Josie Strauss, who was now a widow. "He's so ambitious and so intense."

"Isn't that what drew you to him? After Matt? After the girls? You deserve a good, stable marriage with a winner. You deserve not to have to worry about money."

"All that seems to matter to him is the university."

"That, too, will fade when he retires. Then there'll be only the two of you."

"I wonder. He'll find something else. Intensity is in his DNA. Vanity, too, and pride."

"And what will that something be?"

"I don't know. Something. He says writing."

"There are worse fates. It's better than golf. At least he'll be home."

"Then there are the girls. Julie disliked him even before she met him."

"Well, she'll have to get used to him, won't she? She'll have to see you as a woman and not just a mother. She'll have to accommodate herself to your new life. Don't let her make you choose, Alyce. Don't let her take him away from you. Go for him. Julie will come round once she knows the relationship is forever."

They were on the leather sofa in Alyce's study, with all the memories of her troubled life surrounding them. Softly Josie put her hands on hers.

"Look at me. I was alone since Jack's death two years ago, with no one to talk to, no one to cry with, and no one to be my escort anywhere. Marcia is alone in LA and only remembers to call maybe once a week. Bryan, my son, the lawyer, is in New York, making a bundle. He's caught up in his own family and never calls. No one's perfect. Jack wasn't perfect, but he did love me, and that's all that matters. If David Rosen loves you, you're a very lucky woman. Second chances don't come that often."

20

David and Ron Grillo had breakfast at the Drake Hotel. Grillo was dressed in his presidential uniform: a dark-blue suit from Paul Stuart and a starched-white shirt, a deep-crimson tie from Hermes, and a shining black shoes from Fratelli Rossetti. He looked like a president and talked like a president, but the truth was that he was out of work. Of course, David would not have known that from his manner. He sat tall in his chair with an air of regal self-assurance, as if David were the luckiest man in the world to be offering him a job. *Oh, yes,* David thought. Ron Grillo knew the reason for this breakfast—Mary Henderson had prepared him for David—but he acted as though he had the upper hand.

As David presented his presidential pitch, he scrutinized Grillo's reaction. The man was smiling benignly, sympathetic to Roosevelt's dilemmas and a little condescending to its beleaguered condition. His eyes were twinkling behind heavy, authoritative glasses, as if he were saying kindly, "I feel your pain. I've been there myself. Boy oh boy, you do need me." His chest thrust forward as the remaining waffles and bacon and coffee between them cooled. David felt himself the applicant, and Ronald Grillo was the interviewer. David was irritated at his cockiness, but still, he needed him.

"I can help you. I've been there before. I know how to salvage—"

"Roosevelt doesn't need salvaging."

"That's not what I meant to say. That's not what I meant at all. I can help you reinvent the university. That's your phrase, isn't it? I've read *Finding the Center*. It's a visionary document. We think alike, Dave—out of the box. I can help you implement your dream."

"I know, Ron. That's why I asked to meet."

By the end of the breakfast, the conversation became less awkward, and they were talking like colleagues who might be able to work together. With Alyce Parker and Ronald Grillo, David thought he now had a winning team.

21

Alyce watched Grillo take over the development office like a bear in a beleaguered china shop. He and David worked together seamlessly, largely due to Alyce's sensitivity—her realization that Ron needed to assert his leadership over all fund-raising activities and her acknowledgment that her status was simply as a part-time assistant and that her close association to David was necessary, in her words "to cultivate the garden." She made certain that Ron knew of all her separate meetings with David and the major donors, she always asked his opinion before and afterward, she always deferred to him, and she always left a summary report of each meeting that David and her had alone. "We work together beautifully," Ron boasted to David, as he took credit for all her achievements. She was a friend and colleague rather than a competitor. Ultimately, she let him think that she was his underling and that he was guiding her. "She's a real pro. She really knows her place in the scheme of things."

Alyce knew that David recognized her true value to him as a fund-raiser. She also knew that the way to his willing heart was the university, raising more money than he and Ron Grillo could have alone, sharing David's dream of a reinvented institution, and making herself indispensable to him at work.

Their original compact of keeping a distinction between their business and personal lives had ended before it began, as she allowed their relationship to become more intimate. He stayed with her overnight when the mood was right, and they began to spend weekends together. Still, she knew that beyond his physical desire for her, the university was his personal as well as professional life, and it seemed to transcend everything.

She arranged breakfasts or luncheons several times a week, introducing him to potential benefactors who would serve as building blocks in the slow, arduous, silent phase of the capital campaign they were now planning together. More than once, she gestured to him reprovingly and urged him to be patient. "It will happen, Dave. It's already happening."

Always, meticulously, she kept Ron Grillo informed, until he began to trust her not only as a professional but also as a friend, working on the assumption that she reported to him when, of course, she knew that her ace in the hole was her access to David. But she had a way of making Grillo and the entire development staff feel an important part of whatever she was doing, soliciting their advice and letting them know she was simply there to help as an unobtrusive, part-time adjunct. She made small gestures: she baked muffins for a staff member's birthday, she sent a condolence card for the death of someone's mother, and she shared informational memos with Ron Grillo that were always signed *A* and always ended with a one-liner—"What do you think, Ron?" In time, the development staff and Grillo trusted her as someone who had no intention of threatening their security but, in fact, gave them greater importance in the larger scheme of things. Ron Grillo thought his importance was given a larger dimension because of her proximity to David.

After surveying the trustees and a few wealthy alumni, the cynical, defeatist consultant admitted that the development office was in much better shape than when David first engaged him and that the president might even be able to raise $50 million over five years—but only with Alyce's aggressive, indispensable help and only if they could secure a lead gift; then everything else might, just might, fall into place.

"It will happen, Dave," Alyce kept assuring him. "It just takes time and patience—the cultivation of friends who have been scarcely aware of Roosevelt's existence."

"I don't know that I have the patience to wait that long. Patience is not exactly my long suit."

"You'll have to make it your long suit. You have no choice but to be patient. You're marketing an institution, not just yourself. Institutions are slow to change, and the perception of an institution like Roosevelt is even slower to change."

They were in his darkened office on the eighth floor, and all the other administrators in all the other offices had gone home, or so he thought. She was sitting at the side of his desk, close to him, with her list of donors between them. She leaned forward to explore whom they would see next, and as she did so, she could feel how much he was taken by the scent of her. She knew her blouse gave slight exposure to an inviting cleavage; she could feel herself stir closer to him nervously, wanting him, wavering between caution and abandonment. She could feel one of his hands come over her own, the other lift her chin until they were gazing at each other.

"What's happened to us?" he asked.

She closed her eyes as he kissed her softly, thinking that was all the kiss was meant to be, but then he pressed harder.

She caught her breath, sharing his desire. Then common sense intruded. "Not here, Dave."

"Where?"

"At home, tonight." She pulled away gently, trying not to anger him, and clumsily gathered up her coat to flee. She could not have sex with him in this grungy office, at this desk, or on his worn leather couch, like some two-bit actress in a porno movie. She wanted sentimental music, wine, her favorite diaphanous nightgown, and whispers of comfort and caring before and afterward.

"Don't be angry, Dave. Don't be angry with me."

There was a knock on the door of his outer office that jolted them. He went there. It was frazzled Bob Green. David held the door half open, clearly not inviting him in.

"Are you okay, Dave? I saw your light on and the door locked."

"I'm okay. I'm just finishing up some work."

"Would you like to end the day with a drink? Or dinner? Or both?"

"Thanks, Bob. Some other night."

"I'll even let you pay."

"Some other night, my friend. Go home to your young wife. She's waiting for you. I'll be okay. I just need to finish something up."

A few minutes later, Alyce sneaked through the back door and down the freight elevator. She thought she wasn't being seen, but Bob Green had lingered and was chatting with the night watchman in the lobby. For one split second, Green exchanged glances with her as she fled the building. She could have been a thief in the night—detected but not reported.

22

She found the slightest excuse to brighten his day. She bought him a sweater for the fall season and a turtleneck for winter and sat with him at Brooks Brothers as he tried on a new suit. She left simple notes on his desk: "Good morning" and "Thinking of you" and "Lunch at one o'clock?" Soon they would be having a drink together at the end of the day then a movie. Finally, they had a stroll through Lincoln Park Zoo. By June, she had become not only his consultant but also his partner, and the local gossip columnists were asking the question: "How serious is the relationship between the new president of Roosevelt University and Alyce Parker.

She traveled through these days in constant joy. She was younger it seemed with each passing day, as if she could scarcely believe what was happening to her. She never shared her feelings with Julie, however much her daughter pressed for details, for fear that she would blunt and dull and destroy her growing love for David. But she did confide in her closest friends; she couldn't keep the secret to herself any longer.

Josie Straus continued to encourage her, "You never know if this feeling will come again, Alyce. You just never know. Seize it, seize it. We *are* of a certain age." Bootsie Nathan had doubts because of the difference between Alyce's age and David's—she was seventy-two, he was barely sixty. She was worried about how they would get along once he was retired and had no use for her skills as a fund-raiser. Her other friends were jealous, and some were angry that she had found someone so attractive and so accomplished. Others were annoyed and shocked, so shocked, that she had broken ranks and found a lover so late in life. She and David were now a regular item in *Skylark* and *The Sun Times*. They were a squib in Irv Kupicent's gossip column: "Why is Alyce Parker always smiling? Is it because of her new role as assistant to a certain university president?" The *Tribune* ran a profile of her accomplishments during a lifetime of raising funds for worthy causes and ended with her appointment at Roosevelt and the partnership with David Rosen, ending with a keen perception: "Is this appointment the beginning of a new career devoted to one institution, or is it a new life devoted to one man?"

She continued to shop for her clothing with her personal shopper at Saks, but now she always chose the more youthful dress, the sprightly skirt, and the snugger turtleneck. She changed her hairstyle to let her hair grow just a little darker and a little longer and a little more youthful. *Oh god, I wish I were twelve years younger with the bounce of a sixty-year-old. Give me back those twelve more years,* she prayed. *Twelve. Only twelve, like his age.*

23

Ron Grillo had his own major donors. Within a month of his appointment, he had compiled a list of those he had worked with when he was a president and written a summary and analysis of each one. With aplomb, he marched into David's office with a report he had labored on for thirty days and offered it as though it were a gift. David glanced at the title, "Fund-raising for a $50 Million Campaign," and was taken aback. That night, he read it and was horrified.

"When did you put this together, Ron?" he asked Grillo the next day.

"In the last few weeks. It was easy. I know these people like the back of my hand."

"So you're here to solve all my problems."

"No, oh no." He smiled. "I'm just here to help the cause."

The introduction to the sixty-page document was entitled, "Status of Fund-raising at Roosevelt University," and it presented a scathing review of the current development office and the underperforming trustees. It was followed by profiles of donors who could be solicited only through Ron himself. Finally, it suggested a programmatic way in which fund-raising in general could be dramatically improved.

"All this in one short month?"

Grillo smiled at David with pride.

"Ron, this is wonderful work, and I really appreciate it. But you can't let this document out of your hands."

"Why not?"

Do I have to tell you? David thought, staring at Grillo steadily to indicate who was still in charge of this university. *Are you that insensitive? That tone deaf?*

"Because it's an indictment of the university. It'll make more enemies than friends. It'll unsettle too many people, from trustees to faculty. It's an insult to all of us."

"They need to know the truth, don't they?"

What balls, David seethed. "I'll know when they're ready for the truth."

Grillo truly did not recognize the impact that his report would make, and he took it away, miffed that he had been unappreciated and overruled. Several hours later, he returned to David's office and confessed that he had shared a copy with a trustee he happened to know and copies to his staff so that he could benefit from their collective critiques.

"What in hell were you thinking, Ron? What *are* you doing? Please check with me whenever you do anything that goes public—especially when it involves any of my trustees."

24

"I don't understand that man," David complained to Alyce at dinner. They were at Dee's on Armitage for the comfort of Chinese food to assuage his frustration. He was holding her hands across the table, seeking support and confirmation. "That son of a bitch thinks he's some kind of president in waiting, hoping I'll retire early." He clasped her hands across the table. "Can you imagine someone coming up with a report like the one he showed me after two months on the job? It's as if he's telling me, 'This is the way it ought to be done. Let me show you.'"

"Give him time to settle in, Dave. He's just eager to impress you. I'm sorry I ever brought up the idea of hiring him."

"It's not your fault. I just don't trust him."

"I don't blame you."

"Once a president, always a president," David scoffed. "I can feel him watching my every move, breathing down my neck."

"He's learning from you."

She went on reassuring him that Grillo was no threat to his presidency, that he was a limited man, that she would help him achieve all that he wished in time, and that she would be by his side all the way. At the end of their dinner, she repeated, "We're going to have our $50 million campaign and our campus and whatever else you need to feel fulfilled."

He smiled at her. "Thanks for putting up with my petty insecurities. I'm just wearing thin from work."

She covered his hand. "It's going to be okay, Dave. We're going to make it okay."

25

Alyce made a point of never talking about David with Julie. She knew that the reaction would be negative, and her own response would turn defensive, argumentative, and angry. She would have none of that—not in her life now. She wanted to keep this warm feeling within her as long as possible, and she no longer cared what anybody else thought. This was her private love affair, and she would nurture it as she wished. She vowed to herself that she would keep the subject of Roosevelt University and David Rosen off limits.

But not so with Laura—her dear Laura, vulnerable Laura, and wounded Laura. At forty-five, Alyce's younger daughter had finally found a full-time job at Plunkett's Furniture, and when the company transferred to St. Louis, she went along as its assistant designer. "St. Louis is not exactly Hollywood," she brushed off the state of her pedestrian existence, laughing to her mother, laughing at herself. She was still a girl in Alyce's mind. She was still her favorite—the one-year-old who had stumbled to her in the backyard and uttered her first word, "Flowah." She was busy settling into an apartment as well as recovering from a life of emotional turmoil in Southern California. But as for her mother, Laura wanted her as happy as she had always deserved to be.

"Who gives a damn at what anybody thinks, Mom. Fuck 'em all. No one really cares. It's all gossip. This is *your* life. After what Dad did to you and what I put you through, you deserve a second chance in life."

"I hope I have it."

"Why shouldn't you?"

"I don't know. I'm just frightened that this is all too good to be true, like a dream. It's moving so fast. I'm afraid that he'll call up one day and say, 'You're too old for me. You belong to a social world I don't want in my retirement. You have cultural tastes so different from mine. Your looks are already fading—'"

"Stop it, Mom. Stop all that meaningless crap. All that will fade away if you love each other. You'll never be old. Why, you scarcely look like fifty-two."

"Seventy-two."

"Well, you look fifty-two and act like thirty-two—and that's what counts. Appearances are everything in life. There's not a single wrinkle across your beautiful face. Let your heart go. Stop analyzing everything so much. No one else really cares. It's all gossip to the outside world. He's lucky to have you. Anyone would be lucky to have you."

26

He was. He found every excuse to be with her, at work and afterward, and was warmed by the very thought of her.

Once in midafternoon, when his office door was closed and they were at his desk, their hands crossed inadvertently. He held hers tentatively, then more firmly and eagerly, and he murmured, "Thanks for everything."

"It's mutual."

He drew her closer to him.

"Dave, do you know where we are?"

"In heaven."

"No, we're in your office, and Helen might open the door suddenly."

"Never. She knows that when I'm with you, I'm not to be interrupted."

"You're mad."

"About you."

"Save it until after work, Dr. Rosen."

27

It was toward the end of a long dinner at the International Club of the Drake Hotel, just a few days later, that she fully realized how much she did love him and that there was no going back. He was giving her a new life, but she also knew that he could still break her heart—and she was wary of being hurt. They were with her close friends, Buddy Mayer and John Bryan, CEO of Sara Lee. The place was full of wine and good food. They were feeling no pain and were surrounded by people like themselves, beaming as young romantics do. They considered themselves coconspirators caught in the warm glow of their favorite restaurant and on the brink—she knew they were on the brink—of a breakthrough in every way, in love, and in work.

Fund-raising had become so intertwined with love that the two were by now indistinguishable. For weeks, she had realized her need for him whenever she stopped by his office and he wasn't there. She then felt sudden disappointment at his absence; the twinge of loneliness then lingered afterward. Her dreams at night, he had come to dominate. Then there was this question that always arose within her when she was confronted with even a small decision to make: what would David think? When she dressed in the morning, she wondered whether David would like this skirt or that scarf—he was the man she admired. He had read all the classics and taught abroad and now was lifting a sleepy university from institutional fear. "Lower your expectations," a kind colleague had once warned him, "and you won't be disappointed." Never ever could David Rosen lower his expectations, not of himself at least—and that was what she most admired in him. He went with her to the opera, the symphony, the theater, and the Art Institute providing all the culture she had always loved and wanted and needed. He was twelve years younger, but what did that matter if she already felt and looked and acted twelve years younger?

For six months, she had taken him from one corporate leader to another as she herself began to make the case for Roosevelt, becoming more and more polished and persuasive with each encounter, sharing his passion, and growing increasingly attached to the university and to him. She grew to share his vision of a metropolitan university for Chicago. Roosevelt wasn't pretending to be Northwestern or the University of Chicago but was instead an academic home for minorities and the upwardly mobile, welcoming older part-time students who raced through the Auditorium Building after work in search of a passport to the middle class. It was in the heart of the city; it was a homegrown university where students didn't just study for four years and then leave Chicago but remained to raise their families and create a sense of community, which was rare among big cities. Roosevelt was Chicago—a university for the city. Its fate, she argued on his behalf, was linked to the fate of Chicago, and therefore, it was crucial to business and civic leaders. The case was compelling, and she presented it with the passion and credibility of a lifelong Chicagoan. Now, with the help of Buddy Mayer, her lifelong friend, she was setting the stage for John Bryan to have Sara Lee provide the lead corporate gift. It was bold thinking. Beneath her serene beauty, Alyce Parker had a will of iron that would never allow for defeat.

Bryan was the prime choice among all the CEOs in the city. During the ten years that he had been the head of Sara Lee, the company had grown into a huge success, and he was a hero to stockholders as well as civic leaders. He carried more credibility and respect than any other business leader in town, and engaging him would represent a stunning coup. He had just led a successful campaign for his alma mater, the University of Chicago, and Alyce thought that Buddy might be able to persuade him to make a significant corporate gift to Roosevelt as well. But before she could make that solicitation, she knew that Buddy Mayer herself would have to commit to a lead personal donation to the campaign.

"One domino at a time." She laughed at herself and what she called her Machiavellian strategy. It was eight o'clock, the end of a day of fund-raising, and they were having dinner at Coco Pazzo. "Buddy's our major donor. She'll know she has to make a lead gift if she agrees to make the pitch to John Bryan."

He put his hand over hers, reading her desire for him and reservations about his full commitment, then he brought her hand to his lips. "Alyce Parker, you're magical." Slyly he slipped his other hand under the table between her thighs. "You're bringing out emotions I never thought existed."

"Love or lust?"

"Both."

"Is that frightening for you?" she asked, closing her thighs on the fingers of his hand.

"A little. It's been a long time since I've given myself to someone else."

"Let it go, Dave. There's more to this life than a university. Let's hurry home."

The next morning, after David left, she stood naked before her bathroom mirror like a reborn beauty and smiled and smiled and tried to remember when she had ever been so certain of her feelings about any man—not even when she'd walked down the aisle with Matt and not when she had been pursued by men since Matt's death. How lucky could she be? How often did a woman her age have the chance for rebirth? And as she studied herself in the merciless mirror, all her years faded into distant memories, the signs of aging gone. When had she ever made wanton love? She was indeed an ageless beauty.

At Alyce's behest, Laura came in from St. Louis. She had prepared both daughters for the realistic fact that she was growing increasingly attracted to David and that the relationship was taking on a much more serious turn. But Laura, not Julie, was the one with whom she could open up her heart. She wanted Laura's help in sorting out her thinking before Julie joined them for breakfast the following morning. Julie, she knew, would be difficult and not very helpful in differentiating romance from reality. Life for Julie had become only harsh reality.

A woman of forty-five, a twig with sandy-colored hair that was always loose and disorganized, Laura had retained an infectious sparkle in her eyes and put the worst of her own troubled, confused past behind her.

She listened carefully to how Alyce describe her intense affection for David, as if she was a teenager divulging her most intimate feelings irrepressibly to her closest friend, bubbling over with the enthusiasm of first love.

"He's bright and thoughtful, with a career—a meaningful career—that I can respect. He has more focused ambition than anyone I've ever known. It's scary sometimes. But more than that, far more than that, he's caring and loving, and he loves me. He loves me, oh god, Laura, he loves me." She paused, remembering David holding her naked in his arms just the night before and telling her how much he loved her.

"If he loves you, Mom, that's all that matters. I don't give a shit about his ambition or professional success. How does he feel about you? Does he love you for yourself and not just for your fund-raising? If so, that's all that matters. Is he really in love with you? Or is he using you?"

"Using me? Never. Oh, never. That's what it may have been at first, but we've gone far beyond that. Someone could accuse *me* of using *him*—a job, a helluva catch for someone my age. Why, I'm the envy of all my friends."

"Don't attack me, Mom. You asked me for my honest opinion. I don't want you to be hurt, that's all, after what you've been through with Dad and Julie and me. Just don't let him exploit you. You're too good and kind to be exploited. That's what Julie keeps saying—he's using you, exploiting you, he's taking advantage of you. For once, my cynical, bitchy, self-centered sister may be right."

"She's *not* right," Alyce cried. "David loves me as much as I love him. I know that as I know my own name."

"Well, then that's all that matters. Fuck all your friends— fuck Julie, fuck me. Just go for it. Your old friends will just be jealous that you've found a younger man. They'll just have to get used to your robbing the cradle and dancing until dawn. He sounds terrific. Prince charming in presidential robes. Ooh-la-la. After all that you've been through with Dad, you deserve one love affair in life. Everybody does. Everybody deserves at least one love affair in life."

She brought Laura's thin hands to her face and wept softly into them. It was bizarre and a little disarming. Laura had never seen her mother lose composure, nor had she ever seen her so needy.

"Oh, Laura, bless you," she murmured, kissing her hands again and again. "I never thought this could happen to me anymore in my life. I thought it was all over. I never believed I still possessed these emotions."

But her dream at night, darkened by doubt, contradicted her. She had spoken so self-confidently about David's love for her, but in that dream, incomprehensibly, he was swimming away, farther and farther away, in water that was over her head. Her hands were flailing for him, but he wasn't there. He was swimming away toward the shore, and there he went, running ashore, running from her, fading, no longer needing her—an old, wrinkled woman with dull gray hair who had begun to lose her teeth. Swimming desperately and growing too weak and too old to catch him, she almost drowned.

She awoke into this morbid, distorted image of herself. The nightmare exploded into the glaring light of day, and she screamed after him, "No, no, no, Dave. Come back. I'll be good for you. I'll make your life better. We'll have a life together. We'll stay young together."

Julie drove in from her home in Winnetka, where she lived alone in a small, sterile, immaculate house, bordered by a white picket fence and a front yard garden that Alyce helped her perfect every Saturday morning. She was bringing the pastries for their ceremonial Sunday breakfast. She never dressed in style anymore. Her daily uniform was a pair of black corduroy trousers and a gray sweatshirt that scarcely concealed her swollen breasts—her melons, as she mocked them—and still bore the emblem of her alma mater, Miami University, where her first and only boyfriend had dumped her twenty-five years ago. Soon she intended to have her breasts reduced to ease their uncomfortable heaviness. Once she had a pretty face, framed by black hair and intensified by dark eyes that sparkled with the possibilities of joy, but the experience of having been dumped, to use her word, by that college lover and the unwillingness to develop a single career led to a brittle disposition and an unhealthy attachment to Alyce.

There wasn't a flicker of ambivalence or generosity in her attitude to her mother's new love affair; she considered it not only foolish but also dangerous.

"Should I list the reasons why this is all wrong for you?"

"Why not?" Alyce yielded, annoyed at her always seeking to denigrate David. "You're going to tell me, anyway, aren't you?"

"I'm going to tell you the truth, the unvarnished truth—"

'The whole truth and nothing but the truth."

"Even the unwelcome truth. Even what you don't want to hear. No one else will—certainly not your aging friends or Laura. You're twelve years older than he is, for one thing. Do you really think you'll be able to keep up with him as the years go by?"

"The age difference doesn't seem to bother him."

"Why should it? You're giving his career dynamism while working at slave wages for his third-rate university. Wait a year or two, and you'll see how your age gap widens."

"Please, Julie. I know your heart is in the right place, but you're ruining this for me. We all age at the same rate, don't we? All of us? Even you."

Laura moved to intervene, but Julie's eyes never left her mother's as she redressed her sister. "Oh, be quiet, Laura. You're totally impractical when it comes to things like this. You've screwed up your own life. Don't screw up Mom's."

"Yours is so great? Don't tell me who I am. Don't define me. Why don't you let Mom just enjoy her own life?"

But Julie was relentless. She wouldn't let go. David Rosen played tennis regularly and competitively. Alyce had never touched a tennis racket, and now was her first try to learn how to play (for pleasure) with David. After traveling with privileged professional friends who belonged to the Lakeshore Country Club, Alyce would now be descending into another world she did not fully understand—academic liberals. They're hopelessly cynical and critical. Didn't she see that he was exploiting her? Her talents? Her beauty? Her contacts? Her knowledge of Chicago? All he cared about was himself. And after he was finished with his presidency and they were looking at each other across the breakfast table, both retired, he in his seventies, she in her eighties, what exactly would they have in common? What would be the conversation?

"Does this man love you the way Dad did?" Julie snarled.

"What in God's earth does that mean?"

"Does he love you in spite of everything? Does he know your back is up against the wall financially? Dad was always there for you—"

"Oh, stop the horseshit," Laura snapped in disgust. "Stop rewriting history. Dad was an irresponsible drifter who went from job to job—an alcoholic and a philanderer."

"He was not! He loved Mom. He loved all of us. He had great ambition and drive when he was young. He just had bad luck. Things turned against him—his health, his TB, his heart attack."

"Don't tell me. I grew up in the same fucking house. Dad was a drifter from the start. He was a lousy father and a lousy husband. Take it from an expert who knows. I had the same bum luck. Nice guy, don't get me wrong, especially when he brought back chocolates after each of his one-nighters. But he had no spine. He was an irresponsible bastard of a father. And don't get me started on his cousin Jack."

Jack had molested her when she was eight years old in that dark bedroom at Cedar Lake, where she was sent as an eight-year-old to be chaperoned by Ben and Aunt Joyce because Alyce had to remain in the city at some gala or other. Alyce never talked to Jack again, however much, he denied his violation of Laura.

She watched her two daughters trash each other, dissecting their father and digging up a gory past she wanted to forget. By now, Matt's derelictions or the reasons for them didn't matter. And Jack's molestation was a secret that Alyce and Laura never shared with anyone else, not even with Julie.

"What would you have me do?" She turned to Julie with quiet rage and tears in her eyes. "Grow old along with you?"

"You *are* old. Old. *Old.* Face reality. You're seventy-one!"

"David doesn't seem troubled by our age difference."

"Oh christ, Mother. Can't you see he's using you?"

Her face reddened with anger and despair. Neither her mother nor her sister was listening to her, and with uncontrollable fury, she brushed aside her half-filled cup of coffee, spraying coffee everywhere and sending the cup to the floor, shattering it into shards. She stormed out of the apartment. Laura ran after her to make certain she did no harm to herself or any other driver on the highway.

28

David was warmed by the mere thought of Alyce. His university issues were less onerous because he knew she would come unexpectedly to his office with good news, promising possibilities, suggesting dinner at six when the workday was over, one night a movie, another *La Traviata,* or the symphony or whatever excuse she could invent to be together with him. Soon he was staying at her condo several nights a week, and the image of their bodies entwined carried him through some difficult days.

She bought a tan cardigan for him, and he found a Jensen necklace for her—the first gift he tendered any woman since Debra's death. Others were exchanged, expressions of an intensifying affection for one another. *I love her,* he told himself. Surely he loved her. He measured the moments by when he had last seen her and when she would come to him again. Still . . . still . . . when he swam in his condo pool at the end of a night at his own home and afterward he sat alone there, tossing and turning in bed, he still could feel flickers of uncertainty. *Surely I love her*, he convinced himself. *Surely I'm the luckiest man in the world to have found her—this jewel in the crown of Chicago, this gem in my heart of hearts. I want her. Surely I want her as my partner, my lover. I want us to live in one condo together. But why do I have to convince myself, and do I want her as my wife? That's where this love affair is inevitably leading, as night the day. As a sign of commitment,* she would say. *Everything she does pleases me, and I know my life would be severely diminished without her, but I wonder to what extent I am enthralled by the trappings of her wealth, her status in the city, her sheer beauty and elegance, and her physical passion. I want her as my one permanent lover, but do I want her as my wife? She'll be asking to be my wife. And why would I hesitate? Because I'd be betraying Debra? Or losing my freedom? Or committing myself absolutely to another human being? Or worrying that she is too old for me, accustomed to a standard of living I'll never be able to afford once I'm no longer Mr. President? There are no good, sensible reasons for holding back—and yet I feel the inexplicable need to hold back. Why?*

He remembered a line from Dostoevsky, whom he first began to teach in the old battered classrooms of CCNY and knew so little about life other than the text itself, as though the words had been written for him: "What is hell?" Dostoevsky had asked. "I believe that it is suffering from the inability to love." Now he almost understood the words. He almost understood himself—almost.

All these irreconcilable thoughts swam through him like the crosscurrents of a wayward stream, toward an uncertain destination, seeking resolution. There had always been work to guide him through difficulties in the past; work had always been the ultimate anodyne. It would sustain him again if this woman he had come to love ever were to leave his life. But for now, he could not conceive of a life without her.

29

They were united by their love for each other and the university. The two were indistinguishable—one not possible without the other. She had proposed her plan for their $50 million capital campaign to him, knowing the way to his heart. She would try to pin down Buddy Mayer for a lead gift and ask her to help persuade John Bryan, who owed so much to her father, Nathan Cummings, the founder of Sara Lee. Bryan would be the leader of corporate giving. David would then ask Jerry Stein, his most prominent trustee, to be the chairman of the entire capital campaign but not until she had secured agreement from Buddy and John Bryan. Buddy Mayer was, after all, a Roosevelt trustee, a close friend of Alyce, heiress to the dynasty, and the daughter who, years ago, had championed John Bryan when he was in the competition to become CEO of Sara Lee. Alyce had also worked with Jerry Stein on many a cause and counted him as a friend. Everyone of importance in Chicago, it seemed to David, was Alyce's friend.

"And so the dominoes would fall," she assured him, "one by one."

30

Jerry Stein was a short, thin, wiry man who never seemed short. He was the only original trustee of the university still alive and had served as chairman of the board for many years. At eighty, he was the éminence grise who still held enormous influence over his erstwhile colleagues. As a card-carrying liberal who had led Stein Container Corporation, a major distributor of cardboard boxes, to a receptive world, he was still vigorous and always in demand as a leader of philanthropic causes. When he was an undergraduate at Northwestern, his father needed him in the struggling family business. He was an eager, assiduous student, but he never was able to complete his degree and reluctantly joined the company with his two older brothers, moving into the leadership role and creating a corporation that was now listed among the Fortune 500. He never lost his love of learning and became a devotee of the opera, symphony, Ravinia, and the Museum of Contemporary

Art. He was a Renaissance man without a degree and a business leader now without a portfolio except for the Alzheimer's Foundation. He believed deeply in the idea behind Roosevelt University: upward mobility, social justice, and the elusive American dream of being granted a second chance in life.

Stein was perched behind a large desk in an office reserved for him as former CEO. By his desk was a small overnight traveling valise. He had just returned from Washington, where he was lobbying for federal funds to augment those he had privately raised for the Alzheimer's Foundation. In addition to being short and thin, he was a golf and tennis player still active at the North Shore Country Club and a tightly wound executive who always seemed to have the glimmer of a mischievous smile implanted into his tight lips. He possessed a tendency toward taciturnity—he always made you feel as though you needed to fill the long silences he created. He came to trustee meetings occasionally, but he was always there for consequential decisions. All eyes turned toward him as patriarch of the university family. Indeed, in the two years David knew Jerry Stein, he considered him a mentor and had monthly luncheons with him at the Standard Club to review the progress of their institution.

Stein admired David's *Finding the Center* that projected, as its centerpiece, a thriving new campus in the northwest suburbs, an honors program, an accredited business college, a reinvented college of performing arts, the appointment of new academic deans—and now a capital campaign to make the entire enterprise flourish.

"But not for $50 million," he warned David, who by now had become his friend as well as his protégé. "That's overreach, Dave. You'll embarrass yourself with that kind of unrealistic goal. Roosevelt's never had a campaign anywhere near the magnitude you're considering. It's a small college with no endowment to speak of and an alumni base of limited means. Where's the money going to come from?"

From people like you, David almost blurted out. From the Roosevelt royalty on the golf courses at Rancho Mirage, California, and all the friends the royalty knows. Stein knew that, and he was fully aware that he was being asked for more than avuncular guidance; he was being asked to be a leader in the capital campaign that David encouraged and that Jerry was convinced would not succeed.

David went into a lengthy description of his months with Alyce Parker and the visits to the citywide CEOs and potential donors of consequence.

"I've heard." Stein smiled. "The two of you do get around. You're an item all over town."

"She's a fabulous woman."

"I know. We all know. And now you know." He grinned mischievously. "You've picked a winner, Dave, in every way. Where is your relationship headed? Should I get my tux ready?"

"Not yet. For now, ours is strictly a partnership."

"I'll bet. And my name's not Jerry Stein. Go for it, Dave. Don't let her slip through your fingers. You won't meet a woman quite like Alyce Parker again. When my wife was dying from Alzheimer's Alyce brought her favorite bean soup once a week and sat with Evelyn for hours. Alyce Parker's more than a beauty or a first-rate fund-raiser. Take it from someone who's known her for years. She's compassionate and kind. Like everyone else, I'm half in love with her myself."

"I know. I've come to care for her—"

They smiled knowingly at each other. Jerry had loved and lost and now was married to someone who returned his love, differently but decidedly. In his own recovery, David had discovered a future with Alyce that had become more and more desirable. It had been and would be luminous. When she wasn't with him the memory of her smile radiated through him, as it did now. He loved her as much as he was capable of loving any other human being.

Then his eyes found Jerry Stein's again—the wise, understanding, reassuring eyes of a surrogate father.

Jerry listened diplomatically, even sympathetically, to David's summary of his case for a capital campaign, *Finding the Center*, and tried not to discourage him.

"I've admired your ambition, your aggressiveness, Dave, from the moment you set foot in our second city. Alyce is the smartest appointment you've made in your short time as president. I've worked with her on all sorts of committees over the years. She's the best fund-raiser in town, and the two of you make quite a team. But don't embarrass yourself or her. Neither of you is a miracle worker."

"I may not be, Jerry, but she is. She is. She's helped me enormously. And she's working on a lead gift as we speak."

"And you, my friend," he said, touching David's forearm, "are hopelessly in love with her."

"It shows?"

Jerry Stein smiled benevolently at him. "Just to satisfy my own curiosity, tell me who might be making a lead gift to a campaign that's not even started?"

"A close friend of hers and yours—a trustee."

"Who?"

"You know her well."

"Oh, no . . . not Buddy Mayer?"

"How would you ever guess?"

"I wouldn't. But I do know how close Buddy and Alyce have been over the years. What's holding Buddy back?"

"She wants us to have all our ducks in order and a trustee as chairman of the campaign. The most prestigious trustee, the most respected trustee, the—"

"Keep going." He laughed. "You surely couldn't mean me? Oh no, not me? This old man? As chairman of a capital campaign? Me? At the age of eighty? No, no, no, Mr. President—not at this stage in my waning life. Except for Alzheimer's, this old man has officially retired from philanthropy. All I do now is write checks."

"There has to be one last hurrah, Jerry."

David picked up on the suggestion that Alyce had made to him one night. "Would you do me one small favor?"

"Anything but being chairman. You want me to be your best man at the wedding?"

"Would you talk with our consultant? Help to analyze our problems, if nothing else, and see how far we can push this envelope?"

David reached across the table to shake his elder's hand goodbye. "For now just have a conversation with our consultant. Do it for Roosevelt, Jerry. Do it for me."

Reluctantly he agreed, "For you, for Alyce. But tell your lovely lady, I can't be the chairman. There is a time for everyone to quit."

"I'll tell her."

"And tell her not to forget to invite me to the wedding."

"Front row, center section."

Then the dominoes fell more swiftly than David could ever have anticipated. He and Alyce, Ron Grillo, Alan Archer, and Jerry Stein sat with the consultant, a portly veteran of great certainty with the suggestion of a goatee, and listened to all his pragmatic reasons for moving more cautiously: the university had never mounted a campaign of anything close to $50 million, there was no campaign chairman of stature; no lead gift, no corporate support, no willingness of the trustees to step forward with significant donations, no alumni base of consequence, and the discouraging list went on and on and on.

Alan Archer agreed. As chairman of the board, he felt the university wasn't ready, and David knew the major reason was that the pressure on him would be to make a more significant contribution than he had initially pledged. Ron Grillo championed the effort as though he was its conceptualist and leader, stating that he might not have the resources to move so quickly right now, but with a few more additional staff, he felt they could all pull it off.

"We can't get ahead of our skis," Alan Archer warned everyone. "We're simply not ready for a campaign of this scope. Maybe in a year or two, Dave. Maybe."

David smiled grimly and quietly thanked everyone for coming. He could feel his buoyant expectations fading, but at the same time he could see Alyce smiling at him as if to reassure him, "Don't worry. Don't worry, my love. This isn't over yet. I'll love you whatever happens, but this isn't over yet. We're going to be okay."

"And I will love you," his eyes answered but feeling indeed that the campaign would never be launched.

More was at stake, both of them knew, than the thwarted dreams of an ambitious, overzealous university president.

As the group began to assemble their papers for departure, she asked all of them to pause for just one last moment. David watched Grillo look at her in surprise. He hadn't been informed of what she might say and realized, if only for one passing moment, that his attempt to present himself as commander of their fund-raising effort was pure bluster in everybody's eyes.

"Before we leave, gentlemen, let me try out a different scenario for us to consider."

They turned their skeptical eyes toward her.

"What if I told you that Buddy Mayer was prepared to make a lead gift—I'm speaking of $3 million over five years—and that John Bryan has agreed not only to have Sara Lee make a major donation but to also be the chairman of the corporate drive in our campaign?"

"When did this all happen?" Jerry laughed in disbelief. "Behind our backs? While we were sleeping? There are no contingencies?"

"There are always contingencies, Jerry. You know that." She was sitting next to him and tapped his hand affectionately. "You'll love this one. The only contingency is that you become chairman of the entire campaign."

"Really?" the consultant said in disbelief.

"Really. I'm telling you. We're on the edge. Before we postpone this campaign into a future none of us may live long enough to see, I propose, if Ron agrees, that Jerry speak to Buddy Mayer and John Bryan to see if what I'm saying is true. Remember, if I am right and Jerry does agree to be chairman, we don't have to set a specific goal at this time. This is the safe, silent phase of our campaign— no public announcements, no fanfare. We can hold off on a specific goal until we have one-third of whatever we imagine, privately or together, that goal should be. We can always reduce the final number, if need be. There's no need to frighten anyone, including ourselves, with what may now seem like an outrageous number."

"Alyce Parker," Jerry exploded with laughter. "You are the most charming fund-raiser I have ever known." He turned to David. "Where oh where, David, did you ever find this woman?"

For David, she had become far more than a fund-raiser, far more than a beauty, and far more than anyone he had ever known. If ever he doubted his love for Alyce and wanted her as the center of his entire life now and in the future, it was not at the moment.

She watched Jerry Stein's heart go out to them, smiling softly like a satisfied surrogate father. He agreed to call Buddy Mayer and John Bryan. Still, he insisted that he wasn't making any personal commitment yet.

"I must say," the consultant responded at a second meeting, a little embarrassed by his own negativism but hoping now to preserve a potential consultancy that might actually and incredibly become a full-fledged capital campaign, "what Alyce says makes some sense, especially if everything is kept private and silent until we have a third of our goal in hand."

"Oh lord," Jerry finally acquiesced. "I can't believe I'm doing this—against all common sense. I'll probably live to regret it."

"You won't," David assured him. "We'll use your contacts carefully, just for the big donors. This could be one of the great achievements of your philanthropic career."

"I bet it will be." He laughed. "Chicago's version of the Nobel Prize in philanthropy. The two of you are quite a team, I must say, ganging up on me like this. I don't know how you corralled Buddy Mayer and John Bryan, but I am impressed. I am impressed . . . and pleased for both you lovebirds."

Several days later, Jerry Stein called David. "Alyce wasn't exaggerating. Buddy Mayer and John Bryan are definitely on board—financially. I cannot believe it."

"And?"

"I still think I'm nuts for doing this."

The moment David hung up, he called Alyce to share the news. Before he could thank her for everything she'd done for him, she told him to hurry over. The champagne would be at the ready, she promised, by the time he arrived. "We'll celebrate, my David. This is our turning point. It deserves to be celebrated."

She was dressed simply in brown slacks and a beige sweater. Huddling close to him on the sofa, with champagne glasses in hand, her sensual scent rising through him—a curl of her auburn hair came undone, her eyes grew large with desire, and her cheeks flushed with expectation. More than ever, she had the look of a younger woman. She began to reach out to him, running her slender fingers across his warming face.

"We did it, my love."

"You did it."

He took her into his arms and kissed her until she was breathless.

"Tell me something, Dr. Rosen." She gasped, pulling back a little. "Do you want me strictly for my fund-raising or for myself?"

"What do you think?"

"At this moment, I think you want me for my body."

"And why not? You have a gorgeous body. But there's more going on here. Believe me, Mrs. Parker—much more. You've taught me to love. I know that now."

Her arms went round his neck as if to trap the words.

"What took you so long, my student? Love in the middle of the afternoon?" she smiled. "That's absolutely sinful, Dr. Rosen."

"Touch me."

"Oh god, Dr. Rosen, what is happening to you? Don't you realize you'll be sixty in a week?" She stroked him, laughing. "We must take care of this condition immediately. Would you like to come into my bedroom?"

That night, lying naked beside her naked body, he regained his composure. In the middle of the night, he could no longer sleep. He turned, he tossed, and he watched her dream. The glow of a grateful smile spread across her lovely face. However young she appeared, even without makeup, she was twelve years older than him; however beautiful she was now, that gorgeous face would one day turn pale and surrender to the wrinkles of old age; and however empathetic she was to all people, she did come from a different social class whereas he had entered her world through a presidency that allowed him ephemeral perquisites—a fancy condo and a fancy Jaguar and Paul Stuart clothing and opera tickets and conferences to Japan, China, India, and other exotic lands that he would never have otherwise been able to afford. Now none of that mattered anymore—or so he wanted to believe. He loved her for herself and not for what she could do for him, and he already convinced himself that he was the luckiest man in the world.

The phone awoke them early in the morning.

"It's Julie." She wrapped her naked body in her white robe. "Hold on, Julie," she whispered. "I'll take this in the other room."

"I'm sorry she's called so early."

"Dave, go back to sleep."

"No problem. Say hello for me. Tell her I'm sorry, but I really do love you." And he brought her close to kiss her good morning. "Tell her everything will work out. Tell her I love you for more than your fund-raising, for more than your body."

"Shhh, wise guy."

"Meanwhile I'll be taking a nice hot shower."

Alyce scampered out of the room, knowing she would be chastised by her daughter—for something, for anything. Slowly he rose from the bed, but as he prepared to shower, he could hear their voices rising like a cacophony. He reached over to put the extension phone in its cradle then hesitated, and with one hand, he pressed against the speaker. He listened.

31

"I was really worried, Mom. I called a dozen times last night, but your phone was off the hook. Are you okay?"

"I'm okay, Julie. I just wanted to turn off the world for one night."

She could tell that Julie did not believe her.

"Are you alone, Mom?"

"Why do you ask?"

"I just have the sense that you're not alone."

"Why—?"

"You took my call in your study and not in the bedroom. Last night, you had both phones off the hook. It's not normal. Is he there? Of course. Of course, he's there. And he's been there all night."

"And if he has been?"

"Then you've committed yourself."

"I guess I have." Alyce laughed then drew herself up straight. "Look, Julie. Get one thing straight. I am not your daughter, and you're not my mother. "

"I'm just—"

"I don't care what your good intentions are. This is *my* life. I love David Rosen, and you'd better get used to that fact. I've never loved a man as much as I love him."

"Mom—"

"Please, Julie," she begged, tears replacing the laughter in her eyes. "Leave me alone."

She slammed the phone goodbye, good riddance. But before doing so, she could hear David putting the bedroom extension into its own cradle, she could hear him rising from her bed, and she could hear him showering.

In the kitchen, she prepared breakfast: juice, waffles with maple syrup and blueberries, and brewed coffee. The Sunday *Times* was waiting for them as he joined her. She was reading the front page. She was as naked as a newborn beneath her robe.

He stood behind her and rested his lips on her head.

"Will we survive Julie?"

"You bet we will. You heard it all, you sneaky so and so. You heard me tell her to get a life of her own. I've had enough. She is not going to ruin my life. She's going to have to get used to you and me as one."

"Or else?"

"There won't be a Julie in my life."

"From your lips to God's ears."

"Oh no, Dave. You and I are going to be one. I'll make it so."

They ate their breakfast and lingered over the paper until she was ready for her own shower. Afterward, she was dressed in gray slacks and a black turtleneck. She then came into the kitchen smiling, determined to return to the mood of last night. But silently she cursed her daughter.

The phone rang again.

"Just ignore it," she said. "At some point, my forty-six-year-old child will finally stop calling."

They took the paper into the den with a second cup of coffee. After an hour, when he was deep into the book review section, she shared the thought that had been top of her mind.

"I have an idea."

"Oh, oh, that sounds dangerous."

"How would you like to see a 106-year-old lady?"

"Now that's exactly what I had in mind for a Sunday afternoon."

"No, I'm serious."

"And who is this 106-year-old lady?"

"My mother. I want you to meet her before it's too late. She's a phenomenon."

"You want me to meet your mother? To win her approval?"

"No, not her approval." She laughed. "I don't need that anymore."

"Then why?"

"I don't know. I just want you to meet her. Maybe I just want to show you off."

Her name was Josephine, and she lived in an orderly condo on the eighteenth floor of a high-rise that overlooked Belmont Harbor studded with boats that seemed painted on the lake by Renoir. The dining table before her was a model of order and discipline: on the left side was a stack of unopened envelopes and bills awaiting a response and on her right was *The Chicago Tribune,* which she read religiously during days and evenings that must have seemed endless.

As her full-time Polish caregiver prepared tea for the three of them, she greeted David with a handshake that was firm and strong.

"Alyce has told me all about you."

"All about me? My secrets too?"

"Especially your secrets." She smiled at him flirtatiously. "No, not really. About your success as a president. I remember Roosevelt University when it was first created, just after the war. They used to call it the little red schoolhouse."

"Subversive and sinister in the old days. It's calmed down a good deal and become more main stream." He tried to elicit a smile from her, but she seemed only capable of grimacing. "Over the years, it's become less driven by ideology. It's just another university trying to move working-class students into the middle class."

"A worthy purpose. But it's more than that now, isn't it? You can't fool this old lady." She wagged her long bony finger at him. "Alyce has told me about your ambitious plans, which she's now become so much a part of. I've never seen my daughter so animated. Finally she has a cause that's more than just glitter and glamour and galas."

"Mother—"

"She's been a great help to me," David said in Alyce's defense. "Without her, I couldn't have accomplished half of what I've set out to do. Sometimes you need a little glitter and glamour in your life. At least I do. It's what donors respond to."

"She's been a different woman since she met you. You know that, don't you? See that light in her eyes? You're her white knight."

"Her white knight?" He almost burst into laughter. "White knight?"

"Oh yes," she insisted, without smiling. Her voice lowered, conspiratorially. "You'll see. There are so many things in life that go unsaid."

They bantered on for another few minutes, leaving David with the sense that he had passed a preliminary interview. Alyce led him to a love seat in the living room so that she could be alone with her mother to settle some practical matters, money matters, and family matters. Leaning over him, she kissed his lips softly.

"I'll only be a minute."

But it was more like half an hour, as she and her mother conferred. From his distance, he heard Julie's name, Laura's name, and even Matt's. He did not want to know the gory details, he was no white knight come to rescue the princess from her crumbling castle. As they left the apartment, Alyce gripped his hand to reassure him that she belonged to him more than ever.

"I just thought you needed to see where I came from. Mother's always been austere and cold and distant. Judgmental. Don't take it personally. She's basically a good woman. And her judgment of you is strictly positive. You can see that. White knight. Why, Dave, you're my white knight." She giggled. "Oh dear, what have we come to?"

"She and I are going to be good friends," he assured her, "if I have anything to say about it. She's quite a lady."

They stopped for dinner at Antiprima on Clark Street. A moment after they were settled, it was clear that she was not done with her childhood. She wanted him to know all about her.

"When I was a child, I was chubby. Can you believe that? We had a Lithuanian housekeeper. Even in the depression, after my father had lost his fortune, we had a Lithuanian housekeeper, and the battle-axe scolded me one day for doing something wrong. I was three or four but already full of myself and told her in no uncertain terms, 'I'm the most important person here.' And I was. I made certain I was. It's hard to be an only child. You grow up spoiled and special and pampered, especially if you have a protective, exacting mother like mine—domineering, cold, imperious, demanding, inflexible, but loving. She's loving, too, in her way. She had me become one of the Abbott dancers. I was the best of the Abbott dancers. I had to be the very best, and then there were piano lessons and French lessons and ballet lessons. She was a perfectionist, my mother, and every privation she had ever suffered in her own childhood was to be avoided by me. I was blessed with everything, except a mother's warmth, which mine simply did not possess."

"You don't need to tell me all this, Alyce. I love you as you are. You don't need to go on."

"No, I do. I want you to know me, warts and all. My father was a warm, affectionate man. He was a furrier—well to do, until the market crashed. He was a genial man, a sweet man. Thank God I inherited his disposition. He was the one who held me at three in the morning when I was sick. My mother was afflicted with migraines and long bouts of depression—an emotionally distant woman who always seemed to have allergies of one sort or another and often isolated herself from the world and from me. But she was elegant, mother dear, well dressed, and cultivated. Of all things, she was a cultivated woman, a constant reader, a theatergoer, and a lover of the symphony and the opera.

She always went to the opera without my father, who disliked what he considered artificial theatricality. I was lucky to inherit the right genes from each of them—my father's temperament, my mother's determination and grit and intelligence. Never ever did I think of rebelling. Those were the days when good girls did not rebel."

Hyde Park was self-contained. In a safe community, she went on, and she formed friendships that lasted a lifetime. When she was a teenager, she traveled with her mother to Los Angeles to see relatives and fell in love with the idea of becoming a Hollywood star. Why not? Every pretty girl in America wanted to be a Hollywood star. At Schwabs, the drugstore where Lana Turner was famously discovered, she was sitting with a summer boyfriend at the soda fountain when an agent asked them if they wanted to audition for Joseph Schenck. "Oh," she remembered, plaintively, "I must say I loved the camera, and the camera loved me—at least from the waist up. I could have had a movie career. I know it. I just know it. I could have been in show business. Schenck told me I could have been." She was in fact offered a contract, but her father put the kibosh on that dream. He had seen too many young women in the modeling business sell themselves to the highest bidder, and her mother, of course, agreed. "You didn't rebel in those days. At least I didn't rebel."

"Few people did."

"And so I never had a chance to test my talents."

"Like most of us. I wanted to be Ernest Hemingway. What's new? Life is a series of compromises."

"Is it? Why? Why does it always have to be?"

"It doesn't—not in our case. It won't be in our case."

Hers was a tale of modest privilege. At the University of Chicago, she was a beauty queen, elected Betty Co-Ed, and won a trip to the New York World's Fair, traveling with her mother as chaperone. Despite the attempt at maternal control, Alyce could see the town and was escorted by young men who were taken with her beauty—a handsome, rich son of a real estate dynasty, a young editor at *The New York Times*, others along the way, and inevitably, at home, her high school sweetheart, Matthew Parker, who told her he would wait for her after she'd sowed her wild seeds with those foreigners from New York. "There is a power in female beauty that is sometimes frightening. I've felt it everywhere I've been, like an inner light, a secret power, and a controlling force. I've felt it all my life. It has a magnetizing effect."

As she unraveled her past, she felt that he might think they had so little in common. But that didn't seem to matter at the moment. He touched her lips to silence her. "You don't need to go on. We should live in this moment when *we're* together. We should live each day as though it's the last one of our lives."

In her office at her home, she insisted on completing the family saga, divulging herself for the first time since she'd spoken to her therapist decades before in those long sessions of yesteryear when she was trying to understand why her husband and daughters were disintegrating around her. She could not understand what had gone wrong. In the wider world, she was pure perfection. At home, she had failed as a wife and mother. Or had *she* failed? Was it all *her* fault?

Julie never would marry. The wealthy Florida family of a college classmate with whom she had fallen in love at Miami University checked her father's finances and rejected the (relatively) less affluent girl as unworthy of their son. That heartbreak left a lifelong scar. As bizarre as it had always seemed to Alyce, she tried to comfort Julie by telling her that she, too, had been rejected when she was a kid and for the same reason. Julie hadn't been able to have a healthy relationship with a man. "You have to lower your expectations, and then you won't be disappointed, Julie. There are no white knights in this life." Alyce's remembrances of Matt were quite the opposite of Julie's—a conflict that always arose whenever Julie defended her father, who had inherited a fortune and squandered it in abortive business failures, in alcoholism, and infidelities.

Every Saturday, Alyce would drive to Pine Street in Winnetka to spend a morning with Julie, poking away at the little patches of grass that fronted her white picket house and the few flowers she generously called her garden—her little Garden of Eden. Then they'd have lunch at Frank and Betsy's. Over the years, the bond between them had grown forced and difficult, especially for Alyce, but Julie had drawn it as tight as the proverbial Gordian knot would allow.

32

David listened to Alyce's confessional with a mixture of curiosity, compassion, and love. By now, he had gone beyond analysis. When they came to the entrance to her condo building, she murmured, "Come upstairs, Dave. I need you tonight."

And then they were in the elevator holding hands tightly and in her condo kissing each other. It was as though they had so little time left in their lives and needed to take advantage of this moment. He caressed her hair and cupped her face with tenderness.

"We can't recover the past, Alyce. We have only this moment now and the future. I love you more than I thought I was ever capable of loving anyone."

33

It was time, so Alyce planned to bring Jerry Stein, John Bryan, and Buddy Mayer together with a carefully selected group of CEOs they had been courting for lunch or dinner during the past several months. It was time for Stein, Bryan and Mayer to step up to the plate, announce their gifts, and persuade others to join them in this capital campaign for Roosevelt University.

She organized the dinner for thirty corporate leaders and prospective major donors with the professional aplomb and perfection she brought to everything she did. They all came, the ones they'd met in their plush offices for the past year, some out of genuine interest, and more out of courtesy. They came for Buddy Mayer, John Bryan, Jerry Stone, and Alyce Parker—certainly not for Ronald Grillo, a minor actor in the college circuit of Chicago, and not for David Rosen, who was still a local leader with no historical credentials in Chicago, no lineage, a stranger still to this

Midwestern city. And it was a banner affair. In a private dining room of the Four Seasons, they ate an elegant dinner of shrimp cocktails and rib eye steak, and for the first time David felt that a $50 million goal might not be so quixotic; it might actually be within reach.

After Jerry Stein introduced him, he laid out the case for a metropolitan university more fully than ever before. As a private university, Roosevelt would serve a middle-class student body that would continue to live in Chicago and its suburbs. It would have a musical conservatory that would draw upon part-time faculty from the Chicago Symphony Orchestra, only two blocks from the venerable Auditorium Building that housed the university. It would have a college of education that would be closely connected to the public schools where its graduates would be teaching. It would have an honors college that balanced an open admissions policy, which had always admitted virtually every student who applied. It would seek mergers and acquisitions with other institutions and grow into a great university for the multiethnic population of Chicagoland. And most importantly, as the centerpiece to the entire campaign, it would create a permanent campus in the northwest suburbs, where a vast middle class lived and where major corporations had established world headquarters. Together, these efforts would transform the university. This thirty-page vision, *Finding the Center*, was prefaced by endorsements from Jerry Stein, Buddy Mayer, and John Bryan and bound in a black binder that would have impressed any potential donor.

Jerry Stein rose after David's address and concluded the dinner with a powerful, persuasive, personal encomium.

"I've agreed to be chairman of the campaign because as a lifelong Chicagoan, this university represents the ideals of social justice and ethnic diversity that I deeply believe in. It may not be the University of Chicago or Northwestern, nor should it be, but it is essential to the fabric of our city. When a group of idealists—and I count myself among them—founded Roosevelt in 1945, Chicago was the most segregated city in America. In many ways, it still is. The YMCA College, which became Jefferson College for twelve days and then Roosevelt College upon FDR's death and finally Roosevelt University changed all that and became a haven for people of all backgrounds. It's a private university, with students from a variety of backgrounds, and an institution that can shape its own fate. It graduates students who remain in Chicago and strengthen the city. Now we have a new, first-rate president, with a bold vision, which can connect the university with Chicago and its suburbs still further . . ."

So ran his words as David and Alyce smiled conspiratorially across the dinner table their eyes alive with victory. She knew as never before that he was in love with her.

34

Alyce avoided a confrontation between David and Julie as long as possible, but the time had come for them to meet. In addition to Julie, she wanted him to see her private world—the friends of a lifetime who now lived along the posh north shore. When they drove up to the little immaculate house on the way to the Lake Shore Country Club, Julie was standing at the head of the steps on her porch, a singular lonely dark figure dressed in a loose black dress that hid her growing heaviness. She was backlit by a dim forlorn lamp in the living room and seemed eerie, David thought miserably, dreading this moment and knowing it had the potential for fireworks—and worse.

David moved to join Alyce as she opened her car door, but she held him back. "Stay here, Dave. It will be better this way."

She stood with Julie at the foot of the porch steps, and after they exchanged kisses that were followed by what seemed to him some testy admonitions, he watched Alyce bring her reluctant daughter slowly down the steps and along the path to greet him. As he opened the car door for her, Julie mumbled words that resembled good evening. She settled in the rear seat, slinking a little like a reluctant, moody teenager dragged to an affair she did not want to attend. Alyce touched David's right thigh to assure him that everything would be all right and she'd make everything all right. This temperamental daughter shouldn't rattle him.

In silent tension, they drove through the dark, rich north shore night, out of Winnnetka and by Glencoe as though proceeding toward the funeral of a friend. David glanced through the rear view mirror to encounter Julie glaring at him with hostile, resentful eyes—a greeting that would have frozen anyone else more vulnerable. *I need this treatment*, he thought, *the way I need a hole in the head.*

The Lake Shore Country Club sits atop a little hill that rolls gently down to the eastern shore of Lake Michigan, between the affluent communities of Glencoe and Highland Park. When you enter the expansive dining room, you know you've arrived at some privileged, rare private world reserved for only those who have prospered. For Alyce, it had always been a second home. As they weaved their way toward the table she'd reserved for them, David whispered, "What is the average age of these diners?"

"Nasty, nasty," she hissed at him. "You're talking about my friends. I haven't asked them. Don't you dare say what you're thinking."

"Is this an old-age home?"

She flinched and clutched his hand remonstratively. "Careful, buddy boy. This is my generation you're condemning."

"Well, it certainly isn't a lost generation."

"No. It's the one that flourished after the Second World War. It's the great generation. It's my generation."

"The affluent generation."

"Be that as it may. Wealth is nothing to be ashamed of."

Behind them trailed the petulant Julie Parker, dragged along on an invisible leash.

All those clustered round the table were successful professionals of one sort or another: a retired lawyer, a physician who was still practicing, a venture capitalist, and an accountant. They were lifelong friends who, like Alyce and her family, had migrated with their wives and children years ago from the South Side of Chicago to the north shore. They all seemed in terribly good shape—golfers and tennis players in retirement, all with the flattest of stomachs who must have visited their personal trainers at the local gym several times a week. Some of their wives had worked outside the home early in their marriages, but now that seemed pointless. There was enough money to go around, and all of them were volunteers for one worthy organization or another. Squirming among them at the large round table sat a rigid Julie assuming a posture that stubbornly suggested she was being chained to her chair. She was compelled by her mother to attend this important introductory dinner of her lover to her friends. Surreptitiously and distrustfully, Alyce could see David watching her every movement, waiting for her to pounce. She felt she could not control the dynamics of those closest to her.

The conversation was genial enough for a while, as her friends welcomed David, the president of a worthy if struggling second-rate university for the poor and middle class, into their coterie. With a degree from Columbia and a long list of publications as well as the presidency, he drew the respect of these prosperous friends.

But then, inevitably, the talk suddenly turned sour.

"Roosevelt?" the accountant remembered. "I took a course there one summer in the early fifties—when it was known as the little red schoolhouse."

"Well, it's come a long way since then," Alyce said defensively.

Julie smirked. "Really? Tell me. How has it changed? Why would anyone go to Roosevelt when there's the U of C and Northwestern nearby?"

Everyone chuckled, anticipating an outburst. They had seen this movie starring Julie Parker before.

"Did you ever think that it might be a matter of money?" David suggested. Alyce blinked, perched to protect him. She was fearful that Julie would make the conversation personal. "They might not have enough money, even if they were qualified."

"Or the grades. If they were smart enough, there would always be scholarships, wouldn't there?"

Alyce could read David's mind: *Fuck you,* he was silently protesting: *Who needs this shit, you calculating, miserable bitch.*

Then the conversation turned political. The lawyer initiated a discussion of the Clinton controversy that was on everybody's lips. Bill Clinton had just appeared with Hillary on sixty minutes, defending himself against the charge of adultery. The lawyer, Jack Dawkins, who was senior counsel at his firm, couldn't see what all the fuss was about.

"Who cares what he does in his private life?"

"I do," Julie exploded. "I do. A lot of people do. The man is not morally fit to be president."

Everyone's eyes suddenly turned to her. Alyce sent warning signals that were just short of overt anger, but Julie was uncontrollable.

"Well, he isn't. He's a whoremaster hillbilly from Arkansas."

"Anything else?" The doctor smiled.

"I'm sorry. I don't know who I dislike more—Bill or Hillary. I can't for the life of me understand how she can sit there on television before millions of people and defend the scumbag. She's an enabler. She's complicit."

"She's his wife, that's why," the doctor's spouse objected. "For better or worse, she's his wife. You have heard of that marriage vow, haven't you—for better or worse? If every wife walked out on her husband because of an adulterous affair, there wouldn't be too many marriages left—certainly few presidential marriages."

"Speak for yourself, Mrs. Rogers. That's a feeble excuse, and you know it. She's as bad as he is."

"Come on, Julie," the wife of the venture capitalist chided her. "Lighten up." She and the others had clearly heard this kind of tirade before and weren't shocked. Alyce had heard it, too, all the time, but at this moment, she wanted to strangle her daughter.

"You sound so American tonight," David finally had to say, empathizing with his loved one. "So puritanical."

"Well, I'm not ashamed of sounding American. Are you? Are you?"

The lawyer smiled at her as though she were a rebellious, petulant teenager. Then in an attempt to lower the temperature, he turned to David. "What do you think, Dave, of the Clinton affair?"

"I'm wary of speaking, for fear I might be indicted."

"What *do* you think?" Julie leaned forward, staring through him as though no one else existed at the table in that vast, sumptuous dining room.

Alyce glared at her daughter and excoriated her silently. *Stop being bitchy, Julie,* her eyes told her. *Stop it, stop it. Stop ruining my life.*

"Well, I guess I agree with Jack. I think it's irrelevant to his presidency."

"So that's what we've come to," Julie protested in contempt. "Now it's irrelevant. Nothing is relevant anymore in this society. Everyone is so sophisticated, like the people from New York. The latest thing is to tolerate adultery. Bill Clinton is a scumbag, pure and simple. He doesn't deserve to be elected president."

All eyes turned to the menu, except for those of Alyce and David. She was looking across the table at him plaintively, smiling apologetically, saying silently, "I'm sorry. I'm so sorry, Dave. I didn't mean to put you through this." Her face had gone sallow with shame, but her friends were accustomed to Julie's periodic outbursts, and the dinner proceeded with some degree of civility, as Julie sulked and remained dangerously silent, a time bomb waiting to explode. Alyce, too, remained unnaturally quiet, avoiding Julie's eyes, although it was clear that a storm was brewing within her and between them.

The return to Julie's house was a silent, tense ride. Like a teenager in the midst of a temper tantrum, Julie slammed the car door when she left without saying good night or goodbye, and Alyce spent the drive to the city slumped in her seat in stoic withdrawal. Only once in that endless journey home did she exhibit a reaction. It was not an apology for Julie but a lament, a cry, a plea that she uttered in the midst of the beautiful trees and high hedges and perfect gardens and stately homes that surrounded them on the winding road back into the city—a supplication for understanding her dilemma. Exhausted, she sat back against the seat beside him in furtive tears, and said softly, "I have so much to give to someone who will love me."

"I know that, Alyce. I count myself a blessed man to have found you. We'll work this out but not tonight. It can't be tonight. We're both exhausted and fraught."

At her condo driveway, he turned to her in the car and said, "I think I ought to sleep in my own place tonight."

"As you wish." Before she left the car annoyed, she turned to him. "Thanks for coming. I tried, Dave. I wanted it to be better. Now you've seen my situation at its worst."

"Alyce—"

"Don't say it. I'll be okay. I've been in this position before, but you are right. We shouldn't be together tonight. Come for brunch tomorrow morning so that we can talk."

"Of course. I'm sorry," he started, and she could see him almost reversing his decision, wavering, and sensing that if he loved her, he would stay to console her, he would hold her in the night, and he would assure her that everything would be all right. That's what she needed at the moment. "But I haven't the wherewithal, the energy—"

She raised her hand to stop him. "It's too late for apologies. We'll talk in the morning."

Will Julie destroy this love affair she feared? Will she stand between David and me? Where does she think I'll find another man like him at this late stage of my life? I'll have a profession that is perfect for me. Security. Someone who wants me so much. Someone who makes me feel eternally young. I can't let her do this to me, not now, not at my age.

It was midnight. The phone rang. She was reluctant to answer. Was it Julie? David?

"How are you? Forgive me. It was cruel of me. I should have stayed with you. Should I come over now?"

She sighed with relief.

"No. I'll be okay," she lied. "Come tomorrow morning."

"You're sure?"

"I'm sure."

"I'm coming over."

"No, Dave. I, too, really need to be alone tonight. I'll be okay in the morning. You'll love me in the morning."

35

I am one insensitive bastard for leaving her alone, he berated himself. *That daughter is an impossible twerp. She's probably on the phone with Alyce right now or will be tomorrow and the days after, poisoning the love that Alyce and I have for each other.* But she must be accommodated, the bitch, he must accommodate her. Alyce would never leave her. He had to figure out some form of modus vivendi if he wanted this love affair to continue. And he did want it to continue. Oh god, he wanted it to go on forever.

He'd never known these country club types before coming to Chicago. But they, too, were an extension of his relationship with Alyce and her friends of a lifetime. He had to give a little. He was a different man from the one he'd been before his presidency. But even then, he was an opportunistic academic. To be honest, he chastised himself—*Don't airbrush your history.* Wasn't he the one who insisted that they should live at One Magnificent Mile and wasn't he the one who wanted a Jaguar and a suit from Paul Stuart to match his sudden affluence and power and prestige? Wouldn't he be the one to move into Alyce's rich apartment? After all these years of a life marked by scholarship, his presidency had prepared him for her. He hadn't read a book purely for pleasure in months.

He wandered around his condo and realized how central Alyce had become in his life. There were notes and reminders from her on his desk; a list of donors they still had to see; a birthday card with her inscription, "Love, always—your Alyce;" a photograph of them at some charity event, ever youthful and ever vibrant, smiling as though the world were theirs; a sweater and a watch that she had bought for him; and a Valentine's card. Without her, he would be a lonely figure—successful and important and alone.

So he dismissed this disastrous evening as an unfortunate event for Alyce. She had tried. Her friends would become his friends. They were decent people, after all, a little right of center politically but good, hardworking, and successful friends. Her children were the essential problem; still, he was confident that he could work his way around their resistance to him. His presidency was all about working out problems. Why couldn't he transfer that skill to his personal life? He kept convincing himself that it would all work out. He would make it work out.

In the morning, she was full of remorse.

"You don't have to say anymore," he assured her. "We'll keep Julie at a distance—for now. I'll leave her in your ever-loving maternal arms."

"Aren't you kind . . . I've been thinking all night."

"That can be dangerous. Don't start, Alyce. We don't have to relive the evening—"

"We need to get away."

"Where to?"

"How does Puerto Vallarta sound to you?"

Suddenly, the phone rang, but she didn't answer. It rang and rang, and he smiled and said, "It's beginning to sound better and better with every ring of that telephone. It's my understanding that no one ever calls you in Puerto Vallarta."

36

The week away was the tonic she wanted both of them to have: a warm sun, cool breeze, and fireworks from the freighter on Banderas Bay after a late dinner by the ocean, as they watched lovers and families strolling along malecon. She had planned each day carefully and chosen favorite restaurants that she had once enjoyed with Matt on prior trips to this tourist getaway in Southwestern Mexico. They slept late and ate breakfast on the hotel terrace and walked the beach and sipped mojitos before lunch at La Palapa—that exotic restaurant on the sand, located a few feet from the bay. In the evening, they wound their way up the stairs of the treed Café des Artistes, a garden spot that seemed to float in air and embrace Spanish stars that winked at them through the trees.

This had been her winter hideaway with Matt for so many years; this had been their island retreat. For the first few years, they'd stayed in a big house on the bay, with a servant and a cook and a swimming pool that their two girls frolicked in on large white rubber swans; then as that extravaganza became prohibitively expensive, she found a modest hotel. After that, there no winter vacation spot at all as Matt's business ventures took a tailspin from which they never recovered.

She closed her eyes against the past and opened them now on her future—David. She kept him in her spell. She knew, in all modesty, that she was this gorgeous woman whom patrons and waiters clearly recognized as someone out of the ordinary, the most beautiful and, therefore, most important woman wherever they went. "Is she a movie star?" They would whisper to their partners. "Is she a well-known model or celebrity?" And through it all, she knew that she had reclaimed David, not just for her beauty or her fund-raising or her connections, but for herself.

Only once in that idyllic retreat from the world did she quarrel with him, but it was the essential quarrel. They were at the outdoor restaurant, Vitae Oceanfront Bistro, which faced the bay and the family *flaneurs* that passed them by. It was ten o'clock in the evening. They'd finished their dinner and were sipping cappuccinos under a moon as bright as it had ever been. The iridescent stars glowed like sparklers far off in the distance where the Four Seasons and other five-star hotels suddenly seemed so close she could touch them, close enough to stay the next time they would come to Puerto Vallarta.

She was holding his hands across the table and looking at him with more affection than she had ever shared with any man. The aperitif, the dinner, the glass of wine, and lemon tart only intensified her feelings. Whatever difficulties Julie had presented and would present had disappeared in the cool night air. All their own disagreements seemed petty in this idyllic setting, and she knew there was no going back for either of them.

"We're very lucky, Dave, to have found each other at this stage of our lives."

He nodded and brought her hands to his lips to kiss them.

"I love you," she murmured, holding his eyes hypnotically with her own.

"I echo the sentiment."

"Do you? Do you really, Dave?"

"I do. Why would you doubt it?"

"As in marriage? As in living our lives together?"

She watched him bridle for a nanosecond; she had caught him unawares, like the proverbial deer confronting headlights on a country road.

"Marriage?" he blurted. "Is marriage essential? Is living together essential?"

She withdrew her hands from his.

"*Essential?* What do you mean? What else could it be? It certainly is essential for me."

This moment, which had been emerging for weeks in her mind at least, was one that she could see he wasn't quite ready for.

"We're not kids any longer," he said warily, letting silence hover between them for more than a critical moment. "What about a compromise? How about continuing as we are and seeing each other as we do, sharing expenses when we travel? What's wrong with our current arrangement?"

This was the response she'd feared she might encounter. "No, no, no, not for me—never." Tears welled up in her eyes. "You don't seem to understand, Dave. This is a very big deal for me."

"Deal?"

"Don't mock me."

"Well, it's a very big deal for me too."

"No, not so much for you it seems. It's not a big deal for you, or you wouldn't even think of living apart from me. If you loved me, you'd want marriage, commitment—everything." Hurt and feeling rejected, she restrained the tears that were rising to her eyes. She waited a long time before she spoke. "I've been badly hurt in my life, Dave, and I don't want to be hurt again. For me, marriage is total commitment, not some living arrangement. Corny, I know, maybe, I don't care. Call me puritanical. For me, it's true, and that's all that matters. Living the way we do now, apart at night and together during the day and on occasion together for an entire evening, is fun. It's convenient. It demands nothing of us, but it's not commitment. It's not marriage."

"Come on, Alyce," he said too quickly, speaking out of character. "I can hear the violins playing in the background."

She stood indignantly, and threw her napkin down. A silver spoon clattered, and a glass spilled water across the table.

"I'm walking back to the hotel."

"Alyce—"

"No, leave me alone. I'm not some bargaining chip. These are not negotiations. This is not a *deal*."

"Alyce—"

She brushed aside what she anticipated would be an attempt at appeasement, but she saw that he had revealed himself. Was Julie right after all? Was she merely his fund-raiser—no more, no less? His sexual gratification? His mistress?

"Just leave me alone," she cried. "I can't talk to you now."

Across the malecon, she stumbled toward their hotel. Uncontrollable tears were blinding her eyes. She was crying like a child until she had no more tears to shed. Every night of this vacation, she had slept naked in his arms. She was a wanton woman surrendering herself completely. Once he had asked her to go to dinner without a bra or panties beneath her dress, and she'd acquiesced. It was an adolescent fantasy for him, if not for her, why not? The other day, they went to the nude beach when she didn't really want to go—another fantasy of his, why not? At night, there was anything he desired, anything that made his heart grow faster, reinvented, more youthful,I and now he was unwilling to take the next obvious step toward marriage. Slowly she slipped on pajamas, trying to sober up from her fantasy of permanent love and telling herself to act her age.

So, she thought, *this whole affair has been no more than a dream.*

Minutes later, she could hear him fumbling with the key to the door then circling the room like some ominous black cat in the dark. He was coming close to her, withdrawing and drifting to the patio to stare at stars that belonged to other lovers, returning to the bed and sitting beside her while she kept her back rigidly against him. She could feel his hand caressing her arm tentatively, gently, asking forgiveness, but unlike her usual compliant self, she tightened and recoiled from him.

"Don't misunderstand me, Alyce," he murmured to the back of her body. "I'm sorry for my insensitivity. There were no violins. They weren't playing after all. I'm just trying to be practical."

She didn't move.

"Julie hates my existence without even knowing me," he tried to explain to her. "She calls you twice a day. You're at her house every Saturday. She's your daughter, and at some point, you're going to have to choose between the two of us."

For the next few minutes, he went through the reasons why they ought to pause before they married and entangled themselves in legalities: the disparity in their ages, the financial complications with daughters who were barely able to support themselves, and the loss of independence. The list went on, but she barely heard him. As she listened to all the other reasons, they seemed specious and self-serving. Slowly she turned toward him, her eyes awash in tears.

"You don't know me very well, do you, Dave?"

"I do, but I want to avoid any problems—"

"There won't be any problems," she snapped. "If I say I love you, it's not some sentimental lyric from a popular song." She sat up rigidly in the bed and looked at him closely. "Do you love me, Dave?"

"You doubt it?"

"You've never say so."

"Yes," he murmured, "I do . . . I love you. You're a remarkable woman—"

"Don't tell me how remarkable I am. Everyone tells me how remarkable I am. Just tell me that you love me—and mean it."

"I love you," he answered and meant it.

They were bleary-eyed the next morning but relieved that they had crossed the Rubicon of their relationship and were reborn and in love again. But she did not hesitate. She began to discuss wedding plans. They would have a large affair in the Lake Shore Country Club on a Sunday afternoon in May and invite all the important people in town as well as their families and closest friends. It would be the wedding of weddings. She asked only one favor of him.

"I want you to meet my Laura first."

"Oh, dear. Another daughter to test my commitment. Is she the litmus test?"

"No, no. There won't be any trouble with Laura, not now. She's been through hell and back. She's gone far beyond adolescent self-centeredness and a failed marriage. She cares only about my happiness. Laura's the love of my life."

37

The trip had resolved any doubts David might have had toward marriage. If it was the commitment Alyce needed, well, then, he would submit. He wasn't letting her go because she had to marry and have a home together. He loved her too much to fuss about a ceremony. There were always children to complicate a second marriage. He regretted having no children of his own to create his own sense of a family. Their absence had left a void throughout his marriage to Debra that they never fully overcame, and that left him especially lonely after her death. That pang of emptiness returned now with a vengeance. He had no one to support him, except Alyce. She was his family now, and she was all that he had. She was precious. He didn't want to lose her over what he considered a mere ceremony—a marriage. It was their love for each other that mattered.

But for the one quarrel with Alyce, their vacation had been perfect. She'd shed her years in the southern sun.

During vacation, they'd taken a boat trip along the bay, walked in the sand like young lovers, gone to the casino where he won enough money to pay for their trip, and more meaningful than any other gesture, he'd caressed her body and murmured in the middle of the morning, "It doesn't get any better than this. Hold this moment, Alyce. Don't let it slip away from us. Never doubt my love for you." He'd bought her a native necklace and then a bracelet. Only her virtues counted now. She was always thinking of what would please him, suggesting off-beat restaurants when they returned to Chicago, calling at midnight to say good night to him and always ending with the three key words, "I love you." *Nothing,* he vowed to himself, *is going to tarnish this love affair. No daughter will prevent me from making this marriage work.*

When he first met Laura in Alyce's condo, he never would have guessed the history and depth of her tribulations. They were buried within her by now, far down where scars don't show and memories lie too deep for tears. She was a pretty woman of forty-five, with bobbed blond hair and the engaging smile of her father, pencil thin to the point of emaciation, an independent iconoclast who was already suffering from a case of kidney failure—the result of those wasted years in the Hollywood of the seventies. She talked tough, but at bottom, she seemed kind and gentle, a fragile bird with wounded wings.

Alyce had prepared him. Laura loved her more than anyone in the world, she said, and knew how much she owed her for having been nearby when her light was low. She didn't want her mother hurt in these last years of her life and was pleased to see her so happy. If some university president was the one who could make her feel so loved and complete, she was content. Not her choice, but no matter what, it was her mother's life. Unlike Julie, she felt that it wasn't her business to intervene or judge.

David studied her surreptitiously as she sat at the dinner table facing Alyce and him. He was determined to get along with her. But within moments after their dinner, the relationship was tested—before he could figure out what made her tick. The inevitable topic was Clinton's impeachment trial. Laura's reaction was as different from Julie's as any liberal and conservative perspectives could possibly be.

"Who cares whether she gave him a blow job in the Oval Office? What's that got to do with running the country?"

David flinched, but then realized, as Alyce had warned him, that the whole point of Laura's irreverence was to see what it would take to rattle him. Alyce had sent up signals. Laura liked to play the role of provocateur. She had the mouth of a longshoreman but the heart of an angel.

"Given a little more discretion"—he laughed—"I basically agree with you. But remember, the Oval Office is, after all, *our* Oval office."

"Oh, horseshit. You're an ally of Julie. She's got this high-minded notion that Clinton's private behavior has something to do with his public performance. What a crock of shit! We'd never elect anyone to office if that were the case."

Behind her bravado and bluster, Alyce had told him, was her recently discovered kidney failure. Laura put on a brave front, but it scared her more than she was willing to admit—her coarse manner, Alyce smiled at her daughter's roughhewn eccentricities, as if to forgive them, was no more than a mask for the misery of her life.

Tomorrow Alyce and Laura would be seeing a specialist to determine whether Laura needed a transplant. David felt genuine empathy for this battle-worn woman, but he also realized that these daughters, each in her own way, would be formidable adversaries once he married Alyce.

In the silence of his condo, after his visit with Laura, he grew ambivalent about the marriage, especially about the daughters, especially about Julie, but now he could see about Laura as well. There were, there would be so many complications. He didn't want to be without Alyce, but she didn't come to him unencumbered, and somewhere in the depths of him, he felt that given the ultimate choice between those daughters and him, she would choose the daughters. In the end, it would always have to be the daughters. At the same time, at this moment, he knew that she would not accept anything short of their living together as husband and wife. I can't prevent a petty resistance of daughters, who have become used to owning their mother completely, but I can understand it, I can empathize with it, and I can be more tolerant and be larger than their fears.

He dreamed that night, and throughout his troubled sleep, he couldn't help but remember Debra's keen desire to have children and her inability to conceive. There had been so many abortive attempts, so many miscarriages, so many heartbreaks, and then her stubborn resistance to adopt any children that were not her own biologically. Their marriage had been a perfect match, or so it seemed in retrospect, except for the absence of a child, of children. That was like a silent, steady current running just beneath the surface of their happiness. What would have happened to them if they had raised two kids of their own? Would they have moved to Great Neck, where Debra wanted to live once they had a family and continue to enjoy the intoxicating life of faculty parties and theater and concerts and exhibitions in the city where they both worked—and then share the joy of watching their children grow? He wondered sometimes. When the opportunity to be president of a university in Chicago, a city they'd visited just twice in their lives, presented itself, would he have had the courage to break their kids' hearts by having them leave their high school friends and would he have been selfish enough to ask Debra to quit her job as leader of 114 advisers in the high schools of New York? Well, without kids, in any case, he'd asked her to sacrifice her blossoming career for his. Would their kids have been as screwed up as Alyce's if she had lived and agreed to adopt? If he and Debra had had the children she wanted, they would be grown by now, a comfort to him in his older years, sound and solid because Debra was always sound and solid, his rock of Gibraltar as he always said. He would be able to confide in them, and they would provide perspective and would care.

When Alyce called him in the morning, she had good news. Laura's kidney deficiency could be treated by medications, although the doctor would have to continue monitoring her condition closely. She was animated and buoyant, and in a few moments, she slipped into some of the plans she had been making for their wedding— always a step or two ahead of him. Somewhere between her enthusiasm and his own hesitant response, he realized—they both realized—that she was largely talking to herself. She paused apprehensively.

"Has something happened, Dave? Is my enthusiasm frightening you?"

"No, no," he lied. "Not at all. Your enthusiasm's infectious."

"I'll bet it is." She laughed nervously. "Something's wrong. Tell me what's wrong."

"Nothing's wrong."

"I know you too well. What is it?"

He hesitated. "Twelve years—"

"Twelve years, three months, and two days."

"No hours? No minutes?" He laughed. They both laughed, and their difference in age went up in meaningless smoke—a joke that no longer mattered, even though she knew it would provide gossip among her crowd and be a constant reminder of her daughters. Age? Aging? Didn't some corny poet coin the cliché that love was in the eyes of the beholder?

"I promise never to be sick," she vowed. "I promise never to age. I promise never to lose my beauty. I promise never to lose interest in all that matters to you."

"Really? You promise with such confidence—as if you were in control of your life, defying fate and planning to live forever like your mother. Do you plan on being immortal, Alyce Parker, my ageless Alyce Parker? I only mentioned our difference in age because it's been on my mind as a concern."

"It's a concern only if we make it so."

But he didn't believe her. Debra had never been sick a day of her life either—until the age of fifty when the cancer struck, at fifty-three when her right breast was removed, and at fifty-seven when she died.

Why had he never shared Debra with Alyce? Why had he kept their love a secret from her and the world? As irrational as it might seem, he'd felt disclosure would be betrayal. That first love was too private and too precious to share.

"Are you sure you want to leave all your assets to Alyce?" his lawyer wondered. It made him raise his heavy eyebrows skeptically. "Are you sure you want to use me as your attorney?" David had never written a prenuptial agreement with Debra. It would not have occurred to him to write one, for they assumed their marriage would last forever. The lawyer repeated the question several times to make certain that David understood exactly what he was signing away. He was clearly surprised that a man of such accomplishments did not have a sense of greater caution about his private financial affairs. There had always been pension plans for insurance wherever David had worked and a simple will written only a few years ago that left everything to Debra as it would now leave everything to Alyce. Why would he complicate matters? Still, his lawyer looked at David with an almost imperceptible smile of condescension and wondered how naive a man with a PhD could be—a man who had risen to a university presidency?

"Are you sure you want to leave everything to Alyce?"

"I'm sure of it."

Who else would it go to? Where else? He never gave the matter another thought.

Alyce signed a prenup, too, with the same attorney, which at David's insistence divided her estate between her two girls and left him out of it completely. "I'll never need your millions," he chided her, "but they will."

38

The afternoon wedding was the most elaborate in the history of the Lake Shore Country Club. Twenty-five tables were perfectly arranged for the 250 guests who had been invited. The place was stately but intimate, with elaborate candelabras, fine silverware, flowers everywhere, exquisite wine from the Loire Valley, and elaborate water glasses from some Scandinavian country. All were basking in the sunshine of that day in spring, Sunday, June 10, 1992. It was considered an Alyce Parker tour de force—an Alyce Parker special. She was at the peak of her career and fame. A burnished beauty, her eyes darted everywhere and then concentrated benevolently on her interlocutor and really listened to what he was saying. In the corner of this large elegant dining room, Stanley Paul presided over an abbreviated band. He was the conductor for Chicago's socially elite group of instrumentalists and was an old friend of Alyce. The group was poised to play nostalgically and romantically throughout the sunny afternoon: Glenn Miller, Tommy Dorsey, Benny Goodman, Artie Shaw, maybe the Beatles or Paul Simon, and surely Joni Mitchell, Alyce's favorite—the singer Laura had introduced her to and that subsequently she had always identified with.

"There'll be no clouds in our lives," Alyce murmured to her husband as they danced alone in the ballroom. "They belong to our past."

"Because of you."

"And you."

She kissed him on the lips as everyone smiled with affirmation or envy or nostalgia, then she looked into his eyes with the kind of unreserved joy every woman craves and every man is grateful for. "Oh god, Dave, where did you ever come from?"

His arms tightened round her to guarantee, without saying a word, that he shared her love and was now completely hers.

An hour before the party began, there had been the briefest of vows exchanged. Alyce had come from a secularized Jewish family on the South Side of Chicago, the kind that observes only three holy days in the year—a ritual she still maintained but mocked gently by calling it Judaism lite. David's parents, so he'd told her, had moved from orthodoxy to conservatism and then he emulated his coolly scientific older brother, who had died just a few months before Debora passed away. He had forsaken all religion and thought of himself as a secular, atheistic Jew. "It's the culture that must be preserved," his father had railed against his brother's precocious protestations in the early war years when Mark was a smartass adolescent entering Princeton. David, at the time, was a child of twelve, and Hitler was at his most powerful. "My father had failed religiously with Mark and tried hard with me," he'd told Alyce, "and in part, it worked. But I've come to believe that there is no God up there, my Alyce, only stars. There is no God, surely, but there is a culture worth preserving."

"And here on earth?"

"There's you."

As she'd listened to him, Alyce feared his adamant atheism. She thought it was too hard, too certain, too absolute, and even too arrogant. She called herself an agnostic, insisting that there was too much mystery and magic in those stars for nothing to be beyond them. But at their wedding, with all their families and friends surrounding them and now joining them on the dance floor, these distinctions seemed incidental and unimportant— abstractions that others debate to no purpose.

Clustered in a corner of the banquet hall were David's former colleagues at City College and their leader, Ed Bartoli, now the president at the College of Staten Island. He was David's oldest friend and mentor and the man who had persuaded him to enter administration when he was at a turning point in his career. Alyce wanted to know Ed and his wife and all these other friends she'd heard so much about, for they'd been at the critical center of David's past.

Her mother, Josephine, sat properly upright in her wheelchair. *A handsome queen, who would be a proper lady until her last breath,* Alyce thought. Josephine was smiling faintly as though she almost approved of the proceedings, and Laura served as her mother's matron of honor and keeper of the flame. Laura had scurried about the room all morning like a dutiful daughter, seeking with the maître d' to create the perfect wedding and making certain that everything was in order for her mother's big day. Off in the shadowy distance at the doorway, lingering isolated, was peevish Julie in a simple gray dress. She was clearly not prepared for the wedding, sulking silently and clutching Duchess, as if that devoted puppy was all that remained of the fading relationship with her mother.

The ceremony, which Alyce had arranged to be as simple and short as possible, having ordered the secularized rabbi to speak only in English and to avoid the word *god* at all costs, was over in moments as she heard cars arriving in the parking lot and early guests gathering in the anteroom to loosen up on cocktails and hors d'oeuvres. The rabbi ended his duties by reading brief remarks prepared by David and followed then by a simple wish for the couple's good luck and future happiness. He watched benignly as David and Alyce kissed each other with an abandonment not expected of older lovers. She could feel David turned toward her, dazzled by her sheer physical beauty—with the pink cocktail dress that framed her perfect figure, the long smooth unwrinkled neck, the face that was perfect in all its contours, and those eyes that sparkled up at him as though she was the happiest human being on earth.

This, thought Alyce, *is my last chance at love.*

> We looked at love from both sides now
> From give and take and still somehow
> It's love's illusions I recall
> Tears and fears and feeling proud,
> To say "I love you" right out loud
> Dreams and schemes and circus crowds
> I've looked at life that way

Slow music of other times drew them toward even greater intimacy, as Alyce surrendered to him. The tunes of their separate generations now belonged to both of them. They danced to "I'm in the Mood for Love" (a tender song of her youth), "Hey, Jude" (his), and all their other favorite songs of the forties and fifties and sixties. Family members and friends and David's colleagues, old and new, smiled upon her with generosity and approval. "She deserved this happiness," they seemed to say. She deserved to be at the center of their world. When the band struck up Glenn Miller's "Little Brown Jug." She was more than ready for it. Her feet were syncopating to the infectious music, and her legs were fairly floating in the air like the twelve-year-old Abbott dancer—the shortest, most talented of the troupe, and everyone's favorite. As she now remembered, she was young, young, eternally young when she was on that stage of the Chicago Theater so many years ago, but now she was young again. She always told herself that in another way she was reinvented and reborn. Alyce Parker was an ageless beauty. In that spacious ballroom, where she had spent so many evenings of her life, she could feel everyone's approbation, and she loved it. Illusion had become reality.

David and Alyce stood in a corner of the room with the group of CCNY friends, outsiders to this sumptuous party. Proud of his new wife, stunning and poised as she was, David introduced Alyce to them one by one.

"Quite a life you lead now," Ed Bartoli chided him. "You've come a long way from East Flatbush."

"Yes," said his wife, Rose, a small, stout, effervescent woman, who, along with Ed, had hosted annual Christmas parties at their presidential mansion on Grymes Hill in

Staten Island, where there was a view of Wall Street and Manhattan in the distance. "You have to come back."

Alyce could see a wave of nostalgia flood through David. She knew these former colleagues were his essential past, with political values he still cherished. He had told her of the turbulent struggle for equal rights at the City College of the sixties and seventies in the era of open admissions. These couples were the residual idealists of academe, and he used to be at one with them. Now she watched him cringe at the view he must have thought they had of him, as well intentioned as they were. After all, they had come from the East to help him celebrate his new life. She could see that they felt a distance to him now. They were culturally uncomfortable in this country club setting, whereas David clearly fit in. She held his arm tightly, reading his mind and assuring him he was the same man they had once known. But as she glanced at all the other guests of the newfound, comfortable world in which he thrived, she could see that wasn't true. David had become a convert to luxury and power and status. That was the David she truly loved—the presidential David.

Rose Bartoli turned to Alyce and cupped her hands warmly. "We're so happy for you. You have quite a man here. Come to New York with him for a visit."

"Yes, Dave." Alyce turned to him. "Take me there. I want to see where you began."

"It's a long way from this country club, let me tell you," smirked Tom Quinn, the current chairman of the English department, a hardscrabble Irish liberal cynic, and Shakespearean scholar. His eyes roved the room, trying not to judge the new world of David Rosen, although this world of the wealthy was one that David, too, had always condemned without knowing it, defensively and jealously perhaps, along with all the others in his coterie.

"Take me there, Dave."

There? Where was there? Where was his true home?

"Oh, Dave," Alyce interrupted his mixed memories, eager to bridge past and present and coordinate and organize everybody's joy. "We have to have a reunion a year from now so that I can see where it all began. Isn't there a world famous steak house in Brooklyn?"

"Peter Luger's in Williamsburg," Rose Bartoli confirmed. "Across the Williamsburg Bridge from Manhattan. It's a fantastic place! We always find an excuse to eat there."

"Peter Luger's. Peter Luger's. I've heard of it. Yes, yes, yes. Let's make a date for a year from now—all of us. And the next day, we'll visit East Flatbush, Dave, to see where you grew up."

He smiled at her with gratitude. She could adjust to any group and, immediately, almost imperceptibly, become its center and its vital force. He was glad that these aging figures out of his past had come to help celebrate his new life, to witness his success, and to embrace his wife. Who would not love Alyce Parker?

Across the dining room, in front of the band, was the call to dinner by David's vice president for Development, Ron Grillo, who, by now, had become enamored of Alyce and grateful to David for having kept him in the loop of all their dazzling fund-raising. Most of all, he was thankful for David's letting him lay claim to some of its success so that he might find a presidency elsewhere and then retire with dignity to his condominium in Palm Beach. Ron was serving as MC of the affair. This was the ultimate courtesy that David and Alyce could tender him, and his chest expanded with pride.

"The time has come for all good folk to dine. A cake will follow, and speeches will follow—long, ponderous, presidential, sentimental speeches. No, no, I didn't say that. This is definitely not a fundraising event, folks, so everyone can relax for the moment. We've restricted every speaker to two minutes—except our president, who has three minutes. Please, my friends, find your seats. The band will continue to keep some of you on your feet, especially Alyce Parker, who is an alumna. All of you know this, I'm sure. She's the most famous alumna of the nationally recognized Abbott Street dancers. Please find your seats. Our Roosevelt students, who are serving as ushers and usherettes, will help you if you're lost."

And they did find their seats. The rabbi offered some nondescript, ecumenical words over the breaking of the bread that could have been a blessing or a greeting or a coronation of any denomination, and everyone soon was concentrating on shrimp cocktails and Sancerre and copperhead salmon from the fanciest fishery in Highland Park. Dessert was the elaborate wedding cake, but before David and Alyce cut it, they did need to say a word or two, individually. Alyce never left her eyes drift from David. She watched him with all the love any man could want.

"Thanks for coming," David beamed. "Alyce and I are living examples that there are second lives in America. I never thought there would be a second one in mine."

"I echo Dave's remarks," Alyce choked like a girl. "I've never been so happy in my life."

From the corner of her eye, she thought she glimpsed Julie outside a window of the club, glaring at her and stalking her. Startled, frightened, and incredulous, she could not believe her eyes. *No, that can't be my Julie. It has to be a figment of my imagination.* Julie would never be so brazen. But Duchess was indeed there, clutched in her arms, trying to lurch away toward her true mother on the other side of the windowpane, so far away, yet so close. *No, it can't be. It's an optical illusion. It's a momentary nightmare.* And sure enough—when she looked again, the witchlike figure was gone, and in her place stood David—her future in whatever few years remained to her. David Rosen was the love of her life.

Before these hundreds of people, she cried.

"Please, dear friends," she urged them. "Share our happiness."

In the limousine he'd hired for the trip to town with their travel bags in the trunk, he held her close to him and mused about their spectacular wedding. It had been an ideal setting for his well-meaning buddies from the past and new friends who wanted to help him in whatever new enterprise he and Alyce contemplated. Could he ask for anything more? The wedding was the culmination of a lifetime of achievements, professionally and personally, and he knew that Alyce was central to its ending. As he held her in his arms, he considered himself the luckiest man in the world.

And she? Never had she imagined herself so fortunate to find David at this stage of her life—a university president, a man of means, a traveler, a cultivated man, and a lover who adored her. She had all she ever wanted: emotional and financial security and prestige and adulation. But the one thought she never did share with him was a nagging fear:

growing old before his very eyes. She had to do everything she could to remain ageless and beautiful. It had always been the source of her power; it would have to remain so now, more than ever.

That night at the Four Seasons, she entangled him with limbs, thighs, and arms that had been strengthened by daily exercise. In the midst of their lovemaking, it must have been midnight, and they couldn't seem to have enough of each other. The phone rang demandingly. It was Julie, of course—their mutual fate. She wanted to apologize. She would have been there. She had every intention of being there. She had her dress all laid out, but she was suddenly plagued by this awful migraine and needed to rest in the darkest of rooms all day and night.

"Julie, were you at the window, outside the club, watching everything and holding Duchess in your arms?"

"No," she cried. "I told you. I couldn't come as much as I wanted to."

"Then it was an illusion after all."

"What was?"

"Nothing. Nothing at all."

"Well, how did the wedding go?" she asked eagerly, preparing for a long conversation.

Alyce closed her eyes. *Good god*, she thought, *not on my wedding night*.

"How did it go?" Julie repeated. She craved the gossip about the people who had come from all walks of life. What were his former friends from New York like? Snobs? Tough? Condescending? Outsiders? She wanted to know. She needed to know. Was it all that Alyce had hoped for?

"Give me all the gory details, Mom. I'm so sorry I couldn't be with you."

"It's midnight, Julie, for God's sake," she mumbled, as she lay bare in David's arms. "I'm exhausted. We'll talk in the morning."

But they never did talk. In the morning, she and David were off to Santa Fe for their three-day honeymoon, leaving no hotel number with the daughters or anyone else.

39

David was buoyed by the wedding and honeymoon. He was blindly in love with the most beautiful woman in Chicago— sharp and intelligent, beloved by everybody, with a *joie de vivre* that was infectious. She was in love with life and in love with him—what more could he ask for? He was luckier than he thought he would ever be. The wheel of fortune had turned in his favor, and he was only sixty, with years ahead to spend with Alyce. If she lived to her mother's age of one hundred seven, he would be ninety-five, but that would never happen. Longevity was not one of his ancestral gifts. He didn't care about the differences in their age. If he had her for the next fifteen or twenty years of his life, he would be more than satisfied. For now, he was relatively rich and certainly prestigious and important and respected, and on his arm was this elegant woman who sparkled every day and every night. He remembered the sayings: live for the moment, seize the day, live every day as if it is the last day of your life, and every day of your life is extra.

For the moment, he told himself that this was his mantra, and she agreed. They were arrested in time. The wedding had been perfect, from the floral arrangements and luncheon, from the music and dizzying dancing, and from the spring sunshine that cast its glow throughout the dining room. Perfect. All of it was perfect. The honeymoon was too, as they strolled among the galleries of Santa Fe and ate Mexican food in all of its finest restaurants. His New York friends were still his friends, but he could see that they were fading from view. They were now veterans of another life, ready to retire. He would never meet them the following year at Peter Luger's; he would never return to Brooklyn or to City College or anywhere else from his receding past. He had transcended his origins and entered Alyce's world willingly and comfortably. He was proud that he had risen in social status.

They bought a larger condo in Alyce's building on Astor Street, across from the cardinal's mansion and close to Lincoln Park, where they walked every day in the late afternoons of spring and summer in 1993.

What had been two condos now became one. The original apartment included a fair-sized modernized kitchen and an elegant living room that separated a book-lined den they never used, her office with all her mementoes, and finally, their bedroom and her bathroom—her own bathroom, where all the deep secrets of her ageless beauty were hidden.

On the south side of the condo, walled off by a friendly door, was a distinct wing—a hallway that led to his study with its fax machine and books from a scholarly and teaching career that was no more now than a fading memory.

Adjacent to his private office was a guest bedroom with portraits of smiling adolescents, Julie and Laura, above each twin bed and a bathroom that was his alone.

They lived in the same extended condo but were separated by discrete sections—two condos made one. After dinner, they spent the next three hours apart: he with his mountain of projects and she with phone calls to friends and her daughters, arranging for Sunday musicales in their home, setting their fund-raising schedule and their reservations for every pleasure—Steppenwolf, Goodman, and Writers theater; the Symphony; the Lyric Opera; the Chicago Humanities Festival—and watching her favorite television shows. The marriage was highly satisfying during the first several years in which the relationship fulfilled their separate needs. They had scarcely any arguments, and their love deepened. One anniversary was celebrated at Les Nomades, a second at Mount Everest, and a third was to be at Laserre's in Paris. The months raced by, and neither of them seemed to have changed—if anything, they were more in love than when they first married.

Often at night, as he warmed to Alyce's body, he marveled at how, as an insecure kid, he had risen from the barely middle-class streets of East Flatbush in Brooklyn to Astor Street in the Gold Coast of Chicago and from a mediocre student to the presidency of a university. He watched her sleep with a smile on her lips, dreaming his same dream of contentment. He thought to himself, *Hold this moment forever. Never let this moment change.*

And Alyce? She awoke each day with a radiant smile that ran through her body naturally, with matters to arrange and reservations to be confirmed. She had an appointment at Saks with her personal shopper who had picked out the gown she would wear at the next gala—this one featuring Barbara Cook.

The enlarged condo was ideal for entertaining, and David was grateful for it, despite its exorbitant expense. He and Alyce put together intimate, catered Sunday afternoon musicales in the living room with students and faculty from the Chicago Musical College who performed like professionals. "Why," Bootsie Nathan and her other friends, whom Alyce made a point of inviting, exclaimed, "I never knew there was so much talent in the Chicago Musical College. These musicians are as gifted as those of Northwestern and DePaul. It's the best-kept secret in Chicago."

Wherever they went, they were one—David and Alyce, Alyce and David. She kept her surname, which disappointed him, but she explained that she was so well-known as Alyce Parker that by now, the name was her identity. She couldn't be Alyce Rosen, not even Alyce Parker Rosen. At times, he wondered at her need for independence. Was it a safeguard against the future? The prenup agreement; the closeness she still felt toward friends who didn't want to be too close to Roosevelt; their separate names; and one daughter still hostile to him, the other indifferent—were these the small obstacles toward unconditional love that could one day unravel? No, he refused to believe these warning signals that suggested their differences, and moments of fleeting doubt always yielded to the joy he found in her.

He took her on travels to exotic lands, all on Roosevelt's dime and the currency of foreign educators and administrators who invited them to their countries.

One program followed another, increasing enrollments significantly: an MBA for international students in Japan and China and South Korea and India and Nigeria, visiting with Alyce to these and other countries like a high-paid academic salesman and searching always for more and more students who might come to his enrollment-driven university, underwritten by their own governments.

In Cyprus, he tried to forge a liaison with American hotels on the island that offered internships for students pursuing degrees in hospitality management, a new program in the business college. With Greece, in Salonika, he promoted faculty exchanges in the hope of luring students who wanted desperately to study anywhere in America.

"You've given this success meaning," he told her as they sat on the patio of Hotel Sheraton in Nicosia, sipping calvados after dinner as the sun set and gazing out at the sand and sea.

"You don't need me, Dave, not for these foreign excursions. I'm just an added burden and expense. A trinket."

"Really? Who else would I have cocktails with at the end of the day?"

"Some local charmer. Some beautiful, young lady."

"Some young chick? No, no. I prefer my women seasoned."

She tapped his hand with faux reprobation. "I'll take that as a compliment, young man. Am I salt or pepper, thyme, rosemary, or ambrosia?"

"Definitely ambrosia—if I know what that word means."

He knew that without her by his side, all his master building would be no more than pedestrian, the lonely work of a driven president, some Sisyphus rolling his rock up the hill. With her, their adventures were a never-ending presidential honeymoon.

They were a president and a stunning wife who represented a relatively small Midwestern university no one had ever heard of, but they were treated like royalty wherever they went. Alyce's beauty did not hurt, and he took pride in the power it radiated. It was an indispensable weapon. In nondescript conference rooms, at opposite sides of spare wooden tables, David would face a friendly local bureaucrat from the chamber of commerce or school system or mayor's office as he boasted of the academic achievements of his students while Alyce waited dutifully and modestly on a hardback wooden chair behind them and sipped tea patiently.

Only once did he have a significant quarrel with her on his foreign excursions, but it was a whopper, and it cut to the core of differences between them that were emerging. In an extravagant mood, when she was making their travel arrangements, she'd organized a personal interlude in Hong Kong. It had nothing to do with work, and they stayed at the five-star, lavish Peninsula Hotel. It was an extravagance he would never have considered had he been traveling alone. Their room, with its huge windowed wall, overlooked the magnificent Hong Kong harbor. It was lit throughout the night and surely was one of the wonders of the world, with ferries and private yachts cruising beside low-slung freighters that carried food for hungry visitors who had come from across the world to this golden waterway of the Orient. They stood naked at their window all night between bouts of lovemaking. He was amazed at his own vigor and potency. He gazed at the sleepless harbor and the mountains beyond the bay, with the moon hanging like a party lantern in the sky, and then returned to their bed early in the morning, his arm tightening round her slender shoulders to keep her warm.

"It doesn't get any better than this, does it, Dave?"

"We'll keep it this way," he assured her, although he wasn't so certain of his own emotional capacity. "I'll keep it this way for you."

In the early morning, after having stayed up the entire night, transfixed by harbor lights, they lay finally in bed with bodies exhausted from repeated intercourse. At their age, she laughed, their sexuality was absolutely sinful. He heard the envelope creep under the door like an insect. *The bill.* He knew immediately. He staggered naked across the room and slowly opened the envelope.

"Good god," he cried, as if he had been shot. "Do you know what this room costs?"

He could see that she clearly knew. She had arranged all of it.

"Seven hundred and fifty dollars!"

"I thought—"

"You thought *what?*"

"I thought we'd have one magnificent night for ourselves that wasn't related to work—"

"Courtesy of where I work."

"I didn't consider—"

"Who would pay? Of course not. Why would you ever ask that question? You never do. You don't know me very well, do you, Alyce? You take an awful lot for granted. I'd never have the university pay this outlandish bill."

"Oh, don't sound so sanctimonious and pure. The university owes you. It owes me—"

He looked at her with disgust. "You think you're entitled and privileged and now have deep pockets in me. You're an elegant woman who's never had to look at the bill. These superficial appearances conceal our fundamental differences. Your attitude toward this hotel is a perfect example of how far apart our thinking is."

She reached for her robe to hide her nudity from him. He didn't care. He was fuming through the words he uttered.

"Have you no idea how this might look? I would never have thought of having the university pay for this extravagance. You don't know me. You just don't know me. I'm not one of your goddam affluent friends."

"No, you're not. Nor are you as generous as they are."

"Or as wealthy."

"Oh, you have enough money. You have plenty of money. You're just not a generous man."

"Don't tell me who I am. I bought you that oversized apartment we're going back to—four bedrooms and a den, more than I'd ever need or want, lavish beyond my wildest dreams. Pretentious. Listen to me. Listen to me. I come from a background you know nothing about. When I was growing up, as the son of a teacher and the child of a housewife living on a teacher's income, we didn't stay in fancy hotels. We didn't stay in any hotels at all. We never even ate in restaurants."

"Well, we're all grown up now, aren't we? We're not in East Flatbush anymore." Her eyes were now flooded with the sour tears of a lifetime, and he hated himself for his cruelty. "I thought I was doing something nice for both of us, Dave." She stood at the windowed wall with her back to him, naked beneath her robe, as the sun rose over the mountains, which were large and luminous. He hadn't moved from the middle of the room, and stood there frozen in place, crumpling the bill tightly in his fist. "Oh, leave me alone," she muttered resentfully and walked by him toward the bathroom. "I'm taking a long hot shower."

When she reemerged, her body wrapped in a white terry cloth bathrobe, she told him, "I'll pay this bill. No one at the university, including you, dear one, will know this evening ever happened."

She made him feel cheap when he liked to think of himself as generous; she wanted more from him financially than he was capable of offering—more unquestioning, selfless devotion than he possessed, more of everything. It was the first time since their wedding that he looked at her with a sense of doubt at his own inadequacy. She wanted more from him, he feared, than he was capable of.

40

In the morning, she walked alone along the harbor and watched a different sunrise over the mountains. *I knew it can't be*, she brooded. *It's too good to be true. I am that woman destined to be admired, not loved. Well liked, but not loved. Useful, but not loved. And I've tried so hard. What holds him back? Does he suffer from the inability to love unselfishly, or is there something in me that prevents him? Have I idealized love so much that I've asked too much of him?*

When she returned to the hotel room, he was waiting for her impatiently, his luggage packed.

"Let's go to breakfast and then get the hell out of here," he said.

41

In the end, he paid for the hotel bill out of his own pocket—proud that he could afford it. And for all his complaints months later, he remembered with pride that evening at the Peninsula Hotel in Hong Kong as one of the special evenings of his life.

With time, he persuaded himself that the incident was the aberration of an overzealous, well-meaning, loving wife, who, at bottom, thrived in a fantasy world of her own. *There are worse eccentricities in a wife,* he consoled himself. In every way that counted, she satisfied him—if he did not allow himself to think too deeply. She formed the Chicago Board and continued to organize galas at which Tony Bennett, Itzhak Perlman, Kiri Te Kanawa, Harry Belafonte, and others performed. She and David scurried from one event to another; they held private luncheons with one major donor after another; and when David finally grew restless with their comings and goings, he inquired, "When does all this begin to pay off?" She assured him that all their hyperactivity constituted variations on the persistent theme of fund-raising—cultivation, cultivation, cultivation. "Be patient. Be patient my impatient husband. It's beginning to pay off already, with gifts from Buddy Mayer, John Bryan, Al Rubin, and Jerry Stein. More will flow to us now. Sooner than you think—more and more and more. We'll be rich, or at least, the university will be able to buy your second campus. By the time we announce our $50 million campaign, we'll have raised more than a third of that goal."

The seeds did flower, and she proved to be right, as always. These major gifts led to significant contributions from the trustees, eager to participate in a rolling success story. Others followed. "It is"—she laughed triumphantly— "the time-tested domino effect of fund-raising." With the help of a creative architect and conscientious construction workers, they converted Unocal's office compound on its 250-acre corporate site in Schaumburg into a college campus. A spectacular dinner celebrated the opening in September of 1996 on the grounds in front of the main building. The dark sky had threatened rain in the early evening but suddenly cleared as stars emerged from their hiding places behind the clouds and electric-candle-dappled trees, while a sympathetic moon lit the world and bathed the creation of this newborn metropolitan university.

Eight short years into his presidency and David had achieved what he'd set out to do. She was proud of him; he seemed at the peak of his career. There was more, of course. There would always be more, but afterward, in the days and months that followed, despite Ron Grillo's public pride and Alyce's quiet engineering, he began to be weary of his role as an elegant president who always carried with him an invisible tin cup. *The academic salesman,* he derided himself. *The man who made the final ask.* "I may have become a big shot," he told her, "but I know that at the end of the day, I am basically the presidential beggar of Roosevelt University—a salesman in a tuxedo."

"There are worse fates in life," she chided him when he felt particularly sorry for himself.

But he had grown tired of raising money for an institution he would soon be leaving. He was tired of always "making the case."

David had turned sixty-seven, and Alyce was approaching eighty. His discontent first surfaced after they'd returned from yet another Crystal Ball, which was chaired by one of Alyce's closest friends, Josie Straus. They had drunk too much wine, and all his inhibitions, now that they were alone, were gone.

"I think I've gained five pounds tonight," he groused. "In fact, I've gained fifteen pounds since we started this roundelay."

"Roundelay?" And she simulated a dance before him. "Oh, dear, what a fancy, erudite, highfalutin academic term." She twirled her body. "Is this the way a roundelay goes?"

"It's not a dance, my dear. It's a circus—a musical circus."

"Oh, Dave, please don't become literary tonight and show off."

"What should I become?"

"Presidential." She poured the wine. "You should be presidential, even if you don't feel so. Definitely presidential. That's how I like you—presidential." She swayed half-drunkenly and filled the room with the music she loved. "But tonight? Now? You should be a president off duty."

> I dim the lights, and think about you.
> Spend sleepless nights, and think about you.
> You said you loved me, or were you just being kind?
> Or am I losing my mind?

"Our love song," he muttered.

"No, mine, mine alone. You did say you loved me once, didn't you? Or were *you* just being kind?"

He didn't accept her outstretched arms inviting him to dance playfully, even though it would have required little more than a matter of standing still and swaying to the music. He didn't drink the wine she offered. Months of self-indulgence had welled up within him and turned his mood sour and mean. There seemed nothing she could do that would remind him of how lucky a man he was. He wanted to feel cynical; he wanted to tear at her, for no ostensible reason. And though he hated himself for his unwarranted diatribe, he persisted.

"I'm tired of being overweight, of eating and drinking like a pig."

"Try my trainer. He'll get you back into shape."

"I bet he will. But not everyone has your discipline, Alyce my dear. Daily exercise at eleven o'clock."

"Life is too good, is that it, Dave? Too good to satisfy you?"

"I'm so sick of all this shit."

"Of what?"

"Of cuddling up to the rich and famous."

"But you *are* the rich and famous. Who would you rather cuddle up to?"

"Someone who reads a book now and then. Someone who cares about something other than his financial portfolio or the latest dress from Saks Fifth Avenue that's chosen by her personal shopper." He rose and went to her bookshelves. "Look at this," he indicted her. "You've got hundreds of books here and in the den—texts you haven't opened since college and Book of the Club selections with gorgeous covers and unread pages. Are they just part of the furniture? A movie set? The library of a cultivated fund-raiser?"

"Stop, Dave. Stop blabbing. You're on dangerous territory."

> Sometimes I stand in the middle of the floor
> Not going left, not going right

"We're so different." He turned against the music. "Will you turn off that goddamn music? That song is driving me nuts."

"How are we so different?"

"Look at your diary. Look at the poem pasted on the front page of your diary, 'Invictus.' Do you really believe that shit?"

He rose and went to her desk, took the diary in hand, and read mockingly, "It matters not how strait the gate/ How charged with punishments the scroll/I am the master of my fate/I am the captain of my soul. Pablum."

"Put that diary down. I didn't invite you to read it."

"What horseshit."

"Put it down, and never open it again. That diary is my private diary."

"Tell me. Who's the master of your fate? Or anyone's fate? Was Debra master of her fate when she died of cancer at the age of fifty-seven?"

"What's wrong with you, Dave? What's wrong with you tonight?"

"I think our lives are phony and shallow. That's what's wrong."

"That's not true, and you know it. We're raising money for something meaningful, something larger than ourselves. We're reinventing a university for God's sake. What more do you want out of life?"

"Do you really believe that sentimental bullshit? My bullshit? I used to believe it too—the fairy tale of my middle age and, in your case, approaching old age. Then I looked into the mirror and realized I'm not doing it for any higher purpose. I'm doing it to feed my own insatiable ego. And so are you. I look in the mirror now, and what do I see? An aging blimp. What do you see when you look in the mirror, Alyce my dear, after all your makeup is washed away?"

"Someone who's lived a meaningful life. Someone who's given to others."

"And brought up two screwed-up girls."

"Stop it, you bastard. Stop defining me. You don't know me."

"Oh, no?"

"No."

"And tell me, what will you do with the rest of your life? What will I do?"

Even as he attacked her, he hated himself for doing so. She didn't deserve his wrath and self-pity and self-denigration—his burdening her with his own self-disgust. He would always see himself falling short of some elusive perfection; he was filled with all his limitations, his inadequacies, and his failures. She had never lied to him. And if he were honest with himself, what she represented was part of what he'd always wanted for himself—elegance and glamour and wealth and sophistication and power, all the marks of success. In the process of sharing her world, what had he lost? Complexity? Depth? Doubt? Compassion, or was he just feeling sorry for himself?

"David, calm down. You're saying things you'll regret. Calm down, for God's sake. I won't take this abuse. I don't deserve it. Matt had a lot of problems, but he never, never abused me. I'll solve your goddamn petty problems. I'll find you a trainer who will get you back in shape, if that's the biggest problem you have in your life." She tried to laugh, but she couldn't. "I'll call—"

"And join your long parade of faith healers? No, thank you. The personal trainer. The personal shopper. Exercise at eleven each morning. The massage every Monday afternoon. Yoga every other day at ten. The therapist who saved you after your broken marriage. The rabbi. The astrologist. A human pill for every ailment—pop, swallow the pill, and you're cured."

"Astrology? Where did you discover that?"

"Oh, I know all about you—now."

She took a step toward him on the couch and towered soberly above, with an anger that he had never seen before.

"Stop prying into my private affairs, David. That diary is for nobody's eyes but mine. The astrologist is a friend—"

"And what does he—"

"She—"

"What does she tell you? That the sun will rise tomorrow, Orphan Annie?"

"Stop this, Dave."

"Does she tell you where we'll be ten years from now?"

"I won't listen to this. You're being abusive, and I don't deserve it. You're half drunk, and I'm fully drunk and fed up with your abuse. I can't think straight anymore. I'm going to bed. Maybe you ought to sleep in here tonight. Or better still, why don't you sleep in the guest bedroom—in your wing of this condo? The air is purer over there. Just in case you get lost, there's a sign on the entrance way: ambitious narcissist."

42

Alone in her own bed, she regretted her words and feared that she might be losing him. His presidency was stronger than ever, but the marriage, so intertwined with it, was fraying. Still, she wanted to—she had to—hold it together. Were they so fundamentally different, as he accused them of being, that they could no longer be together? "Sorry, Dave," she told him silently, "no apologies. This is who I am—take me or leave me. I have my masseur and my personal shopper and my astrologer. Does that make me weird, a superficial prima donna of the Gold Coast? Don't judge me so quickly. Don't be the academic snob. I do read books, although they may not be the serious tomes you think so important. And I do have friends—those who value me for what I am. What friends have you made in the six years you've been in Chicago?"

In spite of his condescending cruelty, she wanted to hold together this marriage. It provided the security she had always craved, and she was still in love with him. This must merely be a matter of marital adjustment they were going through. What could she do to resurrect the magic they had once felt? Where were they headed in these last few years of his presidency, and what would happen after he retired? What would they say to each other at breakfast once he was retired? What would happen to her friendships? Would they become his? Of course not. What was worse, he had formed none of his own friendships since living in Chicago. Were the two of them so fundamentally different that only the presidency really held them together?

These morbid possibilities coursed through her mind and left her feeling helpless. Inevitably they led to tears, gentle tears at first, then tears that drowned her—the tears of a lifetime. Was she losing him already? And what could she do to recover him?

43

And David? He struggled to sleep in the guest room at the end of the long hallway that separated him from Alyce during the day. There were twin beds in the small room, with portraits of Julie and Laura presiding over each one.

Separate working spaces; separate libraries; separate beds now, for the first time in their marriage; separate wills and financial records, except that he paid all their bills—and he wanted it that way. He was the husband; he was the man of the house. He lay on the bed beneath Laura's portrait and couldn't sleep, cursing himself for having been such a bastard. *She* didn't deserve his abuse, *she* hadn't changed, and *she* was trying to be helpful at work and return the marriage to its former love affair. It was he who was the bastard, as she'd said, and he didn't like what he was becoming.

Had he married her basically for what she could do for him? Was it as simple as that? Was this an institutional marriage after all? Or did he really love her for herself? When that exploitation was no longer needed and when in retirement they confronted each other at breakfast and had the long day ahead to fill, together or apart, would they be able to arrange a life that would satisfy both of them?

What would he do when he finally did decide to retire? Write books that no one else would read? Study articles but have no one to discuss them with? Volunteer for some worthwhile charity? Ambitious narcissist—was that what he really was?

No, he argued with himself. *I'm more than that. I'm better than that. This is a blip in a marriage. I need her, I love her, and I have to find a way of showing her my better angel.*

In the morning, he hesitated before he entered the living room. He could overhear Alyce on her office phone, sobbing, "Laura, Laura, Laura. "What am I going to do?"

David took his coffee into the kitchen and listened to Alyce's voice grow muffled on the telephone. She hung up. The phone rang again; it was Julie. David took a step toward her office but stopped, for fear of being discovered.

"I've never seen him like this. It frightened me. Suddenly, out of nowhere—no, no, nothing physical. He would never do that. He just wouldn't. Please, Julie, don't tell me what he would do and what he wouldn't do. I know him. He's a kind, thoughtful man, and he's not prone to violence. He just had a blowup, a middle-age crisis—the crisis of growing old, the indignity of aging. I know the story all too well."

The lament went on as she tried to defend his behavior. Julie apparently was no comfort, and in a burst of anger, Alyce hung up.

David was standing at her half-open office door, with a cup of cold coffee in hand.

"Can we have breakfast? Can we talk?"

In the kitchen, he caught her trembling at the table. He was standing at the stove, preparing a fresh pot of coffee.

"I'm sorry for last night," he started. "I don't know where all that bile came from."

"Don't apologize. You said what you think of me. Words do matter in life, Dave. You, of all people, should know that. Words can't be taken back . . . ever. They may start as a wound, but they remain a scar, scarcely noticeable but still there."

"That's not what I think of you."

"Of course, it is. You think I've spent my life at one charity ball after another, like some rich, frivolous dame. Is that's all there is to me in your eyes? Is that all you think I am? A shell? Shallow? Well, let me tell you something, my dear. There was a time—"

"Alyce—"

"No. No apologies. You said what you really think of me."

"That's not true. I recognize your talents. And I don't think you're shallow. I was cursing myself last night. I was being unfair to you."

He couldn't restrain her as she reached for a book on the kitchen table.

"I read something in the middle of the night—"

"Come on, Alyce—"

She put on her glasses to read from the novel. "Do you want to hear it? Well, listen, my husband—listen. 'There's so much of life to get through after you realize that none of your dreams will come true.'"

"Do you believe that?"

"I do—this morning. This morning, I believe it."

"Maybe you have to find other dreams."

But she wouldn't return his feeble attempt to make her smile.

As he prepared to leave for the Sunday *Times* and croissants, for what he hoped would be a breakfast of reconciliation, he heard her rustling in the bathroom before her morning shower. What he didn't see after he'd left the apartment was Alyce standing naked in that bathroom, staring into the mirror and crying—crying until her eyes were swollen red.

44

A month later, she took him to Cedar Lake, Wisconsin. She had reconciled herself to David's lingering doubts about her, suppressed them, forgiven them, and tried in time to forget them. He was too important for her to lose. Alyce was determined to make this marriage not only work but thrive. She would let him see this summer retreat, where she and her family had once enjoyed summer weekends and where she thought David might care to spend the summers of his retirement, before she gave it up completely.

Driving north past Kenosha, Milwaukee, and the smaller towns along the Wisconsin coast, she was determined to reveal to him the turning point of her life, in all its morbid details.

"After I sold our home up the hill from the Parker compound, I shared the cottage of Matt's older brother, Ben, and his family, although I rarely went to the lake anymore for personal reasons."

"Which are?"

"I'll tell you when we get there, but first, I want you to see what our situation would look like. It's really only a room in a shared cottage with Ben and Joyce and their kids. You need to decide whether you want me to hold on to it. We could use it during the summers or on weekends, when they're not there."

"As I've said, I doubt it."

"Or we could always sell my part of the house to Ben," she quickly added. "I never did feel quite integrated into Matt's family, partially because they were wealthier but primarily because Matt never developed a career that any of them could respect."

"Well, he was seeking the American holy grail, wasn't he? Wealth. Power. Fame. Status. I know what that feels like, except that he had it within his grasp. I had to fight for all that I acquired."

"Yes, he was pursuing the grail but never finding it. The stuffing had gone out of him. He was tubercular, and then he was a business failure. Finally, he was an alcoholic. He was not exactly the bright young flyboy who proposed to me in the Pump Room when I was all of twenty-one and he was twenty-three."

They arrived in the afternoon and strolled the sloping grounds, down to the expansive lake where kayaks and sailboats drifted by like toy figures—as innocent and charming as a Renoir painting.

"We had some good times here," she recalled, surveying the dock and the boats and the homes across the placid lake. "And we had this nightmare too."

"The one that prevents you from coming here? Tell me."

She led him to the house and slowly answered, "I'll show you."

They returned to the home, and she took him through the Parker rooms until they came to the one that was hers. It had a bed, an antique chest of drawers, a mirror, and an easy chair in a corner of the room. The room looked as though it hadn't been used for many years and was waiting for a renter.

"This is where Matt's cousin, Jack, molested Laura—on that bed."

"*What?* How did that happen?"

"We sent the girls up with Ben and Joyce for the weekend because we had a gala to go to in the city. There was a campfire. Laura had a migraine and went to bed early. Jack violated her and threatened harm if she ever told anyone. Well, months later, she told me—and no one else. She was never the same girl again."

David stood dumfounded.

"And where was Matt in all this? What did he say? What did he do?"

She smiled. "Laura never confided in him. In any event, it wouldn't have mattered. Matt was not one for confrontation. The stuffing went out of him after his TB and the failures in one business after another. I had to deal with all our difficulties."

"Did you confront this Jack?"

"He denied everything, and I never brought the girls to Cedar Lake again. I took Laura to Bruno Bettleheim at the U of C, and he told me to wait until she reached puberty. Well, I did. And then Laura went into a tailspin—drugs, alcohol, the works, boys, and pregnancy. Then marriage and California and more drugs."

"And no else knows about the pedophilia? Not even Matt later?"

"No one else but me—and now you."

They glared at the room, as though they were reviving the scene of what Laura had recreated to her mother: an eight-year-old girl asleep, a dark figure coming by her side, awakening her, consoling her, comforting her, touching her arms and chest and thighs and vagina in that bed— the dark figure of Matt's elderly cousin whom she scarcely knew.

She could feel David's arm bringing her closer to him, waiting a long time to speak.

"Well, we can't come here, that's for sure. Sell the room to Ben and Joyce, and keep the money for yourself. Let's get out of here."

They returned to stroll the grounds again.

"I'd like us to find a summer home of our own. I'll sell my part of the house to Ben, and we'll discover something of our own somewhere else—maybe in Michigan, on the eastern border of Lake Michigan. That's where all the liberals go, or so I'm told."

"Don't exaggerate my wealth."

"No fear. I don't. We'll make it work, one way or the other. Now I'll even be able to contribute to our future."

She took his hand. "See that house on the hill? Come. I want to show you where we first lived when Matt was riding high."

"And you all were happy."

"More or less. But even then, I never did feel secure."

As they approached the house on the hill, he wondered whether they might be intruding on the couple that lived there now; but she assured him, "We won't be intruding.

I know the Griersons. They're both gregarious folk. Loveable. They'll be happy and proud to show us around their homestead. I haven't seen them for years. Besides, I'd like to see what they've done to our home."

An older woman greeted them—Rachel Grierson, dressed in a simple black dress and an apron. She was Alyce's age, but by contrast, she was a wizened and worn woman with little spring in her step. She hugged Alyce. "Alyce Parker, for Lord's sake. You haven't aged at all. Come in, come in. I'm so pleased to see you, after all these years. Good Lord, you do look younger than ever. Don't you ever age?"

"This is my husband, David Rosen."

"Dave to my friends."

"Well, welcome to you too, David Rosen . . . Dave. You've got quite a gal here."

Mrs. Grierson's husband, John, had died the year before. Alyce felt guilty at not having known, but she hadn't been to Cedar Lake for years. Everything seemed strange since Matt's death. Mrs. Grierson was living as an elderly widow now, and she confessed, it did get lonely at times.

"How are Julie and Laura?"

"Oh," Alyce answered hesitantly. "They're just fine. Julie's a surgical nurse at St. Joseph's, and Laura's a home designer for Plunkett's."

"No husbands? No children?"

"I'm afraid not."

Everything seemed smaller to Alyce than when she and Matt had lived in the house during the summers—two bedrooms, an abbreviated living room, a bare kitchen, and a porch that had two chairs and overlooked the Parker compound below. Mrs. Grierson insisted on offering them tea, and they sat in the living room. The two women chatted easily, remembering happy incidents out of the past.

David listened like a bystander and smiled blankly. It seemed to Alyce that he was simply tolerating her nostalgia, but he's really fearing a future of a boisterous family playing riotously across the grassy compound and rolling hills on hot summer days. He had a sense of estrangement from this setting, from the inherited wealth, and from all the indulgences that Matt's inheritance had brought her. She glanced at him occasionally and thought, *This is not my world. This is not where I want to be at any time.*

"That's the kind of person I could have become," Alyce told him after they left Mrs. Grierson. "That house is where Matt wanted me to live with him after we sold our home in Winnetka, but I couldn't. I wouldn't. He went there alone. We finally broke up when I wouldn't go to Cedar Lake with him. I'd had enough. He lived up here until his death, socializing with friends from AA."

"A sad ending—for both of you."

"It was the turning point of my life. We couldn't afford the lavish home in Winnetka any longer. He had become an alcoholic, and after more screaming matches than I care to remember, he agreed to go to AA. We were sitting in the living room, across from each other, in front of the fireplace. I'll never forget that night. I'll never forget that scene. The girls were out of the house. Julie had finally found a career as a surgical nurse and bought a modest home near us."

"And Laura?"

"Poor, confused, wonderful Laura? Oh god, that girl was always breaking my heart. She'd married a cinematographer who took her to Hollywood, where he became a success working with Steven Spielberg, while she hosted wild parties and became a cocaine addict. They finally divorced, and she returned to Chicago as a beaten woman and lived in Julie's house. But that's another story for another day.

"Old age in the Wisconsin winter." David smiled empathetically. "That house might be a bit chilly and lonely in January."

"That was when I found the job at Michael Reese and moved to Astor Street, while Matt left for Cedar Lake to live alone. It was pathetic, but there was no way I was leaving Chicago and spending my old age witnessing his deterioration, catering to him as he became more and more depressed. He hobnobbed with the working class he had never known all his life. We never divorced. On weekends sometimes, I'd visit him. I'd clean up and cook for him like a dutiful wife. I'd even sleep with him, for old time's sake. But he shriveled away and died up there a beaten, broken man.

She glanced at David in the driver's seat, wondering what his reaction might be to her confessions. Why did she need to tell him anything?

"I've been talking too much about myself."

"Not at all. It's good to know what I've inherited."

"You've inherited me." She sidled closer to him. "Am I still worth it?"

"More than ever. I think you decided to survive everything because you knew I was coming along."

"Of course, Sir Galahad. You arrived with the holy grail in hand. All my life has been a preparation for you."

On the way home, they stopped at McDonald's for a burger.

"Well," she asked him, "how does Wisconsin appeal to you?"

"I doubt that Wisconsin ever would appeal to me." He smiled. "And after your story about Laura, less so—for you certainly and for me too. That family would be claustrophobic. It would drive me bananas. Then there would be the ghost of Matt Parker still hovering about the grounds once I do retire. Beneath my extraverted presidency, I'm fundamentally a loner and a very, very proud man."

"Once, I did call you an ambitious narcissist. But you're not a narcissist—you're just terribly ambitious." She smiled, cupping his hands and kissing them. "I'm glad you said that about Cedar Lake. It would be a trial for me too, living so close to a brother-in-law and his family with all the unsavory memories that I've never forgiven Matt for. We'll find a place of our own, Dave. Maybe in Michigan. We can afford it. Have you ever been to St. Jo, Michigan? It's really very lovely, with an expansive white sandy beach and boutique shops and a lake as far as the eye can stretch. This Parker compound in Cedar Lake is too filled with mixed memories."

"And too many relatives."

45

As he watched her dream in bed that night, he wondered whether she thought of him as the man with all the resources and security she'd need for the rest of her life. Was he fundamentally her security? He had already bought the enlarged condo for an exorbitant amount of money. He had given her a necklace for her birthday and a watch for their anniversary. He'd agreed to a prenup that left everything to her, and he was as generous as she could ask for. But he was little more than five years away from retirement now, and the underwritten galas, trips, and dinners that the university had paid for and that they'd grown to assume would no longer be theirs.

Retirement—what *would* he do in his retirement? To teach and write—that's what he'd done before he became an administrative entrepreneur. Teaching, writing, reading, and traveling—what more could he ask for? A companion, a partner, and a lover to share all these pleasures with him—that's what she could be for him and for herself. He had published critical studies and edited anthologies in the sixties and seventies. He always had a project in mind in those days; he'd always needed a project to propel him forward. He had published essays concerned with Negro and Jewish writers, and now he would write a lengthy study of the relationship of Negroes and Jews in American culture. That would be interesting to do. He had already taken notes and made an outline. He would contact his old friend and editor, Tom Gay, with whom he had shared so many financial and critical successes. He would write a proposal and see if he could sign a contract in a year or so—in preparation for his post presidency. Just the thought of a meaningful project that would probably take five years to complete eased his mind. He had something to look forward to, an anchor to confront the anxieties of old age, and it all would be with Alyce, whom he had come to love and appreciate more than ever.

But they were different in so many ways. What would she do when he was alone in his study or off to a library somewhere? What would she do with her time? Fortunately, that would never be a problem. He knew that she was social to a fault. Her friends might not be his, but that was all right, so long as they satisfied her needs.

She was a good woman—Alyce Parker. He kept reassuring himself that she was kind and thoughtful, and she deserved a more loving husband than he had been in recent days. He loved her and knew that if she was gone from his life, he would become a desolate old man. Why would he anticipate an unknown future? He should live now! He should live as though each day was the last day of his life, for every day was extra! He was a university president married to an ageless beauty. What more could he ask for? He was lucky to have Alyce in his life now. She would be there later for him too; she would always be there for him. He had to believe that.

Somewhere he had read that everyone might have no control over 10 percent of their lives—their height, their intelligence, and some of the calamities or sicknesses of their physical existence. But the rest? The rest would be determined by their attitude.

The middle five years of David's presidency proved to be the happiest of their marriage. The university bound them together as husband and wife. The presidency became an aphrodisiac, a heightened, surreal sense of power and love in work and marriage. Never had he enjoyed so much authority over the lives of faculty and staff. Never had he lived so lush in life. His head spun with his material success—a newly bought Jaguar; custom-made suits at Pucci's; travels to Far Eastern and European countries in search of international students; membership in the Economic and Executive Clubs of Chicago, where he wore black tie at hotel dinners with the top executives in town; luncheons at the Chicago University, Standard, and Union League Clubs; and a salary that rose 25 percent each year. Was he worth all these amenities? Was he worth his salary? *Of course,* he convinced himself. The chairman of his board would have recommended an even higher raise each year had David insisted or threatened to leave, but he felt vaguely guilty at his salary compared to that of the lowest-paid full-time faculty member.

His $50 million campaign came in at $75 million, but that wasn't enough for him. He had secured the second campus, but that wasn't enough either. Nothing would ever be enough. One achievement led to the other, and he really did think he was the master of his university. His ambition was insatiable. He remembered a line from the prologue to *The Pardoner's Tale*—"Radix malorum est cupiditas" (the root of all evil is greed). *I am not greedy*, he persuaded himself. He was simply ambitious, and he loved power and status. The annual increases in salary simply came along with his success.

His master plan linked the future of the expanding city with the future of his university. In addition to campuses in the city and suburbs, he and his colleagues developed an honors college, a sophisticated conservatory, a real estate institute, a hospitality management program, an accreditation of the business college, a consortium of local colleges, and a number of universities working with the Chicago public schools. On and on and on. Bigger and better. Megalomania. More and more. Now that the courts had given the university full authority over the 4,200-seat Auditorium Theatre Building, it could become a performing arts mecca for the city. Then perhaps a law school and a biomedical program could follow. Why not? With mergers and acquisitions, why not? It would be bigger and better, with more, more, and more! He was on fire and found the meaning of life in his work and in the marriage that helped to make that work successful. With Alyce by his side, supporting him in every way, he could do anything he wished. He could become anything he ever wanted to be.

As he succeeded, the marriage grew stronger and more intimate than ever. She was the perfect hostess, the gracious partner, and the beautiful wife everyone admired. She was everything he wanted her to be.

46

Their parties rolled on in exuberant excitement, as though they would never end. She was always arranging joy for them. Early on in their marriage, she'd created Chicago Board of local notables who helped her with the annual galas. Itzhak Perlman played in the Auditorium Theatre Council to an audience of four thousand. At noon, before his performance, he called David's office to ask whether there was a good Japanese restaurant in town and would the president, his wife, and a few of their friends care to join him for lunch? David called Alyce to round up four of her friends pronto and race to Kunis on Main Street—and she called in members of the Chicago Club. They spent the afternoon eating tempura and teriyaki and drinking sake and listening to Perlman regale them with one bawdy anecdote after another until six o'clock when he returned to his hotel, changed into a tuxedo, and appeared onstage at eight, transporting an audience with breathtaking violin performances of the *Meditation* from Thais and sonatas of Mozart and Beethoven, as well as encore after encore.

Kiri Te Kanawa's agent sent Alyce a ten-page contract demanding a limousine at the airport, orchids in her hotel room, and perfect acoustics in Symphony Hall—an irritating list of finicky requests that Alyce attended to, assuring David, "She'll be worth it. She'll be worth it, my love." In the end, in her flowing blue gown, Te Kanawa sang like a golden bird. Marilyn Horne was running a high fever and came off the plane in sweat and confined herself to a hotel room all day, uncertain as to whether she could perform that night. Struggling against her illness, she entranced the audience as Alyce, standing nearby in the wings, watched the perspiration dribble down her face. *A trouper she is*, Alyce thought in admiration. She remembered Merriel Abbott's injunction to all her young aspiring dancers, "The show must go on, girls. The show must go on."

Frank Sinatra Jr. was a neurotic who called Alyce steadily for weeks before he came, fussing over details and apologizing for not being as electrifying as his father. He said he would try, and he did. He was far better than she expected him to be. But it was true, he wasn't his father. Then again, who was? Tony Bennett, as natural and unaffected as any star could be, put the microphone on the piano at the end of his performance to show off the amazing acoustics of the Auditorium Theatre Council and made four thousand people feel the intimacy of his voice as he took them on a trip to San Francisco, where he'd left his heart.

All these and more were magical memories for Alyce. She and David lived through them altogether—the center of a social world both of them loved, the stars of stars that embraced a city of friends. But the memories she would never forget were with David after each of the shows—their time alone.

They would stop at the Pump Room on the way home. A three-piece band would be playing, and they would dance until they were the only ones on the floor. She would rest her head on his chest and hear his heart stir with joy and gratitude. All her life, she had idealized this kind of love affair, read about it in magazines and romantic novels, and watched it on the screen. David would look into her eyes, running his hand along her arm with all the love she had ever wanted and engulfing her tiny waist with a firmness that whispered, "You're safe. You're safe with me."

The most successful of the performers was Bill Cosby, long before his infamous fall from stardom. After repeated efforts, the comedian agreed to come, and as with each of the other events, Alyce had to scurry to and fro to hold all the pieces together, trying to satisfy everyone—the guests, the entertainers, herself, but especially David. The Cosby event took place at the Hilton Hotel and was an after-dinner performance in the great ballroom. More people wanted to come than the hotel could accommodate, and it fell to Alyce to handle all complaints from those who ordered tickets too late and had to be turned away.

Three weeks before Cosby appeared, Alyce was at home arranging place cards for the thousand guests who were coming. The cleaning woman had just waxed the floor, and when Alyce hurried from her study to the kitchen, she slipped on the floor and fractured her left arm. Helpless and frightened, she called David, but he was at a meeting off campus. She immediately reached Julie, who said she'd be there at once, and so she was. Alyce's arm had to be put in a cast. In her hospital room, by the time David was able to get there, she was propped up in bed with a broad, guilty smile across her face. Julie was standing by her side like an armed guard who felt the need to wear a perpetual scowl.

"Look at your helpless wife." Alyce laughed. "Look at what I've done to myself. Isn't this cast a wonderful work of art? Get used to it, my love. I'll be wearing it for the next few weeks, right through the Cosby event."

"Maybe we should cancel—"

"Cancel?" She almost leapt from the bed. "Never! Not in a million years! The show must go on."

She could see him smile, probably thinking, almost saying, "What a load of sentimental horseshit—the show must go on." She knew how cynical he could be, but it was all surface; he loved her for what she was—sentimental, romantic, sometimes a little ditsy, but optimistic, idealistic, and strong. *This is what I know he loves in me—my fortitude, my persistency, my loyalty. This show*, she vowed, *will indeed go on.*

Julie held Alyce's hand firmly and then told David that she was staying overnight with her mother and would sleep on a makeshift cot in the room. "These nurses are totally neglectful. She could be dead by the time they come to her."

Alyce could read David's mind and was grateful. He thought it best not to fight with Julie, certainly not while she was suffering. He called from home to say good night privately, but Alyce was with a nurse, then a doctor, then another nurse, and then Julie—the omnipresent Julie. Finally, he reached her.

"I hope I didn't wake you."

"No, sweetheart. Thanks for calling, and thanks for not making a fuss with Julie."

"We'll work out our relationship. She's just overwrought. She'll soon see that I'm really on her team. The important thing is for you to get well. I still think we should cancel the event until you're out of that cast."

But, of course, she would not listen to him.

The next day Laura arrived, and the circle was drawn ever tighter.

47

It's coming, David brooded. The daughters were circling the wagons. Julie was a constant caretaker in their condo and a full-time presence with her mother, phoning whenever apart from her mother for the shortest time and monitoring Alyce's medications. This, he knew, was a preview of coming attractions. These attempts to separate Alyce from him were beginning to assume a pattern. Now was the time to stand firm. Next time, the incident might be truly serious and too late. The ageless beauty had to crumble. Even Alyce Parker, the ageless beauty, had to age.

48

She was a trouper.

"At least my right hand's not affected." She laughed. "That's my writing hand, my working hand."

After her release from the hospital, with her left arm firmly in a cast and held up by a bandaged sling, she made the Cosby evening her total preoccupation, accommodating as many people as she could and apologizing to those who couldn't be included. There were all the details she had to think of in putting the spectacle together—place cards, flowers, favors, a seating plan that put friends with friends, prestige tables for trustees and VIPs, decisions about appetizers and special-order dinners for vegetarians and the religiously orthodox. Several student singers at the conservatory preceded Cosby and amazed the crowd with their operatic voices. Then the superstar casually appeared in a Roosevelt sweatshirt, sauntering on the stage as naturally as if he were entering the home of each guest, with his broad, friendly, infectious smile emanating from his core. His husky voice was inviting the crowd into a conversation rather than a show and raising more money for the university than had ever been raised before.

She treated the cast as a mere nuisance, amazing him with her stoicism in the month she had to wear it. When she had it removed, she threw her arms around him and exclaimed, "Now let's celebrate at Charlie Trotter's. I feel twelve years younger already." She kept their marriage moving on this heightened, thrilling, and surrealistic sky ride. As she helped him raise more money for the university, their love for each other intensified. This was the way to his heart. Their frenzied activity kept Alyce busier than she'd ever been at one of her galas, and she thrived on all of it. She ran to keep up with him; she encouraged him to reach higher and higher. There was no end to what they could achieve together. She simply wanted him to remain president forever. It was what made her happy, and it fulfilled his need for power and status. She felt that it strengthened their marriage.

But Alyce knew that the high life and intoxication of the presidency would inevitably expire; the intensity could not continue at its current wild pace. Indeed David was already preparing to retire in a few years, and she wondered what she would ever do with herself when that awful day arrived. His love was so completely tethered to the university that she worried whether her expectations were unrealistic; she would never satisfy him completely, away from the university. He was a limited man, emotionally limited, but she knew that she could hold his affections if she continued to make him dependent on her. His retirement would come soon, as the night the day, and then they would have only each other. *Will that ever be enough?* She admonished herself for thinking too far in the future. *Live now! I will possess this moment for as long as I can, and perhaps, I can persuade him to ask for another five-year contract?* She smiled devilishly to herself.

49

He came home early one afternoon to hear her playing *The Moonlight Sonata*. He stood at the entrance to the living room and listened in amazement.

"That's beautiful."

She was pleased that he had caught her unaware and pleased that she could please him. There were more arrows in her quiver than he would ever know.

"You never play when I'm here."

"I don't want to distract you. I play in the afternoons when I'm alone."

"Don't stop. I never knew—"

"There are some things about me that you still don't know, Dave. I'm more complicated than you think."

"I never—"

"How could you? I've never played for you before. That's all right. You'll grow to love me for all that I am. I'm saving my other talents and bringing them out one by one to surprise you, like Scherezade. I don't want you to think that ours is strictly an institutional marriage and that I'm strictly your fund-raiser."

He came behind her and put his hands gently on her shoulders.

"I could never think that."

"Oh, you do. You always have. But that's all right. You won't."

"Play, play, play, my Scherazade."

I have been unfair to her, he thought on that night and in the days ahead. *I've seen her through too narrow a lens. She is more complicated than I've believed—more than beautiful, more than useful, more than someone who knows everyone of importance. I'm the one who is limited in taking her for granted and in the inability to reach the goal she wants to achieve—the sublimation of self-interest for someone else. Deep love, unconditional love.*

50

Still, work asserted itself for David.

He cautioned himself not to dream recklessly and impose upon his university more than it could possibly bear. "In dreams," he reminded himself, "begin responsibilities." Indeed, with all its quotidian problems, Roosevelt stubbornly anchored him to reality. The Auditorium Building, which was housed in Roosevelt, was in desperate need of constant repair; a towering new building had to be erected to accommodate his ambitions; the faculty was grossly underpaid; the students needed far more scholarship support than they received; endowed chairs were essential to lure top-notch scholars; the suburban campus needed greater support to attract the multinational corporations that were so nearby— Motorola, All State, Baxter, Abbott, Zurich-American— and the list went on and on. As much as he wished to delegate management to vice presidents, deans, and chairmen so that he could raise the resources essential for them to realize their own individual dreams, he could not avoid the mundane matters of the university that weighed upon him every day. There was no glitter or glory in good management; it was always assumed when it ran smoothly.

Seven black student leaders were in his conference room, complaining that the vice president for finance was denying them funds for an historian and public figure that had expressed anti-Semitic slanders in his work and in public statements. "Those funds were allocated to us without conditions," the leader of the group protested. "We were told we could have any speaker we wished. Freedom of speech, you know. Freedom of choice." He urged the students to consider holding the event off campus to prevent unnecessary demonstrations. Running through his anxious mind were the wealthy Jewish trustees who would protest and even possibly resign if he acquiesced to these strong-minded demands. Tension prevailed at the meeting as he made the case for mutual respect: "How would you feel if another student club invited a racist as a speaker to come on campus?"

Finally, as the student protesters softened, the girlfriend of the leader persuaded everyone that there might be some justice in the president's suggestion. "He's a new president," she argued gently. "Give the guy a chance." After the students had dispersed, the Jewish CFO stormed into David's office, like a man verging on a stroke and accused David of undercutting him. "*You* sign the contract, Dave. *I* can't. *I* won't." *You won't?* David thought, furious at him, but knowing the old timer would retire at the end of the academic year, he decided that a battle with him was not worth having. With pen in hand, he signed the contract himself.

He would recount this kind of fraught issue and others to Alyce at night, in the middle of the day, at the oddest times, and she would respond with the compassion of an understanding wife. There was little she could do about the inner dynamics of his university; that would be noblesse oblige with a vengeance. She knew that the faculty and administration would resent her intrusion as a self-appointed, unelected, unqualified first lady of the university, manipulating her husband's serfs. She kept her distance. She only wanted him to succeed so that their marriage would succeed.

"Don't take everything so personally, Dave," she comforted him one night when he was particularly dispirited. "You can only do so much in a ten-year presidency."

"I—"

"Unless you stay on and negotiate another five-year contract."

"Oh god, no. If I can't turn this tugboat around in ten years, I'll never do it. It'll take someone better than I am."

He watched her try to help in her own steady, quiet, but subtly aggressive, and cunning way. Her thirty-person Chicago Board now included her closest friends in business—a group that agreed to serve only because of her and were so distinguished they eclipsed in prestige David's board of trustees. They helped in all her fund-raising efforts and opened doors she could never have opened alone. Indeed, as the Chicago Board matured, she worried that they might threaten the trustees. She also regretted that possibility, and this became a nagging guilt, although not enough ever to act upon. Once she married David, she probably should have removed herself from the payroll and continued as an unpaid volunteer. He'd told her that this had been the advice of Bob Green and John Anderson as they claimed it looked awkward for her to be paid now that she and David were married. Rumors were spreading across the university, but David never took that guidance from his provost and CFO. He could never ask her to do all the work she did simply as a spouse; it would not be fair. "She deserved every penny she earned," he told them and more. But he did notice, even though it was an action he had encouraged, that she kept her salary apart from their overall private income. *Those funds*, he wondered, *are hers, of course, but they are also being hidden against a rainy day—for her alone.*

As a president, he didn't want to get mired into management where he could have little effect. Tenured faculty members were plaguing him for more perks, students were protesting for this or that restrictive regulation, staff members were seeking marginal increases in their salaries, and deans and vice presidents were arguing for a greater portion of a limited pie. He wanted fast results, and so he turned his immediate attention almost entirely to fund-raising and the preparation for his retirement in three years, when he would be seventy. He scarcely discussed the internal, managerial issues with Alyce, except when he was most discouraged. She always asked about them, trying to help him clarify his thinking, but he really wanted to live with those issues alone, as though they belonged to him. The tedium of daily work was his alone, the glittering galas were hers. However, he found, for all his grumbling, that the galas began to appeal to him as well—a spiffy suit, a sharp tuxedo, dancing till midnight, and a beautiful woman in his arms. He liked to call everyone on a first-name basis, even the mayor and the governor, with the hoopla, the panoply, and the handshaking.

Alyce and David had found activities that were complementary, and they lived in each moment, as gratified as they had hoped to be when they first married.

But his retirement was approaching. In three years, she would be eighty-two and should be ready for retirement herself. *Will she ever be ready for retirement?* he wondered. *Will she want to die without her priceless heels on her slender feet, toe nails pedicured to perfection, and herself dressed in some lavish gown at some never-ending Crystal Ball, where she is at the center of their social universe and admired by everyone for her ageless beauty?*

51

Her daughters wanted her to slow down, to acknowledge her age—seventy-nine already!—and to live like her friends in affluent retirement. Those women marveled at her boundless energy, helping to revitalize the university and keeping up with her energetic, visionary, younger husband. Some were admirers; others were simply jealous of her good luck. Some wished her well; others hated her guts for her good luck.

She didn't care what anyone thought anymore. She only wanted to protect and enhance her marriage. As she whirled in David's arms at one of those galas, she thought, *This must not stop. This moment must never end.*

52

David was a decent, competitive tennis player. He was always hungry to improve. Every Sunday morning, he was on the court with opponents half his age, playing vigorously, playing to win, and playing (so Alyce loved to chide him with an affectionate, forgiving smile) to kill. It became a ritual—tennis, followed by brunch at the Drake and the *Times,* and maybe a movie in the evening that brought them still closer. He was the serious player, and she was the amateur. The entire day always made them feel that the world was right with them. Both of them were certain they had made the wise decision to be together forever, and they knew that they loved each other unconditionally.

In the midst of an aggressive game, a staff member raced to him and said that Mrs. Parker was injured, seriously injured.

She was on the floor, with a helpless crowd surrounding her. The teacher of the group, no more than twenty-five, spoke rapidly and almost incoherently, explaining that it was a routine exercise, but she slipped and fell. "It looks as though there may be broken bones between her knee and her hip. Look. Look there!"

Everyone was waiting apprehensively for the ambulance to arrive. David went past the young teacher and the crowd to kneel beside her. "Oh god, Alyce, my Alyce," he murmured, running his hand gently across her brow, trying to dry her tears. She gazed helplessly at him. He kissed her cheek and brushed her hair and tried to calm her, but to no avail; her violet eyes were blazing with fear and trauma.

"You'll be okay, Alyce. You're going to be okay," he murmured. "It's probably no more than a minor injury—a shock to the system." But he could see that it was indeed a serious wound, especially for an eighty-year-old. His heart went out to her, the love of his life, and he found himself fumbling for words of comfort.

"I'm afraid, Dave. I'm so afraid. It hurts like hell."

"Don't be afraid." There was fear in his own voice as he held her hand to protect her against the worst. "They'll give you something to numb the pain. Don't think the worst. Most injuries seem worse at first than they actually are. Meanwhile, I'm here. I'll be here. I'll be here forever."

"Good god, it hurts."

"How did this crazy thing happen?"

"I don't know, Dave. I'm confused. There was an exercise. I can scarcely remember. I leaped. I tripped. I fell . . ." Tears clouded her vision. "I never used to fall, Dave."

"Forget it. Don't blame yourself. It's just a freak accident. Everyone stumbles in tennis, one way or another. You're going to be okay. Try to control your breathing. Take deep breaths, and inhale slowly . . . slowly . . ."

For a moment, he held his own breath. He was unable to think coherently. *What if she is crippled? Disabled? No, that is impossible. She doesn't deserve this.* Their lives were too good now. He couldn't imagine her less than vital and optimistic. She was the joy in everyone's life, but especially his—the belle of the ball.

She closed her eyes tightly and cursed her failing body, then after a few moments, as she slowly recovered self-control, she considered what needed to be done.

"Call Julie and tell her. She'll be furious if you don't tell her immediately. They're taking me to Illinois Masonic Hospital, but I need to talk to my friend, Eddie Newman at Northwestern. He'll want me to be there, under his care." She looked at David, her eyes flashing and seeking simply to be loved and forgiven for her frailty. With a bitter smile on her lips, she apologized, "I'm sorry, Dave. I guess I'll never grow up to be Billie Jean King."

"There's nothing to be sorry about. This could have happened to anyone at any age." He held her hand, realizing she was in some stage of trauma that was beyond his ability to help. Her whole body was limp and shaking uncontrollably.

"You're going to be okay, Alyce. You're going to be okay. I won't let you be ill." He kissed her softly on her cheek. "Oh god, my Alyce, I love you. How much I do love you." He was in fear. Could he ever live without her?

In the distance, he could hear the screeching ambulance racing near.

"There's the ambulance. I'm coming with you."

"Call Julie. Please, Dave, don't forget to call Julie."

"I'll call her from the hospital."

"Please, Dave. Call her at once. If you don't, she'll be furious, and we'll have another problem on our hands."

In the ambulance, the orderly gave her some sort of sedative that made her drowsy, and then as the pain passed, she slipped into a deep sleep. He looked into her face—a beautiful woman suddenly turned old. The nurse on duty made arrangements for a private room and wheeled her there while David waited in the lobby to be called.

He was frightened. She *was* eighty years old; she didn't belong on a tennis court. He had been selfish for encouraging her to learn the game, assuming that she would always be ageless. In the end, he'd taken her for granted, he'd assumed in so many ways, and he'd used her—her positive disposition, her charm, her generosity, and her worrying about him in so many little, unremembered acts of kindness and of love. She wasn't allowed to die. He wouldn't allow her to die.

When he finally found the courage to phone Julie, she was indeed furious.

"I knew this would happen. Damn it, you fucking shit. I told her it would happen. What the hell is she doing playing tennis at the age of eighty?"

"It can happen to anyone, Julie, at any age."

"Oh, bullshit," she accused him. "It's all your fucking fault. I don't know what she sees in you, you selfish, self-centered, controlling bastard. Tennis at eighty! And all these responsibilities you've thrown at her, at the age of eighty! This accident is entirely your fault. She only took up tennis to please you. Don't you see that? You've driven her to try to stay young forever, feeding the fantasy she has of herself. Now you're driving her to an early death."

He listened to Julie's rant, inclined to tell her to go to hell. Instead, he mumbled, "I'll see you at Northwestern. They're transferring her later in the day to keep her under the care of Eddie Newman. I'll keep you posted until then."

"Oh no, no, no. You won't keep me simply posted. I'll be at Illinois Masonic in twenty minutes."

She is being unfair to me, he thought. *She is childishly cruel and malevolent, but there is an element of truth in all she said.* He had encouraged Alyce to learn tennis; he was responsible in part for this accident. *Julie, too, is scared, and she's found the obvious scapegoat in me. She's also intent on destroying our marriage. I won't let her. I've got to figure out a way of making this troubled woman feel less threatened by me.* And then he grew more frightened. *Alyce doesn't deserve to suffer. She's in love with life too much to suffer.*

He remembered sitting on the hotel balcony and gazing at the Bay of Banderas at midnight. He remembered the nude beach in St. Martins, the restaurant—*What was the name of that bloody restaurant? We ate at a table on the beach, yes, oh yes, it was Las Palapola, and we had spicy crevices with our mojitos and guacamole, and she reached across the table to wipe away the smidgeon of sauce from my cheek.* He remembered walking along the malecon, hand in hand, among families that kept their kids up to God knows what hour and the fireworks from a blazing freighter in the bay, lighting up the starlit sky. *Julie doesn't have the remotest understanding of my feelings. Gently, I will have to make her understand. I will have to find a way of including her in our lives.*

Alyce was kept at Illinois Masonic for the night. In the morning, she would be transferred to Northwestern for surgery. Within half an hour, Julie burst into their private room and rushed to her mother's side. Without acknowledging David, she asked her repeatedly, "What happened, Mother? What in hell has happened to you? Oh god almighty, that's much more than just a bruise. It's much more than a simple bruise." She turned to David with bitterness and hatred. "What the hell have you done to my mother?"

She had already called Laura, who was to arrive from St. Louis late that afternoon or early the next morning. The two daughters would take over now. Julie arranged to sleep in this small room for the night. "Mother shouldn't be alone," she said. "You can't trust these doctors. They never can be found when you need them, or even the nurses on duty. Also, no more tennis," she told her mother. "No more of this young man's sport." Hadn't she warned her mother that one day this would occur? She had to slow down, Julie admonished her again and again given her age.

Alyce smiled plaintively at David, begging him silently to understand and forgive her difficult daughter, at least at this moment of crisis. Julie was simply nervous and upset; she cared too much. Frustrated, angry, and confused, he repressed his animus toward her and was convinced that she did not want to understand him. He wanted to care for his wife alone and to show her how much he loved her. But unable to control the tense situation and witnessing Alyce's plaintive smile, he acquiesced to her desires and stepped outside the room to leave her and Julie alone. From the hallway, he could hear Julie's imperious, grumbling injunctions. "Didn't I tell you this would happen one day? Didn't I warn you it would happen? No, no, you had to listen to *him*. He doesn't give one hoot about you, Mother. He's been using you, and he always will." Her voice grew more intense as she spoke. "I'm taking care of you from now on."

David leaned against the wall that separated them. His body was shaking with anger; he was uncertain of what he could do without upsetting Alyce even more. His natural impulse was to barge back into the room and tell Julie to get the hell out, as she was only making matters worse. Didn't she see how much her mother was suffering? Didn't she realize the stress she was under? Didn't she know that at Alyce's age the stress of a fractured thighbone could lead to a heart attack? He wanted to take charge, but he knew that Alyce would be frightened of a showdown with her daughter, especially at this moment when she was so frail and so anxious. The choice between daughter and second husband was one she did not dare to make and one that he did not wish to force her to make.

But he sensed that something else was at work—something darker and more foreboding. Alyce didn't want Julie to go; she only feared David's anger if she told him so. He knew that. At some primordial level, at this moment of great stress, she seemed to need Julie more than she needed him. Why was that so? What had he not done to gain her full trust? How had he failed her? Had he failed himself? He knew that Alyce would never express her deepest feelings to him, even if she knew what they were. All her life, she had been conflict averse, and he could tell that she loathed having to choose between the two of them.

After a long, silent separation, David returned to the room and kissed his wife good night.

"I'm leaving, Alyce. I'll call to say good night, and I'll return first thing in the morning before surgery and stay throughout the day and night."

"You don't have to," Julie muttered.

"I'll stay with you," he whispered, ignoring Julie, taking Alyce's hand, and kissing it. "All day. Do you want me to bring you back a book? Do you feel like reading? A *New Yorker*? I'll bring a *New Yorker* and your novel. I'll bring in the *Times* and a Hershey's chocolate bar with almonds."

In the bed, Alyce seemed short and old and withered. Her face was clear of all its usual makeup. She seemed so much more than twelve years his senior. But he didn't care. He loved her in spite of her age. All that matters is for her to recover. *Poor woman, rarely a sick day in her life she used to boast—no medications, perfect health, and now? An old woman?*

At home, he watched the news for an hour with a glass of wine held precariously in his trembling hand, suppressing his anger at Julie. He was overwhelmed by the magnitude of Alyce's accident. He called her to talk privately and bid her good night.

Julie answered too fast. "She's asleep. She can't be disturbed."

So that's it, he brooded. Here was her daughter trying in every which way to prevent him from expressing his love for her mother, his wife, the woman who had done so much for him and his university and who would do anything for him personally again. He tried to suppress his resentment. That would be ultimately selfish and self-centered. He had to find a way to reconcile a clash with Julie that he had not initiated or perpetuated or ever wanted.

A half hour later, after what must have been acrimonious words with Julie, Alyce called. "I'm sorry, Dave, that Julie's been so rude. I've sent her out of the room. I'm alone. I'm alone for you. Oh, my dear David, I'm so sorry for what I've done to you."

"You haven't done anything to me. You're what counts now. Don't feel guilty. You're going to get well. You're going to return to whom you were. We'll figure out a way with Julie. One day, you never know, we may be one happy little family. And you and me? We'll continue to be the Fred Astaire and Ginger Rogers at every gala we go to. How are you *really* feeling?"

"Terrible. I'm tired, I'm tired, Dave. I'm tired all the time."

"I'll let you rest. It's hard, I know. It's counter to your entire character, but you have to try to stay calm. Think of our best moments together. Think of champagne at the Café des Artistes. Think of mojitos and shrimp cocktails on the beach at Palapola. Think, if it helps, of me."

"Now that does help."

They held their breath as though they were on the verge of a kiss.

"I'll do everything I can, Alyce, to ingratiate myself to Julie. I know how important it is to you."

"It is. I'm sorry, Dave, but it is. It shouldn't be. It's an albatross, I know, but it is."

He could hear the fatigue in her voice. He murmured, "Good night. Sleep well. Don't worry. We'll work everything out." Before he could completely express his love for her, she had fallen asleep.

He too slept, but fleetingly. In the morning, he stared in the mirror and told himself the truth he had been reluctant to acknowledge. At the moment of crisis, when it truly counted, she had chosen Julie.

In the waiting room, he sat like a stranger apart from Julie, glancing at women's half-clad bodies in the tabloids that featured sex scandals and articles that promised guaranteed weight loss in ten days and the perennial struggle against aging—just exercise, just diet, and just have an upbeat attitude. But he gazed at the photographs without feeling and the articles without reading them. He remained morbidly silent, wondering whom this middle-aged woman, Julie, was and why was she so hostile to him? Had he stolen her mother from her? Or was she simply frightened at the prospect of a declining mother and concerned that Alyce would never be the same woman again?

Eddie Newman, Alyce's primary physician and an old dear friend, came to Julie and him. Short, thin, and full of certitude, he was a brilliant diagnostician who was also a wise guy with a wicked sense of humor. He had only one major flaw as a doctor—a tendency to divulge his patient's illnesses to other patients.

"Will she be able to walk?" Julie asked nervously.

"In time." He turned to David, who had become a social acquaintance. "After I have the first dance, I'll leave her to you, Dave. She's a helluva fighter."

"Watch over her, Eddie. Take care of her."

"Like a hawk. She's my secret girlfriend, did you know that? But her fate is in the hands of Dr. Weaver. He's the one who's doing the surgery."

"How long will it be?" David asked.

"Long. Long for the surgery and then at least an hour in the recovery room. And then sleep, sleep, sleep." He then started to leave.

Julie took his arm. "Tell me the truth, Dr. Newman. Tell me the goddamn truth. Will my mother be okay?"

"Absolutely. She's in good hands, Julie. Try to relax. Anxiety is the worst thing for her to see you have. Stress is a killer. It'll be three hours until you can speak to her again."

"Three hours?" Julie cried.

"That's normal."

Then the surgeon came to reassure them. It was Dr. Weaver—a benevolent, fatherly physician. He looked as though he had performed this procedure at least a hundred times.

"I'll see you directly after the surgery. Don't agitate yourself. This operation is really very routine."

"Unless there are complicating factors," David worried.

"We won't really know until we get in there, Mr. Parker. But no one needs to be agitated. That goes for you too, Julie. Don't fret. This procedure is not uncommon among athletes."

"My mother's not a jock," Julie muttered. "She's no hotshot tennis player."

By the time she had snapped the words, Dr. Weaver had left the two of them alone together.

They sat in the waiting room, ignoring each other. David's mood swung from compassion for Alyce to irritation with Julie. *What a bitch this woman is,* he groused, *short, dumpy, controlling, with worn jeans and a scruffy, baggy, brown sweatshirt that broadcast the bold letters of her alma mater, Miami University, across it.*

What is wrong with this bitter woman? David wondered. *What's the source of her bitchiness and temper? How in God's name do I reach her, accommodate her, and win her over? She's so utterly different from Alyce that someone who doesn't know will never guess they are mother and daughter.*

Alyce old? Alyce dying? Impossible. She was too young to die, too vibrant to age, and too precious to lose. There she was dancing across the floor at the Crystal Ball when he first saw her; skiing down a little slope in Aspen, learning and trying to please him; smiling, always smiling; sitting at a late Vietnamese dinner in Le Colonial on Rush Street; holding hands as they walked along Michigan Avenue, passing all the boutique stores; enjoying the trip to the city of Itsu, near the camp where he worked for a year at the end of the Korean War, just outside Kyoto and that little restaurant where they had to point out to the waiter the exotic dishes they wanted by taking him to the window; bringing David tea and sitting at two in the morning to help him think through some vexing problems in the university; and protecting, caring, and loving him. What had he ever really done for her? How much of his love had he shown, and what in God's name would he ever do without her?

And what had he done to deserve Julie's wrath? His mere existence in her claustrophobic life had bitterly disturbed her. His entry into that tight little world of hers had threatened her absolute claim on her mother. Alyce had told him often of the trauma Julie experienced after a lover at Miami University had dumped her and of the father she still worshipped despite his philandering and alcoholism and inability to hold a job. No new husband and surrogate father would ever satisfy her as a substitute for that idealized father. There was something simplistically Freudian about all these twisted recollections of her childhood, her constant need to eulogize her father, and the compulsion to control her mother. Whatever it was, he knew that she was a threat to his marriage, and he had to find a modus vivendi for them to coexist in Alyce's world. If not, he feared that he would lose Alyce, and he would not let that happen.

Alyce had confided that there had been long periods of therapy for Julie but to no avail. There was Julie's own inability to develop a career as she moved from one job to another like her father, a breast reduction that had discovered cancerous tissue and had led to radiation and residual scars across her flat chest, and a friendless existence in her small nondescript house in Winnetka—a solitary hideaway that was so eerily clean it seemed to lack any semblance of life. This troubled woman had suffered; she was suffering now and terribly afraid. He had to find compassion and understanding for her. There had to be a way to her heart. For now, though, he had room only for Alyce, who was scared to death, lying on the surgical bed with doctors and nurses and machines hovering over her. *She doesn't deserve this*, he thought, *not my Alyce*. She had played tennis only for him; she had done everything to please him. He was now filled with unrelenting guilt.

Laura arrived at noon, and Julie huddled with her in a corner of the room, briefing her. David could see how frightened the younger sister was. Her last and best friend, her mother, and the one she called when she felt most desperate and alone and defenseless, might not be in her life anymore. As he gazed at the two sisters speaking rapidly to each other, he remembered Alyce's heartbreaking story. When they had discovered that Laura had a kidney dysfunction, Alyce had taken her from doctor to doctor in Chicago and New York and LA; she had called every doctor she knew, seeking a definitive diagnosis from Eddie Newman, who concluded sadly, "It's kidney cancer, all right." Now she was hanging in the balance, waiting for a transplant, along with a long list of other transplant candidates nationwide. Alyce had done all she could to maneuver Laura ahead of everyone else on the list but to no avail. She had to wait her turn, and she wasn't used to or satisfied to wait her turn.

Now Julie and Laura sat at one end of the waiting room conferring and he on the other, as if they belonged to different families.

The surgeon, Dr. Weaver, appeared and told them that the operation was a distinct success but that the fractures of Alyce's thigh bones were a serious matter, especially for an eighty-year-old woman. She would have to be in a wheelchair for several months, followed by crutches, and then possibly by the perpetual use of a cane.

"She'll probably have a permanent limp," he warned the three of them, but then he quickly smiled as he grasped for an optimistic outlook. "When I told her my prognosis, she looked at me determinately and said with fire in her eyes, 'That's *your* prognosis, Dr. Weaver. I have my own prognosis. I'll never limp, and I'll never confine myself to crutches or a wheelchair or a cane. Never. Never. I'd rather die first." His smile broadened into affectionate admiration. "With her will, she might just be right. She could recover completely. Who knows? I wouldn't bet against Alyce Parker. She's quite a fighter."

David smiled vacantly, but he knew the doctor was right. He knew this was a turning point in their lives. And then he remembered that other turning point years ago. It was when Debra was being wheeled into the surgical room;

her wan smile of optimism was shown across her face as she'd gazed lovingly at him, just before she had her right breast removed. At the time, she was at the age of fifty-three. Then she died from breast cancer at the age of fifty-seven. Now it was Alyce's turn, except that this was not an act of uncontrollable nature; this had been caused by an accident for which he felt responsible. Kind, generous, intelligent, beautiful, and vivacious—would she now be a crippled old lady as Dr. Weaver intimated? Never. That was inconceivable. When she laughed, a warm light shone through her eyes, a wisp of hair crossed her brow, and he thought of her as eternally young. He recalled the magical moments: when she came into his arms in bed, before and after sleep, before and after sex, and in the middle of the night, he would whisper to her, "I love you. I never realized how much I love you."

Now he needed to care for Alyce as he had for Debra. All the time, alone, and they would grow ever closer as she recuperated. She would have done the same and more for him.

"How long will she be in the hospital?" he asked Dr. Weaver as Julie and Laura hovered close by.

"A week. Maybe less. She's remarkably strong for a woman her age. Her heart's in good shape, thank God, and she has a positive attitude. She could bounce back like new. For all I know, she could live as long as her mother. Who knows? But for now, she'll have to take it easy, stay for a week in the hospital, and then probably need twenty-four-hour care at home."

"I'll take care of her at home," Julie assured everyone. "I'll take care of my mother at home."

David said nothing, but he felt like barking back at her. He was entitled to be the caregiver of his own wife, wasn't he? He was the one to make these decisions. It was he who should be nursing her back to health as much as he could. But he also knew that he had to accommodate to the needs of others, to be in the short term uncharacteristically passive, and that would begin with a healthier attitude toward Julie. That's what Alyce would want. She wanted him to find the best in Julie and discover her virtues— loyalty, devotion, unconditional love for her mother, and whatever he could find.

All that mattered was Alyce and helping her recover. Lines from a poem ran through his mind:

> Grow old along with me,
> The best is yet to be.

He wanted to be optimistic and believe in those words. Oh, how he wanted to believe they were more than wishful poetry.

53

Hours later, the nurses wheeled her on a bed into her room. David, Julie, and Laura rushed to her side as the nurse warned them that Mrs. Parker must rest, "She's been through an ordeal. She's going to need all the rest she can get."

Alyce smiled at all of them faintly. She tried to speak, "I do not recommend—"

"Don't talk, Mother," Julie interrupted her. "Don't exert yourself. You heard the nurse."

Still, she stiffened, smiled, and tried to speak. She could see David make way for her girls and step backward in deference. She could see how hurt he was and her heart went out to him.

"Julie, Laura," she murmured, "let me be with David a moment before he leaves." Alone, she could feel his lips against hers gently, and his head nestled softly between her shoulder and neck. He whispered, "You're going to be all right. You're going to be the way you were." And his warm tears came running down his cheeks.

"Yes, Dave, I'm going to be all right. We're going to be okay."

"I know we will be. I just hate to see you so helpless. What can I do to help you?"

She smiled wanly. "Just love me and put up with my daughters. They're just scared."

"I'm not scared," he lied. "I know you're a fighter."

She could hear Julie and Laura stir outside the room, eager to return to their mother. She nodded to David that they had come to the door and were observing them.

"It's best if you call me," he murmured, "when you're rested and can talk to me in private."

"I will. Tonight, if I'm still awake, and certainly tomorrow, early tomorrow."

"I love you."

"And I love you."

Turning, he confronted Julie and Laura coming toward their mother. He smiled and muttered, "She's all yours."

54

David waited for her call that night, but it never came. In the morning, she apologized, she had felt so tired and gone to sleep early. He could feel the daughters hovering in the room.

"Julie and Laura have been so helpful. They've taken shifts and catered to my every need. Oh, Dave, I've never felt so helpless in my life. I've always been the one in charge—the one you could depend on."

"I'll be there in ten minutes. Can we have some time alone? Send the girls down for some breakfast. They deserve a break. They must be exhausted."

"Ten minutes, my love. How can I wait so long?"

During Alyce's three-week stay in the hospital, he would arrive at eight o'clock in the morning to find Julie ever present; she slept overnight, every night, on a cot that was placed close by her mother's side. He would spend fifteen minutes alone in the room with Alyce and assure her that he was hers whatever happened, that everything would work out in the end, and that he loved her even more than when she had been well and self-sufficient. He would bring her books and magazines and flowers, he would call periodically during the day, and he would be at the ready to do whatever she wanted.

Julie would remain all day and night, and though he resented her proprietorship, he let her cling to her mother, thinking that Alyce would return to him completely once she became well and the distance to these daughters would resume to something like normalcy. Occasionally, he would relieve Julie so that she could attend to her own personal matters at home, and he would sit with Alyce and watch sitcoms until she fell asleep. Julie then would return for her overnight vigil.

This was not the moment for controversy; this was the moment to reach out, to be larger than himself, to tolerate Julie, and to show compassion for Laura. He could afford to be the generous one. He was healthy. He had the comfort of never having to worry about money. He had the prestige of a career that was ending well. The daughters had suffered, for whatever reasons, and he should bring to them whatever compassion he could muster. But in the end, it was really all for Alyce. She was the loved one he wanted to grow old with, whether in health or not.

At the end of this hospital stay, the nurse wheeled Alyce to his car. Julie was clinging to her. She had attended to all the details: renting a wheelchair, buying crutches and a cane, and preparing a welcome home luncheon for the four of them. David told her how grateful he was for her help, which was born of the acceptance that whether he liked it or not, she would continue to be an indispensable part of Alyce's life.

He must create a family out of four fragmented people. Julie and Laura were frustrated spinsters, but they did love and need their mother. Like him, they were scared to death that she might never be the same again.

Alone with Alyce, observing her frailty, David was heartbroken for her. She hated aging and the loss of vitality. She was always tired, always taking naps; she hated becoming dependent on everyone else. For himself, he tried not to think of the worst. The worst was unthinkable. He could not conceive of losing Alyce to her frailty and decline. Without her, he would lose the balance to his hectic life. She was the one who was always able to put his troubles into perspective.

A life without Alyce was unthinkable.

After returning from the hospital, they ate Julie's luncheon with civility and expressed a positive attitude about the future. Julie was particularly pleased that Alyce was out of that prison of a hospital and that now she could take care of her full-time, as it should be.

David remained as cordial as possible, listening for the most part to Alyce and her girls recall their past experiences together and their need to escape to a health spa once Alyce was on her feet again. Afterward, she took a nap and let her daughters clean up. As they prepared to leave, Laura stepped forward and thanked him for all that he'd done. "This has had to be tough for you too."

"I'm okay. I'll be okay. I just want Alyce to get well. You and Julie have been indispensable."

Julie was holding the door, waiting impatiently.

"Come on, Laura," she said. "We need to beat the rush hour home."

David called at different times each day to see how Alyce was faring under Julie's care. After he returned from work, as early in the afternoon as he could get away from work, he would go immediately to their bedroom, where Alyce would be resting or napping. He would sit beside her on the bed, holding her hand and gently stroking her arm and kissing her cheek.

"How's my girl doing?"

"Your girl? Oh god, Dave. Your girl feels like an old lady. Every part of me aches."

"Pain killers? Tylenol? A heating pad? Nothing helps?"

"A little. But I have these splitting headaches that just won't go away."

He took her hand in his. "They will, in time."

She gazed upon him with sad regret.

"Oh, Dave, one night, you're queen of the ball, the next day, you're an old lady."

"You don't look like an old lady to me."

She smiled wanly. "I hope I don't. Tell me something. Tell me the truth. Will you love me when I'm old and gray?"

"You'll never be old and gray. That song was of another generation: 'Will you love me when I'm sixty-four?' What nonsense. Did you ever hear such nonsense? At sixty-four, you were a youthful beauty."

"And now?"

"Now you're a maturing beauty, aging gently, like vintage wine, like a seasoned lady who's had the experience of having lived. Basically, you're an ageless beauty."

"Oh, you lie so well."

"Come now. Have I ever lied to you?"

"No, but don't stop now that you've started."

55

Alyce prevailed upon Julie to discover virtues in David rather than always seek to undermine him. She had established a habit of staying all day with Alyce and making dinner every night for both of them.

"Can't you find anything positive to say about him?"

"I'm sorry, Mother. I know I'm right. The two of you have been a total mismatch from the get-go."

"He brings these flowers every week. He brings flowers for each of us. You can see he's trying. He's always suggesting dinners out or ordering dinners in—whatever I want. You don't have to make dinners for us every night."

"Flowers. Dinners. Mere superficialities. All he really cares about is his work. I want to make dinner for you."

"Julie, stop being mindlessly cruel. Try liking him—for my sake. You have to get used to the fact that I want him as my husband, my partner, and my love for the rest of my life. And he wants me. He may be my last best chance for happiness."

"I hope so, for your sake. But he doesn't deserve you."

"I love him, for God's sakes. I'm not interested in analyzing him. I would do anything for him, and he would for me. I know that."

"I wouldn't be so sure."

"I've been thinking, Julie, and this comes from me alone. I haven't spoken to David at all. Don't make dinner and then stay to eat with us each night and clean up afterward. Leave before he comes home from work. Give us the evening alone. Make dinner, if you like, but leave before he comes home. The two of you shouldn't be together for now. The tension between the two of you upsets me too much. I can't bear the stress. Besides, I do want to spend the entire evening alone with my husband."

"Are you banishing me? Excluding me from your home?"

"No. I just want some time alone with my husband."

"What are you saying? What are you telling me? Deep down, your husband doesn't give a damn about you. Don't you see that? He only cares about himself. He's a total narcissist—"

The front door slammed open. It could have been a scene from a frivolous comedy or bad melodrama. Was he listening from behind the door? In one hand, he bore a huge box of Valentine chocolates; in the other, he had lemon tarts for dessert.

"Am I intruding? I just thought, this is Valentine's Day. We deserve to indulge ourselves."

Alyce reached for him from her wheelchair. "Oh Dave, you are a love. Julie, look—"

Julie was already moving toward the kitchen. She stopped, turned, and offered him the most forlorn smile she could manage. "Thanks. It was thoughtful of you." Then she made her way to the kitchen to prepare their dinner.

As they tried to be civil to one another, Alyce thought to herself, *I'll lose him because of Julie. I know it. In my aging bones, I know it. How much self-sacrifice can I expect of him? How much abuse can I ask him to tolerate?*

56

"It's going to be okay," he assured Alyce as they lay in bed that night. "Cry, cry, my love. You deserve a good cry." He was brushing tears from her eyes as new tears replaced them. "I'll talk to her. I'll make it work."

"How will you ever make it work?"

"At this moment, I don't know how. She's terrified at losing you—that much I do know. I have to find a way of convincing her that it's not true."

"She's gaining a father, not losing a mother. Will that be the pitch?"

"Something like that."

"You know that never works. A biological father is a father and forever the only father."

"I wouldn't know. I've never been one."

"It's too late now, Dave. There's a biological connection that can never be replaced."

"All I can do is try."

"And you'll mean it?"

"I'll try to mean it. And then one day, I may really mean it. We have to be patient. I can't demand her trust. I have to earn it. We just got off to a bad start."

He reached across to her face and cupped it in his hands and kissed her lips. It had been a long time since they'd made love; he couldn't remember how long ago. Suddenly he wanted her—irrationally and selfishly. He pressed harder against her body as he felt eagerness grow within him.

"Oh, Dave," she cried. "I can't. I want to, but I can't. This leg hurts so much."

"I'm sorry—"

"Don't be. You want me, and I'm grateful. I need to be wanted. I need to be touched. I need to be loved. I'll make it up to you when this damn leg is operational."

A few days later, when he returned home, he felt the time had come for rapprochement. Julie was, as always, positioned in the den, watching some sitcom on television while Alyce napped. He sat in the love seat opposite her, expecting her to switch off the program and recognize him, but she simply muttered, "Hi," and sat there, fixated by the gyrations of the actors on the screen.

"How was it today?" he asked.

"Better. Each day is a little better. She walked through the condo today with the aid of the crutches and cane. I think she hates the cane more than the crutches. The cane is a sign of permanent old age to her."

"Great. She is a fighter. If anyone can—"

"I know what she can do. I've known her for fifty-five years."

"Longer than I ever will," he conceded. "You've been a real help, Julie. I want you to know how much I appreciate it." He waited for her to switch off the television set and turn to him. But instead, she kept focused on her program.

He sat there woodenly. "Could you turn off the TV for just a moment?"

She did and then wheeled her chair round to confront him directly and impatiently, her eyes fastened on his like daggers.

"Will you let me take you to lunch tomorrow afternoon?"

"Tomorrow afternoon?"

She was so startled, she hadn't the time to invent a reason for saying no.

"Who will take care of my mother?"

"We can leave her alone for two hours. You did say she's becoming better, didn't you? Independent? Isn't that what you said?"

He wanted to treat her to the Pump Room, but she had dressed down purposely, he knew. She wore her usual uniform: baggy black pants, worn sneakers, and a tired-gray sweatshirt. It was as if she refused to be attractive. She had her mother's eyes and the good bone structure of her mother's face, though she was short and plump. However, a few weeks of dieting could almost make her resemble Alyce more closely when she was forty-seven. He decided against the Pump Room, for fear that she would feel awkward or inferior or hostile. Instead, he took her to Third Coast Café—an informal hideaway a few steps away and below street level on the southwest corner of Dearborn and Goethe, where they ensconced themselves in a corner booth. They could have been father and daughter to any passerby. She sat opposite him stolidly, as though chained to her seat against her will and waited for him to say what he had to say. She ordered nothing but a cup of coffee while he struggled slowly with a Caesar salad. As he nibbled, she watched him, and he, in turn, glanced at her surreptitiously. When their eyes met, they blazed at each other with distrust.

She's an attractive woman, he thought, *or was an attractive woman until she'd had her breast reduction and went out of her way to make herself physically unappealing. She must truly dislike herself to dress this way.* Alyce's wide eyes lingered in hers, and she'd inherited the high cheekbones and dark hair. However, she never did possess Alyce's shine of optimism or warmth or joy in life. In her place were cynicism and a suspicion of the world. She could clearly have done more for herself, but as Alyce once confessed, "She doesn't want to. She doesn't like herself. She doesn't want to look pretty. She's decided not to have a man ever again in her life. I don't know why. A shiftless father whom she still adores in memory? A broken love affair in college when she was a kid? I don't know why. She has a bitter temper—certainly not inherited from me, not even from Matt. She distrusts everyone. It's not you alone. I don't know why. You be the analyst. She's my own daughter, and I don't know why she is this way or what she is or who she is."

"Look, Julie," he tried talking, after they were uncomfortably settled in their places. "I know how upset you are with me for coming into your life and claiming your mother, but can't we try to have a relationship . . . of mutual respect and acceptance? Can't we share the same woman we both care for?"

"I don't just care for my mother. I love my mother."

"We both love her. I'm not a man who wears his heart on his sleeve, but I would do anything for Alyce. And I would be devastated if anything ever happened to her. I'm not trying to steal her from you."

"It sure feels that way."

"Well, I'm not."

She wavered for a moment but then steeled herself against him. She didn't believe a word he said.

"Oh, shit," she finally cried, tossing her napkin on the table. "Is this what you brought me here for? Some peace accord?"

"I asked you here to see how we might get along—for Alyce's sake."

Julie glared at him with distrust. "Don't bullshit me. You drove her like a workhorse with all these fucking galas and fundraising events. Then you've been traveling overseas— for work, not pleasure, always for work, work, work. Then it's tennis at the age of eighty. What's next? Skiing? Pole-vaulting? You've used her—"

"She's loved it."

"She's an old woman, for Christ sakes. She shouldn't be prancing around. She's opened every goddamn golden door in the city to you. You'd be nowhere without her. She's worth more than ten development officers you might appoint. And she sure as hell is worth much more than the crappy crumbs you throw her way for a so-called salary."

"Julie, do me a favor."

"Is this why you brought me here? To buy me off with a lousy cup of coffee? I don't need your presidential bullshit. She's sitting in that apartment all alone right now. Why don't you go back to your university, which is all you really care about, and build your castle in the sky—all by yourself? I'm going back to my mother who needs me."

"Julie, do me a favor. Why don't you go fuck yourself?"

She stood up abruptly and fished a dollar bill from her purse, throwing it on the table. "That's for this lousy cup of coffee."

"Well?" Alyce asked him after Julie was gone for the day. "Success?"

"Not yet. But I'm not done trying. I told you it would take time to earn her trust."

"Good luck. I've been trying to sell you to her ever since we became serious."

"That makes me sound like a commodity."

"To her maybe, but not to me. I intend to grow old, *older*, with you—and you alone. We'll have to find another way, if there is one."

"Be patient. I'm not done trying to work my magic."

But he was still bristling from Julie's contempt for him. *You bitch*, he kept thinking to himself, infuriated with her obstinacy. *You sick, selfish bitch. I've had it with you.*

That, of course, wasn't true—not for a moment.

57

Alyce's recovery was slower than she wished. She had the life force of a fearless fighter who wouldn't accept defeat and stay determined to restore her health and vitality and beauty against all odds, but her mind raced ahead of her aging beauty. She exercised religiously so that her hips and lower back and legs grew stronger. Twice a week, her physical therapist gave her a work over, and once a week, she had a massage at home. She graduated from a wheelchair to crutches to a cane, and then one day, as she laughed, she packed the cane away forever. "Not to be used again, until I'm one hundred and seven."

"Miracle of miracles." He laughed. "You intend to live longer than your mother."

"At least. Tell me, Dave. Will you still love me when I'm one hundred six?"

"Absolutely. I'll be only a youthful ninety-four. Of course I'll love you. At that age, I'll still be planning on taking you to some Crystal Ball."

Still, whenever they went out, she had to sit in the wheelchair, pushed diligently and dutifully by David. She accused him whimsically of exhibiting a certain degree of embarrassment at being with an elderly cripple, but he pooh-poohed her accusation, claiming that she was temporarily disabled and simply transferring her own self-consciousness to him. He would do anything for her. More than ever, he knew in his heart of hearts that to be true. He hated to leave her in the morning; he rushed home as early as possible in the afternoon. He would call her during the days to see how she was feeling, ready to come to her at a moment's notice. He loved her more than ever as a consequence of her accident and her need to depend on him. He would be there for her until the end of their time together, however long or short that might be.

Once, she lamented, "I hate to be so dependent on you, Dave. I hate to be so much of a burden. I've never been a burden to anyone in my entire life."

He kissed her lips and cupped her beautiful, if aging, face in his hand. "If only you knew. You're not the one who's dependent. I'm the dependent one—on you. I'm not sure I'd want to go on if anything ever happened to you."

She was a proud lady. More and more, she hated her illness, she hated her limitations, she hated the loss of her independence, and she hated the little wrinkles insinuating themselves under her eyes and around her once-perfect lips. She hated the specter of old age creeping upon her as though it was a stalker preparing her for death.

I'll lose him to old age, she feared. *I'll lose my beauty, and then what will there be? A wheelchair? A cane?*

David would leave their condo the moment Julie arrived at eight o'clock in the morning and return at five—but only after he'd called Alyce to ask, "Is the coast clear?" Unlike her daughter, she was always dressed for him—happy that she was free of Julie's nagging and unwanted solicitousness throughout the wearisome day. After the dinner that Julie and Alyce had prepared together, she and David would watch television together, like an old married couple. She knew that ordinarily he avoided television, except for one or two news shows, and that he was now sitting with her patiently and tenderly because he didn't want to leave her alone. On her part, she would listen to the frustrations of his presidency, so strange to her nonacademic sensibility, as he spoke of "who's in, who's out / who wins, who loses." Each day, the university seemed to matter less and less.

Alyce was irrepressible and determined to recover as quickly as humanly possible. She began to hold weekly luncheons with the Chicago Board at home in preparation for her next gala. "It's my way of feeling alive, Dave, of being useful, and of showing you how much I love you. It's the one thing I can do for you." Ramsay Lewis, the pianist and local celebrity, was on the board. He had succeeded in persuading Bill Cosby to appear for a return engagement, *pro bono*, and she wanted to make it the biggest blast that Roosevelt or any other institution had ever featured. *"It will be my comeback."* She laughed. *"But, by no means, is it my swan song."*

Sometime during the evening, Laura would phone, and with the bedroom door closed, her voice would be no more than some distant murmur. Alyce would have mutually supportive conversations that always left her smiling and warm inside, but that feeling was inevitably eclipsed by another call later in the evening from nettlesome Julie, who simply wanted to remind Alyce to take this or that pill. "Oh god," Alyce screamed at her once in despair, "life has to be more than the taking of a pill!"

Then the dam broke.

"Stop telling me how to live my life," Alyce finally condemned her older daughter. "No one's forcing me to raise money for Roosevelt, no one's forcing me to organize galas, and no one's making me develop the Chicago Board. I love it. I love it all. No, you're wrong. He's not doing that. He's not what you say he is. You're simply wrong, Julie—and malevolent. You resented him before you even met him. You haven't tried to see one redeeming feature in him. You'll never understand me. I enjoy what I'm doing—*I don't want to retire, goddamn it—ever.* I find meaning in all this activity. It keeps me young. No, no, no, I don't want to slow down. I don't want to become an old lady who sits around reinventing her past and boring everyone with distorted memories—people who have no way of knowing whether the memories are true or not or whether they're just memories turned into fantasies of the past. I want to live in this moment with David. You don't have to keep lecturing me. I'm not your child or your dependent, doddering, old matriarch. I'd rather be in assisted living than in your two-by-four house."

"Okay, okay, I hear you. But I still don't trust him. If you won't live with me while you're convalescing, then I want you to do me one favor."

"Oh, Julie, stop. Please stop."

"Will you install a private line—a second telephone number?"

"What are you talking about?"

"I think he's listening into our conversations."

She looked up to see David at the door. He didn't have to listen to their argument to suspect what they were talking about. He'd heard their wrangling from as far away as his study. Alyce was frightened, startled, and embarrassed.

"I'm hanging up. Julie. Now. No, now. No, no, no! David's here."

She hung up, crushing the phone into its cradle, and then looked up at David. Tears were now blurring her vision.

"My caring, loving daughter who refuses to accept the fact that I'm married."

"Tell me." He smiled. "I heard the wrangling, but not the words. Or shouldn't I ask?"

"It's not enough that she's been with me all day. That's not enough. Now she wants me to install a private phone line."

"So that I won't overhear what she thinks of me?"

"That's more or less the idea."

He wasn't smiling anymore.

"Well, you can tell her to go to hell."

"Dave—"

"Tell her to go fuck herself. And if you don't, I will. I've had enough of her paranoia, her constant assault on our marriage, her interference in our lives, and her treatment of you as her child. There isn't going to be another phone line installed in this house. Not so long as I live here. I've had it, up to here. If you want to talk with her privately, go live with her."

"Dave—"

"I mean it. I'm sick and tired of her bullshit. Tell her to grow up and find a life of her own. Make a decision,

Alyce. At some point, you're going to have to make a choice between her and me. You know that, don't you?'"

Later that night, she sat up in bed, trembling, and she sought guidance, long distance, from Laura. Her younger daughter listened with the patience of someone who simply wanted her mother to be happy after all the troubles her first husband and two girls had brought her in their earlier lives. When Alyce paused for a moment in her diatribe of Julie, Laura simply answered, "Mom, Mom, stop. Stop punishing yourself. If you love him and want him, then tell Julie to go to hell. It's your life. She'll have to find a life of her own."

"Laura—"

"Hold on to him. This feeling you have probably won't come again. It may in fact be your last chance. I'll talk to Julie. I'll tell her to lay off, if you won't."

Afterward, she writhed in bed, mired in self-doubt. When a husband blew his father's fortune on one senseless career after the other and then turned alcoholic; when one daughter couldn't have a normal relationship with a man and suffered from drug addiction, the abandonment of an infant she'd not wanted, and a year in a psychiatric clinic and afterward a bitter Hollywood divorce and more drugs; when the other couldn't form a normal relationship with a man and hung on to her mother like a barnacle; when out of despair, the mother turned more and more to galas and the approval of others, was she a narcissist or someone just trying to find meaning in her own life? Was she escaping responsibilities or craving a life of meaning through philanthropy? Or . . . or is she herself partially responsible for the problems of her family?

An hour passed, and she couldn't sleep for all the guilt she felt. Then she could sense David changing into pajamas and sitting by her side. She knew that he wanted to be kind and understanding. Gently he touched her arm.

"Forgive me," he murmured. "I shouldn't have taken it out on you. She drives you nuts, and then I come along and make it only worse. We'll work it out. Somehow the two of us will work it out."

"Oh god," she said. "Why do I have to be a mother until the day I die?"

"Because you'll always care. And that's what I love about you."

"I don't feel very loved tonight."

He took her in his arms. "You are. You are. Sleep. Don't fret the small stuff. We'll work out everything tomorrow and the day after tomorrow, when we're both rested."

She was wide-awake now, listening to his heavy breathing as he soon fell asleep. She watched his face and worried that she was losing him. *Am I losing him to Julie and his work and our age differences? What are his innermost secrets? Why doesn't he love me as he once did? Or has he ever? Is he incapable of loving me unconditionally? Or have I idealized love so that no one can ever meet my expectations? But then is Julie right after all? Is he self-centered and so consumed by his university that he has no space for me? Or am I expecting too much?*

She stumbled into her study and opened the diary she kept, reading a line that she had inscribed while studying Dostoevsky at the U of C. It was a line she had written fifty years before, faint and fading, and it had now struck her as so true of David: "What is hell? I maintain that hell is suffering from the inability to love."

She did not want to believe that was true of David. He was as affectionate as he could be and as loving as one would want, but something within her sensed that some deeper level of selflessness was missing.

Finally, as always, she blamed herself. Was she losing him only because of Julie or were there other reasons? Her age? Her accident? Her changing face and failing body?

She couldn't sleep and staggered to the bathroom, staring in the mirror at herself. She was unhappy with the way she looked. She looked tired. She looked older. Was she losing her beauty and verging on becoming an irreversibly older woman? Surely aging must be more than what she saw in the mirror. When would she cave in and surrender to old age? Even she, with her fabulous bone structure, her indomitable will, and her joy in living, must at some time surrender to aging. Was this her time? She wasn't ready yet. She wondered whether she should return to New York for a second round of plastic surgery, just a little touch-up before anyone else noticed. Her eyes did have tiny bags surfacing beneath them, her skin was sagging slightly under her chin, her breasts and underarms had lost their firmness, and her stomach was puffy, too puffy, an inch too puffy. However, she could do nothing about it all despite relentless exercises with her personal trainer twice a week and visits to the Ritz Carleton Gym for a swim every morning at the crack of dawn. Her insecurities surfaced and then subsided, like waves in an ocean of tears. She was still a beautiful woman, wasn't she? After all, she comforted herself, *How many women would kill to have my strong bone structure and my dazzling, brilliant eyes, even at my age?*

She went to her study with the sudden need to review her financial folders. The numbers were pathetic: half a million in bonds from the sale of her homes in Winnetka and Wisconsin and ten thousand in a checking account of her own. In the world that mattered to her, she still appeared wealthier than she was. She could still keep up the front, so long as she was married to a university president. David had been giving her a thousand a month for expenses, and he paid for the mortgage. The university picked up so many other expenses—travel and entertainment and luncheons and dinners. She seemed to be a wealthy woman and would appear so for the rest of her life if she stayed with him. So why should she be worried? In an act of trust, when they first married, he'd promised that he would leave all that he was worth to her. So naïve, so generous, he didn't even see the need for a prenuptial agreement. Whatever belonged to him belonged to her. How secure did a woman of eighty need to be? No lawyers required. She realized how dependent she was on him and trusted him to care for her. *So why*, she wondered, *should I feel any sense of insecurity?*

She stared at the family photos above her desk: a youthful Matt in his spotless air force uniform, another of Julie and Laura in the large backyard when they were children, and a family of four with a poodle on each of the laps of Bud and Alyce, beaming. Everyone was beaming; they looked like an ideal, successful American family of four out of a fashion magazine of the fifties or sixties. Tears rolled from Alyce's eyes uncontrollably. What had happened to them? They were so wealthy at the start, so lucky to have had his father buy them their home and build a clothing store that he would leave for Matt to run, so flush with money when they went on the safari to Africa that was financed by skyrocketing Archer stock, so secure, so promising, so handsome a husband, so beautiful a wife, and so pretty their two girls—how could anything possibly go wrong? But Matt drifted from business to business, wasting their wealth and diminishing them, until they had to sell the house and separate.

She leaned against her desk and stared at her dead husband, asking him again and again, as if he were still alive, "What happened to us, Matt? Where did it all go wrong?"

She was startled. David was standing at the door, rubbing his sleepy eyes and watching her cry.

"What's wrong? Is anything wrong? It's three o'clock in the morning."

"I just can't sleep."

He reached for her, but she stood rigidly still, as if she didn't want to be touched.

He looked at the photographs she had been studying and read her thoughts.

"I can't replace Matt any more than you can replace Debra. I can't help you forget that past any more than I can forget my own. But that past is past, Alyce, buried and dead. Now we have each other, with a few more years left to us. Let's not have anyone you quote in that diary, including ourselves, destroy what we have."

"Do you really believe that?"

"It's what I feel. I'm sorry, Alyce, if I'm limited. I know that by now. Maybe what you quote in that diary is right after all. Maybe Dostoevsky had me in mind when he said that hell is someone suffering from the inability to love. Maybe I am that man. I don't think so, I don't want it to be so, but it could be. In any case, I love you as much as I'm capable of loving anyone."

She turned, and with tears awash in her eyes, she fell into his arms and clung tightly to his chest.

"That's all I want, Dave. Please, please, please don't ever leave me."

58

By now, David had learned his limitations. He realized his addictive need for multiple projects all of his adult life, for rising in his career as though that were the full measure of him as a man. Was it? By now, he acknowledged that wasn't necessarily so. Alyce's mocking remark after playing tennis one Sunday morning was so evident to him now: "You don't just play to win, Dave. You play to kill."

All his life, he had played to kill. As the son of a brilliant teacher and the younger brother of a physicist who was out of the house by fifteen and on his way to a Princeton PhD by twenty-one, David had followed by graduating from Columbia with a dissertation, *The Literature of the Civil War*, that he turned into a book he used for tenure at City College. Then he was off to the races: other studies and anthologies for money and the critical study that was to be his magnum opus, *The Heroic Ideal in American Literature*, written in Paris while he was lecturing there and everywhere else throughout Europe. Then he returned home to veer into administration and to rise through the ranks during the tempestuous seventies in New York, writing proposals to fund programs and creating project after project until he accepted the greatest project of all—the presidency of Roosevelt University. Driven to excel, competitive to the end, and racing against all others and himself, he had always played to kill.

Debra had loved the wild ride. She had a separate, fulfilling career and no children. There were just the two of them. Alyce? What were her projects? Galas? Being at the center of an adulating world? *What will happen when the lights go out,* he wondered, *and there are no galas and only Julie, Laura, and him?*

59

For Alyce, there would be the young women who were already coming by for tea or luncheon. They had always admired her for her accomplishments—her triumph over adversity; her outreach to so many organizations; her instinctive leadership whenever she served on a board; her discretion; her positive disposition; her ability to listen patiently; and her elegance, charm, and beauty. She had transitioned into becoming their leader, offering advice when sought and sympathy when needed. It was a role that brought her great satisfaction as a matriarchal figure, and he could see that it was one that would last well into their retirement. That was one of her ways of achieving ageless beauty.

They returned to their social lives, holding musicales for potential donors in their home and featuring gifted student singers. She arranged dinners at the Lake Shore Country Club and in town at the Drake or Four Seasons Hotel;

she ordered subscriptions to the opera and symphony and Steppenwolf and Goodman theaters. She made certain they were invited to the most important galas in town, moving easily among the social circles that counted in the world of philanthropy. Never in her life had she lived so well. Never was she so happy. After several months, she had completely recovered, except for occasional stabs of pain in her thigh, and she and David were once again to be seen everywhere, admired by the young and envied by the elderly.

She managed to keep Julie and Laura at a distance from their glittering lives by seeing them individually, away from David. That was the best way—for now. She knew that the separation was unhealthy and might one day trigger open conflict, but for now, it seemed wise to have a peace accord and let time be the healer. Her daughters loved the separation. David accepted it with some degree of relief. The killer in all things competitive, he seemed relieved to be passive in matters of the heart.

On Saturdays, she visited with Julie, and every third weekend, she did so with Laura in St. Louis, trying to keep their lives apart from them. But that proved difficult, even for Alyce. Julie always found a reason for coming to their condo during the day, resuming the role of her mother's caretaker, and David had to schedule his departures and arrivals in terms of when Julie would be at his home with her mother. He was annoyed; he'd told Alyce sporadically at the incursion, the inconvenience, the sense that he was not in control of his own home. But Alyce could see that the inconvenience, however reluctantly, was acceptable to him—a temporary *modus vivendi,* one less problem when he had so many university issues to deal with. She also knew that these divisions would not be sustainable. Fissures soon appeared and expressed themselves, of all places, in the few religious customs that were important to her.

She went to the temple with Julie on Rosh Hashanah and Yom Kippur, the holiest of holy days, while he worked in his study at home. He was president of a university with a significant number of Jewish students, alumni, and faculty. Julie was quick to criticize him for his insensitivity, but Alyce defended her husband—he had so much work to do.

"None of that," Julie insisted, "excuses him from disrespecting his Jewish faculty and students. He was born Jewish, wasn't he? What *are* his religious roots? Is he one of those so-called secularized Jews? Is he an atheist? I'll bet he's an atheist. They all are—those academics. You're so different from each other, Mother. You would never do that. I don't know how the two of you ever got together."

When Alyce returned from the Kol Nidre service, after fasting all day, she began to see the differences between her and David more clearly. She said good night to Julie and Laura at the front of her condominium building and watched them drive to Julie's home alone—which in and of itself was sad, however difficult Julie had become. In the old days, the family of four would return from the conservative synagogue at sunset and dine on a sumptuous dinner to break the fast together. Reluctantly, she resented David for not being able to accommodate her daughters, difficult as it might have been for him.

"How did it go?" he asked.

She sat on the chair opposite him in his study, dressed in her fashionable beige Dior suit and pleased with the way she looked. He was relaxed in khakis and a dark turtleneck, reading some institutional report or other. He never seemed to cease working. "Work is a trusted friend," he would say then laugh, "in the midst of other woes." Work gave him great satisfaction. He was sorry he couldn't be with her at the synagogue, but there would have been the complications of his being in the company of the girls and all the work that he had to do and his feeling that he was in some artificial setting, faking it all, pretending, and lying to himself. Still, she resented his leaving her to go alone.

She described the evening to him, chatting about the various people who were at the temple—her friends of a lifetime and secular Jews who, like her, appeared in the synagogue only on the high holy days, atoning for the sins they'd committed during the year and asking for God's forgiveness.

"It was a beautiful service. The cantor had a magnificent voice. You should hire her as a voice teacher, Dave. She's a graduate from Juilliard, you know."

"And all your friends were there?"

"All, except Josie Straus. Now that she has the beginnings of Alzheimer's, she no longer leaves the house, poor girl. Jack came alone. He looks like a lost soul without her. Sixty years of a good marriage, God bless them. They've been through absolute hell this past year. I've never seen a woman age so quickly."

"It can happen to any of us."

"I know. There, for the grace of God, go I. Right? I must say, I do enjoy the service. It stills my soul, whatever is left of my poor, battered soul these days. It makes me feel at one with myself."

"Really?"

"Yes. It makes me feel connected."

"To what?"

"A tradition. A community. A god."

"I envy you. I guess I envy you. I lost my faith when I was an adolescent and read the English translation of those prayers. It all seemed to be no more than adulation of a god I could not understand. "Who the hell is this God?" I asked myself. Why does he—or she or it—need so much praise?"

"God's really a nice guy, Dave. Try him out some time. He's on our side."

"I wouldn't bet on that. Not in my experience."

Standing before him, she stared, crushed by his self-centeredness. "I'm sorry you can't even pretend anymore, Dave, not even for me. That would have been a gift. It would have been nice to have you along, holding my hand, walking home from the synagogue, being beside me to simply hold my hand, and pretending that you still loved me."

"I—" he began to defend himself.

She smiled at him forlornly. "Oh well . . . I'll change my costume and put on my robe, and we'll throw together some sort of dinner. I'm starved from having fasted." She couldn't understand his atheism—his belief in nothing that wasn't tangible or couldn't be measured. There were aspects of him that she would never understand.

60

As David listened to her relive the evening at the synagogue, he knew that he should have gone with her. He didn't like himself for being so small, self-centered, and ungenerous. What the hell did he care? For this one night, if he had really anticipated her wishes and sought to please her and make their marriage stronger, he would have bowed to her need for some semblance of a religion. It was so little he could have done for her, but he didn't do it.

Only once had he shared his deepest thoughts about religion with her. They were driving home from the country club along Sheridan Road—a dark winding road under a sky that held no stars or moon and was bordered by mansions and the homes of her life-long friends as well as the home she herself once owned. It was there, on the hill in Winnetka, overlooking her lost world. He started slowly and then became increasingly, irrepressibly confessional.

"The turning point for me against God was Debra's inability to conceive. Unfair punishment, I protested. She wanted children so badly. 'Couples who have no children are more self-centered and selfish,' she insisted. 'They lead incomplete lives.' When I said we should adopt, she wouldn't hear of it and plunged herself into work, leaving my career to me and believing that work would be enough compensation. And it has been for me, I think. But the absence of children also left an invisible scar, the inability to connect with people other than myself, my needs, and my ambitious nature. It's more than narcissism. It's as if I've never developed the ability to connect emotionally. Children might have forced me to connect with others."

"Careful," she'd chided him. "You could have had my children."

"I'm not sure whose fate has turned out better—yours or mine."

"I'm not either. Maybe the best fate would have been children of our own. Of course, it may be a little too late for that."

"Just by a year or two."

"Although we could always adopt Laura's abandoned child."

He looked at her quizzically. A mad thought raced through his mind. *She probably half means it. She probably has had it all figured out.*

"No thanks," he smiled. "I know you've been tracking that boy's progress all these years from afar, but he seems to be doing very well without us."

In his office, after Alyce was fast asleep, he sat and brooded over his pile of projects. He was almost tempted to sweep them from his desk as inadequate—a pending merger with John Marshall Law School, a biomedical program with Rush Presbyterian Medical Center that might just work, the acquisition of a smaller musical school to strengthen his own Chicago Musical College, an honors college, a collaboration with the Chicago public schools, and a recommendation for faculty reappointment and tenure. He also had his to-do list—ten items long. There were no books to be read on that list—none, not even a novel, a book of poetry, or a play to remind him of what he once loved. But it was some comfort that he was approaching that time when he might love that literary world again.

Had he been right when he confessed to Alyce that he hadn't developed emotionally and that there was a short circuit somewhere in his system that controlled his feelings? With no religion and no friends in a city still strange to him, he only had Alyce. There was only Alyce filling the vast void where work and love should be balanced. Whatever else he thought, he knew that Alyce had become indispensable to him.

He found his frustration and reward in work. Enrollments were not rising appreciably, donations had plateaued, and he had no desire for another capital campaign. He knew that he was too near his retirement for still one more bold adventure, but Alyce was not to be deterred. She was busy with the Chicago Board, planning galas that now featured Rosemary Clooney, Michael Feinstein, Marvin Hamlisch, and others. She was coming up with Bill Cosby again. She began to hold luncheon meetings in their condo; she recruited more and more executives until her board was more prestigious than his own board of trustees—some indeed were recruited as trustees. She made her activities star-studded, desirable, fun-filled enterprises, while he felt he was the president of a pedestrian university, balancing budgets, keeping order, forestalling faculty protests, and integrating the entire enterprise. She acted as though she was younger than him.

Still, after all the expenses of Alyce's galas were tallied and after all the hoopla was over, there was little left of clear profit for the university. There were still those sluggish enrollments he depended on, which had to form the trusted foundation for any leap forward.

There was beginning to be a change in Alyce. He could see now that she was growing healthier, with a greater sense of independence now than she had when she emerged from her illness, as if she were stronger, as Hemingway once claimed, where the broken bones had healed. She was ageless and stronger and more independent, as if younger than him. His suspicion of Alyce's motives grew after he noticed that Ron Grillo was attending all her meetings and taking greater charge of all fund-raising activities. When he questioned her, she assured him that Ron's presence was only so that he wouldn't be bothered with all the details.

Then, when he formally announced his retirement, his cynicism turned out to be true. "Did you know," Alan Archer, chairman of the board, confided in him, "that Ron Grillo has been campaigning to be president after you leave. He's been speaking individually to trustees, gaining their support for his candidacy, and taking credit for all the success you've been having. Be careful, Dave. Judas Iscariot is in the wings."

David laughed off Archer's warning with a glib remark, "Someone once told me that 'when you're president, you're in Who's Who, and when you retire, you're who's he?' Isn't that how it goes? Someone's always in the wings, Alan, ready to take your place."

But he was troubled enough to raise the issue with Alyce. She scoffed at the rumor as absurd—the naked ambition of a cunning, opportunistic man who couldn't be trusted. "It'll never happen. The trustees won't allow it to happen."

"I wouldn't count on it."

By breakfast, she had altered her own thinking. "Maybe, Dave, we should keep an open mind about Ron Grillo. Maybe his becoming president isn't such a bad idea, after all."

"You're kidding me."

She looked at him and simply smiled. "No, it would be a natural succession. You never know whom you're going to get when you go outside. I've seen that happen."

Her sudden change of mind surprised him, and then it didn't surprise him. He hadn't paid attention to Ron Grillo, the sneaky bastard. As he immersed himself in university business, he hadn't paid enough attention to Alyce either, and his self-absorption had allowed problems he hadn't foreseen to fester and then flare.

What was happening on his watch? Was he blind? He knew he couldn't trust Ron Grillo, but had it come to the point where he couldn't trust his own wife?

He wanted to end his presidency with a last hurrah. He could never do that with fund-raising and galas alone— that would only be icing on the cake. The mergers and acquisitions with different institutions hadn't worked out, but there was one remaining that was the best of the bunch—a merger with National Louis University. The president had been involved with a sex scandal and the interim who replaced him was about to retire. *Perfect timing*, David thought. And he went in for the kill. After months of lauding the magnificence of a merger, the economies of scale, the doubling of the student body, the pruning of weak faculty to be replaced by young comers who would help to grapple with the thorny issues of the Chicago public schools, and the creation of the largest private university in the country into a partnership with them—after weeks of negotiating, the trustees of National Louis insisted on retaining their autonomy. David was exhausted and began to realize that a private university was fraught with monetary difficulties that weren't so different from those subsidized by the state and equally hard to overcome in a ten-year term as president, which for him was coming to an end. He had given the university a little more status, a sharper image of itself as a metropolitan university, but the heroic vision he'd once dared imagine was far from realized.

And Alyce? He had been distracted from her during the weeks he was working on the failed merger. Then when he returned, he discovered an altogether different Alyce Parker—someone he had never known because he hadn't been watching.

61

Alyce had been going to Madame Danchin for years. The town house that the fortune teller lived in on the west side of the city was paid for by a loyal following of affluent clients. Alyce had always thought of her visit as a peek into her future, but for all her sophistication, a good part was of her believing in it because a good part always turned out to be true. When she returned from her latest visit, she saw that she had inadvertently left the notes of her supernatural session, collected in a blue folder, on her desk. Later, after returning from dinner with her friend, Bootsie Nathan, she noticed that David had rummaged through them.

"Have you been going through my stuff?"

He was sitting at his own desk at the other end of the apartment, with a pile of papers in disarray before him.

"Just a glimpse—a glimpse into your soul. I couldn't stop myself. It's absolutely fascinating. Do you really believe in that crap?"

"It's no business of yours what I believe in. I've been going to her for years. She's a friend. She comforts me."

"Or distresses you. That's a pretty grim fortune she's given you for the next year."

"Please don't go through my personal papers."

"Of a two-bit fortuneteller? You have to be kidding me. Can't you tell this woman is a fraud?"

"She happens to be a highly intelligent woman."

"With a PhD from where did you say?"

"Not everyone has to have a PhD to be intelligent."

"No, but usually they have to have some sort of credential."

"Please don't pry into my personal belongings, Dave. I mean it. I need a private life."

"Why? The one you have isn't enough?"

"Please respect my feelings."

But he couldn't, he was so disappointed in her. A fortuneteller! A charlatan! "Maybe you should give me her address. Maybe I'll see her myself. I need a glimpse into my future."

"What does that mean?"

"Well, isn't that why you saw her?"

"Maybe so, maybe not. Maybe I saw her to give myself some comfort."

"Oh, give me a break, Alyce. You know it's all bullshit."

"Speak for yourself, Dave. Don't speak for me."

When they parted, he thought of her in the worst possible ways: a beauty who had been indulged all her life and whose dream of a happy, little, bourgeois family had surrendered to a life alone; a good woman who had scratched together a living by catering to wealthy patients in a hospital and at night becoming a Crystal Ball leader who was admired by everyone; and a woman who looked as wealthy as her peers but was really barely scratching together a living. A drifting failure of an alcoholic husband and two screwed-up girls—were all that accidental or did she bear some responsibility for what had happened to them?

That was her life, David brooded. He was so different from her. No, they might not be right for each other in the long term, but she was all that he had in his life now and all he could hold on to. He knew how lucky he was. She was kind and generous and loving, but everything about her now seemed glitter and glamour and superficiality. He knew he was being unfair to her, and he disliked himself for finding her limitations rather than embracing her virtues. She deserved better. He still loved her, warts and all. He kept telling himself he still loved her. Besides, who didn't have limitations? Who was he, of all people, to judge her?

62

Alyce, Julie, and Laura planned a long weekend at an expensive spa in Southern California. The trip was at Julie's suggestion, but Alyce was footing the expensive bill. *It is a good idea*, she thought, *although I can scarcely afford it.* The three days away would be a bonding for the three of them and would provide her with long, uninterrupted time to explain why she had to stay with David. It had worked at difficult times in the past; perhaps it would work again. Before Alyce left, she outlined instructions for David's care and feeding of Duchess.

For him, it was an overwhelming responsibility. The truth was that she didn't entirely trust him alone with the dog. He had grown fond of Duchess, but he was so absorbed in his work that he tended to be neglectful. He might forget to feed her, forget to buy more wee-wee pads and forget to walk her in the park. Faithfully he had taken the puppy to the Water Tower for her weekly bath; he had even enjoyed strolling with her, just to break up his solitude. And at night, he found solace in her sleeping at his feet in his study. While Alyce would be gone, he planned to let her sleep on the bed with him, feeling the warmth of her body at his feet. This puppy was indeed a comfort to him.

At the door of her condo, as the airport taxi drew near, the four of them, including David with Duchess in hand, stood waiting awkwardly with valises by their side. Julie and Laura scrambled into the back seat, waving goodbye to the dog, as he kissed Alyce and murmured, "Love you. Take care of yourself." He then helped her to the passenger's seat beside the driver. Finally, he turned to Julie and Laura, bidding them goodbye and mumbling, "Enjoy, enjoy."

When the cab pulled out of the driveway, he was glad to see them gone. A weight had been lifted from his mind.

All went well for the first two days. He was alone, and he liked to be alone. It gave him a sense of liberation and total freedom, but on Saturday, Duchess developed a stomach ailment that refused to pass. The poor dog was moping and groaning, and by eleven o'clock that evening, he knew he had to get her to a veterinarian. Alyce hadn't left the name or address of anyone—or if she had, he'd misplaced it. By eleven o'clock, he realized he must take Duchess to see a doctor or the pet that he himself had grown so fond of could drop dead. But who would be available now? And where? What place would be open close to midnight on a Saturday night? There were all-night kennels, which of course were closed. He was totally unaware of them. Meanwhile, poor Duchess was groaning and writhing on the floor beside him, unable to eat, unable to defecate, pleading for a cure from her master.

He searched the directory for kennels, but when he called, they were closed for the night. Finally, finally, in desperation, he found some place near North Clark Street but was told by the proprietor that he would be shutting down at midnight. Sharp.

"That's it, my friend. It's been a long day and night for those of us who work for a living. Why didn't you call earlier?"

Why didn't he? That would be the rebuke of Julie and probably Alyce too. Their love for Duchess seemed boundless. Alyce and David had left the dog with Julie whenever they traveled together, and Julie had grown intensely fond of her, as though she were her own. If anything happened to this dependent puppy, he would be the one who had allowed her to die. He would be the guilty one.

In the background of that phone call, other dogs were barking in discontent, and it seemed to him like a cacophonous chorus out of hell.

"Could you stay open until I get there? This dog of mine is really ill, and if I don't get her to a vet tonight, anything might happen."

"The vet's gone home."

"Can't you ask him to return? This is really an emergency. I'll pay—"

"Oh, shit. This means I stay up too. How long will it take you to get here?"

"Fifteen minutes at most."

Which wasn't true. At best, if he knew exactly where the kennel was, it would have been half an hour. But he sped through a city whose byways he hadn't fully mastered, not knowing where he was headed, down dark streets of old neighborhoods and then on to a lonely Clark Street, where shops were shuttered and restaurants closed for the night. Why was he so frightened? Why did he feel so helpless yet responsible? For no reason, he remembered the opening lines of *The Divine Comedy*: "I came to myself, in a dark wood, where the direct way was lost." He thought, *If this fucking dog dies on me, everything will be over. Julie will curse me forever as incompetent and uncaring and totally self-absorbed, and Alyce will never forgive me. She'll accuse me of indifference.* More and more, they seemed to be arguing with each other. Everything suddenly depended on Duchess's survival.

The young Hispanic boy, custodian of the kennel, and the old geezer of a veterinarian were waiting for him when he rushed in, Duchess in arm, ten minutes after twelve. Within moments, the vet gave the puppy a shot of something or other and told David it was a minor disorder. They'd keep the dog overnight; she should sleep now with the medicine and sedative he'd given her. By the next afternoon, she should be okay.

"Return tomorrow afternoon, and you'll have a new puppy."

"You have no idea—"

"They do get to you, don't they? These little puppies?"

By the time David retrieved Duchess, she was prancing in his arms, as though she knew she had been reborn. And all afternoon, they played together, rolling on the floor of his study like a father with his baby girl. When Alyce returned on Tuesday, relaxed from days with her daughters in the California sun, Duchess greeted her at the door, barking with enthusiasm and nuzzling her cheek, exuding more love than any human being could ever want.

63

Alyce attended Thanksgiving dinner every year at the lavish Lake Forest home of Matt's younger brother, Bill Parker. Whereas Matt had burned through his father's inheritance, Bill had squirreled it away cautiously and then invested wisely in stocks and bonds, leaving the lucrative family clothing store in the hands of his sons to manage. In retirement, he was a snowbird, spending winters next to the golf course in Rancho Mirage. As an only child, Alyce had always craved a family, and she found it with the Parkers in long summers at the Cedar Lake compound in Wisconsin, before the violation of Laura, and here in Lake Forest for Thanksgiving and Christmas.

For David, on the contrary, those holidays had always meant exotic getaways. Thanksgiving was just another day off, and Christmas was the time to leave the carols and ornaments and city lights to others and escape with Debra to Jamaica or St. Martin to enjoy the winter sun and mojitos and dinner by the beach. But now, he was an adjunct to the cousins of another family, an overtly happy family. He did not mind the ritual. Bill Parker and his extended family were welcoming and respectful of his position, and the Thanksgiving dinner was pleasant enough. The only one who made him feel unwanted in this family was Julie. Alyce and David picked her up on their way to the Parker mansion. On the drive north, she talked directly to Alyce, but only to Alyce, as though he were a deaf and mute chauffeur hired for the night. Throughout the evening, she continued to try to make him feel like an unwanted intruder, but she was discreet enough not to create a scene with Alyce's adopted family—a group of genial folk who found him interesting, affable, and prestigious, a newcomer who possessed special insight into the colleges and universities that their own children were applying to. For Alyce, he could see, these hearty, upper-middle-class Midwesterners were her only family, beyond her daughters, that she could claim.

As they approached Christmas, the differences between David and Alyce grew more evident. They seemed to live separate lives, except for the times they were together to do fund-raising. He lost himself in work and became fully engaged in the creation of a school of real estate with its own advisory board that promised to take advantage of the booming real estate market in Chicago. She had luncheons and some dinners with her vast group of friends and grew stronger and more independent with each passing day. They were together at functions, and in the public's eye, they still sparkled; but both of them knew that the spark was fading, as perhaps it had to with aging and illness and the realization that they had little in common except for the university.

Breakfast was interrupted by the daily phone call from Julie, who was checking in, checking out, and checking up. At night, with her bedroom door closed, Alyce spoke for an hour with her long-lost Laura, divorced and alone in St. Louis, in a voice so low it seemed to him conspiratorial.

David wondered what he and Alyce would have to say to each other once he retired and they sat face-to-face at the breakfast table. Was theirs, after all was said and done, an institutional marriage?

One day, three weeks after Thanksgiving, he returned from work to find a small Christmas tree in her den.

"What's that all about?" he asked, pointing at it antagonistically, as though it were diseased.

"Oh, I finally decided to have my version of a tree this year."

"What for?"

"It's what I've always had, all my life. A small tree—a token of the season. I knew you'd be upset, so I haven't bothered with one until this Christmas, and even now, as you can see, the tree is small. It won't bother you, and it'll stay in my own office. But I feel the need for some reason. Julie and I picked this out today. Isn't it pretty?"

"And what exactly are we celebrating?"

"The Christmas spirit."

"Which is?"

"The holidays. New Year's. An expression of gratitude for what we have."

"Which has nothing to do with religion?"

"Nothing."

"I don't get it," he bore in meanly. "How can you divorce religion from the holidays? This is a Christian holiday—celebrating the birth of Jesus, the Virgin Mary, Joseph, and all the rest of that crap . . . that mythological crap."

"Stop trying to spoil the holidays for me."

"I don't understand you. I really don't understand you. You're a U of C graduate, an English major to boot, a supposedly sophisticated lady, and you still believe in fortunetellers and Christmas trees. What exactly are you searching for?"

"Peace, harmony, community, belief. Right now, I'm searching for a happy marriage."

"Oh," he surrendered. "What a lot of horseshit. I give up."

He left her for his own study in their large condo that once had been two units, separated now by a door that led to his office, a bedroom, and a bathroom—his private quarters.

64

Why did he suddenly care about myths he had so long ago forsaken? Born to parents who were the children of immigrants out of the lower east side of Manhattan, he had studied Hebrew with his father from a large red book at the kitchen table and absorbed virtually nothing. He knew he was a Jew among Italian and Irish Catholics in East Flatbush, Brooklyn, during the thirties and forties, but he had experienced little anti-Semitism, mostly because he'd played touchball and stickball and punchball so well. There were the high holy days and Passover and Purim, and he accepted them blindly, without question, until he was an adolescent and the words in that graying prayer book began to seem meaningless to him. *All this adulation*, he wondered, *for an unresponsive God? A wrathful God.* But the greatest influence on his growing agnosticism and ultimate atheism, before he was able to think for himself about these weighty matters, was his older brother, Mark. He remembered that when his father died of angina pectoris and diabetes, his age was sixty-three. Mark flew in from CERN in Switzerland, where he was spending the year as a research associate. It was four o'clock in the morning when his father died and Mark was standing beside David in his former bedroom in the walkup on Parkside Avenue in Flatbush, gazing up at silent stars. His brother, only four years older but so far ahead of him academically and intellectually, put his arm around David's shoulders and told him, "See those stars? They're only stars, Davey, only stars."

From that moment until now, religion was no more than a collection of fairy tales or fables—some good, some bad, some half-believable, and some preposterous. He could never understand the blind worship of God. So why was he so disturbed by Alyce's need to celebrate, even modestly, a Christian tradition? What did he really care? Was his anger simply directed at a growing dissatisfaction with what he considered her superficiality?

It was all so meaningless. Didn't she realize that? Life was accidental you could die at any moment by a freak accident. You had to create meaning, as Camus once taught him, out of a meaningless universe; you had to create your own morality in a world so seductive to immorality.

He lay in bed beside Alyce and thought of retirement. He had been president for eight years and was tired of the endless cycle of meetings and constant fund-raising, of catering to faculty and donors alike, of dinners with the wealthy rather than with friends, and of racing from one event to another and never finding the time to read or think or write or take time for pleasures other than the narrowly professional. He had guided the university through one successful capital campaign and created a second campus and academic programs that would thrive long after he retired. He had strengthened the university, making it a better institution than it was when he inherited it. What more could one ask for in a career? *Basta!*

Yes, what would you do with your life when you knew your dreams wouldn't come true? As he watched Alyce sleeping contentedly beside him, he wrestled with his discontents.

Lately, he had been turning all her virtues and charming eccentricities into vices and indulgences. Now they came together in a cluster, as if he saw her true character for the first time. Little things began to irritate him: the personal shopper at Saks seemed excessive; the home massage was a frivolity; and the daily exercises, her futile battle against aging was neurotic.

More things became grievances, large and small, to him—the plastic Christmas tree; the fortune teller whom she really believed; the aging country club friends; the young disciples who worshipped her and made him feel like an appendage to a queen; the plastic surgery years ago that had converted her pretty face into a beautiful face; and most irritating of all, her need to represent herself as wealthy when she wasn't financially independent.

What was once so enticing was now irritating. It had not been so with Debra. She would never expect or want these indulgences. Theirs was not an institutional marriage; theirs had been a deep love affair. All Debra ever wanted that she couldn't have were children of their own. He remembered all the times they had lamented this void in their lives, and as always, he cursed himself for not being able to persuade her to adopt.

Alyce turned in the bed, and as if tracking his misgivings of her, she reached out to touch his arm, assuring him that everything would turn out all right once she was truly strong again. She would become whatever he wanted her to be.

He clasped her hand and kissed it. A smile crossed her lips, and before they could speak, she fell back to sleep.

She is a good woman, he thought. *She's always been a good woman despite these petty indulgences. Who doesn't have indulgences of his own? Certainly not me. No, it's I who have changed. I always had all the ambition in the world, but when I became a president, that ambition was gratified by status, power, prestige, and moderate wealth. I've loved it all—all the perks. It was I who chased Alyce Parker. She didn't set out to snare me. Now we face retirement and will have to adjust to each other. The key is to assuage her daughters and create a new family so that Alyce is never forced into making a choice.*

He reached for her hand and kissed it and watched the smile return to her beautiful face. Yes, her face had once again become agelessly beautiful.

All that had remained from the accident were occasional stabs of pain where the bone had broken—osteoporosis too. He could see her grimace at times, but she was a stoic and rarely complained. She was intent on returning their lives to where they were when they were happiest. But even so, he asked himself as he gazed on her contented smile, *Can she adjust to his form of retirement when the music becomes no more than a memory?*

It was a troubling concern that faded quickly in the morning when Alyce came to him with the news about Laura's crisis.

65

"Mom, I've been having these blinding headaches for weeks now, hiccups, and absolute fatigue. I never had them before. I've never been sick. I've never allowed myself to be sick. I used to be able to go through nights without sleep and too many drugs and too much alcohol and too much coke and still feel fresh and ready for a day of work."

"Well, you're not a kid anymore. Have you seen a doctor?"

"He thinks that it might be the flu, but he's not sure."

Her previous doctor had marked her file with the possibility of kidney issues, but for years, she had been careless about annual checkups, and now the doctor was living elsewhere. She had always been as thin as a matchstick, but she had indeed been free of any illness despite the orgies in Southern California that she had shared with her husband—an emerging, gifted cinematographer.

Her primary physician took her blood pressure and was amazed how high it was. "It's a wonder you haven't had a stroke," he scolded her, "or a heart attack." He then sent her to a nephrologist, who told her in no uncertain terms that she had rapidly developing kidney failure, that she had been extremely neglectful, and that she would need to be put on peritoneal dialysis four times a week.

Alyce, distraught and frightened, drove with Julie to St. Louis to be with her. As always, Laura brushed off the gravity of the illness. She didn't want her mother or sister to worry excessively; she was strong and self-reliant now, free of drugs and alcohol and fully employed as the head designer of Plunkett Furniture in St. Louis. However, Alyce brought her back to Chicago to recuperate.

Beneath her bravado, Laura was a frightened kitten. For days, she sat in the dark den of the condo, surrounded by handsome, unread Book of the Month Club selections, and worked on crossword puzzles—the harder, the better. "She is too headstrong for her own good," Alyce told David. "She's always been wild, unpredictable, rebellious, risk-taking, and lovable.

"What," she begged him for an answer, "oh god, what have I done wrong that screwed her up so much? How did I fail as a mother?"

"You haven't failed," he tried to console her. "You're not responsible for your children's behavior. When in God's good name do American children ever grow up?"

66

In the middle of the night, David groped his way to the kitchen for a drink of water. Laura was sitting in a corner of the dimly lit den, working assiduously on *The New York Times* Sunday crossword puzzle, the hardest of them all. From the time he'd met Alyce, he had wanted to find a way to connect with this younger daughter, but Laura was in her own way as inaccessible as Julie, and there never seemed to be the right moment.

He approached the dark den and sat opposite her. She was dressed in her mother's pajamas and robe. He was scarcely able to make out the contours of her face; she seemed so thin, a wisp of a woman who at fifty-four could have been no more than thirty—until you came closer and saw those eyes that fixed themselves upon you, with the sad expression of someone who had lived hard.

"Can't sleep? Is there anything I can get you? Water? Tea?"

"No, I'm okay."

A long silence hovered between them. They scarcely knew each other. As she sat there placidly, she was keeping her eyes fixed on the puzzle.

"It must be a constant pain—this dialysis."

"No problem. No problem at all. I'm okay. I'm going to be okay."

"You are a trouper, Laura."

"I try, don't I? I do try."

There was another extended silence. As he looked at her in the dimly lit den, he wondered who this self-destructive woman was. She had gone through a lot—a molestation at the age of eight; a rebellious, turbulent adolescence of drugs and promiscuity; a dropout from college followed by more drugs and more sex and a baby given up to adoption; a marriage to a man her parents deplored who brought her to Hollywood in the wild seventies and rose professionally as she became more dependent on cocaine, then crack cocaine, and God knows what else; divorce; the return to Winnetka to live with Julie until they quarreled endlessly and Julie told her to find a job or just move out of the house she had worked so hard to buy; Plunkett's as a first-rate, creative store designer; and now stone cold sober, living alone in St. Louis and finally supporting herself but suffering from kidney failure, taking dialysis, and hoping her illness would be cured and that there would be a second chance at life.

The dialysis did work, and Laura returned to St. Louis. Her condition improved, or so it seemed, so long as she continued to administer dialysis faithfully at home every day.

67

"Come, David. I want to take you to a place I visit once a week."

"Another one of your secrets?"

"This is far more important and serious than Madame Danchin or anything else you may have discovered about my private life."

She took him to a coffee shop that sold gelato. A gang of raucous, carefree boys from the Latin school nearby was crowded in a booth across the room from them. This was clearly a daily ritual for them.

"See that short, thin boy at the center of all of them? The handsome one with the curly hair? The one that stands out?"

'What about him?"

"That's my grandson."

"Laura's baby?"

"Snatched from me before I could stop Laura from letting him be adopted. I promised her that I would take care of him until she was able to, but she wouldn't listen. It took months for me to find the agency that had adopted him. But I wouldn't be put down. In the long run, the boy has probably been better off. They found well-to-do parents who could send him to a Montessori elementary school and camp each summer and now the Latin school. He's probably on his way to the Ivy League. He has a better life than we could ever have given him."

"You don't know. Outer trappings can be deceiving."

"Not these. Doesn't he look like a happy youngster?"

Before David could look, the boys had risen and were scampering out of the coffee shop. Her grandson paused for a moment before their booth and exchanged a knowing smile at Alyce. She lifted her hand and was about to respond, but he raced out at the call of his friends.

The encounter affected David more deeply than any of the descriptions Alyce had recounted of her shattered family. He knew how much she cherished children. At visits to other families, she would always participate in the games the young ones were playing. As he'd watched her fix her eyes on her teenage grandson, he could sense her heartbreak at the loss of the boy who could have brought her so much joy.

For David, the days between Thanksgiving and Christmas were fraught with the dissatisfaction of a nonbeliever. Christmas suffocated him more than ever with its commercialized glitter. Carols rang out in suffocating Muzak everywhere across the tinsel, fantasy air of Chicago.

The shop windows along Michigan Avenue glistened with manufactured joy, and inside the emporia were crowds of people who seemed to possess everything they needed. They seemed unbearably happy. Alyce made cookies for the entire development office at the university and for the staff in their condo building. On and on, it went—a constant drumbeat of heightened happiness. She loved it all. David was indifferent, at best. The most irritating of all to him was Julie's constant presence in his home and Alyce's hushed phone calls from their bedroom, which was closed to him until it was time to sleep. Paranoia ran through him like a chill. He felt that the three women were somehow conspiring against him.

His claustrophobic feelings culminated with Christmas dinner when Julie brought in all her holiday CD's and played them back to back, finding perverse pleasure in knowing they would displease him. Laura sat benignly quiet, simply grateful to be healthy for the time being and alive. After an early dinner of ham and sweet potatoes and apple crisp that Julie had made, although there was no ice cream. Vanilla ice cream was absolutely essential for a topping on the crisp, she claimed, and David volunteered to scurry off to Treasure Island, which never closed, to secure Breyer's ice cream that was fat-free. It had to be fat-free.

Alyce, Julie, and Laura prepared this feast all day, chattering while he remained in his study and imagining the highlights of yesteryears. The event closed in on him, and he felt like an outsider in his own home. So intense did his isolated mood become, in fact, he had to excuse himself to take a walk in the December air and save himself from screaming in protest at the way they were excluding him from their tight circle. It was bitter cold along Astor Street, and he had dressed in only a windbreaker. Townhouses glowed with Christmas lights, and the fact that all the good cheer was within doors, celebrated by ostensibly happy families everywhere. The cardinal's estate across the street was so secure and eternal, so certain of itself. All these observations made him feel only lonelier.

All he could think of as he returned home against the bitter Chicago wind with a quart of Breyer's fat-free vanilla ice cream in hand was what he might be able to do to save a marriage that he could feel was slipping away from his grasp, not only because of the daughters but because of Alyce's obvious enjoyment of their shared memories: the extravagant Safari venture; Matt with his triumph in slaying the lion whose head was still high on the wall in her office; Julie's piano recital in elementary school; Laura's high school performance in *The Glass Menagerie*; youthful boyfriends and girlfriends whose names were foreign to him; and the summer Laura almost drowned in Cedar Lake except for Julie's swimming after her and screaming, "Keep your head above water, Laura. I'm coming. I'm coming!" Not only did these memories make him feel alienated, but they underscored all the ways in which he and Alyce were obviously so different—her need to see a fortune teller; the miniature Christmas tree, which was a mere gesture to the season; the country club couples he'd never known before his presidency; her new role as guru to young aspiring Alyce Parkers; their differences in age, widening now as she was definitely old; and more than anything else, Julie and Laura, who were standing between Alyce and him.

As it turned out, the dreaded dialysis was a temporary measure. It did not cure Laura's kidney failure or even stabilize it. A transplant was necessary, and the national waiting list was long, too long. Laura might die while waiting for a replacement. Alyce called everyone she knew and was finally successful when former colleagues at Michael Reese Hospital were able to manipulate the system and move Laura ahead of others. David observed his wife press forward with a tenacity that could not be stopped and admired her persistence. She was a problem solver with an iron will, and nothing would defeat her once she was resolved. A few months later, Laura had a transplant that worked immediately, and she seemed to be restored to full health.

It was a miracle he witnessed, and all of it was due to Alyce. She was indeed a force of nature.

When they weren't looking, when all seemed to be falling into a pattern of galas and university events, when Julie found a job as a surgical nurse and was less present in their lives, when Laura was fully recovered and developed low-key camaraderie with a group of women friends in St. Louis, when David and Alyce were alone together to enjoy the theater and symphony and opera and special events throughout the city where they always met friends, when the great question of the day was what restaurant they should dine in that night or during the weekend or where they should go on vacation, when they were living in suspended happiness, not thinking quite yet of retirement, trying not to surrender to aging, when all seemed right with their world, Alyce was told by the doctors that she had to return to the hospital for a second surgery because her bones were not knitting back adequately.

The three-week wait for a hospital bed was the most agonizing period of their marriage. Julie quit her job and spent time with Alyce during the day. Laura called every night, and David grew increasingly suspicious of how they might be condemning him behind his back. Accustomed to being in charge, he felt controlled, yet he wanted to be a good husband. He wanted to care for his wife as he had cared for Debra; he wanted to be kind and solicitous and tender and whatever else a loving husband should be. Instead, he found himself feeling powerless. Why? Not only because of the daughters hovering over his wife, but perhaps more fundamentally because of his own inability to act forcefully, to behave selflessly, and to come outside of himself and surrender completely to someone who deserved his unconditional love.

On Saturdays, she visited Julie, and late in the evenings she phoned Laura when he was either in his study or asleep. She kept her daughters from him as best she could so that he was forced to be with them only on special occasions. But she couldn't control the irrepressible Julie, who reached her every morning and evening in phone calls that always ended with some querulous admonition, warning Alyce that she shouldn't be running herself ragged. Every conversation finished in an argument until Alyce finally hung up in frustration. But Julie wouldn't be cowed. She followed up immediately with another call that inevitably began with annoyance at her mother for not letting her finish what she was saying during the long telephone conversation, that it was terribly important, and that Alyce had a lot of nerve to cut her off abruptly.

68

Alyce returned to Northwestern Hospital for a second surgery. Her bones were not growing back normally, and she needed a hip joint grafted to the remaining bone with some kind of a rod that ran down her entire thigh. The operation itself was successful, but the day afterward, she had a heart attack that required a stent. She remained jocular throughout the procedure, and after recovery from anesthesia, she again was the good, bright, chipper patient who had no intention of dying that morning or any morning soon. Julie and Laura stood at one side of the bed and David at the other. Each of them was worried as Alyce made light of her condition.

"Will I make it?" She smiled at her old friend, Dr. Eddie Newman.

"You're going to live. You're going to outlast your mother. How old was she when she rolled over and decided to die? One hundred six? You'll outlive her, but you are going to have to be in this lovely room for the next few weeks. There may be complications from the procedure, and we need to keep you on oxygen while we monitor your recovery."

"I ask because if I'm not going to make it, I just want all of you to know that I've had one hell of a time in this life of mine."

"Stop talking nonsense, Mother," Julie scolded. "Of course, you're going to live. What would we do without you?"

"Not argue?"

Her words hung in the air like an accusation, encapsulating the tension between her two daughters and husband that might, each of them knew, have contributed to her heart attack. David took her right hand, limp and cold as it was, and tried to warm it with his own. She scarcely responded and then told him that he ought to go to the university. Everyone would need him there. She was well cared for here.

"I'll be all right, Dave. The girls are taking shifts to stay with me each day and night."

A nurse arrived with three huge pills in hand that made Alyce cringe like a child.

"Oh no," she protested. "I could never get those monsters down. Do you know that I've never taken any pills in my life?"

"It's your choice," Eddie Newman ordered her. "Take those goddamn pills and recover, or don't take them and you'll never leave this hospital alive."

She swallowed hard several times. Within minutes, color returned to her face, and she turned once again to David.

"Go on, dear one. You have important work to do. I'll be all right. I'm exhausted now and just need rest. I don't want to be a drag on you. Besides, the girls will be here. The girls will be here to care of me."

She wanted no difficulties among them; she knew that her daughters would be furious and guilt-ridden if they were denied the opportunity to care for her. She had to assume that David would tolerate and acknowledge her daughters for the sake of her well-being.

"I'm a very sick girl, Dave. I'm eighty-two years old with a heart attack and broken bones. Please understand. I can't have anymore stress in my life. I just can't."

"I don't want to add to your stress, Alyce. I just want to be helpful, supportive, and caring."

"You are, sweetheart, just by being here, and if you just follow my instinct, you will be. I know this is hard for you, but just be patient. We'll have each other afterward for the rest of our lives."

69

David's instinct was to tell those two daughters to go to hell; he was perfectly capable of caring for Alyce alone. He was the husband, he was paying the bills, and he would be with her for the rest of their lives.

After he called her that night and she'd cleared the room, he repeated that he would do anything for her.

"One thing for now. Let my girls feel needed. Let them stay with me. Let's not argue, Dave. My life depends on it."

He had always been in control of decisions and a master at reconciliation of warring parties, and he had always somehow triumphed. But that was business; this was personal. Now he felt not only powerless, but inept and incompetent.

70

Julie and Laura took turns sleeping overnight in Alyce's hospital room. David came early in the morning and left just before curfew at night, but he felt like a visitor rather than a husband, an intruder instead of a man assuming responsibility for his wife. He wondered as to what extent it was his fault, his inability to take charge and his hesitancy at demanding that this was his wife, dammit, the woman he must be caring for in every way, the person he would be living alone with afterward when everybody else was gone, the injured figure he still loved and wanted to continue loving. Her daughters tolerated his presence, but it wasn't until he returned home and Alyce called him late at night so that the two of them could speak privately.

"This will be over soon," she assured him, "and we'll have our lives back, better than ever."

He hesitated.

"They will be better than ever," she repeated, as if trying to convince herself. "David? My David? Are you listening?"

"I hope so, Alyce. I really hope so."

"You don't believe that?"

"I want to believe it. I want it to be so."

"We have to make it so. I just need to regain my strength—to be more like my old self. I'm sorry. It's been all my fault, I realize. I've put you in an impossible situation. I haven't been tough enough with Julie. I can't let her destroy what I've always wanted all my life."

They went on reassuring each other, but when they said good night and wished each other a restful sleep, there was uncertainty in their voices.

As she tried to sleep, she stared at David, closing her eyes while Julie watched her from her corner armchair and imagining a life without him: dinner at home alone, watching TV alone, a nondescript executive escort at a dance, and the persistent, silent fear that she'd fall again and have to be hospitalized once more. In her eighties, with a cane or worse, Laura was withering away, and Julie was dominating her life, even suggesting that they live together now that David was gone. David gone? No. She wasn't letting that happen, but she sensed that it might have begun to happen already. She felt like a woman out of control of her own life.

71

"I have a plan," he told Alyce on the phone after he'd left her alone with Julie in the hospital room.

"Oh?"

"It's called the Julie Solution."

"Not now, Dave. I'm real too tired and weak for serious subjects. Call me in the morning."

"She's with you?"

"You've got it."

Oh christ, he thought. *Are you ever alone? Are you ever free from her—waiting for me?*

"Call in the morning, dear one."

There was such desperation in her voice that he didn't allow himself to be angry. She was frail, and he knew that one heart attack could easily trigger another.

"Try to stay calm," he said. "I know it's hard, but try. Call me in the morning. Call me when you're alone, before she comes in tomorrow."

She called, and after morning greetings and apologies for the night before, she was ready to discuss his "Julie Solution."

"Sounds like you're ready to send her off to an extermination camp. Is that the final solution?"

"No, not at all."

"Then let me guess. The solution is that she's gaining a father, not losing a mother. Is that the gist of it?"

"Something like that. Don't laugh. Don't brush it off. Just listen to me for a moment."

Julie would be welcome to come after he left each morning and before he returned for dinner. She could have all day if she wanted to be with Alyce, but there would be no more preparations for dinners together and cleanup afterward and lingering until eight o'clock every night. He knew it would be hard, and Julie would probably protest like hell. However, in the end, having no choice, she'd have to accept their decision. No ambiguity on their part for *they* were the married couple—no doubt, no guilt, and no wavering. They must have time alone. That wasn't asking too much, was it?

Alyce chuckled and then apologized immediately afterward for not seeming to take him seriously. "I'm sorry, Dave. But you're like Don Quixote tilting at his windmill. It won't work. I just know it won't work."

"Of course it'll work, if we're in it together."

"You're a sweetheart for trying, but you don't know my daughter."

"Oh, I think I know her by now—too well. It's worth trying. We can't go on this way, Alyce. I won't go on. You have to speak to her today. You're coming home in just three days, and she's already making all kinds of arrangements to be in the house all day and night. We can't go back to the way it was. She can't control our lives."

Alyce agreed. She knew the time had come to make a fundamental choice. Reluctantly she murmured, "Just be gentle when you speak to her."

"No. This can't come from me, and it can't come from us together—not at first. She has to know that *you* mean it."

"I'm not sure I have the energy to do this, Dave. I scarcely have the energy to breathe."

"You have more spunk than you realize. And I'll be here to support you, if anything goes awry. I'll talk with her then, alone or with you, and we'll make whatever accommodations seem necessary."

"You're right," she agreed reluctantly, frightened at what she knew would be the outcome. She didn't want any more conflict. She wanted to live free of stress. "The time has come."

72

At the door, Julie stood, smirking. Had she overheard this plot against her? Was she outside the door, listening and ready to retaliate? Alyce and David hung up quickly like guilty spies caught unaware in an act of intrigue. But Julie was in good humor. She had taken care of everything: buying a wheelchair and soft coverlet and a pretty dress for leaving the hospital and crutches and a cane, just in case Alyce ever needed one. She and Laura planned on preparing a lavish luncheon as her welcome home. She was bursting with ideas of how they'd make her recovery as easy as possible, but in the middle of one of her effervescent monologues, Alyce stopped her in midsentence.

"Hold on, Julie."

"What's wrong? Doesn't that all sound great?"

"Of course, it does. And thoughtful of you. But it's all beyond anything that's necessary. David and I have been talking about how we'd like to live when I'm released from this prison."

"Oh?"

"Sit down, please, Julie, and listen to me—and don't overreact."

"I don't need to sit. I think I know what's coming."

"Listen to me. For once, please listen to me. We have a marriage that I want to protect. I want you to know that. I love David very much, and I don't want him to leave me because of some petty squabble that I know we can resolve—if only you'll try."

"Me? Try?" Her entire body tightened. "Are you telling me that I haven't tried? What about him? What more does he want from me?"

"I'm not speaking for David. I'm speaking for myself."

"I'll bet you are."

"We need guidelines until things get resolved. I am not going to subject myself to anymore stress, Julie. You must know that."

As she presented David's solution, Alyce could see Julie grow stiff with fear and anger and resistance. She knew her daughter well enough to know that there was an explosion on the way.

"You're telling me I'm not to come until he's left for the day and not to prepare dinner or eat with you or clean up for you? You're telling me I shouldn't worry about your medications? Are you basically telling me that I'm not welcome in your home?"

"I didn't say that, Julie."

"Well, it sure sounds that way. Who's going to care for you? *Him?* Give me a break. Who's going to cook for you?

Him? He can't cook. I'm the only one who can take care of you."

By now, she was beyond control.

"Julie, please stop. I feel too weak to fight with you. I haven't the strength. And you're too wrought up to be rational."

"Oh, screw both of you. You're the ones who won't listen to reason. You want him? You can have him."

And before Alyce could respond, Julie burst out from the room in panic. She called the nurse and told her to have someone find her daughter before she left for the parking garage. She should not be behind the wheel of a car in her state of mind. But Julie had already fled the hospital and the garage as well. She was out there somewhere on the expressway, panic-stricken.

Alyce called David.

"Stay calm," he warned her, trying to remain calm himself. "I'll track her down. I'll find her. I'll speak to her."

"You must, David. You don't know my girl. She's so stubborn and single-minded. You have no idea of what she's capable of. You just don't know her. Once—"

"I'll find her and speak to her. I'll settle her down. Just take care of yourself."

After he left, Alyce realized how dependent she was on him, how much he loved her, and how he was trying to keep them together. He had shed whatever narcissism he might have had once and now was hers.

73

He tried to reach her all morning, but the only voice he heard was an answering service: "This is Julie Parker. I'm not available now. Please leave your number, and I'll get back to you as soon as I can."

He continued to try but to no avail, and his frustration with her only grew. Finally, at twelve o'clock, she decided to answer.

"Julie—"

She hung up.

He tried again. When she picked up the phone, he spoke quickly. "Julie, we need to speak as soon as possible."

Silence, protracted silence.

"Will you meet me for lunch at Betsy and Frank? At one o'clock?"

After another long silence, she muttered, "What for?"

"I can't say what I want to say on the phone. I need to see you. This is much too important to both of us. Betsy and Frank? One o'clock? Can you meet me there?"

"This is a waste of your time."

"Can you see me?"

"Oh shit, if you say so. I'll be there."

She was in her usual uniform when he arrived: a green sweatshirt with Miami University emblazoned on it, blue jeans worn at the knees with the fabric torn a little, and tired sneakers. She was short and plump, on the verge of being obese, and she was looking as though she hadn't had a full-night sleep for a long time.

"What Alyce and I are asking for is simply a little time alone."

He waited for a response, a counterargument, shouting, screaming, and anything, but she simply glared at him with disdain so that he fell inarticulate before her morbid silence. Her body stiffened, suppressing the fury and resentment that lodged like poison within her.

"Especially at night."

"And who's going to take care of her?"

"I will."

"To buy her medicines? To cook? To care for her at night?"

"I'll come home early. She's done enough for me in our time together."

"You bet she has. And what's she got in return? A tennis accident that's left her with broken bones and a heart attack."

Fuck you, you bitch, he thought. *I've had it. Why am I sitting here kissing your ass? Why should I be the victim of your neuroses?*

Julie glowered at him; her entire body was trembling with tears. He watched her rise and flee the restaurant before he had time to compose himself.

74

Alyce was relieved to know that Julie was safe and that she could now try to reason with her. In long conversations, she assured both daughters that once she was on her way to full recovery, everything would return to the way it was. Having no choice, they acceded. It was clear that this was the way Alyce herself wanted her life to be. At the same time, she prevailed upon David to let them help take her from the hospital and make the lavish luncheon they had planned for her homecoming. It was important that they not break ties irrevocably.

"Of course," he agreed. "I'm in no position to keep them from you. I don't want to. I don't want you to feel you have to make a choice."

That was disingenuous. She had already made her choice. She wanted this marriage to last for the rest of her life. Without David, there would be no joy, just the prospect of becoming an aging matriarch who was tended to by two overzealous daughters.

75

When David wheeled Alyce into their condo, Julia and Laura were at each side of the wheelchair. The sun blazed through the window, with a view of the lake: schooners and sailboats moving lazily along still waters, a clear blue sky, and a friendly sun. To the south and west, the towers of the city she loved so much loomed large and powerful.

Their home was immaculate. David had made certain to have the cleaning woman come the day before so that it would be immaculate.

"Oh, David, what a beautiful apartment this is! I'll buy it."

"You won't have to buy it. You own it."

Within moments, Julie and Laura were fussing in the kitchen and dining room, putting together the feast they had prepared. Like guests in their own home, David and Alyce waited patiently and generously in the den and let them feel useful.

"Thanks for putting up with your aging invalid of a wife."

"You don't look aged to me."

But he was only trying to assuage her. She knew that she had grayed in the hospital and that she was thin and frail and withered—her porcelain skin was now without the shine it once wore. She was an old woman now. Old—what an ugly word. She was now trapped in a wheelchair and in need of crutches and, probably, forever a cane. Would he love her as he had when she was queen of the Crystal Ball? What did she offer him now that she was no longer beautiful?

In an almost inaudible voice, she murmured to him, "Today will be over soon. Tonight and tomorrow and the day after, our lives will be our own—our very own."

Julie was at the entrance to the den, beaming. "Luncheon is being served in the main dining room."

Julie and Laura chattered on, recalling memories that he had no way of sharing: the quiet evenings at Cedar Lake and the house on the hill when Laura was a toddler and stumbled toward her mother in the large backyard with a single tulip in her hand and uttered her first word "Flowah."

Alyce tried to draw David into the conversation, but he told her not to be concerned. He found these stories fascinating.

"I'll bet you do." She smiled. "I was just wondering, how are things at the university?"

"You don't want to know. They're terribly boring."

"That's impossible." She took his hand in hers. "A university is never boring."

He glanced at Julie and Laura, as if to indicate that he had no intention of marring their nostalgia. "I think it best that I save my own war stories for another time."

The four of them sat there awkwardly until Julie rose with delight and served a strawberry tart for dessert. Then more remembrances of things past and chatter and clean up afterward as David wheeled Alyce back to the den.

"I think I ought to return to the university and leave the rest of the day to the three of you."

"Dave, you don't have to do this."

"It's best this way. Trust me."

76

She did, and after he was gone, she spent the afternoon with her girls, listening to their selective remembrances: Julie being cheerleader in her senior year at high school; Laura with a mini-exhibition of her water colors; Alyce playing Chopin at a family gathering; the dogs, one after the other, in the evening having eaten a packet of ex-lax that Alyce inadvertently left on the kitchen table and defecated on the living room carpet when they returned; and their high school graduations, the last times they were together as a family where everyone dressed to the nines and everyone was happy. It was a picture postcard of a happy family.

Julie and Laura insisted on making dinner for them. Alyce acquiesced, having no energy to object. She just wanted peace and quiet and the time to recover and be a loving wife to David and a devoted mother to Julie and Laura. Was that asking too much? Peace and quiet until she recovered? She shooed the girls off before David returned, kissing them goodbye, thanking them for everything, and repeating that they were indispensable to her.

After they'd left, she slipped into the deepest, darkest sleep marked by doubt. *I can't lose David,* she vowed to herself. *It took me a lifetime to find him, and I can't lose him now. I want to live my dying days with him. I want him to be as he was that night at the Café des Artistes in Puerto Vallarta—buoyant and charming and witty and young and handsome among those moonlit thick trees, admiring her along with all the others in the restaurant and being awed by her beauty while listening to the pianist on the ground floor play the song she had requested: "There's someone I'm longing to see / someone to watch over me."*

Why oh why couldn't the kids keep an open mind and see him as I do? Since the tennis accident, he had been so attentive and gentle and loving, caring less about the university and more about her and bringing home desserts, flowers, and whatever would please her. Why was he such a threat to them? Why did it have to be either/or?

Tears welled into her eyes, but then she surrendered to a sleep that had no dreams. When she awoke an hour later, David was sitting on the bed beside her, kissing her cheek. He had clearly been studying her for some time.

"How's my girl?"

"Your girl is feeling stronger. She's rested up for you. Julie and Laura left dinner, Dave—"

"Don't worry."

"It's their last gesture until we send them a signal otherwise. Tomorrow and thereafter, we're on our own. Hold me. Hold me tight."

For that moment, they did believe that they were one again.

77

The days and nights ahead fell into a pattern. Julie was almost true to their agreement. She came to the condo in midmorning and left before David returned from the university, but inevitably she would call at nine o'clock to see how Alyce was feeling, to check in on what her dinner had been like, and to ask if she should pick up any medications or might be helpful in any way possible before she came the next morning.

When Alyce returned from the bedroom, where she always took the phone calls, David ignored the interruptions, and they settled into evenings of watching sitcoms together. They were predicated on Alice's conviction that laughter was a form of therapy. Sitting there side by side on the sofa, he tolerated the programs but feared they could be a forecast of vapid retirement—no more projects to fret about and no more travels to anticipate, just silly sitcoms to lighten the burden of whatever aging might bring.

Alyce had the regimen of a Trojan during her convalescence. On Mondays, the German physical therapist arrived for a two-hour session; on Tuesdays came the Irish masseuse to give her a thorough massage; and Thursdays brought the Jewish therapist, whom she had seen during many dark days in the past. They worked through her lingering depression. Each morning, she did as many sit-ups and push-ups as she could tolerate. Each afternoon, there was an hour's nap, and when she awoke, she dressed for David, who came home with prepared food for their dinner and the news of his busy day. Afterward, he maneuvered her in the wheelchair through nearby Lincoln Park before the sun set behind the city towers to the west and sat contentedly beside her on a bench.

"You're quite a trouper, Alyce," he said in admiration, "a real fighter. No, no, it's true. It's absolutely true. I've never seen anyone quite like you. Nothing can keep you down." Gently he took her hand in his and kissed it.

"I need to be up and doing," she explained. "It's in my nature. I'm going to slay this dragon if it's the last thing I do. I plan on holding meetings of my gala committee at home, if that's all right—the gala committee of the Chicago Board, to plan for the Cosby extravaganza. It'll lift my spirits more than any medicine might do, Dave. Ramsay Lewis has agreed to be my cochair. He's the one who got Bill Cosby to come again—free of charge. Cosby had promised him. But that will happen only if we can attract a thousand people and raise a million dollars."

"Good god, you're incredible." He kissed her hand again and then her cheek and finally her lips. "You're a force of nature."

"The most important thing in the end is that I'm *your* force nature."

78

Each of the following weeks, the gala committee of the Chicago Board met in their dining room to enjoy a working luncheon, prepared and served by a caterer. By now, the board included CEOs and vice presidents and was more impressive than those who were university trustees. They all pledged tables for the gala and took responsibility for identifying friends who would follow suit. Alyce created the mood of a fun-filled, exuberant time together that also served a worthy cause—scholarships for gifted artists in the Chicago Musical College.

Ron Grillo joined them as their direct connection to the university itself. But Alyce knew that his motives for being there weren't entirely pure. With so little staff, he could raise only ordinary amounts of money; it was Alyce who was the breadwinner, and the galas had proved that year after year. Ron wanted to be seen as more than just part of the action. He needed to be its hero.

She knew Grillo had a more personal motive in needing to push his way into the center of plans for this gala. Once David announced his intention to retire, Grillo sought the guidance of several trustees as to the wisdom of becoming a presidential candidate. Now he wanted to gain the support of the Chicago Board, many of whom could become members of his own board of trustees. When Alyce alerted David to his machinations, he mocked Grillo's blatant opportunism. "He won't become the next president. The trustees will conduct a national search, and trust me, Ron won't be among the finalists."

Still Ron Grillo tried. At a meeting of the Cosby committee, he recommended that the gala be dedicated to Alyce and that a note should be sent by him to all the key players in Chicago. The board members thought it was a fabulous idea and agreed that he would have an incredible response. "The whole city will want to come now." Ramsay Lewis laughed. "We won't have room for everybody."

After the caterers had left, Grillo lingered with Alyce in the den.

"I want you to know one thing, Alyce. Whatever happens, you'll always have a job in development—at least so long as I'm in charge."

She listened to him, and though she did not entirely trust him, she was flattered.

"You're kind. It was thoughtful of you to suggest dedicating the gala to me."

"It's the least we can do. I want to write a tribute and show it to you before we mail it out."

Moments later, they stood at the door, and he kissed her goodbye on the cheek. For a passing moment, she sensed that the kiss was more than just a kiss—it was the hint of an invitation to sex. As he entered the elevator, he smiled and said, "It was a good meeting, Alyce. Everything you touch is charmed. This is going to be one helluva gala."

When he was gone, she went to the bedroom to nap. A warm sense of gratitude radiated her entire being and she thought, *I haven't felt this good since my first accident. It's gratifying to be appreciated by so many prominent people, to be adulated, and to be loved.* Ron Grillo may have had his own motives, but she was flattered nevertheless. She didn't care. She needed confirmation of her value; she needed it again and again.

In the mirror, she studied herself. There might be a few wrinkles, but they could still be hidden. There were slight pouches under her eyes, but makeup would bury them. There were also other signs of aging—tightened lips and a chin and neck and upper arms with flesh that had grown just a little flabby. She'd have to see her plastic surgeon, Dr. Gilmore, in New York to have a touch-up—but by and large, for an old battle-axe, she smiled at herself, she wasn't doing too badly. The ageless beauty, the infectious vivacity, was returning, and with it came that magnetic power of attraction.

She described the meeting to David, and he was clearly pleased it had brought her so much joy and made her feel so needed.

But for whatever reason, she never did mention the conversation with Ron Grillo afterward.

79

Ron Grillo's note that the gala was dedicated to Alyce had the positive response expected. More friends wanted to come than the Hilton Hotel could accommodate. In the end, 1,500 people in black tie and gown swelled into the cavernous ballroom. Stanley Paul and his ten-piece band were playing to the music of a bygone era, and each table was shining with roses and candles glowing throughout the room with all the magic Alyce could create. This was to be her masterpiece.

Julie couldn't attend; she didn't feel well. She thought her mother was crazy to take on a gala of this scope, and besides, who else would take care of Duchess? But Laura was there to escort her mother in a wheelchair. Alyce had first insisted that she could brave the event without the wheelchair and dance away the night with David, but he agreed with her daughters that she wasn't steady enough to be on her feet, no less dance until dawn.

There was a red carpet flanked by young violinists from Roosevelt's Chicago Musical College that ran up the steps into the ballroom. At the entrance, Laura stood protectively by Alyce, with David opposite them, and welcomed each couple as they approached, a little like royalty greeting the populace. In the corner stood a photographer prepared to memorialize each couple.

When they settled into their seats near the bandstand, David opened his program and read the tribute to Alyce for the first time.

"This Crystal Ball is dedicated to Alyce Parker, a woman who has dedicated her career to the betterment of Chicago. From fund-raising for the Lincoln Park Zoo to Michael Reese Hospital, from a host of philanthropic efforts in support of Roosevelt University. She has always committed herself to the well-being of others. Tonight she is our queen, and we are grateful for everything she has done for the university and the greater Chicago community" (Dr. Ronald J. Grillo, vice president of Development for the Chicago Board of Roosevelt University).

Son of a bitch, David silently cursed his underling. *Sneaky, clandestine, unscrupulous, opportunistic son of a bitch. He had never been consulted about the tribute. Is something going on with Alyce and Grillo? Neither had ever hinted at the tribute. Maybe she didn't know this was coming. Grillo never even consulted with me, the president and the one he reports to. What a blind, ignorant, stupid fool I've been.* When he turned to the next table, Grillo had been waiting for his reaction, and as their eyes connected, he winked in triumph as though he assumed that David's reaction would be no more than gratitude.

Before David could put his anger into perspective, the others at his table—Chairman Alan Archer and his wife, Elise; Mayor Daley and Maggie; Buddy Mayer and her escort, John Bryan, and his wife, Jerry Stein, and Marion— were alive with chatter and proposing a champagne toast to Alyce. He had no choice but to be convivial.

Bill Cosby appeared after dessert, dressed like an undergraduate in jeans and a sweatshirt that bore the logo of Roosevelt University, sending the glow of his smile throughout the room. With microphone in hand, he moved among the crowd, spoke to individuals, teased them, thanked them for coming, and wound up at David's table, towering over Alyce with that infectious grin.

"Remember Lincoln telling Harriet Beecher Stowe that 'You must be the little lady who started the Civil War?' Well, here is the lady who started the Crystal Ball and helped to put together this fabulous evening: The Crystal Ball Queen, Alyce Parker."

Everyone stood and applauded their queen—her feistiness and fortitude and refusal to yield to the ravages of time and illness, a model for all the other women in the room.

"Someone told me that she wouldn't be playing in the US Tennis Open this year because of a slight injury she incurred on the court. Well, tonight she's almost completely recovered. She promised me this first dance, and with her husband's permission, I'd like to cash in that IOU."

Gently Cosby helped Alyce rise from her wheelchair. With a moment's hesitation, Alyce was in his arms, and they were dancing slowly to the song she had reserved for David.

There's a somebody I'm longin' to see

I hope that he turns out to be
Someone who'll watch over me

After several turns, Cosby brought her back to David as though she were a gift, and they finished the dance together. Joyous, grateful tears were rising through Alyce's body to her eyes.

I'm a little lamb who's lost in the wood
I know I could, always be good
To one who'll watch over me.

At home, at one o'clock in the morning, she and David collapsed on chairs in the den. Alyce's gorgeous scarlet gown was flowing from her, cinched at the waist, full in the bosom, a striking accent to those brilliant eyes that had always lit up every room she ever entered.

"That was the best of my best. Bill Cosby was in fabulous form. What a talent he is."

"Without you, Alyce, it wouldn't have happened."

She knew that was true, and she thanked him, almost formally, "My last hurrah. My swan song."

"I doubt that it's the last. What would you do without the Crystal Ball? You looked as though you were just beginning a second chapter in your life."

"I'm exhausted," she confessed. "I need a good night's sleep. Is anything wrong, David? You look as though something's wrong."

"Nothing. Nothing's wrong."

But then he couldn't control himself. As she started to leave the room, he asked her quietly, "Is anything going on with you and Ron Grillo?"

"What do you mean?"

"You know what I mean. The dedication."

"Oh!" She chuckled half-heartedly. "*That.* Wasn't it thoughtful of Ron to think of that?"

"Very much so."

"Is that what's bothering you?"

"That's all? Without consulting me? Without mentioning it to me? Without my approval?"

"We thought that you'd be pleasantly surprised."

"Come on, stop bullshitting me, Alyce. What is going on?"

"It's true. We thought you'd be pleased and grateful."

"Stop being disingenuous."

"Oh, what a fancy word."

"You do know that he's doing everything he can to succeed me. He's talking to trustees. He's doing everything he can to get my job."

She stood, wavered a little, and pulled her gown close to her. For a moment, he thought she might faint. But Alyce Parker was stronger than he would ever know.

"I don't need this abuse," she said. "I'm going to sleep."

80

He brooded alone in the den, listening to her prepare for sleep. Then there was the silence of self-satisfaction. He looked at the walls of the book-lined den and seemed to see her mind for the first time. All Book of the Month Club selections were still in their jackets as spanking new as when they had first arrived, all unread. He went to his own study in that large apartment and sat among his stack of reports waiting to be read and worn books with marginalia out of another time when he aspired to be a scholar—books that he had written himself and notes for another he planned to write in retirement, if he still had the energy or the desire to write it. It was as though he were returning to his real home when he entered his study.

They were so different; they were so alike. But without the university holding them together as they sat at breakfast and confronting each other alone in retirement, what would they have to say to each other?

Three days later, the one-page contract crossed David's desk for his signature. He could not believe it. Ron Grillo had signed up Alyce for three years, without his knowledge or approval. Alyce had signed it; Grillo had signed it. In addition to his having appointed her unilaterally, Grillo had raised her salary by 10 percent.

"What is this all about?" David asked his vice president for Development, holding the contract in his trembling fingers. "Who authorized you to sign this without consulting me?"

"I thought I wouldn't need authorization—not after a benefit that brought in $2 million."

"Two million gross—a helluva lot less after all the bills are paid."

"Still—"

"Does John Andersen know about this?"

"Of course he does," he answered, superciliously, as though there had been a transfer in the power dynamic between the two of them.

He knew that Grillo had been warming up trustees to the idea that when David retired at the end of the following year, he, Ronald Grillo, past president of another university and a close friend of Alyce's, could be David's natural successor, and his chief fund-raising assistant would be Alyce Parker.

"Yes," Grillo almost sneered. "He doesn't like it either. Surprise, surprise. He sent Alyce's contract on to you and told me to speak with you directly."

"Thanks for the courtesy, Ron. Thanks a whole lot. Why the hell did you go ahead on your own, without consulting me and without even having the courtesy to speak with me first?"

"Alyce was very nervous. She was afraid to approach you directly about her reappointment. And to be honest, I wanted to be sure a three-year contract would secure her job after the new president comes on board."

Don't bullshit me, David recoiled, looking at him angrily and thinking the worst of his insubordination. *I know what you've been up to. I know you've been cottoning up to my trustees, currying their favor. I know you're thinking of the presidency after my retirement as yours. You've been lining up the trustees one after the other, you son-of-a-bitch.* But he contained his anger. "You do know the position you've put me in, don't you? Just the other week, Andersen questioned me about her being on the payroll at all. He always has from the moment Alyce came on as a consultant."

"I know," he chuckled. "John Andersen is our institutional scrooge, isn't he? Maybe he should have gone to the gala and gotten a taste of what she's brought to this university."

"Don't change the subject, Ron. You've put me in an awful position."

"You don't have to approve it. You're still the president. You can let her work elsewhere. My own opinion—"

"I didn't ask for your opinion."

"I'd keep her is my opinion, whatever difficulties the two of you are going through. She's invaluable."

David glared at him. "Look, Ron. You know that if I want to kill your presidential aspirations, I can—and any aspirations you may have to go anywhere else. A search committee will always consult with me for any job you pursue. I can kill your career. So please don't fuck around with me. I've been around the barn a couple of times."

That night, when he confronted Alyce, she told him that if he objected to her contract, he'd have a minor rebellion on his hands. Everyone wanted her to stay. The friends she'd made at the university, all the staff in the development office, and her self-created Chicago Board of Volunteers would probably rise up in protest if they ever learned that personal considerations were why he would not reappoint her. They would threaten to go to the chairman of the board of trustees, Alan Archer, a close friend of hers, and have her reappointed over his objection. It would be a mess, and he'd appear petty, vindictive, and less than generous.

"Don't you think I deserve a reappointment after all that I've done?"

"It doesn't seem to matter what I think anymore, does it? You're doing all this behind my back. You're one cunning woman."

"Just pragmatic." She smiled devilishly. "If I don't take care of myself, who will?"

"What kind of goddamn marriage is this any way?" he protested. "I thought you were retiring with me. I thought we were still married."

"We are, but that doesn't mean that we have to retire at the same time. You may be tired of your presidency, but I'm just getting started fund-raising."

81

Both Julie and Laura urged her to divorce him. Alyce was stronger than she'd been since her surgeries and heart attack, and they told her that David's retirement into solitude would be nothing but a disaster for her. She would always need to socialize through the hurly-burly of fund-raising and galas, not sit in the shadow of an aging, isolated, would-be writer.

"I sure as hell hate to see you work at all," Julie argued, "but it's a whole lot better than being with him. You don't need him. If he won't sign the contract now, Ron Grillo or any new president will sign you up in a heartbeat. Then you'll earn what you truly deserve."

She knew that was true, but she also knew that she wasn't ready to leave David.

He was cooling toward her. She felt that would have to happen one day, and now it had happened. He was furious at her for signing the contract behind his back.

A twelve-year difference in age seems like nothing when you're in your forties or fifties; in your early eighties, it's a lifetime. He no longer loved her, if ever he really did love her. When she'd felt vulnerable, recovering from her fall and surgery, she'd ignored all his deficits. Now they only seemed magnified.

All she had ever asked of him was unconditional love. Was that too much to ask? Probably. He might have considered her beautiful and vibrant and commanding ten years ago, but now at eighty-two she was indisputably old, with health problems and recalcitrant daughters. She sensed that she was losing him. He had married her strictly out of expedience and used her for his own professional purposes. Julie was right about that. *It is finally a marriage of convenience,* she told herself, *an institutional marriage.* He was resentful of her girls. They had never become his stepdaughters and had never accepted him as her husband. If they had been his biological children, the entire relationship would have been different, and their troubles, joys, and fears would have been truly shared. There is the hard truth of it: you can sever a friendship, you can end a marriage, but you can never divorce your children.

Her girls were the love of her life, but they were also albatrosses too heavy to bear. Laura had discounted Matt long ago as an unreliable father in every way; she loathed him for his irresponsibility. Julie, who was aware of all his imperfections—his alcoholism and his inability to maintain his inheritance or carve out a career, still worshiped him, and that needy sentiment had grown only more idealized with time.

All these thoughts roiled through Alyce's mind, as she remained with Julie during the day and lay beside David at night, as she walked alone through Lincoln Park during cool spring afternoons alone with Duchess, and as she tried to defend him to her daughters. In turn, she sought to make him understand that he could never be the father they'd always wanted because he was not their father.

She concentrated on David. He turned in the bed and faced her in his sleep, his expression filled with pain. He must have been in the midst of his own private dream or nightmare, but she wondered, *Can it possibly be?* She had thought he was her last best hope at love, but Julie and Laura made it impossible for that to happen. Now the moment had come, so late in life, for her to make her Hobson's choice. But she knew there was no choice. There was only acceptance.

82

In a short time, the inevitable occurred. Julie had been more or less faithful to David's compromise. She had come to the house after he went to work and left before he returned. But soon she could not help herself. She was buying some groceries for dinners and beginning to cook for them. From David's point of view, it was once again intrusive. When he objected and Alyce told her so, she retreated, but all three of them knew it was a temporary standoff until collision occurred.

Every Sunday morning, he continued to play doubles at the Midtown Tennis Club with three men half his age. At seventy, he still felt young and vigorous. Except for ephemeral ailments, he had never been sick or hospitalized, and he used to joke, a little arrogantly, that he didn't have time to kill. As a lucky man, he still took no pills.

Tennis was his affirmation of perpetual youth. He played intensely, with a preternatural need to win, and after two hours on the court, he would return to take Alyce to brunch. One Sunday, as another attempt to create peace in the family, he invited both girls to join Alyce and him, but when he returned from tennis, he knew immediately that he had entered a combat zone. Reconciliation at the Drake Hotel wasn't happening that day.

The scene he confronted was different from any he could have imagined: three women in the midst of a furious argument frozen suddenly by his entrance, as if they had been captured unaware in some ghoulish photograph. Alyce was in her office chair and her daughters opposite on the sofa. Laura was watching Julie, who had clearly been ranting. Arrested by David in the midst of her diatribe, she hesitated for only a heartbeat. She stood imperiously. "If you want him," she barked at her mother, "you can have him." She glared at David as she brushed by him. For one mad, melodramatic moment, he was afraid that she might pull a pistol from her purse to annihilate him. Instead, she raced across the living room and was out the door without a word.

"Let me have the keys to your car," Laura told her mother. "She shouldn't be driving."

When Laura was gone, David sat on the sofa and touched Alyce's trembling hand gently and tentatively.

"What did I do to provoke this outburst?"

"You've done nothing, Dave."

"What can I do?"

"You can't do anything. She's impossible."

"Apologize," he said. "That's what I should do. I should apologize for my existence."

Self-pity—he hated himself for the feeling.

She didn't respond. He went to his quarters on the other side of the condo and showered away his tennis sweat and dressed in Sunday casuals: khaki trousers and a black golf shirt, with an inscription of Bellagio, the Las Vegas Hotel, where they had once gone for a wild weekend. There, she had reserved an expensive suite, and he had won $2,500 at the blackjack table to help pay for it. He had called Las Vegas garish beyond words and the Chihuly glass ceilings over the top creations, but she reminded him later that he had enjoyed himself when he was there. Laughing at himself, he had always talked about it afterward, but nevertheless, he was enjoying the thought that he could afford this kind of extravagance.

He blamed neither of them—they were simply different creatures brought together by an institution that seemed, for a time, to satisfy their lifelong needs.

That time was coming to an end.

The irreversible moment occurred just three days later when David returned from the university. He had finished acquiring the largest gift of his presidency which was $5 million. It was the reward of a year's effort that he and Alyce had collaborated on, and he felt more buoyant than ever. The acquisition had begun when he'd noticed that an alumna, Florence Miner, had increased her annual gift from one hundred to a thousand dollars. For the past year, they courted her, and he finally wrote a proposal for a computer center named after her brother Robert Miner, the cofounder of Oracle who had bequeathed her a billion dollars. He and Alyce had flown West more than once and visited her in her Tiburon mansion overlooking

San Francisco Bay to secure the gift. Alyce had been the humanizing presence that made the success possible.

Now David raced home to share the good news and suggested that they celebrate with dinner at the Four Seasons Hotel, but instead of finding her alone, he was greeted at the door by a strange elderly woman. For a moment, he thought he had the wrong address, but then he checked the number on the door—21C. The condo was his.

"Dr. Rosen? I'm Katrina."

David looked at Alyce, perched on an easy chair in the den.

"Katrina will be here to help for a little while," she apologized, "but only if you agree. Julie arranged for her to be my caregiver."

Katrina quickly retreated into the kitchen, leaving them alone.

"When did all this happen?"

"Last week. Julie saw how hard my convalescence has been on you. She worried about our meals and my medications. It's much too much for you to handle, Dave, a university presidency and an invalid like me. She's right. I need someone. I don't want to be a burden on you."

"You're not a burden—"

"Sometimes it seems that way."

"And who's supposed to pay for Katrina?"

"I'll pay."

"I'll bet you will." He regretted his malevolence the moment the words emerged from his lips.

Before she could answer, the phone rang. David grabbed it.

"Is Mom there?"

"Julie, what in hell do you think you're doing, arranging for a caregiver?"

"Oh, relax. I thought it would make your lives easier."

"Without even consulting me? Without warning me? Who's going to pay for this woman? You?"

"Well, you wouldn't let me care for Mom, so—"

"Will you please stay out of our fucking lives?"

"Oh, be quiet, you skinflint. You just don't appreciate the least little thing I try to do."

"No, I don't. Get the hell out of our lives and find a life of your own."

She was about to curse him again when he slammed the phone down. Alyce stared at him helplessly.

"Don't be so angry with us, Dave. I'm sorry. It's all my fault. I should have warned you in advance, but I was afraid of this reaction."

He sat across the room from her, breathing deeply to suppress his fury. Beyond his anger, he was ashamed that his first response was the cost of a caregiver. That was mean, that was petty, that was not his true nature, but it was his immediate response and his way of expressing resentment. He felt used when he should have tendered generosity.

He softened his voice. "Yes, you should have asked me first. Look, Alyce, I don't give a damn about the money. It's just the feeling of being excluded—of things being done behind my back without consulting me." Then for the longest time, he stared at her in silence until he found the right words. "Are we on the same team, Alyce?"

She did not answer him.

"Alyce, are we?"

"I'm too weak for this, Dave. I don't feel well. I do need care—full-time." She looked as helpless as a child. "There's a dinner that Katrina's prepared for you in the kitchen. Your favorite dinner—veal scallopini. I'm sorry I can't join you. I'm going to bed. I'm exhausted. I just can't handle all this stress."

He watched her go in the kitchen and listened to her ask Katrina to leave; she would call the good woman after she talked with her husband.

83

For Alyce, the dream was over. All she had ever wanted—but wasn't that everything?—was absolute love, the commitment of someone who not only admired but loved her so deeply he would tolerate her daughters, her own loss of beauty, her little idiosyncrasies, her frailty, and her aging. What was lacking within her that could not create the bridge to comity and have her dream come true?

Or is a dream a dream because it rarely does come true?

84

On the following Saturday morning, when David was working at home, he received a fax that shocked him to his core and into recognition of the inevitable:

Dear Alyce,
Please review the following draft of your divorce decree before your meeting with Mike on Monday morning.

Keep up your spirits, dear one. You'll get through this.

As ever,
Diana

He stared at the document for a long time, shaken and saddened, feeling impotent. But once the sudden shock had abated, he wasn't surprised. He read it and reread it, but his mind was filled with thoughts that lay too deep for tears. Gobbledygook and legalese. His eyes glazed over. She did not want any portion of his salary or pension or retirement bonus, but she did insist on claiming the condominium for which he had paid. He couldn't read the details with any sense of reason. Words, words, self-protective words. Later, when he had composed himself, he would study the details.

He took the fax to Alyce in the dining room. She was immersed in the *Chicago Tribune*, drinking her final cup of breakfast coffee with confidence and poise and calm.

"What's this all about?"

She looked at the fax, and the smile vanished from her face. But her eyes never left his. She was certain, she was determined, and she had made up her mind irrevocably.

"Diana made a mistake by sending it directly to your fax machine. I'm sorry. It should have gone to mine. I wanted to tell you myself before you read it."

He stared at her with disbelief.

"I'm divorcing you."

"What? What have I done now?"

"Nothing. You've done nothing. This current arrangement just won't work out."

He began to speak, but she raised her hand to stop him.

"I'm sorry I'm still in a wheelchair, Dave. I'm sorry for having daughters. I'm sorry it's come to this."

"What the hell am I supposed to do if we get divorced?" he protested angrily, thinking for the moment only of himself. "You're the one with all the friends."

"Oh, you'll find someone. You'll find someone in a minute." And she snapped her fingers. "Men always do. I'm the one who will be left alone."

"So that's the end of this nine-year love affair?"

"Love affair? Is that what we're calling it now?" She smiled at him with mild condescension. "You never loved me, Dave. You used me."

"Oh, please. You sound like Julie. That's not true, and you know it. We used each other. And we loved each other too, didn't we?"

"Not unconditionally. Never unconditionally."

"Give me a break. That sounds like something out of *Cosmopolitan*. This is insane. You're being prompted by Julie and Laura—"

"No, I haven't been."

"You're acting presumptuously," he said, almost desperately. "Give this time. You'll be out of that wheelchair in a week."

"And then I'll be walking with a cane."

"So what? Who cares? Give this time. Give this three months before you sign our lives away."

But she refused. She wasn't listening to him anymore.

85

Alyce had been reluctant to divorce, but she knew no other solution. He was a cold man, she had concluded, unable to transcend the limitations of her daughters, unable to love her in spite of them or her own physical incapacities.

In the end, the marriage couldn't continue. She had fallen in love with him hard, when she thought that love would not have been possible anymore in her life. She had wanted him to be the incarnation of some imagined, idealized love, hoping he would bring her unconditional love, but when it was tested, it wasn't there. He was a cold man, insensitive when it really counted, self-centered, and an opportunist obsessed with work. He was . . . he was . . . inadequate to her insatiable needs.

She divulged all these pent-up, conflicting emotions to her close friend, Bootsie Nathan, as they sipped high tea at the Drake one late afternoon. Bootsie had been married to Myron Nathan, who went to Brown with Matt

Parker and had died just a year ago. She knew Alyce since their childhood in Hyde Park, and they'd always been confessional with each other and as close almost as biological sisters. This matter had been different—the secrets of her disintegrating marriage had been too painful to share—until now.

"You have no choice," Bootsie told her after listening sympathetically to Alyce's lament. "Biology *is* destiny after all, isn't it? Where did I learn that? When all is said and done, Julie and Laura are your daughters. You'll get through this Alyce. No—you will, you will. I did. We all do, one way or the other."

"You have grandchildren."

"Yes. That is a blessing, isn't it? But it's still very lonely without Myron. At our age, you do the best you can. You live each day as though it's the last day of your life. I'm lucky I have enough money to live alone with a caregiver, but I'm one step away from an assisted living facility—believe me."

86

John Andersen, David's vice president for finance, ended his weekly Monday morning meeting by saying he had one last sensitive matter to discuss. He was a tall, lanky Minnesotan who had been a close ally throughout David's reinvention of the university; he had come from the world of banking and enjoyed everyone's respect. It was clear, as he fumbled for the proper tone, that he was the designated hitter for this awkward conversation.

"The rumors about you and Alyce are gathering steam, Dave."

"Really?" Dave snapped. "I couldn't care less about what anyone says or thinks. It's a private matter."

"It would be if Alyce didn't work here."

"She's only a consultant."

"A paid consultant. And that makes all the difference." He hesitated, and David could see that he loathed the role he had been asked to assume, but he was the fiscal conscience of the university. So many people looked to him for stability; so many admired him. "Bob Green and I would like to speak to her about stepping down if you guys decide it's quits before you begin this last year of your presidency."

"Not yet," David stopped him, alarmed. "She shouldn't be punished for something that has nothing to do with her professional performance. She's too valuable to let go. Sign her up for two years—my final year and the first of my successor. Let him determine her future. You'd know what I mean if you had been at the last gala."

"We weren't invited."

Andersen immediately regretted the jab and was on the verge of an apology, but David raised his hand to stop him.

"That's not necessary, John. I know your importance to this university. I appreciate everything you've done to keep my dreams in check. I didn't send out the invitations."

87

"I don't know what we can do now," Harry Lieberman told him, leafing slowly through the prenuptial agreement that David had signed nine years ego. Lieberman was a matrimonial attorney who had become a casual acquaintance and now was handling his divorce case. He was very short and compact, with a grin of perennial success across his lips. His black hair was flattened by pomade, and he was known as a killer in court. "I don't know what you were thinking, Dave, or who was giving you advice at that time."

"Her lawyer."

"*Her* lawyer?" He couldn't help but smile superciliously at David's naivete. "You have to be kidding. Really? A university president with responsibilities of all sorts, a university with an attorney of its own—and you let *her* attorney draw up your prenuptial agreement?"

"Don't rub it in, Harry. I don't know why I was so naive. I was married to the same woman for thirty-five years, and we never thought it would end. I didn't think this marriage would end either. I didn't even know what a prenuptial agreement was, believe it or not. I just never thought of taking care of mundane stuff like this."

"You're a romantic."

"In spades."

"Well, I'll do my best, Dave, but you really have handcuffed me. Her lawyers are claiming that you should turn over half the assets you've accumulated in your investments during the marriage and half of your retirement bonus. They want the condo as well."

"All of me." David smiled, embarrassed, his voice singing the song with sotto voce that was rising through him: "Why not take all of me? / You took the best. / Why not take the rest?"

"This is no joking matter, Dave. You were naive. I've talked with her attorneys. I don't think there's much room for negotiation. They want everything. That daughter Julie, especially. She's a bulldog. She's Alyce's real attorney. One tough, tenacious bitch."

"You tell me."

88

"Everyone knows you've given that university the sparkle it never had. He may have been successful in some of his so-called academic projects, but you've given it class and panache and a public image."

"Stop it, Julie. Be fair. He's been good to me. He's been generous. He's taken me all over the world and let me do whatever I wished. The galas. The musicales here. He's been good to me. I owe him as much as he owes me. Don't take this marriage and sully it."

"Then why in hell are you divorcing him?"

"Because he doesn't love me as much as I need to be loved. Because he's coldly ambitious." *Because of you too, Julie.* "I don't want to hear your tirades any longer. I don't want to argue with anyone anymore. I can't keep up with either of you in my weakened condition. I'm always short of breath. I'm always tired. I finally realized that ours was an institutional marriage."

But she knew that was only half the reason—and perhaps the less important half. At night, alone in bed, she wondered why in fact she was divorcing him. Most marriages are compromises after all; most have conflicts between children and stepfathers. Why should she expect hers to be ideal? Perhaps he'd be more loving and attentive in retirement, when the burning need to succeed finally abated and he could concentrate completely on her. Perhaps. She still loved him for his intensity and ambition; it had a frightening power, commensurate almost to her beauty, and she feared its absence. Without it every day would be like a living death.

No, she knew there was more, if she were honest with herself. The deeper, more clawing reason for divorcing him was her girls. Just a few weeks ago, Julie had discovered that she had contracted breast cancer in situ and, against the doctor's advice, had decided to have breast reduction. Alyce had spent considerable time with her as she endured chemotherapy, then lost her hair and had to wear a wig. She stayed with Julie at her home for several days and nights a week, which created even more tension in the marriage as David lived alone. He tried to be compassionate, but she knew he still carried resentment at Julie's arbitrary hiring of Katrina, whom David reluctantly had agreed to keep as a caretaker, and now he was resentful at her days and night alone with Julie.

Alyce and Julie argued continually, and the major source of their arguments was David. Julie hated him. He was selfish and uncaring and opportunistic; he didn't love Alyce. He never had, and he'd just used her. And Laura? She too was alone, having survived a kidney transplant. She was needy, so needy of attention. Alyce was on the phone each night or visiting her on weekends in St. Louis. It was overwhelming and more than she could handle, and David always seemed to be at an emotional distance. She was recovering from her heart attack and still needing all the support she could find in her husband, but he wasn't there for her and the only solution was divorce. The loneliness within their marriage was like an open wound and more than she could bear.

On Valentine's Day, he moved out of their condo on Astor Street. All that was left was the settlement of assets.

You can break up with friends, she thought like someone trapped in a family she hadn't asked for. Tears were streaming down her face as she struggled vainly to sleep. *You can divorce a husband. But you can't divorce your children— not if you're a mother.*

She wore an understated black suit for the divorce proceedings and appeared as the beleaguered, helpless, aging victim. She sat quietly in her wheelchair in Judge Ann Rabinowitz's chambers. She seemed shorter than her normal height and older than her years; she was crunched between her two lawyers who guarded her protectively on each side. David and Harry Lieberman sat stoically across the room, and Judge Rabinowitz was securely upright behind her desk in judicial robes. She was in her fifties and could have been Alyce's daughter; indeed, the families had casually known each other during their Hyde Park days. Was there a slight conflict of interest and impartiality? Of course, there was none, but that didn't prevent the judge from chatting with Alyce about the good old days.

"We don't have to go to trial, do we, my friends? It's my understanding that Alyce is finally asking for only the condo."

"And that's against our better judgment," one of her lawyers snarled.

"It's also my understanding that Mr. Rosen has agreed to that settlement."

"Reluctantly." Harry Lieberman smiled.

Alyce returned his smile almost flirtatiously, like an echo of her old charm and of memories at functions in the Standard Club when she'd interacted with him socially. It was the oasis for upper-middle-class Jews in the days when they weren't admitted into the Chicago Club.

"It would be so nice to split our opera tickets," Alyce smiled like a forlorn victim. "I'll miss the opera."

She presented herself as someone who was still recovering from her long illness and would have solicited sympathy from the harshest of critics. It was certainly more than David ever would.

89

He watched her throughout the divorce hearing and thought cynically that she must have rehearsed this performance for days. She had taken on the role of a beleaguered, self-sacrificing wife and had thoroughly convinced the judge of her dilemma.

After the proceedings, as Lieberman said goodbye to David outside his office building on LaSalle Street, he smiled benevolently at his client and tried to console him. "In the long run, you'll be okay, David. Men always wind up ahead in a divorce like this one, if not at the start financially. It's the women who suffer, especially at Alyce's age." And then he added, sniggering just a little, "But you may have to work another year before you retire. We could have done better. I know how you feel, but you really did handcuff me with that goddamn prenup agreement."

David felt disgusted with the legal fees. He could still hear the meter ticking whenever he called Lieberman for no more than a moment—the hassling over his financial assets, Alyce's passion to hold onto the condo, and the messy details of a divorce that left him wasted and defeated and guilt-ridden. Through all of Alyce's convalescence, he should have been more loving and understanding. He could have found a way, if he had really tried, of accommodating Julie and Laura and of not possessing their mother completely. Someone else would have been more generous. Someone else would have cared more. He owed Alyce so much he could never repay all that he owed her. He was too self-demanding, selfish, and self-absorbed—*Oh god, I could have done so much more for her if I had only loved her more.* There was a dimension missing in him, a final reservoir of compassion that should have transcended their trivial differences.

He was living now in a one-bedroom rental in the rather tired gray Hotel Seneca on Chestnut Street, just across from the rear of the snazzier Ritz Carleton. He had found several buddies to play tennis with him on the outdoor courts each day behind the Museum of Contemporary Art and ate breakfast alone afterward in the basement cafe of the Seneca, which resembled a waiting room on concrete steps to purgatory. Work was all consuming and all that he had to live for; it lifted him for sporadic moments from depression. In one year, after his presidency was over, he would have to find a life beyond visible power. He would write literary criticism, read books about truth and beauty, travel to lands unseen, and meet someone new—perhaps someone younger who had no daughters and wasn't so needy. Who knew what the future would bring?

He hated the idea that Alyce was still present in the life of the university, like a shadow cast across his presidency, a beautiful, reenergized, aging woman, still adding members to her Chicago Board and preparing for leadership of still another gala that was like an adjunct to the core mission of his university. Indeed, all her fund-raising activities were like a wholly owned subsidiary of his university. But he kept a distance from all that she did, appearing in her company only when absolutely necessary.

In this strained twilight of a public career, he wanted to leave his presidency in triumph. When a retired mogul approached him with the idea of creating a school of real estate, he seized the opportunity, and within a year, there was an advisory board, a curriculum, and an entering class. When he learned that the president of the National Louis College of Education had been forced to retire because of a sex scandal, he seized the possibility of a merger that would create the largest college of education in the nation, a private university working on the gritty problems of public education, collaborating in the neighborhoods with pre-K programs, and becoming a model for how universities and the schools might work together. But at the last moment, trustees of National Louis turned him down because they thought they would lose their historic identity, and they sought a new president of their own.

A success or a defeat—it was all part of the excitement of being the leader of any large enterprise. It was a masquerade ball of a career in which one would wonder, *Who's in / who's out, who wins / who loses*. But beneath it all, he was still troubled by the divorce and knew that somehow he had failed. There must have been some defect within his personal character that had contributed to the breakdown. He should have tried harder, been more empathetic, and loved Alyce more. But slowly he realized that however limited he might have been emotionally, they were different in so many ways and had come together accidentally: he was an academic, while she was a socialite; he stemmed from a far more modest background economically, the second son of a schoolteacher, while she was the only child of a furrier who traveled among the well-to-do. The list could go on. There were always differences between two people who would love each other that needed to be overcome, and if it hadn't been for Julie, the marriage would have worked, blossomed, and thrived. He needed to believe that. They would have grown old together, closer in age because they truly would have depended on each other. Their love would have grown deeper and more meaningful than ever.

He wandered the street absently, strode down a Michigan Avenue, which was brightly lit by fabulous emporia—and saw nothing. He meandered to the lake and strolled along the endless beach front, staring at Navy Pier in the distance, the silver Ferris wheel aglow in the dark, the cruise boats that escorted party revelers halfway across the lake at midnight, the moon with its seductive halo, the stars that lit up the sky like diamonds, the lovers that passed him by in his neighborhood of Streeterville, and then he would return to the gray furnished apartment on the third floor of Hotel Seneca.

He knew that he was carrying a low-lying depression, the aftershock that comes with any divorce, and he finally decided to see an analyst to help him sort out the essence of why he still should be suffering from guilt.

Dr. Gordon had an office on the eighth floor of the Garland Building on Wabash Avenue. David found it eerie. It was nothing but one large room, with a small desk that separated the two men, a leather couch, two worn chairs, a small silent clock that only Dr. Gordon could see, and a standing lamp by his chair that was dimly lit and threatened to expire at any moment like an old worn candle. It was a dark, spooky space, almost like that of a fortune teller's and encouraged David to travel far inside his marriage to a place where he had never been. The details rolled out and the analyst listened patiently, interrupting rarely.

When David recalled the scene of his return from the tennis courts to find Alyce, Julie, and Laura embroiled in a battle over him, Gordon simply murmured, "Did you ever feel that she might just be jealous that you were younger and that she would not keep up with your pace?" That was true, but he knew that was only a part of the reason for their breakup. The analyst was simply trying to soothe him and free him of guilt. When he described Alyce's childhood, her family, her marriage to Matt Parker, the perfect family they had wanted to create and how it had all unraveled, Gordon suggested that she was probably searching for some kind of idealized love with David, that she had craved the center of attention all her life and was suffering from a deep-seated narcissism, and that her beauty and vivacity were a form of personal power she was terrified of losing.

And David? Had he been questing, like Don Quixote, for some heroic ideal that could never be achieved, fostered in childhood by a brilliant brother and father he could never measure up to? And that quest, Gordon suggested, might be his own form of narcissism.

Gobbledegook. Psychobabble. But perhaps, it was not wildly off the mark.

After six weeks of analysis, he emerged more whole than when he had begun, convinced that there are some human differences that could never be reconciled. The analyst had given him permission to feel guiltless. He'd suggested that this had been a marriage of convenience, maybe of expedience; they had been a mismatch except for the raising of funds, the galas, and the dinners at all the hotels. Her daughters had never invited him into their tight family circle, and that was the bridge he could not overcome and the cross he could not bear. He would always wonder what he could have done that he had failed to do.

Work was not sufficient to fill the last days of his presidency. They lacked the promise of possibility and, more urgently, the human touch. Why struggle during the day if you have no one to tell your stories to at night?

And so a year before the end of his career, he put an ad in *The New York Review of Books*:

I'm a retired professor of English, interested in all forms of culture—serious books, classical music, contemporary theater, traveling to anywhere in the world, but especially to Paris. I'm still youthful, as I approach seventy, a tennis player, a walker in the city, a man who has all the time in the world for a woman in her fifties or sixties who would like to join me at this stage of life—in Chicago or New York.

90

Alyce was relieved that she would be living in the large apartment on Astor Street. Initially, she had wanted more from the settlement—a good portion of David's salary during the nine years of their marriage as well as half of the increases in his equities, but she refrained her lawyers from being confrontational. She was not a ruthless woman. David had been good to her, and she did not want to end the relationship in utter bitterness. In addition, she assured herself that she would soon be working fulltime, thanks to Ron Grillo.

She no longer needed a wheelchair, but she was still fragile and wobbly when she tried to walk unaided. She resorted reluctantly to a cane. "But only as an affectation," she told her friends, laughing blithely, swinging it around like an assault weapon, and carrying the fabulous smile that lit up every room she had ever entered (a tribute by David that she always cherished). It was a mixture of empathy and joy and beauty and self-confidence and (he later added cynically when his love for her was fading) a touch of narcissism.

The aftermath of her aging beauty struck her when she entered the International Room of the Drake Hotel for dinner with her friend Bootsie Nathan. They were two elderly women. It was the same restaurant where she had clinched the deal and where Buddy Mayer and John Bryan had agreed to be leaders of the capital campaign and where she and David, sitting across the lavish table from one another, had exchanged glances of success and knew that they were in love and where now, only a few years later, she entered that same room and no one even turned an eye to notice her.

Her last years were marked by tragedies worse than any mother should ever have to endure.

Julie's breast cancer was arrested for a short time by a double mastectomy, but it returned with a vengeance. After she'd had the surgery, the affected lymph nodes required more chemotherapy, which were then aggravated by the hot flashes of menopause that persisted and left her bathing in sweat and constant pain. In desperation, she had hormone replacement therapy, risky as it was, but the cancer returned and the radiation she endured reactivated a prior case of shingles. It was as if a plague had invaded her body, determined to destroy her, and was rapidly metastasizing throughout her organs. Her blistering temper raged on, directed at her mother; she had turned out to be an angry, deeply frustrated woman in her fifties, unwilling to go gently into that dark night.

She wanted to move in with Alyce.

"It won't work, Julie. We're at each other's throat too much. We'll destroy each other."

"I'm destroyed already, Mother. It's either that or a nursing home."

They existed together, but before they could adjust to their new life, it was Laura's tragic turn. Her kidney transplant was a dramatic success, and they thought she'd live her final years quietly in St. Louis. She did so for a while, but she developed lung cancer, which she had kept secret for months in an attempt to spare her mother and sister. One day, she called them from her hospital bed to say that she had contracted pneumonia. When Alyce and Julie arrived, they were amazed to discover that in fact, Laura had developed a life-threatening lung cancer and was already on radiation. Julie screamed at the young doctor, "You must be crazy. Can't you see how sick my sister is? She's dying, for God's sake. She's dying. She should be in hospice." But the doctor kept assuring them that with additional radiation, Laura would recover. She never did.

Those days and nights with Laura were nightmarish, so Alyce would remember, a journey from purgatory into hell. Laura sat in an armchair in her little living room, shorter and thinner than ever and terrified of death. At fifty-five, she was looking already like an emaciated ghost. With only one bed and a secondhand couch in that woebegone apartment, she slept with Alyce, while Julie used the sofa. She couldn't sleep. She needed help with the bathroom; she asked for guidance down the stairs to the kitchen in the morning; and deep into the night, she kept murmuring to Alyce, "I'm going to die, Mom. I shouldn't have to die. I'm too young to die. I'm sorry for having hurt you so much. I'm so sorry for everything. I wanted so much to make up for all the hurt I've done." And then just before she went to sleep forever, she gave Alyce permission to seek out her grandson, who now would be twenty, not realizing that Alyce had been quietly observing the boy grow into manhood without ever telling her. Finally, she asked her mother to have her buried in the family cemetery at Rosehill, next to the place that Alyce had set aside for herself.

Julie died two years later, having suffered in acute pain during her last days from shingles and menopause and a cancer that had finally spread to her bones and affected her brain. Her last days at Thanksgiving and Christmas with Alyce were marked by dinners ordered in from the Women's Athletic Club. She sat at her mother's dining table before mounds of food, nibbling at the edges of what should have been sumptuous dinners, but the food didn't matter anymore. She was finally alone with her mother. It was the way Julie had always wished it to be—the two of them together.

Another woman would have disintegrated after these tragedies and reluctantly accepted her fate. But not Alyce Parker—not even at the age of eighty-seven. She did suffer a yearlong depression after the death of her daughters when nothing in life seemed to have any importance anymore. It was the first time in her life she endured such prolonged sadness, but like the proverbial phoenix risen from the ashes, she emerged into the land of the living alone and found solace in volunteer work. In honor of Laura, she secured funding from all the wealthy friends she knew and created a Kidney Mobile that tested people for diabetes and kidney failure. She remained on the board of the Lincoln Park Zoo and asked for permission to have two little stone sculptures erected and dedicated to Julie and Laura. At the

Crystal Ball, she now appeared as an aged figure, revered but more and more marginal with each subsequent event. Her photos continued to appear in the *Tribune* and *Sun Times* and *Skyline* as someone to be admired, and for her ninetieth birthday, she had friends arrange a magnificent gathering of celebrities at the Lake Shore Country Club to pay tribute to her.

She continued to be a mentor for many young feminists, and they looked up to her as an older model of a woman who had struggled her way through the most difficult of circumstances and was still serving others. One of her acolytes made a film of her delivering an address that provided selective recollections of her life: she was standing securely on her own two feet, dressed in a white Dior suit, she was genial, she was self-effacing, and she was humorous. She was indeed an aging beauty who was already aged, confessional about her tragedies, although she omitted many of the darker moments (most essentially the conflict between David and her daughters) and transformed others. *Why not?* she convinced herself. *I've always been a woman with the glass half-full.*

She knew she was presenting the romanticized story of her life, as she wanted it to be remembered—a recreation for the world to admire. Then she wrote a book that defined her life and published it for all her friends and disciples, who were shrinking, alas, in number with each passing day. The memoir was self-congratulatory and narcissistic, but it carried the force of a feisty, beautiful woman who had lived to be noticed and admired all her life. When she came to the few brief pages devoted to her marriage with David, she acknowledged his virtues, she lauded his achievements, but she also considered him a cold man, unable to provide the empathy she craved. She acknowledged that he loved her, but he couldn't gratify all her insatiable needs. If her life had not been perfect, she made it so in in her memoir.

91

David observed Alyce's tribulations from afar, although he lived no more than half a mile away in a more modest high-rise on Lake Shore Drive. He suffered from the guilt of someone who felt that somehow he should have found reconciliation with her daughters and accused himself of lacking the core characteristics of patience and tolerance and understanding and kindness and other virtues that would have obviated his own inherent selfishness and need to possess Alyce for himself alone. So he berated himself.

But he also knew he was not completely at fault; he had tried with all the love that he possessed. Wasn't that enough? He had wanted the marriage to last, but the daughters wouldn't yield, and Alyce had finally made her choice. Theirs was a mismatch from the start. He had given her nine years that were the most gratifying of her life, and they had enjoyed a love that was almost strong enough to survive the conflict with her girls.

Many women answered his ad—cultured, well-spoken, attractive, and financially independent—academics mostly, each of whom had been touched by disappointment in some earlier relationship. None of them caught his eye as Alyce had that magical first night at the Crystal Ball.

None of them—until he sat across from his future wife in the restaurant of the Art Institute. She smiled through him with gentle, approving eyes, as though she had been waiting for him all her life. It was an attractive smile that promised security and unconditional love. She was an elementary school teacher, a modest woman, a cultivated woman, and a kind woman, with a sparkle in her eyes that was ageless.

When they read Alyce's obituary in the *Tribune*, dead at the age of ninety-nine, he turned to her and said, "I can't believe we were ever married. It all must have been a dream."

ACKNOWLEDGMENTS

Thanks to my good friend, Earl Schub, for an early reading of *Aging Beauty*; to Fred Shafer, my friend and editor, for helping revise several drafts; to Catherine Garber of Fergus Garber Young Architects, who was kind enough to design the cover; and, most of all, to my loving wife, Jody, who has helped me create this novel, watched it develop and always believed in me.

CPSIA information can be obtained
at www.ICGtesting.com
Printed in the USA
FSHW021425300419
57709FS

9 781796 020120